SUMMARY

Ending up in a wheelchair wasn't part of Rory's plan. But Daralyn, a family friend with a horrific past, needs a Master who can help her thrive in a world that terrifies her. Her desperate need to trust, her eyes full of hunger for what love should be, are keeping him up at night.

He's determined to be the Dom to give her that. Strength is in a man's will, not his body. No matter what, she's going to find everything she needs in his arms.

IN HIS ARMS

A Nature of Desire Series Novel

JOEY W. HILL

SWP Digital & Print Edition publication September 2020 by Story Witch Press, 452 Mattamushkeet Dr., Little River, South Carolina 29566, USA

The following material contains graphic sexual content meant for mature readers. Reader discretion is advised.

Digital ISBN: 978-1-951544-04-1

Print ISBN: 978-1-951544-05-8

ACKNOWLEDGMENTS

Part of the joy of writing relationships in romance is the ability to "idealize" some aspects of a love story. However, the best romances know when to tap into the realities of falling in love. As such, it was vital to me to represent a paraplegic Dom hero in a way that respects the real-life paraplegic men out there, navigating their own relationships.

To do that, I had invaluable help. Thank you to the team of readers—some disabled themselves, others who were caregivers or had access to family members in wheelchairs—who reviewed parts of this story or answered questions. A special thanks to Jeanne for letting me take almost verbatim her thought about Rory realizing that being a sexual Dominant is something that transcends the body, something any submissive paying attention will recognize (smile).

Thank you also to the disabled people who have crafted videos to help others like them learn to navigate the daily how-tos of life in a wheelchair. These videos were an incredible resource for an author. While the written word done right can paint an unforgettable picture, for practical skills, nothing beats a visual. These videos also kept me from badgering my reader team with endless minutiae like: "how would you take off your pants?" "how would you open a door?" etc. A particular thanks to Richard of Wheels2Walking, as his videos became a key resource for Rory and Daralyn's story.

Daralyn presented her own kind of challenge. I thank my physician resource who answered the questions I had about her that can't really be posted online without law enforcement taking a much closer look at you, lol – but I'm very glad they would, to confirm I'm simply an author looking for accuracy in her story.

I hope you all fall in love with Rory and Daralyn. However, as always, any shortcomings in the story are entirely the fault of the author – not those who helped me bring Rory and Daralyn's story to life!

CHAPTER ONE

*S*he'd been getting paler by the hour. As her departure time drew closer, he was worried she might pass out.

Rory pushed his chair a few inches to the right. Just enough to study her from his vantage point at the front counter without looking like that was what he was doing.

Daralyn stood before the mirror in the back of the store, where they sold outerwear and work shoes. Someone else would think she was fussing over her appearance, but he knew she rarely looked at herself.

He noticed everything about her. Every emotion transmitted through body language—a change in the angle of her chin, the light of her eyes. The rate of her pulse, the tiny beat of it in that pocket at the base of her throat, and how her breath made the slight curves of her breasts rise and fall.

Last Christmas, he'd kissed her under the mistletoe, in front of his well-meaning family who'd engineered the event. He remembered every detail of that, too. One of her nervous, chapped hands had fallen onto his biceps, her fingers tightening. He'd wanted to pull her into his lap, right there in front of everyone. Not because he wanted to disrespect her, but because he ached to do what a man with two functioning legs could do. Hold his girl flush against him, cradle her in his arms as he kissed her. Feel the give of her body as she trusted his strength enough, wanted it enough, to melt into him.

1

Not long before that Christmas, when he had thoughts like that about her, he'd put them away, appalled at himself. Since she was fifteen, she'd mostly lived with his family. But then Marcus had pointed out the obvious, and it had stuck to his brain cells like gum.

Marcus was his brother's...husband. Yeah, Rory was small-town enough that saying it, even in his head, still felt weird. But Thomas was happy, and Marcus was a decent guy. When he wasn't being a prick. So Rory was cool with his brother being gay, though he still reserved his right to block any images in his head of guys getting it on with each other.

A couple days after that Christmas, Rory had been in the driveway in front of the house, watching his mom and Daralyn say goodbye to Rory's sister, Les, who was headed back to medical school. Marcus was standing beside him.

"You know she's not your sister, right?" he said.

"I'm pretty sure she is," Rory responded. "There are pictures of me holding her as a baby."

"You know how easy it is to head slap a guy in a wheelchair?" When Marcus swept a palm toward him to demonstrate, Rory lifted a quick fist to block, and then cocked it to strike.

"About as easy as it is for one to punch you in the nuts."

Marcus dropped his hand with a chuckle, but then he sobered. "You know I meant Daralyn. She's twenty. You can treat her as a woman, Rory. A woman you want, with a man's hunger."

Marcus didn't know everything going through Rory's head when he was around her. At least he thought he didn't. Because then Marcus demonstrated the uncanny insight Thomas had complained about, more than once.

"When you think about her, I'm betting a couple things happen in your head and your cock."

At Rory's narrow look, Marcus shrugged and adopted a Southern drawl. "The two are connected like biscuits and gravy, boy."

"Asshole," Rory muttered.

A slight smile played on Marcus's mouth, but his intent green eyes remained fixed on Rory. "You want to protect her like it's the only thing in life that matters. And you want to make her yours in ways that you're worried are wrong. They're not, and when you want to know why, you'll come find me to talk it out. Don't be proud. Desire

2

can cover a fuck-ton of ground, but wanting to fly won't keep you from crashing if you don't learn how a plane works. Even if you're willing to risk yourself, you can't risk your passenger. She's everything, right?"

Coming back to the present, Rory pensively tapped his push rim. He knew about being out of control, not having enough knowledge about what was ahead, and how crazy that could make a guy. But whatever this was, it was still a jumble between his head, his gut, and yes, his sexual desire for her. Even as, at other times, it was like a straight line between two points.

Biscuits and gravy. Shit.

He pushed out from behind the counter "Daralyn."

She turned, gave him an absent, jittery smile, and immediately came his way. Her glossy hair, the rich brown of a house wren's back, was in a ponytail, the bundle of natural curls bobbing against her exposed neck as she moved. Depending on the light, her hazel eyes had touches of blue or amber scattered through the golden-green irises.

The blue shirt she wore had a scoop neckline and lace band at the bottom that hugged her narrow hips in jeans. A feminine ensemble that enhanced her body without being intentionally sexy.

She wasn't girl-next-door. She was fragile angel, bewildered by the world in which she'd been dropped, like a puppy tied in a sack with a stone weight.

He knew that kind of anger on her behalf wasn't useful, but her life had been a total shitstorm up until she was fifteen. When her father died, God rot him, and her uncle took off shortly thereafter, their closely knit rural North Carolina community had realized, to its shame, what had been happening in that rundown house for years. But until Daralyn came to live with them, even Rory's mother, Elaine, who'd been first to notice the situation, hadn't realized the worst of it.

Some predators knew how to shape their victims to add to their camouflage. Her father and uncle had fucking excelled at that.

Her father must have been the brains, though, since the uncle had been caught a year later in Roanoke Rapids, assaulting a young girl within a block of her school. Rory kept hoping the son of a bitch would be killed in prison before his seven-year sentence was up.

"Do you need something before I go?" Daralyn asked. She had a breathy voice. When she had to raise her volume, her gaze would dart back and forth like a startled deer. "I can... I mean, I don't have to go. I'm sure the first day is orientation, really, and..."

"You're going."

Her attention flitted to his face and then over his shoulder, somewhere else. She'd meet and hold Thomas's gaze, or his sister's. His mother's. But not Marcus's. And not Rory's. Not without a different level of effort.

He couldn't say why that was significant, but a primal part of him responded to it, tightening his heart in his chest. He also realized he'd said the words not just as encouragement, but as a command.

You want to make her yours in ways that you think might be wrong. They're not, and when you want to know why, you'll come find me to talk it out...

He was losing his mind to some weirdness Marcus had planted there. He tried easing his tone, no matter that it felt like he was backing away from something important, something she actually needed. He gestured to her. "C' mere. I have something for you."

He liked seeing the curiosity in her eyes. With how quiet she was, some people thought she wasn't smart. But since she'd started working here, she'd learned everything about running his family's farm supply and general store. She knew where every item was and could give helpful guidance to customers, whether it was about how much grain to feed a horse, or what kind of tool was needed for a home or farm repair.

When they'd decided to employ her, at first they thought she wasn't going to work out. She wouldn't ask them any questions, though she was clearly anxious and frustrated when she didn't know something. Then Thomas told her straight out, "Daralyn, the more questions you ask, the more you learn from Rory and me, or Mom, the better you'll be at this."

She'd mulled that over, a frown creasing her brow. "I'll be more helpful to you?"

Thomas started to speak, and Rory knew he was going to assure her she'd have a job no matter what, but some part of him knew that fear wasn't why she was asking the question. Rory spoke up before his older brother got it out.

"Yes. Tons more helpful."

She hadn't hesitated to ask a question ever since.

As Rory leaned back to reach behind the counter, her gaze slid over his upper body, the stretch of his T-shirt over his chest and shoulders. Even though she was quick to turn her eyes elsewhere when she noted his attention, her cheeks pinkened.

Gaining weight and spread was almost inevitable when a guy ended up in a chair, so much so the first wheelchair was often made wider to allow for it. He'd been an athlete before his accident. Over time, he'd built himself back to prime shape through adaptive sports, lifting at the gym, and religious dedication to the fucking hell of never-ending PT. He was never gladder for his commitment to all that than when he saw her sneaking those looks.

He had a recumbent bike he operated with his arms, and his weekly workouts included marathons on the county roads. Neighbors would shout encouragement as he passed their homes. His few old high school buddies who still lived in the area would come by in their pickups and razz him, pretend like they were going to nudge him off into a ditch.

Fuck, he loved those guys.

"Since you'll be at school from four to nine," he said to her, "you'll need dinner."

"You made me dinner?" Her eyes widened.

He snorted. "Yeah, if I wanted to poison you. Mom made it. I provided the lunch box."

His mother was a feeder, and she liked to cook. She particularly liked to feed Daralyn, who'd been skin and bones when she'd come to them. She'd filled out some, in nice ways, but she was still an indifferent eater.

He'd figured out at least one food she liked, though. His contribution to the lunch box was three miniature Reese's peanut butter cups. He'd tucked them next to the small container of soup and half a sandwich on homemade bread. Mom would have given her way more, but they'd all learned they couldn't give Daralyn too much. It seemed to overwhelm her, and she'd eat nothing. But she'd tackle small amounts.

She'd find out about the contents later. Right now she was enchanted by the lunch box.

"Holly Hobbie," she said, cracking the beat-up 1979 metal container. "Where did you find it?"

"Greenwald Reardon's place." Greenwald ran an old antique and junk shop off the interstate.

"I love it." She gazed at the blue bonneted girl in a patchwork dress, standing in a field, holding a fistful of feathery wheat grass. "Thank you. I'll be sure and thank your mother for making me dinner. That was really nice."

Her smile was what had convinced Rory that Daralyn was an angel. It lit up every dark place he had inside him. As she took the box from his hands, he made sure their fingers brushed, just to feel the little quiver in them, see the quick flick of her lashes toward him.

His feelings weren't a saving-the-damsel-in-distress thing, either. Hell, sometimes he wanted to drop on his knees to *her*, feel her arms around him, because he was pretty damn sure she'd survived something none of the rest of them could. It fucking awed him.

"That girl's smile is God's miracle," his mother had murmured once.

Rory didn't have his mother's faith, not by a long shot, but he couldn't argue with that one. He'd been told it was a miracle he hadn't died when the tractor rolled over him. He hadn't felt that way at first. Truth, he'd been a little bitch about it all, wallowing in his own pity. Which he'd learned was normal, a stages of grief thing. But Daralyn's smile made him ashamed of indulging in even a second of that shit.

He'd had a loving family and friends who'd supported him, every step of the way. She'd spent her first fifteen years with people who never cared what she wanted, except to use it against her. No one in her corner.

She glanced at the vintage Coca-Cola clock on the back wall. It said three-fifteen, and her ride to the community college was coming at three-thirty. Just like that, the nervousness was back. Double the strength.

"I guess..." Her voice quavered, her eyes slammed shut, and her knees buckled.

"Shit." He hit the brake locks on his chair and grabbed her elbow. He couldn't stop the fall, but he slowed it down. She went to one knee by his feet, but her kneecap glanced off his carbon footplate and his steel-toed work shoe.

"Darn it," she whispered.

He heard the helpless despair that turned the gee-golly-whiz word into a profound oath of self-condemnation. And he refused to allow her to go there.

"Breathe through it," he said. "Just breathe. You're fine." He gathered up her long, thick ponytail so he could reach her nape, knead it with strong fingers. He wanted to soothe, be gentle. But seeing her on one knee before him, her head bowed, other reactions surfaced. He could feel her breath against his abdomen. Her hand was gripping his knee.

What surged up in him was too certain and powerful to be wrong. He might question it later, but not now.

He tightened his hold on her hair, let her feel the pull against her scalp. Her breath stilled, and the hand on his knee curled. He could see her fingers pressing into his leg. Yeah, he'd somehow known she'd react that way. He caressed her neck with a firmer, sure-fingered stroke.

"You're going to school, and you're not only going to be fine, you're going to love it, do great things with the stuff you learn. Become a rocket scientist or something. Straighten up for me."

She lifted her head and shoulders, bracing her hand on his thigh to stand. Instead of letting her make it all the way to her feet, he grasped her under the arms and brought her forward. He'd intended to turn her sideways, but her knees naturally parted, and he kept the forward motion, lifting her so she straddled him. Since his chair didn't have arms, her legs slid past his hips, her calves finding a natural resting spot on the wheels.

Hell...finally. He had some elusive traces of sensation at the tops of his thighs, enough to conjure what her backside would feel like, pressed against his lap. Her thighs and knees brushed against his hips, his waist. That input from his nerve endings to his brain was heaven.

Even more importantly, having her legs spread loosely around him distracted her, which seemed to pull her away from her worries. Maybe he could get a straight answer out of her, help drive them away completely.

"So what's the problem?" he asked bluntly. She blinked, moistening her bottom lip. Her hands were on his biceps, teasing a million responses from his flesh.

Stop thinking about that. Think about her.

"Tell me, Daralyn."

7

She gestured helplessly around her. "I'm okay here with... At the store."

She'd been about to say, "With you." But as much as he loved knowing she felt safe with him, the crumpling of her features, reflecting the defeat her fears created within her, was a bigger concern to him.

Everyone wanted to be needed. But being needed through wanting and craving was way different from being needed as a place to hide from the unknown. He knew about that kind of fear. The first months after his accident, it had kept him paralyzed in ways that turned his wheelchair into a prison.

"When I'm here, and it's not time to leave, I get excited, thinking about going to school." She was trying hard to steady her voice. Trying not to shake. Her fingers continued to curl against his flesh, convulsive kneading. "Happy, even. Now it's time to do it, and I'm thinking about the people, the noise, all of it. It's like walking along the edge of the ocean, my feet in it. It looks so amazing and big. One part of me thinks being in it would be wonderful. But then I think about getting swept away from shore so I can't get back. Untethered... Unmoored."

She pronounced the word carefully. She kept a journal, and he'd seen her make entries when she heard words she liked or didn't know. At fifteen, she'd been close to illiterate. Learning to read had been the first thing that had brought her out of her shell. He remembered her and Les sitting on Les's bed, Les going over English basics with her.

Sometimes he wondered if he was being fair, wanting her. Maybe her first true relationship should be with someone fresh and new, who could see her as she was now, rather than a culmination of her past.

He'd quizzed himself on that, ruthlessly. Was he going after her, interested in her, because she *had* been broken? Did he want her because he could feel powerful with her in a way he couldn't anymore with the confident cheerleaders who'd once fawned over him? They'd loved his six-foot height and strong legs, his ability to pick them up and tease them.

And what about her? Was she drawn to him because he was safe? Known?

Yet as he looked at her pale face, felt her anxiety, he knew he wasn't going to back off. He had an idea, supported by that gut feeling he'd had when he'd tightened his hand in her hair.

Still holding her in his lap, he fished out several more things from behind the counter. He'd had to shorten a length of chain for Kenny Fisher earlier in the week, and he'd dropped the eight-inch remnant behind the counter. It wasn't a girl's bracelet kind of chain, but 3mm links, extra durable hardware. Retrieving that, a spool of wire and the pair of small pliers with them, he nodded toward her left hand. "Hold it out to me. Palm up."

An authoritative tone, easy as breathing. It was the way he talked to the seasonal help, the high school kids who helped unload Christmas trees in December.

But they sure as hell didn't respond the way she did. He exhaled the command and she inhaled it, responding by lifting her arm.

She had a scar on it. The discoloration was faint, but the puckering of the skin was noticeable on a six-inch track of tender skin under her forearm. He thought it was a burn scar, but Daralyn had never offered any information about the old injury. Since it didn't seem to bug her, and her worst scars were on the inside, making her self-conscious about one on the outside didn't seem to serve a useful purpose.

He looped the chain around her wrist, figured out the length he needed, then removed it again. Sliding off his class ring, he laid it in her palm. "Hold onto that a minute."

His initials were stamped in black on the square middle, his school name outlining it, the school's mascot and graduation year on the dark gold sides. Her fingers closed over it, one of them slipping inside the ring to anchor it in her palm. She caressed the silky inside of the metal as if seeking the heat of his body. Maybe he was just imagining that, but the surge of feeling in his chest said he was right.

He used the chain and wire to form a bracelet, the ring the connecting centerpiece. After he fastened it on her, he ran his callused fingers over and around the whole thing to ensure nothing was jabbing her. As he caressed the soft skin, her pulse rate increased.

Registering the reaction, he glanced up, deliberately letting his gaze roam over her features. She had silky eyebrows, a fair forehead and straight nose. Then there were those very distracting pale pink lips. He wanted to place the heat of his mouth over them.

Her lashes swept down over her cheeks, but her wrist stayed willingly in his grasp. He kept his thumb coursing over that velvet stretch of skin below the bracelet as her fingers trembled. The chain was snug enough she would be aware of it there, the class ring a heavy, masculine weight at her pulse point. She'd folded her fingers forward, so one of her fingertips rested inside it again.

"Daralyn." His voice had roughened, and he kept it that way. "Do you think about that kiss at Christmas?"

Her lips parted, her cheeks getting that charming pink color.

"Look at me."

He didn't think he was breathing when her gaze raised to his, held. The golden-green color had deepened, the pupils big and dark. "Tell me," he said softly.

"Yes. I do."

"Every night?"

Her eyes sparkled a little, showing some spirit he liked. A lot. "I have other things to think about than just that."

"That wasn't a no. I plan on kissing you again, really soon. So if you die of a panic attack, I won't get that chance."

Her lips curved, her eyes lighting in a way that shot heat straight through every nerve-rich part of his body.

"Okay."

Though it was the last thing he wanted to do, he guided her to her feet. When her gaze fell naturally to his lap, she quickly looked away.

No big surprise, the pressure of her body had inspired a reaction. While he took immense pleasure in thinking about her gorgeous ass being on his lap, he couldn't get hard from just the thinking. Psychogenic erections, the term for that, weren't something he could have any more. But reflexogenic, caused by direct physical contact to his cock? Damn straight.

The press of her lips together, the significant sudden absence of that trembling in her fingers, told him she wasn't upset by it. In a polite world, he'd make things easy by pretending he hadn't noticed her noticing. He wasn't feeling polite. Instead, when his steady, silent regard brought her gaze back to his, he locked her into a full acknowledgement of it.

She's a woman now. As Marcus had said.

A crackle of gravel in the parking lot outside told him the community transport van for the college had arrived. But she still didn't look away. It was as if she knew he had to tell her she could. His reaction to that was so strong, he considered pulling her on his lap again.

But Marcus had been right about that other thing. *She's everything.* Her happiness, her well-being.

"Daralyn," he said in measured tones, gripping his push rims so he didn't reach for her instead. "Go on before you miss your ride."

She swallowed. Turning away, she collected her backpack and picked up the lunch box. When she reached the door, she pulled it open, making the shop bells mounted over it ring. The chain on her wrist clinked against the knob.

"See you in a while," she said, shooting him a shy glance.

"You sure will."

A small smile, and she stepped out, letting the door close behind her.

He moved to the window. At the open door of the roomy passenger van, she hesitated. There were five people in it, in addition to the driver. Since Daralyn had her head lowered, as if she were thinking, he got ready to go out there and give her reinforcement if she needed it.

Then she curled her fingers over the chain, the ring. Taking a deep breath, she gripped the rail and mounted the steps into the vehicle. When the door closed, she had settled gingerly into a seat next to a nerdy-looking guy staring at his phone.

The van pulled away, trundling out of the parking lot and accelerating once it was on the paved road.

He sat in an empty store, his heart aching, desire coursing through him. She'd been gone five seconds, but the Daralyn-sized empty space in the store had the density of a black hole.

Truth Number One. He wanted her, and he didn't want to hold back on that any longer.

Truth Number Two. Maybe he was channeling some bizarre Fifty Shades thing that he'd absorbed by falling asleep to late night TV, but that didn't fit. He wanted to say that kind of thing wasn't him or her, but their reaction to one another during those odd moments said otherwise. And yeah, he'd looked at some of this stuff online, but he hoped like hell he'd stumbled on the wrong places, because he'd seen things he... Fuck, he didn't even want those things in his head.

But some of it *hadn't* repelled him. Just the opposite. That disturbed him more than the stuff that had.

That brought him to Truth Number Three. He needed to talk to Marcus. Because there was another reason Marcus's words had taken up residence in his head. The online sites had helped Rory realize it, too.

Marcus wasn't "just" Thomas's husband.

Marcus and Thomas split their time between Marcus's penthouse in New York City and a 1940s farmhouse they'd bought here. A few months back, Rory had come by to see Thomas. He'd used the ramp that Thomas and Marcus had included in the house updates right after they purchased it to access the porch.

Seeing the front door standing open behind the screen, Rory had pushed into the living room, calling out. Nothing. The house was empty. They weren't in the nearby barn, where Thomas had his loft art studio and Marcus his home office, but the cars were under the port. Which meant they were likely on the back porch.

The door to that was open, allowing a cross breeze through the house. Because the adjacent windows were also open, he glimpsed Marcus and Thomas before they were aware of him.

Thomas was against the wooden porch railing, clutching it on either side of him in white knuckled hands. Marcus had him pressed up against it. His strong hand was wrapped around Thomas's throat as his lips cruised over his cheek.

Rory started to retreat, fast, but before he did, he heard Thomas utter a single word.

Rory hadn't needed to see Marcus's face that day to know what expression it wore. The satisfied growl of response had told him.

The fevered look Thomas sent toward Marcus was one Rory wanted to see on Daralyn's face. And that word... Rory had never heard it used by anyone in his world. Yet it had come back to him again and again since then. Only in his imaginings it came from Daralyn's lips, said in the same way Thomas had said it to Marcus.

With desperate yearning, but also an absolute certainty that the person who owned that word could answer that yearning and desperation.

"Master."

So yeah, he needed to talk to Marcus. No matter his aversion to learning more about his brother's sex life than he really wanted to know, he wouldn't dive deeper into uncharted territory with just a gut feeling. No way was he going to risk fucking with Daralyn's head.

That said, he also didn't want to treat her like china. He knew better than most not to assume someone was too fragile to handle something because of what they'd been through.

The way she'd teased him just now, about having other things to think about than that kiss? That had been damn close to flirting. Like she might one day feel safe enough to mouth off at him, the playful way a woman did when she felt safe with a man.

He wanted to kill her uncle and father for treating her the ways they had, but she'd been stronger than the both of them. He believed in her strength.

He was a man who wanted to treat Daralyn like a woman. She could tease, defy or confront him all she wanted. He'd never hurt her. He'd celebrate that confidence, even as he'd challenge it, in ways she might just crave. Maybe she needed that.

He had an unsettling feeling he sure as hell did.

CHAPTER TWO

*A*fter he closed the store for the day, Rory decided to settle himself by doing his evening workout, a few miles on his bike on the Hickman Road loop. Then he transferred to his regular chair and headed for Thomas and Marcus's place.

By road, they were a few miles away, but as the crow flew, it was a matter of crossing several fields. During the growing season, they offered sweet potato, watermelon or squash crops. When they were little, he and his siblings played with kids on those farms, so they'd worn down a regular path between the fields. Now there was a paved pedestrian and bike path, part of a county-wide greenway project funded by taxes.

As Rory left the path and crossed the road to Marcus and Thomas's driveway, his gaze went to the guest house on their property. Daralyn's house.

When Thomas and Marcus bought the Hill place, it had included a rambling farmhouse, a barn and an outbuilding, plus a few fenced acres. The outbuilding had been renovated into a guest house that included a bedroom, living area, kitchenette and bath, as well as a screened patio. All cozy-sized, the whole place about a thousand square feet.

They'd offered it to Daralyn, her first home on her own. In exchange, she cleaned Marcus and Thomas's place and house-sat for them when they were in New York. Despite her protests, they also paid her for that work.

She loved the little house, and had decorated it to her tastes. Strings of white lights lit up the patio area, more noticeable with the sun going down. She'd bought up a bunch of dollar store hummingbird and flower solar lights, which provided a small rainbow starfield in the bed of pansies that fronted the porch. Shepherd's hooks held chimes that danced over the flowers when the wind blew.

Thomas and Marcus encouraged her to stay in the main house during their New York absences, but she only used their kitchen on occasion, for the cooking that couldn't be done in her kitchenette. The flat screen didn't interest her. She'd watch short bursts of TV with Rory's family, usually excusing herself partway through a program, and she had no interest in having a television herself. He'd never seen her make it through a full movie, even one she seemed to enjoy.

She preferred to read her books. Most nights, if he went by there on his bike ride, which he usually did, he'd see her on the patio. She'd be curled in a chair, reading, her head bent in concentration, her hair falling softly along her face. She still moved her lips when she read, because the words didn't come easy or fast.

She always lifted her head when he came by, and would wave. He didn't usually interrupt her, but he liked to confirm that she was all right.

It wasn't about her physical safety. Crime wasn't a big issue in their town. A little vandalism and petty theft were the extent of it. Or Mrs. Marten reporting her goat Molly missing again, although she was always found in someone's garden.

The only serious crime that occurred in their county was the kind that could happen anywhere, to anyone. Out in the country or in a big city, to the rich or to the poor.

Al Moorfield had lived in their town most of his life. When Al died, his son, Oscar, and his maternal half-brother Burton, had moved in. They'd come from Nashville. Oscar had explained that he was a widower with one child, a six-year-old daughter, and they'd wanted to move out of the city. He lived on a military pension and was a disabled veteran with a prosthetic leg.

He said he homeschooled his daughter, so the only time Daralyn had been seen was when they came to town with her in their company. She'd been a tiny, skittish shadow in baggy clothes, her uncle's hand firmly clamped on her shoulder.

They did bring her to the Baptist church, even though they discouraged conversation with anyone, and went home without attending any of the Sunday afternoon socials.

Though they were considered "somewhat peculiar," people assumed they were okay. They made regular church appearances and had roots in town, which were reinforced as they settled in and years passed without them causing any waves. The first thing made them "seem" like good people, and the last two meant they'd earned the right to be left alone, no matter how eccentric they seemed.

In hindsight, they'd all been clueless about something that should have been so fucking obvious.

Daralyn had been out of that hellhole for five years now, so Rory didn't know why he was getting himself worked up thinking about it. Maybe because the more he went over what had happened before she got into the van today, the more certain he became that he should have gone with her.

The rhythmic sound of an axe being swung told him Thomas was behind the house. Marcus would be close to where Thomas was.

Rory pushed himself up the ramp onto the porch and followed it to the back.

Marcus was on the phone, no surprise. He owned a gallery in New York, and was always scouting talent, promoting talent, buying or selling. Rory's mother had once tartly suggested he have the cell surgically implanted into the side of his head. Marcus had told her he'd thought about it, but it would mess up his hair.

When Rory came around the corner, he saw Marcus was in one of the roomy rockers, painted a clean white with a blue patterned seat cushion. He wasn't relaxed in it, though. He leaned forward with a tablet under his long fingertips while he spoke in the strong, smooth voice that fit the rest of him.

He glanced Rory's way and gave him an absent nod, gesturing toward the backyard. Thomas was currently stripped down to jeans, splitting cords of wood for the stove and fireplace inside.

Rory shook his head, and pointed to Marcus. A flicker of surprise went through Marcus's green eyes, but he inclined his head and held up five fingers. A few minutes, then.

Rory positioned himself at a companionable but polite distance and settled back. An electrified fence enclosed several acres, in order to give grazing room to the two cows, one female goat and a wandering pig with the girth of one of the cows. A flock of chickens hung around near their coop, clucking or roosting. Thomas had planted a garden back here, a hobby patch by local standards. It was enough to provide him and Marcus with some fresh vegetables in season, though, and flowers for Daralyn to cut for table vases. The vegetables were done for the fall, but a few flowers were still holding out, since they weren't likely to get a prolonged cold spell until sometime in November.

In a couple weeks, Marcus had a fundraiser slash new talent scouting opportunity coming up. Since he was talking to whoever was on the phone about a silent auction, it sounded like his call was about that.

Rory had never been to New York City. He couldn't imagine living there, all those people crammed together. But when Marcus or Thomas talked about the museums and art, the little coffee houses and colorful people on the streets, or parks like the elevated High Line or the view from the Rockefeller Center observation deck, Rory saw how closely Daralyn listened.

Thanks to his adaptive challenge group, Rory was comfortable traveling, having gone on several trips with them. While he still preferred visiting wide-open spaces, versus crowded cities to broaden his cultural horizons, he'd be okay doing things like that with her.

He returned his attention to his reason for being here. Rory was as inflexibly straight as a railroad tie, but there was no denying his brother-in-law was insanely good-looking. His dark hair fell to his shoulders and over his forehead, feathering and layering perfectly without any apparent effort. His features were chiseled, mouth firm. Those piercing green-like-sea-glass eyes could make a woman of any age forget what language she spoke. Rory had seen it, any time Marcus came into the store. Even his mom or Les, both used to being around him now, could still sometimes be caught just staring at him, as if he wasn't entirely real.

Rory wondered if they'd ever noticed that was how Marcus looked at Thomas. He expected they had, because as much as women liked a pretty face, it was the emotional stuff that really won their hearts.

Marcus's obvious love for Thomas, his possessiveness combined with his devotion to his well-being, elevated the female attention for Marcus to a whole different level of adoration.

Women.

Daralyn sometimes went completely mute around Marcus, but Rory suspected there were other reasons for that. Though Marcus always spoke to her kindly, he never asked her anything that could be phrased as a statement. "Daralyn, I'd like a cup of coffee." "Daralyn, I'll drive you home."

Marcus clicked off the phone and removed the earpiece, putting it on the table with his phone and tablet. He stretched out his long legs and settled deeper into the chair, cracking his neck. As he picked up his half-full wine glass, his eyes shifted with undisguised appreciation to Thomas swinging the axe, the roll of muscles, the stretch of the jeans over ass and thigh.

"Could you pretend he's my sister and not ogle him like that when I'm around?"

One of Daralyn's words. Ogle. Ogling. She usually put them in a sentence to help her remember the meaning. Rory wondered what sentence she'd used for that one.

Marcus slanted him an amused glance. "Sexist prick."

"Yeah, whatever. You know what I'm saying."

"Well, my only other option is to ogle you." Marcus tossed him a look. "Showing up all sweaty and muscular, with your masculine stench."

"Control your lust, you twisted perv."

Part of their usual banter, so all good. But when Rory attempted his usual fuck-off grin, he could tell Marcus registered it was a little forced, thanks to the sudden bout of nerves. Shit, this was stupid. He said it straight out before he could change his mind.

"So you said to come talk to you when it's time. About Daralyn. I'm here to talk. If now's good."

Marcus's gaze could go from neutral pleasant to cool and laser-focused in a blink. Rory had seen it fluster Thomas, though Thomas was no pushover. The part of Rory that had him here now understood why that look could unsettle Thomas, the way Rory's similar expression could do the same to Daralyn. It made him feel better, more reassured, while at the same time...unmoored. Daralyn's new word. He almost smiled at the thought.

"Okay," Marcus said. "Where do you want to start?"

Rory told him about what had happened before she left for school. Some of it wasn't easy, because though it sounded general enough, the things he'd said and done, the chain around her wrist, had a motivation that became more blatantly clear under Marcus's intent regard.

"I know it's important for her to get out there and make things happen for herself," Rory said, shifting. "But there's this feeling in my gut when I know she needs more...structure, for lack of a better word. It's like she's asking me for that, in a way without words."

In the extended pause between them, Rory wondered if he'd totally misinterpreted the situation, what Marcus had been trying to tell him that day in the driveway. Marcus removed that concern with one question.

"What did your gut tell you today?"

"That I should have gone with her," Rory said instantly. "I'm wondering if she's pushing herself too much, out of some misguided idea that she owes us proof that our faith in her isn't unfounded."

He shook his head. "I went through that. Thinking I had to prove myself to everyone by rejecting any help." He probably still had too much of that, but he recognized when it went in a destructive direction. Mostly. "Sorry. I'm getting off track."

"Not necessarily." Marcus tapped the rim of his wine glass. "It's all related. By giving her the bracelet, you made your first real step toward calling your relationship what it is. Acknowledging where it's headed. How much do you know about the look of that?"

Rory knew he was going to redden to the roots of his brown hair, but the hell with it. "I've looked at things online. Some interesting stuff. Some scary and repulsive things."

"Well, it's the Internet. Equal capacity for both."

Rory lifted a shoulder, met Marcus's gaze. "I also heard Thomas call you something once. And when I look at Daralyn...or rather, when she looks at me...I think I feel that. No, that's chickenshit. I know it. But I don't know shit about any of this, so how can I feel that so strong?"

Marcus's eyes flickered. "Thomas didn't need a manual to know he preferred men. That came from his gut, his heart. His cock. His mind. That said, do you know how to read anything other than a farmer's almanac?"

"Don't be a dick."

Marcus's lips tugged in a smile. "I'm going to send a couple books to your tablet. That way you don't have to worry about your mother seeing shocking print material in your sock drawer when she does your laundry."

"She won't let me do my laundry," Rory muttered defensively. "She says I do it wrong."

"Rory, Les is in medical school and Thomas doesn't live at home. You pay your share of the bills and live with your mother to take care of her. There's a big difference in that."

"We take care of each other," Rory said. He appreciated Marcus's comment, though. He'd razz Rory about plenty of things, but not that.

He could transfer himself out of his chair into a bed, a shower, a bathroom. All the basics required to make living on his own an option, but it had taken time to get to that place, mentally and physically. During that time, his mother had helped care for him, encouraged him, dealt with his bullshit and his temper.

Once he moved past that, he could have lived elsewhere, but to prove what? He and Thomas had talked about it, talked about their dad and what he would have wanted.

Elaine wasn't helpless or feeble. Hell, she wasn't even elderly, not really. Marcus didn't appreciate the reminder, since there was about a fourteen-year age difference between him and Thomas, but Elaine wasn't much more than a decade or so older than Marcus. She had an active social life, volunteered regularly for their church, and was an avid gardener. She pitched in at the store whenever needed, though Rory had made sure she could start giving more of her efforts to her church and community work, finally enjoy with her friends the leisure time she'd earned a hundred times over.

Yet for all that, he, Thomas and Les all felt better having someone at home with her. The nest had emptied out fast, and their father had died shortly before that started happening. The house was always in need of repairs, with several outbuildings and a food garden that covered about an acre. Way more than one person could maintain.

While the store and Thomas were both making enough to hire people to fix some of the stuff, Rory and his mom were of the same mind on that. If they could do it themselves, there was no need to waste the money.

The day might come when Rory would get his own place nearby, like Marcus and Thomas had done, but for now, this arrangement worked. Though she'd never hold her children back by saying so, Elaine liked having someone in the house other than just herself.

"You're starting to embrace this side of yourself, whether you realize it or not," Marcus said. "There are theories about this stuff possibly being hereditary."

Rory's brow creased. "You lost me."

"We were with you at dinner a couple weeks ago. Your mom was tired, and it was time to clear the table, wash the dishes. Elaine was doing that thing she does, wanting her sons not to be bothered while she flitted around them. You told her to sit down and drink her coffee while you and Thomas cleared. She sat."

Rory tried to remember. "I wasn't disrespectful about it."

"Not in the least. But you were adamant, and firm. Firm in a way she responded to."

"Are you saying my mother..."

"I'm saying Thomas told me your father was a very authoritative person. Your mother loved him, fit with him. Thomas said as you're getting older, you're acting more like your dad. I'm not going to plant any whips-and-chains images of your parents—"

"Hell, thanks for that. You just did."

Marcus's eyes sparkled. "It was likely more subtle for them anyway, disguised by their time period, the father as head of household, things like that. But my point is, your father's behavior and mannerisms groomed something already within you."

Thomas came up the steps, picking up the bottle of water left there. He leaned against the porch rail. "Hey. When did you get here? Are you..."

He trailed off at Marcus's significant glance.

Rory realized he was regarding Marcus in an almost mirror pose. Unblinking, his jaw set, back straight, his overall demeanor reflecting a watchful casualness. It was the posture of someone talking to a peer.

Thomas looked from Marcus to Rory and back. A corner of his

mouth twitched, and he shook his head. "Don't know how I ever missed it," he muttered.

"He's your brother," Marcus replied. "So..."

"Yeah. Right. Eww." Thomas shuddered, but as he turned to leave, he bumped Rory's foot with one of his own, nodded to him and headed back down the steps.

"Hunh." Rory watched his brother move to the wood pile, lean his ass against it and gaze out at the field, taking his break while giving them their privacy. "So he already knows."

"Soon as I started pointing out the things in you I'd noticed. We've talked about it a couple times, when you might come talk to me. If you would."

"Probably why I waited. Everything I learn from you I might have to visualize for Thomas." Rory echoed his brother's mock shudder. "Eww."

Marcus's firm lips curved. "Keep that in mind. I have a multitude of ways to traumatize you, because I've had your brother in every possible..."

"Nope. Lalalalala..."

Marcus grinned and brought the conversation back to topic. "You love her."

"Yeah. I do." Simple, straightforward.

"How much?" Marcus's face went blank, no cues. Which meant Rory looked for the answer inside the limitless well of feeling the question inspired.

"Like whatever God is," he said. "More than I understand or know, but want to spend a lifetime finding out."

At the surprise in Marcus's face, Rory lifted a shoulder. "My mother's belief in God looks different from mine or Thomas's, but she and my dad taught us the important parts. It's there, if you listen for it. When this happened to me," he touched the push rim of his chair, "I had to become a way more active listener."

"Well said."

"Thanks." Uncomfortable with the praise, Rory pressed on. "You're going to give me books, homework. Okay, fine. But tell me the traps and pitfalls. I don't want to do the wrong thing."

"You're going to do the wrong thing, make mistakes."

"She's had enough of that in her life. I want to do my damnedest not to add to it. Tell me where it's likely to happen."

Marcus pursed his lips. "Fair enough. There's a fine line between being an alpha asshole and being the Dom a sub needs. So you coming here today, to try and learn, that's smart. Daralyn is a submissive with a lot of unknowns, in terms of how she'll react to any relationship, let alone a Dom/sub one. You'll need to be even more intuitive than most Doms on picking up cues."

"I can do that." He already was. And though they both knew what they were talking about, Marcus actively using the language—Doms, subs—took it to a different level. Made it real. He was really doing this, going down this road. No more hypotheticals. "What else?"

"Don't back away from your instincts by second guessing yourself," Marcus said bluntly. "Which often happens because you're worrying about the first mistake. It's trickier terrain, because sometimes the way you need to react looks a lot like the alpha asshole."

"Hmm." Rory thought that through. "Like when Thomas told you that the two of you were done, and not to come after him. But you did anyway."

"You do pay attention, Padawan. Better than I give you credit for."

"So how do you know when you've stepped into the shit of the first mistake?"

"You don't always. But when police and restraining orders get involved, it's a good bet that you're in that territory." Marcus chuckled. "Seriously, just read what I send you, stay aware of her cues, and follow your instincts. But no matter how you try, Rory, you *are* going to make mistakes. Don't overreact to them. Just think it through, and change the strategy. Don't abort and retreat when it's not necessary. That can be equally bad. There's a reason they put a safety net under the high wire. It cushions the fall, helps a person get back up there again."

He'd had to learn the same lesson for his chair. Mistakes happened, and getting bogged down in the failure or embarrassment didn't help anything.

"Okay." He pushed his wheel forward and back, thinking. "Should I...uh...go to one of those clubs?"

When he'd looked at that kind of thing online, it hadn't grabbed him. Marcus's suggestion about his parents might be unsettling, but the structure he'd described struck a very real chord. Maybe the truth for him and Daralyn was somewhere in that realm.

"One day, if you want to, sure," Marcus responded. "But what's between you and Daralyn at this moment might not be ready for that. If the reading material isn't enough, though, there's a BDSM group in Charlotte. They hold a Dom/sub 101 class every month, and it doesn't matter if they have one attendee or fifty, the class happens. You can go to one by yourself, or with Thomas and me."

Marcus offered him a pointed look. "Just keep in mind, while the building blocks are essential, a big part of it is beyond knowledge or understanding. It's feeling and instinct. It's learning to find the balance. Plus working on trusting yourself and her."

He tipped his head toward Thomas, sending his husband and submissive a warm glance. "That's the biggest key of all."

Another good thing about Marcus; the guy didn't beat a dead horse. He knew when enough had been said for the time being. Thomas returned to the porch soon after that, and Rory hung with them for a short while. They talked about more casual things. When Marcus and Thomas shifted to dinner plans, Rory declined the invitation to join, deciding to head for home.

As they went inside, Thomas gave him the fond mix of *you're a shit-head* and *I've got your back* older brother look. Marcus held the door for him, then nodded before he stepped in behind Thomas. The look he sent Rory was different, but one Rory might as well go ahead and call what it was.

Dom to Dom.

He pushed himself around the side of the house, headed for the access ramp. About the time he reached it, a pickup truck slowed down on the road. It belonged to Ralph Peterson, the farmer who lived near Marcus and Thomas.

When the truck came to a full stop about fifty feet past the house, Daralyn emerged from the passenger side. She said something to Ralph, raised her hand in farewell.

As she turned, she had her head down. She made a beeline for her little house, her backpack hugged close to her body. She didn't look toward the main house, as if that would keep her from being noticed. Rory suspected it was also why she'd had Ralph drop her farther down the road.

By the time she'd reached her door, Rory heard the front screen door squeak open behind him. Their footsteps told him Thomas and Marcus had moved around the corner to join him.

"She's home pretty early," Thomas said. "Her classes weren't supposed to finish until nine."

"Yeah. Damn it." More of the anger bled into his voice than he'd intended. Thomas put a hand on his shoulder.

"Don't get after her about it. It's bound to be tough--"

"You think I'm pissed at her?" Rory shrugged off his hand, glared at his brother. "Damn it, I knew this afternoon. This was too much, too soon. She needed a backup."

"Rory, she has to stumble," Thomas said. "You can't catch her every time she falls."

"I can't catch her at all, most the time. So it makes it even worse when I don't catch her when I know I can."

"Maybe you should give her the night," his brother persisted. "Talk to her about it tomorrow, when you feel less worked up about it, too."

Rory glanced at Marcus's face, which had gone expressionless. Letting Rory figure it out. Make the decision.

"Yeah. Maybe." As he took the ramp to the ground level, he was pointed toward the road and home, but he didn't head that way. He thought of the backpack, full of supplies she'd picked out with such excitement and pleasure. Les had gone with her, when his sister was home for her last break.

Marcus and Thomas had given Daralyn the community college tuition as a Christmas gift, but Daralyn had missed the winter, spring and summer registration periods. When she'd finally signed up for the fall classes, it had been after doubling up on her bi-monthly sessions with her psychiatrist. Even so, this was going to feel like a major setback to her. But it wasn't.

He turned away from the road and headed for the guesthouse.

Thomas started to call after him, but Marcus put a hand on his shoulder. "Let him go, pet." He sent Thomas a significant look. "It's begun now. You don't get between Master and sub when they're in session."

"You think that's what this is."

"It feels that way. Life exists between Lloyd Dobler and Dr. Seuss, after all."

Thomas blinked, his dark brown eyes reflecting that endearing puzzlement that happened when Marcus threw a wrench in the workings of his brilliant artistic mind. "Say what?"

Marcus quirked a brow. "'I'm looking for a dare to be great situation,' versus 'To the world you may be one person; but to one person you may be the world.' But it all goes back to Lloyd. I think he knew they were one and the same. The dare to be great situation was being the person his heroine needed. Becoming the one."

Thomas shook his head. "Eighties movies and Dr. Seuss. You never fail to surprise."

"Long and short, let it play out. Trust your brother. Trust Daralyn."

"I do. I just don't want either one hurt. He's still got so much anger in him sometimes." Thomas sighed, looking toward the guest house. "His attitude has improved by leaps and bounds, but Mom worries he's still vulnerable to emotional bumps in the road that can throw him for a loop physically. I'd say that's a Mom thing, but I feel it too. He's so invested in Daralyn already. What if staying here, being with him, isn't what's best for her?"

Marcus shifted, his body brushing Thomas's in support. "If he truly loves her, and yeah, I think he's already way past halfway there, he'll know that, maybe even before she does. If that's what she needs, he'll let her go."

"How do you know that?"

Marcus met his gaze. "Because I love you. And if me letting you go had truly been the right thing for you, for your happiness, I would have. Even if it had killed me."

Thomas's eyes went to heat. In less than a blink, he had his hand on Marcus's biceps in a solid grip. "There's no world where that would have been the right thing for me," he said.

Marcus's jaw flexed, but he gave Thomas's nape a hard squeeze. It was the answer he was always glad to hear, down to his soul, but it didn't make his own statement any less true. Letting Thomas go would have destroyed him. Not physically. He would have kept going, being who he was, but something inside would have died and never lived again.

If that was the depth of feeling Rory and Daralyn were on their way to sharing, Marcus shared Thomas's worry.

He hoped to God Rory wouldn't have to face that choice. Because Thomas was right. Nothing could knock a person down harder than that, and make you never want to get up again.

CHAPTER THREE

*D*aralyn stared at the legs of her kitchen table. It was a yard sale bargain Elaine had found. She and Daralyn had painted it a pale green, and Daralyn had stenciled the legs so a vine with tiny white flowers was climbing up them.

Her backpack was at her feet, and she was curled up over herself, her head in her hands. She didn't have the energy to move, even as she despised herself for that immobility.

So much had changed, so much hadn't. Each day brought new challenges, but each challenge was just as hard as the last. Would it ever be easier? Why, after five years, did she still stand in darkness in broad daylight? A weighted darkness no one else could see.

She was smothered by it. Silently.

We hear a peep out of you, girl, you stay in that hole another hour.

Dr. Taylor, her psychiatrist, had coaxed Daralyn to talk about it.

No one else can see the darkness, so it's not real. But it's the most real thing. Because it stands between me and everything else.

Everything else you want? Dr. Taylor asked.

Everything else. Just everything else.

In the meantime, she was losing things her survival instinct told her it was too dangerous to lose. Like awareness of her surroundings.

"Daralyn."

She snapped up straight. She hadn't heard him open the door, his chair moving over the threshold.

She didn't have to look his way to feel his presence. There was a heat around him that could fill a room, surround her. And his eyes...if she looked at his dark brown eyes, she found something there that she wanted to be as real as that darkness, because then maybe she'd have a shelter from it. She felt that way when she was around him.

"I knocked, but I could tell you didn't hear me."

She would have ended up in the cellar for a couple hours for not paying attention. Maybe had her next meal taken away.

She kept her face down, because he'd see she'd been crying. But she hadn't been expecting him here, and didn't know what to say. Which might explain the utter nonsense that started to come out of her mouth.

"I'm sure the tuition can be refunded, and you all can use it for something else. And the books and these notebooks, I can use them for other things, maybe study them at home and learn—"

"Stop," he said.

"It's okay. Really. I'm fine. I just...I'll be at work tomorrow. It will be okay."

He moved toward her, and she surged up and around the table, retreating. What was she thinking? But before her unthinkable act could fluster her, he came to a halt, met her gaze with an even, steady look.

"Are you running from me, Daralyn?"

She'd seen him get frustrated about his ability to maneuver easily in close quarters. But the loss of that ability had taught him to rely on other methods. Effective ones.

She stammered to silence and gripped the hem of her shirt in nervous hands, but otherwise she stopped moving. With a satisfied nod, he came to her, stopped so she was standing by the side of his chair.

"What happened?" He took her hand, tugged so he moved her back to her seat in the kitchen. "Sit down and tell me."

I couldn't do what's so easy for everyone else. Again. No matter how much faith you all have in me, no matter how much I try, I can't seem to make it into the light. The cold and dark are always waiting.

"Hey." He'd touched her face, had kept her hand clasped in his other one. "Don't get so frustrated. You're fine. Remember? You just told me so."

He was teasing her gently, his lips curving above the well-groomed short beard that covered his jaw. She couldn't smile, so she stared at their linked fingers. She loved his hands. Strong, chapped from the work he did around the farm and at the store. He was wearing a T-shirt, so she could see the fine lengths of his forearms, the biceps that flexed when he pushed his chair. She could get ridiculously mesmerized watching that.

She wanted to tell him what had happened, she realized. He was good at that, too, helping her unlock the things in herself that kept her from saying what was happening in her head.

"I thought I could do it," she said. "For a few minutes, it was exciting. Then there was the noise, and someone was shouting across the courtyard. So many things, from so many different directions. I went to my first class and all the chairs were taken except one in the back, and there were so many people between me and it. The teacher started talking, and...I don't know. It felt like too much. I couldn't breathe. So I left, and everyone was staring at me..."

Her words faded away. His fingers were stroking hers, lying along her wrist, playing with the chain. Sensation ran up her arm, through her upper body.

She twitched. "I...do you mind if I get up and cook some eggs?"

She needed to move, and fortunately he nodded, moving back to give her room to get past him. She felt his attention as she pulled out the container of eggs she'd gathered from Thomas and Marcus's laying hens.

"What did you do after that?" he asked.

"I sat in the courtyard." She slid her skillet to the right burner of the small stove. "I figured I'd wait there until the van came back for us at nine-fifteen. But then I saw Mr. Peterson. He's taking a class about soil enrichment for his watermelons, and it finished at six-thirty. I asked him if he was heading home and he was, so he gave me a ride. He didn't talk, just played music on his radio. I closed my eyes and he hummed along. It was nice."

Mr. Peterson was better than most about that. He was a quiet person, too. While many people knew she wasn't a talker, it didn't stop them from purposefully trying to draw her out sometimes, making her anxiety rise.

She gripped the rubber sleeve on the skillet handle and stared miserably into the dark bottom, at the slick coating of oil she'd put in it. "I failed."

A glance his way showed those brown eyes with a reproving look to them. "How did you fail? You got in the van, went into the classroom. Maybe you just need someone to go with you the first few times."

"I have to do it by myself."

"Why?"

She tightened her hold on the handle. The oil was starting to warm, blending with the seasoning cooked into the cast iron. It was a reassuring smell. "Because...because everyone else can."

"And you want to be able to do it, too. That's a good reason." He considered. "But what if the first time I ever went to physical therapy, I'd said fuck off, I've got this. I'm going to pull myself up on my weak-ass arms, with a body that works much differently, and do these workouts without a spotter."

"You would have gotten hurt." She set her jaw. "But it's not like that. It's been five years..."

"After spending the first fifteen years of your life without any real help or support," he countered firmly. "You haven't been sitting on your ass. You've learned to read and write, started working in the store, doing a million things you didn't know how to do. None of it has come easy. We've seen you struggle. But you keep pushing yourself to do more."

Because it was like a slap in the face, how she tried and yet fell short, at things so easy for everyone else. Dr. Taylor could tell her all sorts of reasons why, connected to her childhood, her uncle and father. She talked about a gap that needed to be crossed, but it wasn't a gap. It was an impenetrable wall that needed to be knocked down with equipment Daralyn didn't have.

She'd said that Daralyn would have it, in time. But it got so tiring to fail so often.

"Daralyn." He'd drawn close, and reached past her, cutting the heat down and moving the skillet off the burner. She started at the realization she'd been about to burn the oil, but he touched her arm. "Look at me."

Tears were dripping down her nose. He pulled a paper towel off the roll and blotted them, cupping her face. "You're killing me, honey," he murmured. "You're so much stronger than you realize. But I get it."

He gave her a wry look. "So I'm at Red's gym, not having one of my better days, and I'm dragging myself along the parallel bars. While I do that, some guy dead lifting three hundred pounds moves from that station, grabs water, tosses the cup away and moves to another piece of equipment. It's so easy for him. I get why it's not easy for me. But still, it tears me down sometimes.

"Then Red says to me, 'Hauling your ass up onto these bars takes perseverance. Because it's not to sculpt yourself a cute ass or reach a fitness goal. It's to keep a body healthy that's permanently lost half its mobility. And that's more than perseverance. It's also courage. Courage ain't pretty or easy, and it's not like in the movies. It's like the song says. It's a cold and broken hallelujah.'"

"In the song, it's love that's a cold and broken hallelujah," she said. "Not courage."

He tugged her hair. "Same difference. Remember when you tried to do that weekend orientation field trip thing the college hosted?"

She'd come home early and fast on that as well, but Elaine and Les had been quick to reassure her that it was just too soon to be away for a whole weekend.

"A bunch of people in a new environment, new stuff to learn..." He shrugged. "It's totally okay to have a spotter for a while."

He was acting like everything was okay. It wasn't such a big deal. She knew it was. Yet she found the energy to respond, to feel less weighted down by what had happened, enough to engage in the conversation, wipe away the tears herself.

She frowned. "A spotter?"

"Someone to go with you to the campus. Sit with you in the class, or maybe just hang around nearby, like in the courtyard. Someone you can touch base with if things get to be too much." A half smile touched his mouth. "Like having a therapy dog. Minus the tail and floppy ears."

She laid her hand on the chain he'd put around her wrist. "Like this. A touchstone."

It had startled her when he'd done that. But it had helped, the pressure of those links. Yet that, too, reminded her she'd failed. Even when he'd given her a tool to help.

"I'm sorry," she said, telling him that.

His expression became slightly harder, but not in a mean way. She knew what mean looked like. "There's nothing to apologize for. You think football players win their first game just because they have all the right equipment? No. It takes skill and practice. The equipment just helps them keep getting back on the field. Now, how about a spotter? Nothing wrong with having that. A few weeks down the road, you'll tell me to stay home, that you've got this."

Surprise rippled through her. "You'd be my spotter? What about the store?"

"Your classes are three nights a week," he said. "Amanda can help cover the store mid-afternoon until the six o'clock closing, and Mom will pitch in when she can't. All we need is someone to watch the register and answer basic questions. I'll have my cell and they can text if something comes up they don't know. "

She frowned. "Johnny knows the farm end of things better. Maybe he should cover instead of Amanda.'

"Yeah. But Amanda needs the money for that pharmacy tech certification she's doing."

"I know that," she said quickly. Too quickly. "I was just thinking... Johnny also needs some extra money."

"So he does." Johnny Hill, one of the many Hills in their county, including the family who had once owned Thomas and Marcus's house, regularly helped out at the store. "But he isn't as pretty," Rory noted. "People might not buy as much, or be as forgiving if he doesn't know stuff off the top of his head like we do."

Her eyes narrowed. She'd picked up the skillet to move it back on the burner, and set it back down on the stove with more force than intended. She jumped at the noise. Darting a glance his way, she saw his eyes were twinkling.

Slowly, she turned to face him. "You said that to tease me."

He did that more often now at the store. Kept her smiling, sometimes even getting her to tease him back, though it still startled her when she did it, like discovering a room in her house she hadn't even known was there.

"She'd actually be good in the store," Rory pointed out. "I wasn't teasing about that."

"No. The pretty part."

"Yeah. On that I was maybe teasing you." He cocked his head. "It got you riled. A riled woman has a special light to her. My dad used to say that to my mom when she was getting worked up. It usually made her smile. Unless his timing was off, in which case she might swing a skillet like that at his head."

"Hmph." She moved to the sink, lifted the bottle of dish liquid.

"Don't—"

But she'd already pivoted and squirted it, a strong blue stream that hit him mid-chest and could penetrate his shirt like cold fingers.

She'd done it so quickly, her impulsiveness hit her a beat after the fact, giving her a surge of near-terror and an inexplicable burst of laughter, captured somewhere under her breastbone. He put his hands on his push rims.

"Give me that bottle."

She scampered in front of the table as he pursued, but she had to be quick. His current chair was designed for optimal maneuverability. She remembered the day he'd been working on it in the back shop of the store, how he'd explained it to her. He'd had the casters drawn to the inside of the main wheels, which made the chair less stable, but gave it a smaller width and minimal turning radius. Just like an experienced bike rider didn't need training wheels or a heavier frame, instead preferring a stripped-down sports bike, an advanced wheelchair user like himself didn't need the additional stability.

However, a small space was a small space, and it worked against him. It worked against her, too. She'd slipped by him into her bedroom, and that was where she made her mistake, because now he blocked the door. The only way out was the window.

He gave her an amused look as she eyed it. "Really?"

She shrugged, but realized he'd done it. He'd really made her feel better. The school stuff was still there, but he was right. It was just a bump in the road, not a major thing. And he'd said he'd go with her.

If he went with her, she could do it. Maybe she should be ashamed about that. Or maybe she could trust him when he said that it was nothing to be ashamed of at all.

Her bed was between them. She was considering her next move, which might be dashing over the top of it if he tried to come around, but then he took a different tactic. One she had a really hard time resisting, especially when the smile on his face gave way to something else. Something quiet and considering. Intent.

"Come here," he said, holding out his hand.

When he used that tone, other things happened to her. Everything inside became still, and her thoughts and movements aligned, focused on what he was telling her. That was happening more and more, too, when she was around him.

Now she came out from behind the bed. Instead of taking her hand, he closed a hand around her wrist, above the bracelet.

"I should spank you," he said quietly. "What do you think of that?"

She suspected he'd intended it to come out teasing, a joke. But her reaction wasn't that way at all. That stillness expanded, even as her heart thudded a little more powerfully and her fingers curved over his on her wrist. Her breath was short and quick in her throat.

She'd never been spanked. She'd only seen it shown on TV, a parent doing it to prove they cared about a child by offering discipline, structure, love.

She also remembered the stories about him and his sister Les routinely wrestling as kids. Mostly it had been one-sided, him wrestling her to the ground when the mood took him. He'd said Les was a scrappy and dirty fighter, so once he had her down, he'd slap her ass, giving her a spanking like his parents, just to make her madder.

Thinking about those two things together gave Daralyn an odd mix of feelings, emotional and physical. Her fingers had tightened further over his, and his gaze had gone heated. It moved from her fingers, up to her parted lips.

"I think you like the idea," he said. "I know I do."

She couldn't speak, but she couldn't look away, and when he put pressure on his grip, his eyes on hers telling her what he wanted, she accepted his will. She lowered her gaze and nodded, just the slightest of movements.

After he locked his brakes, he brought her down over his lap. Slowly. She could sense he was watching her carefully, hardwired to determine if she had any negative feelings about it. She knew he cared about her, wouldn't want to hurt her. She felt nothing but a desire for him to hold her like this, do what he'd threatened so playfully. But her response to it wasn't playful. It wasn't bad, either.

Only Rory could take her from tears to an impulsive playfulness to something she couldn't describe, but most everyone would think she couldn't handle.

Her ponytail tumbled forward over her shoulder. He put one hand in the center of her back, below her shoulder blades. Her bra strap was under her shirt, under his palm, an intimacy that increased her awareness of his touch. She thought about him unhooking it, getting it out of the way so her breasts would press against his thighs. He had some sensation toward the top of them. She'd heard him mention that and wondered if he would feel her nipples against his skin as intensely as she felt the pressure of his legs now, through the thin shirt she wore.

He loosened the band around her ponytail, letting her hair fall free over her shoulders. As she curled her fingers over his push rim, her other hand dropped to his shin to latch onto his jeans. Her hold constricted when he stroked through her hair. As she inhaled, she could smell the fragrant dishwashing liquid on his shirt front, mixed with his warm male scent.

She had a full-length mirror in here. Les and his mother had added it to the room. By adjusting the chair a few inches, he could now see her fully, how she was stroking his shin, the little movements of her fingers. He made a noise of pleasure and approval, so she didn't stop. She rested her cheek on his leg.

"So how many swats does squirting me earn?"

The question, issued in a tone of dry humor, summoned a small smile, then a little giggle when he tickled her sides, making her squirm. She went still again as he dug his fingers deeper into her hair.

"I've thought about brushing this," he said, low. "I'd have you kneel at my feet while I do it. Maybe with you wearing nothing but a robe."

He'd never talked to her like that, and her mind ran wild with the possibilities, even as her body flattened under the petting. He'd turned his attention to the hand on her back, and what was below it. He molded his palm over her buttocks, traced the middle seam of her jeans, separating the cheeks. It didn't do that when she was standing, her body too thin and the jeans too loose.

There was a quiver going through her, little shivers of the flesh. He was treating her like a woman.

He lifted his hand and gave her a firm smack at the widest part of

36

her backside, sweeping upward. If she'd been naked, the impact would have made the cheeks wobble.

A little gasp broke from her, her thighs wanting to loosen. He did it again. She opened her hand, closed it on his shin, on the wheel rim. The sensation was indescribable. She wanted to wiggle but remain motionless, all at once.

He did it five times. Feelings ricocheted around her insides like fired bullets, full of heat and urgency to find a target. When he started to lift her, she couldn't make herself loosen her grip on his jeans leg. With a chuckle, he gently disengaged her. His voice was husky to her ears. Weighed down with hunger.

"Like lifting one of the barn cats off my lap."

He brought her to her feet, shifting his grip back to her wrist, a loose clasp above the chain. As he rubbed a thoughtful circle over her pulse with his thumb, her hair fell forward around her face, and he brushed it back, gave her a look.

"You gonna squirt me with dishwashing liquid again?"

His smile inspired an uncertain one of her own. She felt unsteady, everything throbbing. "I don't know. Maybe."

"Good answer. Best answer possible. I'm taking you to dinner Friday," he said. "All right?"

She lifted her gaze to him. "Okay. Yes."

"Wear a dress and leave your hair down, fixing it the way you did for church last week."

Now he'd surprised her enough she ventured a question. "Why?"

He smiled a smile that didn't reach his eyes. A whole lot of other things took up the space there as he looked at her. "Because during the service, the morning sun came through the windows. The light touched your hair and haloed you in different colors, like the angel you are."

He tightened his grip, watched her lips part again. "I haven't been able to stop thinking about it ever since."

CHAPTER FOUR

*T*wo days later, they were facing another school day. And Rory was still thinking about the night in her cottage with every other breath.

The whole world would have wondered if he'd lost his mind, proceeding like he had, with the spanking and everything attached to that. Sex had to have all sorts of confusing, possibly traumatic implications for her. Yet he thought of how many people treated him like he was an egg, capable of breaking with the slightest pressure.

Daralyn wasn't an egg. She was fragile, and she'd been through hell. But she'd damn well earned the right to be treated like a woman, when that desire was so clearly showing itself. And she deserved that right from someone who would chop off his two functioning limbs to keep from hurting her.

No, he hadn't known if spanking her was a good idea, no matter how much he'd liked it or she'd seemed to. But Marcus's words had filled his mind. *Don't second guess your instincts.* His instincts had said he should move forward with learning what felt good to her.

Any concern he might have had about whether even playful corporal punishment would summon bad memories for her had been relieved by the clear signs of her interest and arousal at the idea. It sure as hell got him going. The air in the room had become thick and heavy, things slowing down so he could hear her breath, short and quick in her throat.

He recalled the way her breasts had pushed up against his thigh, causing the neckline of the shirt to gap. Over the cup of her bra, he'd been able to see the pink circle hinting at her nipple. He'd wanted to play with it. Use his mouth and suckle it deep.

Need had surged through him, a desire to plumb this feeling for them both, see how deep and broad it was. Fortunately, he'd had the good sense to rein it back. Though stopping after five swats was more difficult than tying a string to one of his teeth and attaching it to a swinging door, he had done it. There was a sharp sweetness to taking just a taste.

He remembered her intriguing reluctance to let Amanda Brewster pick up the slack at the store. He and Amanda had dated in high school. After he'd landed in the chair, they'd reconnected for a short time. But that hadn't been about a relationship, not that way. She'd just been a friend from high school who'd been there when he needed...a spotter. For the thing a guy felt the most uncertain about, after losing a lot of his functionality below the belt line.

As a result of that initial experience, and everything he'd built upon and around it since, he could see the possibilities for a relationship far more clearly. Particularly one with the remarkable woman he was about to take to school.

Daralyn had put her books together, checked her supplies, and was emerging from the restroom, just as Elaine was coming in the front door, ready to take over until closing hours. Daralyn had changed out of her work clothes into the same pretty blue shirt and new dark blue jeans she'd had on the other day. He imagined she'd hung the outfit back up in the closet, keeping it ready for this second attempt.

She'd also put his bracelet back on.

The day after the night in the cottage, when she came in to work, he'd called her up to the counter, had her extend her wrist. He'd seen the flash of dismay when he'd taken out the pliers. He liked knowing she didn't want to take it off, but he placed his hand over it, caressing her wrist and the top of her hand.

"I don't want you wearing this at work, because it isn't safe to wear jewelry while operating store equipment, like the knife sharpener and chain cutter."

"Of course." Her expression had gone blank. "And...you probably want your ring back."

"Long as you have it, I know where it is." In preparation for this moment, he'd found a clip and added it to the bracelet, showing it to her so she knew it would be easy to put it back on herself. Then he laid the whole thing into her palm and folded her fingers over it. "You can keep it, long as you need it. If you feel better wearing it for school or when it's not a danger to you to have it on, that's fine by me."

Though it gave him intense pleasure to see it on her, he wouldn't tell her that, because he was interested in seeing how much she would wear it for herself. She'd tucked it in her pocket that day, and since then he'd noted she put her hand in there pretty often. Now, while wearing it, she was worrying the ring with two fingers, rolling it against the heel of her palm. She was paler than when she'd gone into the restroom, but she was holding.

He could deal with that. Despite his mother moving behind the counter, setting her stuff down, he met Daralyn's eyes as if they were the only two people here, and gestured to bring her over to him.

He closed his hand over her wrist, the bracelet, gave them both a light press. "It's going to be a good night," he said.

He saw a little color come back. "You'll be there."

"I'll be there."

She drew a breath and gave him a ghost of a smile, but it was there.

Rory glanced over his shoulder at his mom. From how studiously she was changing the login on the cash register, he knew she was taking in every detail. He bit back his own smile. "You got this, Mom?"

"Why do you always ask me that? I was working in this store side by side with your father—"

"Way back when you were carrying Thomas. You would have had him right here behind the counter and gotten right back to work, if Dad hadn't insisted on that hospital nonsense. I know." He flashed her a grin. "But that was before you got old."

She picked up the fly swatter hanging by the register and threatened him with it. "I can still work three people your age under the table," she retorted, but her eyes twinkled. "Off with you two."

"I'm really sorry about—" Daralyn started, and then stopped as Rory applied pressure to her wrist. Her gaze snapped to him.

"I asked my mother to come in and help. My decision. Right?"

Her mouth opened. Closed. He didn't dare look at his mother. If she was as surprised as Daralyn, he didn't want to dilute the moment with self-consciousness.

"Let's go," he said. "Do you have your stuff?"

Daralyn hesitated, then nodded. "Yes, Rory."

∼

As she went toward his van, they were side by side. He opened the passenger door for her and she hoisted herself into the seat, putting the backpack between her feet. "Thank you."

A flashback cut through his mind. Him, after one of the football games, with his girlfriend at the time, Emily Waters. When Rory obtained his license, Dad had let him have one of the farm pickups to run around in. Rather than letting Emily step on the running plate and put herself into the seat, Rory had done it, lifting her with all those easily won muscles from farming and football. He remembered her flush and bright eyes, her laughter, as he set her down. He'd tugged her hair, given her a grin.

Forcing himself not to recollect the negative things down that road, he reached up and clasped Daralyn's braid, tugged it. She smiled, which made him feel better, too.

He closed the door and came around. A remote opened the side door, laid down the ramp. He rolled in, transferred himself out of his chair to the driver's seat. After he turned it on its swivel to position himself, he locked it in place. The movement brushed his shoulder against her. Figuring *what the hell*, he stroked her hair off her neck, laid a kiss on her collar bone. Her breath drew in, a little shudder, her cheek brushing against his temple. Then he casually straightened, turning over the ignition.

As he drove the hand-controlled vehicle, he prompted conversation about tonight's classes. It helped distract her, though he could feel her studying him as they talked. That was okay. If the kiss had distracted her as well, it would add to the things keeping her stress down to a manageable level.

Yeah, it was all selfless on his part.

It didn't take too long to get there. Their small annex community college fondly took him back to memories of high school. Probably because it had been set up in the old middle school building that dated back to the eighties. Their county didn't rate a lot of funding for new buildings, so they'd made do with this one. He'd been here before for other town events, and knew the place had ramps, but nothing fancy, like the ADA-mandated mechanized doors of newer campuses. And since it wasn't a large community college, there weren't many handicap spaces, but at least they were easy to find, and he was in luck tonight, because a couple of them were open, including the one that provided a wider space for a vehicle with a ramp.

He saw a bunch of people toting backpacks, scrolling through tablets or phones. Everyone moving this way and that, in groups or alone. The main difference between this scene and high school was the mix of age groups, but fifty percent or more were in their late teens or early twenties.

As he took in the scene, he was aware of the ball of tension in his gut, but he knew what it was, and it was okay. He'd been so focused on helping Daralyn, he'd forgotten the one drawback for him, when around a bunch of unfamiliar people. While interacting with new customers or delivery drivers he hadn't met before, he got small doses of it. But surrounded by a sizeable number of people close to his own age, he felt it more keenly.

The glances in his direction, quickly cutting away to avoid direct eye contact. The bright wattage smiles of someone making a conscious effort to acknowledge him more directly than they would a "normal" stranger, perversely so he wouldn't feel like he was being treated differently.

He wasn't sure which reaction he preferred, or where the happy medium was, but it didn't matter. This wasn't about him. It was about Daralyn.

They crossed the open courtyard, the hub for students coming and going to their various destinations. He saw plenty of outdoor tables where he could set himself up. He pointed them out to her, so she'd know where to find him. "Take me to your first class," he told her. "So I'll know where to find you."

That won him another small smile. They moved toward the building in question. A bearded thirty-something in flannel shirt and work shoes held the door open. Probably here for a continuing education class in his chosen blue-collar field, like Peterson had been. Or maybe for a computer class to head in a different direction.

The man's brown eyes were on Rory's chair, not on Daralyn, so as Rory gestured to Daralyn to precede him and she complied, the guy gave her the stink eye. He thought she'd stepped in front of a handicapped guy. Thankfully, she missed it, her mind gripped by what was ahead. But Rory wasn't going to let anyone think Daralyn would do something like that. He nodded to the guy as he passed through the open door. "Thanks for holding the door for my girl."

The man's face cleared, then he grinned at Rory's casual remark.

Rory caught up to Daralyn, who was waiting for him. It was louder in the hallway, more people in a contained space. The chair helped, people making a conscious effort to give them a path. She stuck close, her hand on his shoulder. He gripped it briefly, letting her know it could stay there before he pushed forward. Then they reached the open door to her classroom.

He'd made sure they'd arrived early enough she wouldn't have the same experience with crowded seating she'd had last time. Nobody better at advanced logistical planning than a member of the disabled tribe. Pi, one of the guys in his adaptive sports challenge group, called them that.

Glancing up, Rory's smile disappeared as he saw Daralyn had become noticeably paler. He pinched her arm lightly, drawing her gaze. "Don't forget to breathe," he advised. "Else you'll look like a blueberry and a crow will swoop down and try to swallow you."

She punched him in the arm, little more than a brush of her knuckles. He'd have Les work with her on that. When it came to punching her big brothers, Les could give Rocky knockout lessons. During his sister's last visit, Rory had claimed to have permanent bruising from the punches she'd landed when they were much younger. "Maybe when you get to be a big-time doctor, you can fix those," he'd told her.

"Maybe I'll become a brain surgeon and remove yours, replace it with a rock," Les rebounded. "It will be more functional."

"You can donate the brain to science," Thomas had put in. "As a medical anomaly—a brain with the intelligence of a rotting turnip."

As he captured Daralyn's hand, Rory shared that memory with her, earning another weak smile. "I'll be in the courtyard if you need me," he reminded her. "You can text me as much as you want."

Her gaze skittered around the room. Her hand was also getting colder. "Hey." He drew her attention back to him. "Just think of them as customers at the store. You don't have a bit of trouble talking to them."

"Now." She grimaced. "And that's because I always have you or one of your family as backup."

"Well, that's what I'll be. Right there in the courtyard. But I can sit in here instead if you want."

She set her chin, gripping her books tighter. "No, I can do it."

"I know you can, but if you change your mind, just text me. Hey. Daralyn, look at me. I mean it."

Her eyes came to him. He saw the struggle there, to stay calm, to make this work, to be more than she thought she could be, to try, when all she really wanted to do was run back to the safety of a much smaller world. It was really enough, it really was, and...

He tugged on her hand, reeling her in until she came down to him, and he could lay his hand alongside her face, thread his fingers into her hair. He put his mouth on hers. Held her like that, with heat and firmness, then let his fingertips move just enough to stroke her behind the ear, find the delicate flesh below, register the skip of her heartbeat through her pulse.

As he eased her back, the focus in her hazel eyes was now fully on him, just as he'd intended. "You've got this," he repeated. Not as a persuasion or wishful thinking, but as an absolute certainty. "Keep your head up. Make eye contact. Don't hide. You don't have to hide. Not ever."

She moistened her lips, her gaze on his mouth. He'd given her something else to think about, and it made his own heart thump harder to see it.

Slowly, she straightened, and looked toward the classroom. A few more people had moved past them, come in to take a seat, but there were still plenty of chairs available close to the door. He watched her lift her chin, tighten her hand on the backpack strap on her shoulder. She sent him one last quick look. "On your first day of school, were you nervous?"

"Everyone is."

"Did your parents say anything to help?"

"Yeah. Dad said, 'Behave yourself, boy. Or I'll strap your ass when you get home.' Kind of makes me hope you don't behave."

Giving her startled expression a wicked grin, he nodded. "Go on in and sit down."

There was that minute hesitation, but hand to God, he felt like a proud parent himself when he saw her make the decision. She took one step forward, then another. She walked straight to the corner desk at the very front of the room. The one closest to the door. As she slid into it, her gaze went to the white board, and latched onto it. This was some kind of civics class, so a slide of the Bill of Rights was projected onto the board. She started reading it, slowly, her lips moving.

The teacher slid past Rory. He was a skinny thirty-something guy in khakis and a crisp shirt with thin blue stripes. The wire-rimmed glasses completed the educator look. Rory knew he was the teacher because he went to the desk up front and set his briefcase upon it.

Daralyn looked toward Rory once more, enough time for him to give her a nod, and then the teacher moved to close the door. Class was beginning.

He headed to the courtyard. The halls were emptying out, but the doors had a push bar on the inside, so he brought his chair close enough, pushed it open, and gripped the frame to bring his chair up against the door, lever it open with his caster, and maneuver through. It wasn't the smoothest looking operation, but he was way better at it now than he'd been at the beginning, when he'd banged his elbows and knees. Not that he felt the knee impact, but an injury there was of greater concern than anything above the waist. He had to stay hyper-aware of whatever came in contact with his legs, for cuts or injuries he couldn't feel.

The pull side took only a little backward momentum, a good yank. He liked that side because it made it easier for him to open the door for a woman. That is, if he did a quick brake lock so the resistance from the door didn't roll his chair forward and mash her against it.

Challenges like that had enabled his earliest physical therapist, Lucille, aka The She-Bitch-From-Hell, to successfully introduce him to his first adaptive sport, wheelchair basketball. After a particular grueling session, where he'd considered his greatest accomplishment to be not breaking down and bawling like a baby at how freaking weak he was, she'd taken him out in the back of the center. They had a track and several basketball courts, one of which was in use for an informal scrimmage. Every guy playing was on wheels.

"There's more than basketball happening," she'd pointed out. "See how smoothly they handle their chairs? One handed, two handed... they become one with them. You can hate and resist the equipment that gives you options, Rory, like your chair. Or it can become your best friend."

"Stupid. That's just stupid." But his attention had reluctantly remained on the basketball players, the way they did wheelies in the chair, taking the casters off the ground as they spun, their center of balance flawless.

Or not so much. When one player toppled, something that, at that point, had terrified Rory, the guy swore, but it was a good-natured oath. No different from a guy going up toe-to-toe with another guy at the hoop and getting knocked on his ass. One guy nudged his chair back over to him, and the player pulled himself back in it on his own. In less than a minute, they were back to playing, no muss, no fuss.

A couple days later he was asking her what kinds of exercises would get him out on the court with them.

He knew why those early days were coming up in his head right now. A lot of the things going through Daralyn's head he could see so clearly because he'd been there.

A comfort zone was bliss. It was also stagnation. The death of hope.

He stopped at a table where a kid who looked like he hadn't been long out of high school was reading. He had a shock of red hair, a silver cuff earring and wore mostly black. "Hey, where'd you get the Funyuns?" Rory asked.

"Over there." The kid waved to his left without looking up. "Vending machine next to the restroom. But stay away from the protein bars. They've been in there since the fall of the Roman Empire, and they taste like it."

"Who are you kidding? That's the way all protein bars taste."

The kid grinned and looked up with bright blue eyes. He did a double take. "Oh. Yeah."

Rory ignored the full stop and eyed him critically, the well-developed biceps and shoulders. "Where do you work out?"

"Wherever I can. Right now at a buddy's garage." The guy was now looking past the chair, studying Rory right back. "How about you?"

"Home gym, but I've got a personal trainer, Red, down at—"

"Martin's Gym." The kid whistled. "Yeah, I did a couple sessions with him. He's tough."

"Don't I know it. I was walking before I started going to him."

The young man blanched. At Rory's grin, he chuckled and held out a fist for a bump. "Good one. I'm Brandt. Hey, I'll split the Funyuns with you. Half the fat..."

After Brandt headed off for his class, Rory settled in with his paperwork, spreading it out on the table. But before he started on that, he texted Daralyn a dozen emojis that looked like red roses.

A few minutes later, she returned a smiley face, a heart, and a knight on horseback, with a lance. He had to admit that made him feel pretty damn good, and not just because it showed him the most important thing, that she was doing okay.

When the doors started opening about ninety minutes later, signaling the end of the first class, he had her lunch box out and waiting. He saw her emerge, find him, and her already encouragingly happy expression brightened. She started talking to him about ten feet away.

"Did you know that the Constitution came from a document signed almost a *thousand* years ago? The Magna Carta..."

Since she'd never obtained a high school diploma, getting her general credits to qualify for that was her first step in community college. He'd graduated middle of his class, an indifferent student. Even his friends who were much better students had seen school as a social outlet and the means to get into a good college. The adult students here, working their classes in between work and kids, were climbing a ladder to better opportunities.

How many of them had ever set all that aside long enough to be as delighted as Daralyn was, simply for the chance to sit in a classroom and learn?

Was it the sadism of fate that had put a woman with her intelligence in such a terrible position for most of her childhood? Or had it been a gift of mercy that helped her survive? Who better understood just how amazing flying was, than a bird who'd always been caged?

Didn't matter if it had been in the cage since hatching out of the egg. Thousands of years of flying couldn't be bred out of a creature born with wings. It would call to something in their very blood and bone, if they had the chance to embrace it again.

Seeing the world through her eyes, her excitement, was like being able to fly himself.

"Daralyn." An unfamiliar voice broke her off mid-sentence.

As Rory turned toward it, he saw the teacher of her civics class approaching their table. He carried a slim, dog-eared paperback. "Turns out, I did have it in my file cabinet. This is an old text, but it's one of the best I've found. It examines the historic motivations and environment that existed during the time each constitutional article and amendment was formulated."

When he offered the book, she hesitated. "That's so kind. I don't read very fast, Mr. Reid. Maybe I could look through it when I'm between periods here, so I can give it back to you before I leave for the day."

"It's all right. Take it, and take your time with it. I haven't had someone so interested in constitutional history since I had my own first class on it." He smiled at her.

Yeah, he was her teacher. Yeah, Rory was glad she was excited about civics. But the teacher had eyes—four of them—and they were all noticing just how pretty she was. A pretty, eager, adult student.

Rory told himself it wasn't because he was in a wheelchair that the guy hadn't given him the quick assessing glance any other guy would, if he saw a man sitting with a woman who'd caught his interest. Even so, the ugly thing sitting in his gut said it was. A man with only half a body wasn't really a man anyway, right? Probably in the "friend zone" at best. Not serious competition.

"Thank you," she said, taking the book like she'd been offered treasure. Who the hell wouldn't be fascinated by her? No artifice, just pure sincerity. With deep hazel eyes, shiny long hair and a shy smile that made any guy with balls want to keep that smile turned his way.

"Mr. Reid—" she began.

"Joe is fine," he assured her.

Not even remotely fine, asshole.

48

But Rory couldn't miss the possibilities here. Smart guy, lots of things to teach, with an unassuming, relaxed personality that would work really well with Daralyn.

Plus a whole body. One whose operator wouldn't have to think twice about how to open a door for her.

Shut the fuck up, he told that pathetic inner voice. Once, it had been his constant companion. Now, not so much, but it liked to surface at annoying times.

"Joe," she said. "This is Rory Wilder. He's my friend, and my boss."

Joe turned to Rory. As Rory offered a hand, their eyes met, a whole lot of messages going back and forth.

Rory tried not to be petty, but he couldn't help but notice Joe had a limp-wristed handshake. He couldn't call it a true read, though, since Joe had that typical brief hesitation, as if worried Rory might break if he shook his hand wrong.

"Nice to meet you, Joe," he said, trying to sound pleasant. "Sounds like you're a good teacher."

"Some students remind you that you start this gig wanting to be a good teacher." Joe shrugged, offered an easy smile. "Thanks for that reminder, Daralyn. See you in a couple days."

It helped Rory more than he wanted to admit that the second Joe turned away, Daralyn's attention went a hundred percent to the book she cradled in her hands. "That was so nice of him," she said. "I'm going to try and read this before my next class with him, so I can return it."

"It sounds like you can take a little longer if you need to."

She looked up, glanced at Joe's retreating form. Then she returned her gaze to Rory and gave him an absent smile, her mind full of all sorts of new ideas.

Rory nudged her lunchbox at her, trying to keep his amiable expression fixed in place. "Go ahead and eat something, since your six-o'clock class won't let out until seven-thirty."

"Oh, right." She set the book carefully out of range of the food, and unpacked her thermos and sandwich. She unwrapped the sandwich and broke off a nibble. "Want half? I won't eat all this."

She wouldn't, much as he wished she would, so he took the other half. Six to six-thirty was apparently dinner time. Some of the students had brought their own, like Daralyn. Others lined up in front of the food court options.

"Is this a lot like high school?" she asked.

He hadn't looked away from her profile as she took it all in. Now she looked at him, realized he was gazing at her, and smiled uncertainly, making him wonder what she saw in his expression. He made a conscious effort to add warmth to it.

"Yeah. And no. In high school, the people you're hanging with are your close friends. You have stuff in common, like me and the football team. Or Les and her fellow science geeks. Thomas...he always seemed to be everyone's friend, but not, if that makes sense. Though I didn't get why then, I do now."

"Why?" She chewed a bite of her sandwich slowly, her attention fixed on him.

"He couldn't be who he was. A guy who liked guys. So it was sort of a mask. He was a nice guy; that part wasn't a mask. He was good-looking enough to be popular, so those things kept him from being treated like an outcast."

"Yes. I can see that." She put down the sandwich, studied it. "My uncle and father didn't take me into town much, but I knew the rules when we were together. 'Don't talk to anyone. Don't wander off.' If I broke the rules, they wouldn't take me back except for church, not for a long, long time, not that we went that often anyway. So when I met people in town I knew, like Thomas or Les, or you, I had to act the right way."

He swallowed back the anger her earlier life always incited. She didn't need that. He responded in a steady voice. "How did you feel like acting?"

"Like I wasn't there," she said honestly. Her gaze moved to where his hand rested on the table, traveled up to his shoulder, touched his face and moved away. "I didn't feel real, so pretending I was felt... uncomfortable. Being in town was different from being at home, which was good, but I was afraid, too, which made me think being invisible would be better. If that makes sense."

"It does." As he touched her hand, she brightened.

"Tell me a high school story. Something you did with your friends."

"You've heard all the sports stories, probably more than anyone wants to. Including me."

His friends had visited a lot in those early days, telling way too many nostalgic stories about being on the football field. Talk about rubbing his nose in it, though he knew that hadn't been their intent. They just hadn't known what else to say, and reliving their glory days seemed the best option. He'd known she listened from her room sometimes, the door cracked.

"Something other than sports," she said.

"Girls?"

She frowned. "No."

That gave him a boost he'd needed. "Sure?"

Her eyes narrowed. "You're teasing me because I don't have a skillet."

He chuckled. "Trying. What I really want to do is rip off Joe's legs so I can have a fair fight for your interest. I don't have any cool books about the history of the Constitution."

She looked as if he'd dashed cold water in her face. "What?"

He waved a hand. "I'm kidding."

"You think he was..."

"I think you're a beautiful woman who's really interested in what he's teaching. He's going to test the waters. He's an adult, you're an adult."

"No. I'm going to go give this back to him."

"Hey, Daralyn." Startled by her reaction, he managed to snag her wrist before she jumped up. "You've done nothing wrong. Neither has he. It's just normal guy-girl stuff. If he asks you out, you just say—"

"I'm with you. I belong to you."

Talk about being caught off balance. He hadn't seen that one coming, let alone the force with which she blurted it out.

She stopped at his reaction, took a breath. "I'm so sorry. I interrupted. What were you about to say?"

"I was about to say..." He was neck deep in treacherous waters, with no clue about all the dangers that lay within them, so he spoke carefully. "That if you were interested, you'd say yes. If not, you'd tell him you're not, that you just really like his class and what you're learning in it."

She stared at him. "You... I don't belong to you?"

"Daralyn, why do you think you belong to me?"

"Because you touched me...that way. You've kissed me."

"Yeah, but you can choose to be with me. When a guy kisses you, it's not like a brand or something."

Even if it had felt exactly that way to him.

Her gaze dropped back to the book. She traced it with nervous fingers. He had no idea where she'd gone in her head until she lifted it, looked at him with that unflinching honesty he'd just praised.

"Do you want me to belong to you?"

He did. He wasn't sure if he should say so, yet it came out of his mouth before he could stop it. "Yeah. But I want—"

"Then that's all that matters. I need to get to my next class."

Before he could get out another word, she'd shouldered her backpack, grabbed the book and fled.

CHAPTER FIVE

*H*e decided the best course of action was to behave as he had before that baffling conversation. He sent her more emojis for the next class, received some tentative ones in return. She didn't come back between her second and third classes, though she texted him and said she was going over the homework assignment with the professor, because she had some questions.

At five minutes until nine, he'd put away his laptop and paperwork, satisfied with the amount he'd completed. When she emerged a few minutes later, he was relieved to find she'd reverted to the excitement she'd displayed after Joe's class.

On the way home, she talked about the things she'd learned, the people she'd met. No more Joes, but he was sure she'd been noticed by all her instructors. She'd kept the teachers hopping with her questions.

As he was pulling into the driveway at Marcus and Thomas's, she at last broke off, giving him a sheepish look. "Sorry. I was jabbering like the mockingbirds."

"Not even close. Those noisy bastards could win medals."

When he put his hand over hers, folded in her lap, she adjusted her double grip and wrapped it around his hand. The chain bracelet pressed into his skin, and her fingers were light, like bird bones. While they were never warm, they weren't cold, like they became when she was upset.

"Thank you," she said seriously, looking at him. "You were right. It made all the difference, knowing you were there. I won't need it for long, I promise."

"I'll be there however long you need me. Don't worry about that. It worked out good. That end-of-day paperwork I always put off got done."

"I can help more with that."

"You do plenty already. And you're an investment. Mom says you'll learn stuff, probably put us on some high-tech system that will eliminate paperwork altogether."

He grinned at her, and she smiled back. Her fingers played over his, and he shifted to capture them, hold them still with a firm grip.

She met his gaze, lowered hers. "If you don't need to get home... would you like to come in for some coffee or hot chocolate?"

"Yeah, I'd like that. You can keep telling me about the school stuff. If you're not too tired."

"I'm not sure if I'll sleep at all tonight." Her eyes went bright again. "I'm just so full of everything I saw and heard..."

As she spoke, he smiled some more and swiveled around on the driver's seat to transfer himself to his waiting chair.

He rarely had to tell Daralyn anything twice, and when they'd returned to the school parking lot, he'd told her to wait for him to open the car door for her, coming or going. Now she didn't stir until he came around to do that.

When he gave her a nod of approval, that light in her eyes got a different kind of shine. She took the hand he offered and, delicately as a deer, slipped out and onto her feet next to him.

A light was on in the living room at Marcus and Thomas's, and he could see Thomas stretched out watching TV. Rory didn't see Marcus, but his Mercedes was there next to Thomas's classic Chevy Nova, so he was elsewhere in the house.

Rory opened the screen door to Daralyn's patio and followed her into the house. She shifted one of the two kitchen chairs to the wall, giving him a spot at the table, before she moved to the pantry.

"Coffee or hot chocolate? I can do the chocolate with skim milk."

"Hot chocolate sounds good. Tell me more about the science class. You didn't finish talking about that one."

He propped an elbow on the table as he watched her. He listened, responding and asking questions, yet he suspected her awareness of how he was looking at her was growing. Could she sense the energy coming off him, building in the small space between them once again as he inhaled her scent, followed the sweep of her hair over her shoulder? He studied the little bumps her bra strap made under her shirt, the way the denim stretched over her backside when she bent to pull out the saucepan. The capable movements of her hands as she made hot chocolate with milk, using the stove instead of the microwave.

Listening to the sound of her voice, those breathy syllables, he wanted to close his eyes, let it soak into him. But he wanted to see her too. He liked that she could feel the intensity of his gaze. He liked seeing her get a little nervous for good reasons.

When the hot chocolate was ready, she put his mug on the table and sat down beside him with her own. She took a breath. "You look like you might want to talk about something," she said.

"Yeah. I do." He reached out, cupped her face, and laid his mouth on hers.

She made a surprised and pleased noise, but it was nothing next to what surged through him. The strength of it told him how much he'd thought about doing this, all night, ever since he'd kissed her throat when they left for the school. How he'd denied himself for those few hours was a miracle of deprivation. He wanted to pull her on his lap, but he didn't. He kept it right there, elbow on the corner of the table, his hand hooked with hers on the edge.

She wanted more, was pressing into it as she made a little sound in the back of her throat. Tension shivered through her as she struggled between giving into the kiss, giving him what he seemed to be demanding from her, and leashing her natural response, reining it back. What she thought wasn't allowed.

He wanted to tell her anything was allowed with him, anything she wanted, but he knew the dangers of going down that path with her. Daralyn never framed things in terms of her own wants and desires. Asking her what she wanted, pushing her to express that, was a sure way to send her into a panic attack. They'd all learned that the hard way.

With effort, he broke the kiss, keeping it easy but lingering, running his thumb along her delicate jaw. She was staring at him. When he dropped his hand to the table, palm up, he noted she put her braceleted wrist, not her hand, in his grasp. As he gripped it, she settled, resulting in a surge of feelings hard to describe. He just knew they were the exact right ones for the moment.

"What's going on in your head?" he asked. "Tell me."

"No one looks at me the way you do. Like I'm something in an art gallery, interesting and special, and almost too beautiful to touch."

"I want to touch you. A lot. Tell me more about what you're thinking. You can't say anything wrong."

She pressed her lips together. "There's this feeling when you look at me, like I'm about to feel something I've never felt, and I'm scared. But excited, too. Happy. I feel like I can talk to you, say these things in my head that don't make sense, they're so jumbled, but when you look at me the way you're looking at me, there's this steady calm in your eyes that comes inside of me. It unjumbles those thoughts, makes sense of them."

He considered himself decently experienced with girls. He'd lost his virginity as soon as he could take the beat-up truck down one of the many back roads that all the teens knew. He hadn't been naturally smooth with females, but being a football player had helped improve his fumbling tongue-tied state. He'd learned the basics, how to navigate the often awkward signals and baffling clues men and women dropped for one another in the dating game. The things they struggled to say or not say.

Not in a million years would any of them have opened their hearts this baldly, spoken such simple, emotional truths about what they were feeling. She had no experience with playing coy or being worried about what he thought of her. Not that way. It was a humbling gift of innocent trust.

And heartbreaking that she'd managed to express it so well, without crossing into the territory they all knew was dangerous for her.

Thinking about what Marcus had said about watching for cues, Rory knew she'd taught him to do that early on. Uniquely preparing them for the direction this relationship seemed to want to go.

He brought her into his lap, her hair tumbling over the arm he had around her back, holding her securely. He gathered all those thick locks in one hand and twisted them, his knuckles pressed to her neck.

He liked knowing she'd put herself in his hands. What she'd said about Joe and belonging to Rory, he knew there was something wrong there. But he wanted the words to be wholly, perfectly true. Because the gift of her giving herself to him on every level, wanting to belong to him, whether she could say it with words or not, was what he wanted.

Slow. Easy. He was in love with a woman who was unable to say what she wanted. Talk about a minefield.

But he wasn't going to deny her pleasure because of how her uncle and father had fucked up her head. He slid his thumb beneath her neckline and hooked it under her bra strap to discover cool, soft skin. He caressed her shoulder and collar bone as he met her gaze. "Take off your shirt."

No hesitation, and no apprehension, only desire in her multicolored eyes. She straightened in his lap, arched as she brought the shirt off, set it aside. The feel of her skin against his arm was something he wouldn't get tired of any time soon, so he settled her back into the cradle of it and enjoyed looking at the small curves cupped in pale blue cotton. He tightened his hold to bring her close enough he could brush his lips over one quivering mound. Still steady and slow, not going for the nipple. Just everywhere near it. Her hand had hooked over his shoulder, her fingers digging into his shirt.

He went beneath the loose waistband of her jeans to find the nip of her waist, molded his palm over it and her hip bone, his fingertips against the elastic of her panties.

She started trembling harder as he petted her with a light touch that moved in lines and circles. Over her hip and side, up to her rib cage, around to her bare back. He unhooked the bra one-handed, pressed his palm to the ridge of her spine there.

He didn't give a damn about getting to the "good stuff," as his buddies had often called it. It was all good stuff, and he wanted her to know it. He was content to spend his energy studying her every reaction, making sure they were doing all right.

He left the loosened bra where it was and lowered his touch to slip the button of her jeans, trace the edge of her panties below her navel.

She bit her lip, and one hand had dropped to his knee, fingers gripping the seam of his jeans in a sudden death grip, indicating the wrong kind of tension.

"It's okay," he said quietly. "Don't worry. Talk to me."

"When you touch me," she said hesitantly, "it feels good. But I'm not sure about...between my legs."

Not unexpected. "How about taking off the jeans? I just want to hold you in my lap in nothing but your panties. That's all we'll do." He didn't want to spook her. Make her think he was going to ask too much, too soon. The way she nodded, her expression easing, settled his concerns.

"Good," he murmured. "I want to look. Feel how wet you are."

The concerns he'd thought he'd reversed snapped into a full locking of her muscles, so violent she bucked herself off his lap. He caught her before she could fall, but she scrambled away, stumbling over his feet. She was a few paces away in a jarring blink, standing in the doorway of her bedroom.

"I'm sorry," she stammered. "I'm so sorry. I can't help it."

"It's okay." He kept his voice calm while his mind sifted rapidly through the past few seconds. When he'd spoken, he'd moved his touch up, his fingertips gliding along and above her navel. Because he'd moved away from the area causing her worry, back toward something she'd seemed to like having him touch, he knew it was his words, not the contact, that had caused her abrupt reaction.

He pushed toward her, wanting to soothe, but she retreated fully into the room, so he stopped at the threshold.

"I..." She closed her eyes, shook her head. Her hands were fisted at her sides. "I thought it would be okay. I'm so sorry..."

"You don't need to say you're sorry, baby. You've done nothing wrong."

She gave him a wild, despairing look. What concerned him the most was she looked like a trapped animal. The bra was loose, showing her breasts, her jeans open and barely snagged around her hips, but she seemed unconcerned about that. Then he thought about where he was, in front of the door. All the mixed messages about choice, and the still untapped mystery of her mind on that subject in particular, told him he had to make sure she understood.

If she *could* understand. That was the most unsettling thought of all.

"I don't want to leave, but if you need me to go, Daralyn, I can go. It's all right." It was the last thing he wanted to do, and he wasn't even sure if it was the right thing to do. He'd still make sure she knew she had that option. He always wanted her to know that.

Problem was, he didn't think words were what would help her understand that. And he'd just made the mistake he'd warned himself about. He'd asked her to tell him what she wanted. Or needed, which fell in the same category.

Her expression became more desperate and torn. She was rigid, and she'd crossed her arms over herself. Now she was fighting to talk and couldn't, her breath starting to rasp.

Fuck. A panic attack. Whatever else was going on here, that took priority.

"We're all right," he said, backing the chair so he wasn't blocking the doorway. "Breathe. Sit down on the bed for me. I need you to sit down and breathe."

She sank down on it, and bowed her head. Her back was to him, the stiff curve of it showing the stark lines of her vertebrae. When she shivered, he wanted to go to her, wrap his arms around her, but the opening between the wall and the bed on that side was too narrow for his chair. Whether it was intentional, so he couldn't easily reach her, or unintentional, it accomplished the same thing. Keeping him at arm's length.

The helpless rage he felt was the kind he knew too well. He'd take it out on his punching bag later. For now, he kept murmuring to her, even as his heart hurt, even when she curled forward over herself, as if her own pain was more than she could bear "Daralyn," he said softly.

"I'm so sorry, Rory. So sorry."

"There is nothing to be sorry about. We're okay, you and me. Nothing is wrong. Nothing that can't be fixed."

Her shoulders hunched. He wasn't sure if she heard him. "I'll see you at the store tomorrow," she said. "It will be fine."

Another of her cues. She couldn't say what she wanted, but if she said something was fine, it meant she was spinning herself up. Unless he backed off, it would get worse.

Leaving her like this was counter to everything he wanted to be for her, do for her. But just like he'd known he should have accompanied her to her first day at school, his gut told him it was time to back off. He was going to knock that fucking punching bag off its hook.

The thought helped him keep the frustration out of his voice. He hoped. "I'm going, but first, how about you take your robe off the hook on the closet there, put it on? You're cold, and I don't want you to be cold."

After a long second, she rose stiffly. She had her back to him when she let the bra slide off her shoulders and plucked the pink plush robe off the hook. It had hearts embroidered on it. Marcus and Thomas had given it to her for Valentine's Day.

When she wrapped herself in it, she sank back down on the bed. Back still to him, her arms wrapped over herself. She was rocking.

He clutched his push rims in tense fists. "You can call me if you need me, okay? Tell me you're hearing me, Daralyn."

He didn't know if it was for her benefit or his, which only increased his frustration, but she did respond.

"Yes. I hear you." Her voice was strained, like she was trying to be heard over a storm wind. She repeated herself. "I'll see you at the store tomorrow. Okay?"

"Okay," he said.

Uncertain, he took his time making his way to the front door. Closing it behind him was like slamming his heart in a car door. Her bedroom only had one window, and it faced the back field. Not great terrain for him to get his chair back there. Otherwise, he would have camped out, made sure she was all right, even if that made him a peeping Tom.

Everything told him he needed to be in there with her, even as he knew he also had to send her the message that things could go bad between them and still be okay. She had the room to make choices.

But what the hell had happened?

Elaine had already gone to bed, which was good. Rory wasn't in the mood to talk. He stared blankly at the TV screen for a while, then prepared for bed. When he was still studying the walls at 2 am, he pulled himself into his chair, and went into the kitchen.

Mom had left apple pie out, draped with cellophane. He cut

himself a small piece of the dessert and heated it. While he had to be careful about his fats and things that could mess up his digestive system, the day he had to pass up his mom's pie for good, life might not be worth living anymore.

Before his accident, like anyone else, he'd only seen the mobility issue when it came to people in wheelchairs. Being in the chair required a much more aware and intimate relationship with his health, his bodily functions, his diet. Circulation, heart issues, skin checks, bowel programs, catheters...things that didn't come up too often in movies about people in wheelchairs.

Even the mobility stuff only hit the surface. He'd had to learn to do so many things differently in a world structured around people being able to stand and walk. Doors, stairs, countertops. Dropping your keys on the floor, getting up and down, in and out. Traveling, driving. Opening the door for a woman.

Most people didn't think twice about attending their sister's high school graduation dinner on the twentieth floor of a building with a fancy rooftop restaurant. They didn't think about how, if there was a fire alarm and the elevators were shut down, someone would have to help them get down all those stairs, likely risking their own lives with the delay.

Before his accident, he'd have seen himself as the guy who helped that hapless loser get out. Disabled people were called heroes when they participated in a marathon. Jumped out of an airplane. As if striving to be what you wished you could be—the norm, physically—for just a moment more, was heroic. Inspiration porn.

We don't see ourselves like that. We're just people like anyone else.

But they didn't get to be the people who ran into a fire and pulled out the unconscious kid. Or picked up a gun to fight for their country.

Fuck, who was he kidding with this rambling? He was circling around what he was really thinking about. He kept seeing how defeated she'd looked when he left her. He wouldn't have left an animal in the woods in that kind of shape.

He'd read some of the books Marcus had given him. A bunch of stuff in it had turned him on, but it had seesawed with a sinking feeling of doubt. How could a sub feel safe and protected, trust that he had her, when he couldn't even pick her up, carry her into a bedroom, lay her down, him on top of her...

Stupid, yeah, but that was something he'd dreamed about doing with Daralyn. Stretching out upon her, making love to her that way. He just knew it would make her feel safe and loved, being surrounded that way. He ached when he thought of it.

What had happened in her kitchen had felt like such a natural step in their relationship, so sweet and good. But in a heartbeat, he'd stepped hip deep into a swamp he hadn't seen coming, when he should have, right? He'd checked in on her mood, her body language, all the way there. And yet it had been good...until it had gone bad.

There was so much shit he didn't know when it came to her. How in the hell was he going to figure it out, avoid hurting her like this?

He hadn't been big on therapy for himself, until he'd discovered that not only had his body needed re-training, his mind had as well, to cope with the huge change his damaged spinal cord had brought to his life.

Daralyn had been under the care of a psychiatrist for five years, and he wondered if this would be the upcoming topic. Or did she talk about any of it? His own counselor had told him, "We're not mind readers, Rory. We can deduce a lot from our studies of people in similar situations, but there will be things unique to who you are, how you're experiencing your loss of mobility. In order for me to help you with that, you have to talk to me."

Daralyn had gone on a mile a minute with him about the Magna Carta tonight, but when it became about something difficult, she went mute. He'd graduated a C-student, and he hadn't attended college. He was good at math, anything with numbers, but he'd read books only when required for school. Even then, his dad had to threaten his younger son's life to keep him from taking advantage of the Cliff notes his friends snuck around and bought. Sports, fishing, hunting, tinkering with engines or hanging out with his friends; all of those things had rated higher in Rory's priorities than books.

Yet, as his interest in Daralyn had evolved into a man's desire, he turned to book learning. Psychology stuff. While his intent had been to learn more about trauma victims, he'd been surprised to discover things about himself, his family, the way they related to one another, healthy versus unhealthy behaviors. Apparently, what was just day-to-day for the rest of them was a complete science.

It was fascinating, though he could see how people could get too carried away with it and not rely on their most important tool for figuring things out about one another. The way he'd learned most things.

Common sense. Paying attention.

While he was eaten up with guilt about what had happened in her bedroom, something penetrated his self-flagellation and told him to look closer.

On the surface, it seemed like she'd been afraid of him touching her too sexually, between her legs specifically. Anyone with a brain would expect that reaction from a woman with a history of childhood trauma and abuse. But he kept going over it in his head, and something was off about it.

His fists closed on the table on either side of the untouched pie. "Damn it," he muttered.

He swung away from the kitchen table and went out to the porch. His intent had been to give himself another view, some fresh air, but across the darkened fields, he saw a light on in Marcus and Thomas's barn loft. Thomas was having one of his middle of the night creative inspirations. Which meant Marcus would be in his downstairs office, even if he was just asleep on the couch. The two of them didn't spend much time apart if they didn't have to do so.

Returning to the kitchen, Rory drew his phone out of his T-shirt pocket. Spun it on the table a couple times, then he typed in a text.

You up?

A minute later, the phone buzzed a short note.

Need something?

He thought about it. Yeah, he did. But to honor the guy code, he responded a different way first.

Just confirming your vampire hours. If you're done sucking blood out of your latest vic, do you have a few minutes?

It wasn't blood that got sucked, but yeah, I have time.

He was off his game. He'd walked right into that one.

Now traumatized. Thanks, asshat. Can I call?

The phone started vibrating, and Rory picked up.

"What's up?" Marcus asked without any preliminaries. His voice sounded a little thick, confirming he'd been asleep. Guilt stabbed Rory, but remembering the anguish in Daralyn's face, he pressed on. He'd be with her at the store in a few hours. He had to figure this out.

"Did you, uh, see her any tonight?"

"Not really. We were on the porch around her usual bedtime. She pulled some laundry off the line behind her house and waved at us. Then she scurried back into her cottage like a mouse expecting a cat to pounce on her." Marcus paused. "Is she okay? Do I need to go check on her?"

"Is her light off?" He couldn't see the guest cottage clearly from the porch.

"It went off around eleven. Something happen after you two got back?"

"Yeah. Something went kind of wrong, and I'm trying to wrap my head around it." It welled up, the frustration, the anger. "Damn it, Marcus, she's got so much shit going on. Instead of having ten panic attacks a day, she has one or two a week now. That's how we measure her progress."

"That *is* progress," Marcus said. "And it's way more than that. She barely talked those first couple of years. Now she's pretty comfortable talking to family. She handles store customers on her own. In a reserved way, but still friendly."

"I know," he snapped. "That's not what I'm saying."

Marcus had every right to get impatient with him, because he wasn't making any sense. Rory braced himself for a deserved dose of New York sarcasm.

"Rory," Marcus said quietly. "What's the issue?"

"I'm the first relationship she's had. That should be enough. Why am I trying to pile the Dom thing on top of it?"

"Because you are a Dom. And she's undeniably a sub. Maybe your gut knows she'll handle a Dom/sub relationship better than a vanilla one. That's why you keep gravitating that way."

"Or maybe it will set her back five years because the dickhead who wants her doesn't know what the fuck he's doing." He took a breath. "It may be too soon. I think I should back off. Just be her friend. Leave the rest out of it."

Less chance of fucking up that way. Fucking her up worse. It scraped him raw inside, thinking of not kissing her sweet mouth again. Closing his hands over her soft flesh. Seeing his touch make her eyes get confused with arousal. Instead of a single knife in the heart, all those thoughts together were like being thrown up against a wall of blades.

"I can help her go to school, get stronger." He closed his eyes, his fist on the table back in a clench, but he forced out the words, no matter that his voice was as harsh as a winter wind. "She might be better with someone else."

A long pause. "Yeah," Marcus said. "You may be right. There are plenty of guys at the community college. Smart, getting degrees. They'll be able to relate to her better. And they can take her dancing."

"I can take her dancing." Rory stared into space. "Prick."

"Chickenshit." But Marcus said it without any heat. "You remember when your mom decided Thomas and Daralyn would be the perfect match?"

"Yeah. Mom thought she was saving Thomas's soul from the devil. Who, coincidentally, looked a lot like you."

"I think she's come around on that."

"She's accepted Thomas is gay. Not so sure she's changed her mind about you being the devil."

Snark aside, Rory remembered when his mother had pushed Thomas and Daralyn together. Thomas had been the first man Daralyn had felt comfortable around, though that hadn't been a surprise to anyone. Thomas had a calm core to him that could settle the most aggressive of beasts. Like Marcus. Or win the trust of the most shy. Like Daralyn.

In no time, his mother had practically had Thomas and Daralyn engaged, at least in her mind. She'd wanted to deny Thomas was gay, head it off before it reached the point of no return. She'd come a long way since then, seeing past the religious doctrine she'd followed all her life to what God really was. That was the way she'd put it.

Marcus had decided to ignore his devil comment. "Thomas wasn't your mother's only issue," he continued. "Daralyn didn't see Thomas as a threat."

"And I am?"

"You know that's not what I mean. There are two types of male threat to a woman. One is the bad kind. The other is the kind that gets her flustered, aroused. I suspect your mother worried Daralyn would never be able to handle a relationship with normal sexual expectations. But Thomas told me that every time Elaine pushed him and Daralyn together around you, you acted like an asshole. More than usual. Why was that?"

Truth? She'd made an impression on him from the first time she'd stayed with them. When she was sent away for the short period before the courts got a clue and awarded permanent guardianship to his parents, he'd felt her absence. A lot. Which should have told him something, because he and Emily had been a hot item back then.

He wouldn't brush Marcus off with more bullshit when he was trying to help. "One night, she and Les were watching this movie in Les's room. Chick flick, one of those Nicholas Sparks things. The one with Scott Eastwood."

"Great ass. He's a looker, just like his dad was at that age."

"Gross. Any*how*," Rory said with emphasis, over Marcus's chuckle, "My room was at an angle from theirs, and I could see Daralyn. During those gushy love scenes, she'd touch her lips, and get this look on her face. It said to me she wanted something like that, no matter what her fucked-up family had done to her. And I thought, damn it all, why should Mom or anyone else think it's okay to make her settle for something less? And now..."

He shook his head. "I feel it even stronger. She should be loved the way a woman wants to be loved. Not have to run from it all her life. The fuckers who did this to her shouldn't get to take that from her."

Marcus was quiet a moment. "Rory, you've just defined what true love is. When you love someone, you won't let them settle for less than what they truly want. You encourage them to embrace who they are, no matter how scary that can be. The most important thing to you is her, what she feels and what she wants. Right?"

"Yeah."

"That kind of love allows room for mistakes." Humor entered his voice. "A man making mistakes around a woman is inevitable. You know that, because common sense isn't your problem. Patience is. Your temper is. Believing in yourself."

Rory tapped his wheel, thinking. "No offense, but you love her, too. How do I know your advice isn't based on the same wishful thinking as my attempts to make this work with her?"

In the ensuing silence, Rory could hear a faint drone. Probably a space heater running, warding off the autumn chill in the barn office.

"There came a time I had a crisis of faith," Marcus said. "I thought I might not be what Thomas needed. I told myself I should give up, let him have his life down here, with all of you. Me not be a part of it. Later I realized the biggest part of that didn't have a damn thing to do with what Thomas did or didn't need. It had to do with my belief in myself. Whether I could hold up my end of the relationship, be what he needed. It was about my fear of failing him. Not loving him the way he deserved."

Another pause. "So don't fucking make this about protecting her when it's not."

Marcus had never spoken so frankly to him, or with such rough emotion in his voice it lingered like a full-on kick in the balls. Remembering the time Marcus meant only increased the impact.

Rory's father had died, and his tractor accident had happened soon after. Both events were the double whammy that brought Thomas home. For a time he'd settled into running the store, pretending his time in New York as a struggling artist had never existed. While the specter of Marcus had been a dark blip on his mother's Catholic radar, Rory had had his head up his own ass, wrestling with anger and self-pity, adding weight to the Thomas guilt-train.

Only Les had seen what was so obvious, that everything that fueled their brother's soul was dying right in front of their eyes. Yet it had all been such a clusterfuck, Rory could see how Marcus might have doubted himself, whether he was the best thing for Thomas.

Now Thomas was finally living the life he'd wanted to live. One that included his family and his art, with his love for Marcus at the center of it. He was healthy and strong, just all around better for having Marcus in his life.

He should say that straight out, but he and Marcus had rules in their mutual give-each-other-shit society. Marcus had just bent them all out of shape to give Rory what he needed tonight. Better not to take it any further, or they'd end up on some touchy-feely talk show.

Fortunately, Marcus had resumed in his normal clipped, no-bullshit tone. "If you back off, then you're doing what your mom was doing, denying Daralyn all the choices she could have."

Rory could see that. He still had to voice his deepest concern. "I get all that. But what if I'm in the way, blocking her view to those other choices?"

"You're in a wheelchair. She's standing. You're not blocking the view to anything."

"Man, you are such a dick."

"Thank you. I put serious effort into it." Marcus chuckled, then sobered. "Rory, you're right. I may not know shit, either, but I'll tell you what my gut says, and I'm betting yours does, too. A Dom usually has a certain amount of arrogance in his arsenal. Same thing that drives a surgeon, a pilot, or anyone who has someone else's well-being resting in their hands during a key moment. You have every right to take your shot with her. You have every right to be at the front of the line."

He liked hearing that, but... "This isn't just about me."

"No, but instead of thinking of you and her in separate boxes, on separate paths, think about both of you, together. When you're around one another, there's a thread there. One that's grown into a damn rope. We all see it, including you. When you came over here and I asked if you loved her, you gave me a pretty over the top answer, but I didn't doubt you meant it as you said it."

Rustling noises suggested Marcus had gotten to his feet. Once awake, Marcus had to be moving. Rory expected he'd just disrupted the guy's sleep for most of the rest of the night. He'd have to make that up to him, damn it.

"You going to give me any specifics, or are we going to keep talking generalities?" Marcus asked. "What happened to get you to this place in your head?"

"I'm not going to disrespect her by talking to you about specifics."

"Give me the high level."

"She was responding to something the way I expected. And then suddenly she wasn't. On the surface, with her background, it makes total sense, but I think there's more to it. I think I'm missing something."

"That's what a good Dom does, Rory," Marcus said. "He looks deeper than the obvious. If there's anyone in the world who needs a Dom with that kind of radar, it's Daralyn. To her psychiatrist, she's a puzzle of behaviors, treatment options. Dr. Taylor is great for her, and

Daralyn needs her approach. But she needs yours as well. Stick with your perspective. Set your worries aside. What do you want to do?"

He thought. "I want to dig. I want to figure out what's really going on."

"Then that's what you do. If she had a rough day today, give her some breathing room. If you set the boat rocking, settle it down, put it back on an even keel, then go after the problem. Or, in terms you'll understand, wait until the rains have passed to dig the hole, so the shovel doesn't clog it up with mud."

"Farm analogies. Next thing, you'll be saying *y'all* and wearing overalls."

"You just reminded me why I need to get my ass back above the Mason Dixon. Before I fucking forget how to be a New Yorker."

"What's sad is you say that like it's a bad thing."

"Shithead. One last thing. Try not to get pissed off about her father and uncle around her. She can't use the anger."

"I know. But it's tough."

"Tell me about it. You and I prefer violence to handle asshole behavior. But your brother? He's better than anyone I know at looking past the anger and hate and seeing the people behind it. Like your mom. I literally wanted to kill her a couple times. He saw her pain, her confusion, and that became more important to him than stepping on her to get to the relationship we wanted to have. It took time and pain to get there, but because we took the harder route, we are where we are right now, all of us in a better place. You could express all that rage you have on Daralyn's behalf, but what does that do for her? How does that help her love you and you love her in a healthy way?"

Rory thought about it. "Didn't you get all of this from years of experience with the Dom and sub stuff?"

"Some of it, and that's why it's important to mentor with an experienced Dom, the way you're doing. But it's more than that." Marcus sighed. "Thomas and I might be Master and sub, but we learn from each other. If we're doing it right, we grow in love with one another, like any other couple out there. Talk to her, Rory. Read everything she gives you, from the words that come out of her mouth, to every bit of body language. The things she doesn't do or say, as much as those she does. You're asking yourself the right questions, and reaching out when you need help. That's all the way it should be."

"Okay. Thanks. I appreciate it."

Marcus grunted. "I do twenty hours of community service a month. Helping the handicapped and all that. Mentally handicapped, that is."

"Pansy."

"Cripdick."

Rory clicked off. Much as he hated to admit it, his brother's husband was becoming something he never would have expected.

A good friend.

CHAPTER SIX

*R*ory glanced over as Daralyn put a cup of coffee at his elbow. Then she was gone, headed for the trio of women chatting at the handmade quilt display, even though they hadn't signaled a need for help. That didn't necessarily mean she was avoiding him. From watching his mother and Les manage the tourist traffic, she'd learned they bought more if there was a smoothly inserted comment about the women who'd made the quilts, some backstory to reinforce their authenticity.

They hadn't had any one-on-one time. When Rory opened the door this morning, a customer had already been waiting. Mr. Hernandez had needed a replacement part for his tractor, so that he didn't lose daylight on the field he had to work today. More customers had arrived on his heels, a steady flow until ten-thirty. Then this vanload of church ladies had arrived from Asheville. The store had been a planned stop on their meandering tour to the beach.

In their few interactions since she'd arrived a few minutes behind him, Daralyn had been friendly, pleasant, acting as if nothing had happened. But she avoided eye contact, more than usual, and stayed in a flurry of activity. Which was as big an alarm flag to him as the giant Stars and Stripes that flew over the car dealership in town.

Up until today, she'd developed a pleasant habit of incidental contact, brushing against his shoulder or knees as she came behind

71

the counter to get things. Laying her hand on his shoulder to steady herself as she reached up to retrieve something from a shelf.

Today she was giving him a wide berth, as if touching him might turn her into a frog.

He'd considered several ways of dealing with it, and had settled on the one that made the most sense to him. To break the brittle wall of self-consciousness around her, he picked a couple times to call her over, request her help with a customer. He talked to her in his usual way, teasing her a little. Touched her arm or hand like he might normally do while making a point, before moving on smoothly, as if all was good. Normal, the way it should be.

She began to relax, act more like herself. By early afternoon, they were pretty much where they'd been before yesterday. The only time he put a hitch in her stride was when she was taking off. She worked until two today, part of the modified schedule he and his mother had imposed upon her, so she didn't burn the candle at both ends on her schoolwork.

"Remember, I'm taking you to dinner tonight," he said. "I'll pick you up at six."

"Oh. Yes. Fine." She looked as if she might say more, but then she slipped out the door. He pushed his chair to the window to watch her pedal her bicycle to the road. She liked riding it to and from the store on the good weather days.

He'd taught her to ride a bike. Well, it had been a group effort, Thomas explaining the basics, Les demonstrating, but he'd been the one to stick next to her on the bike, since he could run the fastest. He smiled. He'd been her spotter.

He remembered when he'd put his hand on the seat to steady her, his fingers curled near her buttocks, his body leaned in as he held one of the handlebars.

She'd turned her head toward him once or twice, her ponytail swiping him. She'd stumbled through an apology, but he'd just rubbed his jaw where it itched and smiled.

"Focus on your balance," he said. "I'll be holding onto the bike until you find it. Don't worry about anything but that, okay? I'll take care of the rest."

He brought himself back to the present. She usually ate her lunch with him, but she'd made an excuse about not being hungry, that she'd eat when she went home.

If they'd moved too fast, he'd slow it down. But after last night's conversation with Marcus, he was resolved. He wasn't going to stop unless he had a more compelling reason than his fears. She deserved more courage from him than that. He watched her hair flutter over her shoulders, the straight line of her back as she pedaled, the slight movement of her hips. God, everything about her called to him.

You have every right to be at the front of the line.

Marcus was right. He damn well did.

He was taking her to The Purple Swan in Florence, one of those bistro style places where the portions were small and overpriced. The food was good, though, and the inside was decorated nice.

It had once been a typical diner which did breakfast and lunch, offering cardiac attack, man-sized entrees for five bucks a plate. Once the bypass was finished, cutting Florence out of a big chunk of beach traffic, the town business owners had been smart enough to revamp the way Rory and his family had done. A crop of trendy-styled places had sprung up, touched with a small town flair. The combination tempted city people to detour.

Daralyn had been to The Purple Swan with his mother and Les, to celebrate Les's birthday, followed by some shopping in the local array of "quaint" stores, as his mother put it. What had stuck in his mind was Elaine mentioning how enchanted Daralyn seemed by the restaurant's décor and that she'd eaten most of the small portion she'd been served. That was good enough for him.

He'd called ahead and confirmed access logistics and whether the optimal seating locations would accommodate a wheelchair. Nothing could cast a pall on an evening like finding out the place was so jammed with people and tables a wheelchair patron would get stuck in a back corner near the restrooms, server's station or a noisy kitchen access.

After he closed up the store, he went home, took a shower, got dressed. It took him longer than most people to get ready for things, especially when he wanted to look his best, so he'd done his workout early this morning, rather than at the end of the day like he usually did.

Elaine was home, but headed for her book club at six. She knew about the date but, to her credit, she didn't make a big deal of it, though he saw her doing the mom secret smile thing. When he came into the kitchen, he had his suit coat folded over his lap. He hadn't yet tied his tie, the two silky ends draped on either side of the collar, the shirt open a couple buttons.

As usual, his mother looked attractively put together. Except for the unsettling year after their father's death, she always emerged from her room in the morning fully dressed in flattering outfits, her dyed dark hair curled and arranged, her makeup in place. Tonight, she'd dressed up a bit. Even if he hadn't already known, it would have reminded him it was book club night.

Her eyes sparkled as they lighted on him. "You look very handsome. Want me to help with the tie?"

"I'll do it. But if I ever meet the guy who invented a noose as a fashion statement, I'll string him up with one." Rory winked at her as he popped the collar and started the process. He'd typically check himself in a mirror after, but Mom was better for that. "How many bottles of wine are you ladies planning to finish off tonight? Sorry, I meant books."

She sniffed. "I noticed you had a tear in your sock when I did the laundry yesterday. Everything okay?"

She'd learned not to hover so much, but she'd still ask. A mom was going to be a mom, no matter if he was in his twenties or his fifties.

"Yes, ma'am. Caught my ankle on the metal shelf edge in that back corner of the store, where it's hard to maneuver. I checked and it didn't even leave a scrape." He shot her a wink. "A little higher up and it would have caught my pants. I'd have a good start on those fancy hundred-dollar jeans the kids run to the store to get."

Not that his were much cheaper. His day-to-day jeans were designed for the wheelchair disabled, with no back pockets, and a lined seat with no seams that could rub against his skin and cause sores. But from the front and sides they still looked like anyone else's jeans.

"Just so they rest on your backside the way they should," his mother said primly.

"But I was looking forward to wearing them belted around my thighs." He grinned at her. "For me, that'd make dressing in the morning a lot easier."

She snorted, and surveyed him as he finished with the tie, putting his collar down. "Good?" he asked.

"Perfect. Your father never could do that without help. Must have skipped a generation, because your grandfather could do it in his sleep." She closed the distance between them and put her fingers on the tie, smoothing it, and him beneath, then touched his face, his brushed hair.

"I won't go on," she promised in that way that told him she would, with very little encouragement. "But I'm glad you asked her to dinner. You're helping her see she deserves that kind of attention from a man."

"Well, I'm likely a better choice for that than Thomas."

Shit, he hadn't meant to go there, but her wording had raised his hackles. Like he was some kind of hands-on app to help Daralyn learn how to date.

Elaine's lips pressed together, but before she could say anything, he closed a hand over hers. "Sorry," he said. "I didn't need to say that."

"The truth is the truth," she said.

He'd reversed their hands, was holding hers firmly. "I'm nervous, and that turns me into an inconsiderate jerk," he said. "She matters to me, Mom. I'm not doing this as a community service."

"I know." Elaine took a breath. "I'm just...I'm trying not to do what I did with the two of them. Make you feel like I'm expecting something that doesn't fit with what you truly want. Who you truly are."

Fair enough. He should have known better than to react to everything through the lens of what was going on with him. That was a surefire method to convince himself he was being treated differently because he was in a chair. Sometimes yeah, it *was* that, but a surprising number of times, it wasn't. It just took stepping outside his own head to see it.

"Think I should take her flowers?"

Elaine looked toward the kitchen table. She'd already assembled a small bouquet for him from her flower garden, the base in a damp paper towel wrapped with green paper, tied with a yellow ribbon. "Will that do?"

She really hadn't meant what he thought she had. From the light in her eyes, he could tell she was genuinely happy about him and Daralyn spending the evening together.

"Thanks, Mom."

"Anytime. I'm off to my book club. Have fun." She managed to bite back, "Don't be late" before she said it.

Once he'd passed twenty-one, plus achieved the physical shape where he could have lived on his own if he'd chosen to do so, he'd had a sit-down with her. As a grown man, his comings and goings were his decision. But because he knew she worried, he usually texted her his ETA, and updated it if it changed. A compromise, him respecting her love for him, and her respecting his age and independence.

But as she picked up her purse and looked at him, he could tell there was something else, and he addressed it. "I'll have a care with her," he said. "I wouldn't do anything in the world to hurt her."

"I know that, son." She took a breath, gave him a quick smile, and slipped out the door.

He could feel her worry. For him and Daralyn both, and for so many things. But though he and his mother still butted heads at times, her care was a gift he'd learned never to take for granted. And not just for himself.

Daralyn had never experienced the gift of a mother's love, not until she was fifteen. It had helped save her. For that reason and so many more, Rory would never give his mom too much shit for being a mom.

Finally growing up had given him the skills and resources to take care of those he loved. Which meant not just the obvious things, but their feelings, too.

~

When he didn't see Marcus's car at the house, Rory remembered he and Thomas had driven to Charlotte earlier in the day for some art party networking thing. They'd be back later tonight.

Daralyn was standing by the road waiting for him, something she'd have done to be considerate to him. Which he appreciated, but he'd be telling her not to do that in the future when he picked her up for a date. She deserved to have a man come to the door for her, just like any other woman.

The look of her got his heartrate going. Maybe there were more glamorous women in the world, but he couldn't care less about that. She'd left her hair down, as he'd requested, and it was in loose curls on her shoulders and down her back, shorter pieces wisping around her face. She wore a yellow dress with a V-neckline and little buttons down the front. He imagined getting a glimpse of sweet curves cradled in lace when she bent over her menu. He didn't think that in a creep kind of way. It was just another part of her he appreciated, that unconscious femaleness that made her Daralyn.

As he slowed next to her, he saw she also wore a gold necklace with a pendant on it, a sunflower in gold and green metal. She'd probably found it on one of those shopping trips with his mom or sister. When Elaine's sunflowers grew tall and sunny in the summer, they were Daralyn's favorite flower. She'd stand beneath them, her head tilted back, face wreathed with a smile as she reached up to touch the over weighted blooms, making them sway.

He wanted to get out and open her door for her, but it would be kind of obnoxious, making her wait while he did that. He wished he could lean over far enough to open the door from the inside for her, but he'd end up overbalanced and on the floor. So when she got in on her own, he settled for taking her hand and showing her in his expression how much he felt the next three words.

"You look beautiful," he said.

The gold and green pendant picked up those colors in her hazel eyes as they brightened. She smiled, but her hand was cold, and he could feel a little tremor. "Nervous?" he asked.

"Yes. It's never been just the two of us for dinner." She looked down at their clasped hands and seemed at a loss to say anything else. She wasn't wearing the chain bracelet, but he knew she wore it to give her courage for class. He took it as an encouraging sign she didn't feel like she needed that, despite her nervousness.

Her gaze lighted on the bouquet. He'd pulled a glass from the kitchen that would fit snugly in one of his cupholders, and set it up there as a vase to hold it.

"For you," he confirmed. "Full disclosure—Mom cut and arranged them, but she was on the same page with me. I wanted to bring you flowers tonight."

As her gaze dwelled on the bouquet, a mix of emotions in her face, he lifted her hand to his lips and kissed it, which drew her attention back to his face. When she would have shifted her gaze away, he told her by the touch on her chin, her cheek, that he wanted her eyes to stay locked with his. When she complied, he ran a thumb over her lips, the curve of her cheek.

He'd been nervous too. He'd been out on his own to plenty of places, but this was the first time, since he'd ended up in the chair, that he'd taken a woman out to a nice dinner. With Amanda he'd stayed in his comfort zone. A pizza place where his friends hung out, or other familiar stomping grounds.

He was in charge this evening, taking care of someone precious to him. But when he touched her, and he had her full attention like this, the nerves disappeared. It was as if he had a direct line to what was going on in her head, and why her hand had that coldness to it.

"Daralyn, you don't have to worry about anything tonight. I've got you. All right?"

She pressed her lips together, which inadvertently moved them against his fingertips. When she realized that, she did a little start, but then, at his look, she did it deliberately, nuzzling against his touch, those eyes wide and full of so many things. It terrified and humbled him, even as he wanted to roar it out to the world.

She said she belonged to me.

He reined that back, because he couldn't ignore the troublesome side to her declaration, something he would have to pursue at some point. But not now. "You haven't answered me," he said. "You're not worrying about anything tonight. Got it?"

"Okay. Yes." She gave him that smile again, a little easier.

He waited for her to put her seatbelt on, and pulled away from the curb. "We're going to The Purple Swan. Les said you really liked the desserts. I think we should start with those and work backwards."

Her smile grew brighter as he winked at her. "But having dessert at the end makes it something to anticipate," she pointed out.

Yes, it surely did.

She hesitated. "I think I'm nervous because...I've never been on a date."

He hadn't even thought of that. Here he was, being antsy about it being a fancier deal, while for her, pretty much all of it was a first, wasn't it? It gave him a full stop, realizing it.

When he'd kissed her the other night, that had likely been her first real kiss.

He wasn't counting anything her father and uncle had done to her, and pushed the repulsive thought away before he could get trapped there.

"We're going to have a great time," he told her.

"I already am," she responded.

He'd told her she looked beautiful.

Daralyn held that to herself like a promise, a desperate hope that things would go well tonight. She wouldn't have a panic attack, or do something to embarrass him. Several times while getting dressed, she'd considered all the things that could go wrong, and it had almost overwhelmed her enough to do something she would never do; tell someone she couldn't do something she'd been asked to do.

Dr. Taylor told her to break things down into bite-sized pieces, rather than trying to take everything at once. Rory had said the same thing to her at the store, more than once.

He looked really handsome. He always did, but tonight, he wore a suit, complete with a white dress shirt and a tie. His hair was neatly trimmed on his neck, layered on the sides, with that light feathering of brown strands across his sun-lined brow. His beard's soft gleam made her want to touch, stroke.

He had thick lashes and fierce brows, a lot like Thomas. His eyes... the first time she'd tried one of the Lindt dark chocolate squares that Elaine kept in a jar on her kitchen counter, she'd turned it over and over in her fingertips, and thought of Rory's eyes. They could get even darker when he was angry, or stirred up. Aroused.

She knew what that looked like now, for him. And she couldn't stop thinking about it.

So much had happened between them in what seemed like such a short time, but it wasn't short at all. She'd been thinking about him a long time, even before he'd kissed her under the mistletoe that past Christmas. She thought he had been thinking about her too, because when they worked in the store, she saw him looking at her certain ways. If they were behind the cash register counter together, he would look at her, their faces so close, because even with him seated, the difference in their heights didn't require him to look up much at all to look her in the eye.

It was as if there was a heat there between them, drawing them together.

But for all those months since their kiss at Christmas, he hadn't acted on it, and it wasn't her place to initiate anything. She was a mess of emotions most days, unless she completely shut down, something she'd promised Dr. Taylor she would try not to do. Back before she came to live with the Wilder family, she existed day to day by creating rooms in her head where she could go, while the parts of her that could work on autopilot did. She hadn't known that was what it was called, autopilot, but she thought auto-plod made more sense. It wasn't like flying at all. Just a constant slog through a choking mud that stayed the same, that you hoped stayed the same, because it could become concrete really fast.

Things could always be worse.

Even if Rory had wanted to pursue anything with her, she knew why he hadn't. She'd experienced a setback after that Christmas, her panic attacks taking over again when Dr. Taylor had her do test runs, visiting places that were outside her comfort zones. So many things piled on top of that lovely kiss, squashing the few little scenarios she'd created in her mind of where it could go from there.

She'd given up hope, figured it was a lost opportunity, and focused on getting the confidence she needed to start school. The ache of "could-have-beens" with Rory had been added to her vast chest of other could-have-beens. But that one had lingered outside the box, edged with a particularly sharp regret. Maybe because she saw him every day, while the other could-have-beens were already well out of reach.

She'd rallied, found the confidence she needed to finally start school. Rory had not only helped her make that final step, he'd shown her he'd never lost interest at all. Hope was not lost. Those possibilities were back in the front of her mind. When she looked at him, a full garden bloomed inside her, rivaling the lovely bouquet he'd thought to bring for her.

Since he used hand controls to drive, he couldn't continuously hold her hand, but she was glad for how often he did anyway, like at stop lights. The looks he sent her, a mix of heat and intensity, made her hand quiver inside the grip of his.

Her mind cycled back to last night, when he'd touched her. And before that, when he'd...spanked her. She'd thought of little else, a constant mix of images and feelings while she was lying in bed, working at the store with him, studying through the afternoon. He'd stayed so calm and patient with her. Particularly last night. She could tell how much he'd wanted to hold her after she'd been so confused and upset. She wished she could have figured out how to accept that, but the panic took her. She hadn't meant to move where he couldn't reach her in her bedroom.

His calmness with her didn't have that smooth detachment backed by well-meaning concern, like she'd experienced when her fate was being decided by a parade of officials in the child welfare system. She'd seen the flash of anger and impatience in his eyes. But not with her. Not in the least. She studied him closely, a lot, and knew the difference.

He was an active, restless type of person, who met challenges with a physical response. His frustration usually had to do with something he couldn't change, but wished fiercely to do so. He was a man who fully appreciated the simplicity of picking up a hammer to drive in a nail. He was unfailingly gentle and patient with her, but last night he'd been less gentle...and she kept thinking about it.

He'd turned down his music when he pulled up to her place. She didn't care much for TV, but she liked music, as long as it wasn't too loud. Rory was what Les called an "old school" country fan. Hank Williams, the Carters, Gene Autry--the preferred playlist for terrorists torturing hostages, according to Marcus. She liked the old, tinny sounds of the music, though. There was a quiet around it, just a voice and a few instruments amid the low-level static from the original recording.

Hearing the faint tones of the music, even with the volume turned down, reassured her. He kept music as a background at the store. He never asked her if she'd like to listen to something else, because he knew those kinds of questions caused her problems. Even so, she'd noticed he'd tried different genres on different days and somehow figured out which ones she liked. The stations and playlists she hadn't liked, he'd never chosen more than once.

He pulled up to The Purple Swan. She hadn't cared where they were going, but knowing he'd specifically chosen it because he thought she liked the restaurant meant things.

Before he left his seat, he tugged her hand so she leaned toward him. When he cupped her cheek, his large hand threaded into her hair so his fingertips could curve against her neck, which gave her the dual sense of tumbling through clouds and resting safely in his grip at once.

He met her mouth with his own, and she melted into it with a little sigh of relief. He answered it with a deep sound of satisfaction, teasing her mouth with his lips, his tongue. That was new, and she welcomed it, with a shudder through her core. She curved her hand over his forearm to hold on as his mouth sent her world spinning.

When he drew back, he didn't go far, those dark eyes so close. "Thank you for coming to dinner with me."

"Thank you for kissing me."

His brown eyes twinkled. "The gift giver doesn't normally thank the person for accepting the gift."

She had to think about that one, and when she figured it out, her cheeks warmed. His mouth curved in that firm near-smile. "I love the way you blush. Stay there."

He transferred himself to his chair with the ease of long practice, though she knew it hadn't been easy at all at first. When he came around to her side, opening her door, he offered her a hand to help her out. He kept her hand, but nodded toward the restaurant.

"Meet me at the door?" he asked.

The ramp started on the side of the building, coming around to the front.

"Can I stay with you?"

She saw that pleased him, and was glad for it. When they reached the ramp, he gestured ahead of him. "Not wide enough for side by side," he said.

"Then I'll follow right behind you."

"View's better for me if you walk ahead." He shot her a grin and she wondered if she was going to blush all night.

He'd been teasing her, but he also meant it. She was aware of his eyes on her with every step. As they reached the door, another couple had arrived. The man opened it for his wife, and then gestured to Daralyn. She glanced at Rory, and he gave her a nod, then offered the guy a thanks as he followed her in.

He handled things like that fine. but she knew it still bugged him. The man was in his seventies, a person Rory would have held the door for, as a sign of respect for his elders. But the man held the door for him, compassion for someone with limited mobility.

If they did something like this again, she'd adjust so that when they came off the ramp into a wider space, she was beside or behind Rory, so he could hold the door for her.

He and his family had done many similar things for her, adjusting their habits and routines to help her develop those things for herself in the way she could best manage it. But that wasn't why she wanted to do it. It was the thing inside her that told her she wanted to meet his every action like a dance partner, a give and take of motion that made them seem as if nature had brought them together for that. She'd never danced before, but that was what it looked like, when she'd seen it in glimpses on television.

The hostess seated them. Just like the last time she was here, Daralyn was delighted by the mural on the back wall, swans floating in a lavender tinted lake, reflecting the hue of the clouds above. Their waitress introduced herself as Lobelia.

"Do all the waitresses use purple flower names?" Daralyn asked. Lobelia was about Daralyn's age, with abundant dark hair bound up with a lavender scarf. It matched the restaurant attire of black slacks and purple blouse.

"Not everyone realizes it is a purple flower," Lobelia said, with an easy smile. "And no ma'am. It's my real name."

She took their drink orders, and then Daralyn was looking at the menu. "What looks good?" Rory asked.

He did, but she didn't say that. Most people's way of interacting was so unconscious and natural, but from listening to them a lot, she knew the things she thought, the way she thought them, would be considered out of place if she said them aloud.

"Daralyn." He'd held her hand from the moment they'd sat down and now he squeezed it again, drawing her gaze. "What I'm looking at looks good to me, too."

She bit her lip. "Was I that obvious?"

"I made a guess, and I'm glad I'm not wrong, because I would have sounded like a conceited ass." His wry smile didn't dilute what was in his gaze. "I'm not complaining. You don't look me in the eye much, but when you do, I think you should take a good, long look. See what's there."

He reached out with the other hand, touched her jaw, so she lifted her gaze. "It's difficult," she said low. "When I look, I can't look away. I get lost there...in the right ways."

He stared at her, and a muscle flexed in his jaw. "I'm sorry," she said, dropping her gaze again. "Dr. Taylor says I need to talk, try to work on not being afraid to speak my mind. But when I do, I tend to say—"

"The truth. Unembellished, straight from your heart. I get what Dr. Taylor wants you to do, and it's smart. But Daralyn..." that insistent touch on her jaw again, reminding her to bring her eyes back up. She didn't know why it was particularly hard to meet Rory's gaze, but when he clearly wanted her to do so, it was easier. She drew in a breath because his dark brown gaze held powerful things. "When it comes to you and me," he said, "You say it just like you think it. Understand me?"

She swallowed. "When you talk like that, I get really lost."

His gaze sharpened, spearing her straight through the heart. "That's not lost. That means you've come straight to me."

The drinks were brought, and the main task she'd dreaded was here. What to order. She couldn't waste food, but everything except appetizers would have portions far too big for her. And then there was the worst part. Having to choose. Nothing could paralyze her more.

Rory said he needed a few more minutes and sent the waitress away. He gestured to the menu. "Since I've never been here before, tell me what looks good."

She could handle that. It was like a customer asking her the best item for a job. She mentioned several entrees that had caught her attention the last time she'd been here, including the things Les and

Elaine had ordered and discussed. She'd ordered what Les had, so if she had leftovers, Les could have them.

She reached out impulsively, traced a healing scratch on the back of his hand, resting on the tablecloth. "How did you do that?"

"Hell if I know. Probably digging in the nail bin. Oh, wait. Mrs. Schwartz," he remembered. "She has that fancy manicure where she can't touch anything."

"And Mr. Schwartz is always sending her out when he's in the middle of a project, to pick up something for him," she finished.

"Or to get her out of his hair. She does like to backseat drive on the home improvement projects."

They were smiling at each other when the waitress returned. Lobelia looked at her expectantly, but Rory spoke.

"She'll have the fried chicken marsala," he said. "Ask the chef to half the portion size and box it up, hold it in the kitchen until we get ready to leave. That okay?"

Lobelia glanced between them and nodded. "You got it. And you, sir?"

"Lean sirloin with the vegetable soup. What's good on the dessert menu?"

"Apple tart with a butter cake base. You could die happy eating it. Comes with hand churned vanilla ice cream."

"We'll try to leave room for that," Rory said.

He'd chosen the thing on the menu for her that she would have ordered for herself, if she was capable of doing that. Suddenly, she was choked up, the tears stinging her gaze bringing a wave of terror. Her hands fell to her lap, clutching one another, and a shudder ran through her shoulders as she ducked her head. No. Not here. Not here.

"We're good," Rory said quietly to Lobelia. "Thanks."

The waitress withdrew with a curious look. *Darn it.* Every time she thought she could handle something new, these totally random emotions hit her like a two-by-four. Like how her first day at school had gone. But Rory had helped her rally, go at it again. And he did it now, too.

"Breathe," he murmured. "Just breathe. No matter what happens, you're fine. We're all good."

She sent him a desperate look, then directed it elsewhere, like a bird landing only briefly on a bush, but he was having none of that. Once more, as persistent as breathing itself, he brought her attention back to his face by cupping her cheek, making her look at him. Which meant she saw his expression was relaxed. He wasn't concerned in that way that made her feel so self-conscious, like she needed to pull herself together to make everyone stop worrying.

"You know," he said conversationally, "In the beginning, I didn't want to go out in the chair. I thought about people staring. Having to deal with obstacles. Or something embarrassing happening. Mom and Thomas made me do it. Very first place they ever took me was McDonald's, just like when Les and me were little and Mom and Dad were teaching us how to behave at a public restaurant." His lips twisted. "It was freaking terrifying."

He ran a thumb over her palm, even as he adjusted into a more relaxed position in his chair. "Then these kids headed for the play area outside. They squeezed past me, in that impatient way kids can do. One of them put his hand on my arm, on my push rim, as he wiggled past. Didn't think a damn thing about it. I was just another adult to get past so he could go play."

Humor crossed his expression. "His mom made this horrified gasp, had him come back and apologize, which kind of ruined it, but I held onto that really important revelation. I wasn't the center of the universe. Just another person doing their thing."

She was holding onto the look in his eyes, the touch on her face. She pressed her cheek into it, closed her eyes, trying to absorb his heat, wanting to sink into it.

When she opened them, he was still watching her. "I shared something kind of personal," he said casually, "so maybe you can do the same. Why do you have difficulty eating?"

Her gut tightened up. "You'll get angry."

"I'm not going to be angry at you."

"I know. But I...I don't want to make you angry or sad about my family."

His gaze flickered, as if the comment had particular meaning for him. He lifted a shoulder. "I appreciate you caring for me like that. But I want you to tell me, Daralyn, if you can."

She sighed. "My father and uncle said it was expensive to feed me, and I'd better not ever waste food, or eat a mouthful more than I needed to. Sometimes they'd make me so nervous while I was eating... I'd throw it up. Then they'd be really angry."

She didn't want to go back to that place in her head right now. She'd shifted her gaze to the mural. She could create a room that looked just like that in her head, go there...

"Daralyn."

She looked up, and he was close again. His lips brushed over hers, making them part. That warm swirl happened in her belly as he gazed at her, so close his face was all there was. "Thank you for telling me. Don't go away. Stay here with me. Tonight, that's the only thing I'm going to ask you about your life before you came to live with us. I promise. And since it was tough, I'm going to give you a standing quid pro quo. You can ask me any question, no matter how uncomfortable you think it would be for me."

"Quid pro quo." She tried that one out on her tongue. "It means..."

"Sort of tit for tat. You gave me something, so I give you back something of equal value."

"Oh." She pulled her notebook out of her purse and had him spell it, so she could write it down, carefully forming the letters before she tucked it away again. "All right. Can I bank my question? I need to think about what to ask."

Amusement had wreathed his face as he watched her, and it was still there. "It's a standing offer. And when I ask you a question, if you don't feel like you can answer it, that's okay. Just say 'pass.'"

"I'll always answer you, Rory." Because when he posed a question to her, she had to answer him in some acceptable way.

As a child, she hadn't known what a choice was. Her uncle and father didn't give her that option for anything they told her to do.

Ever.

Dr. Taylor spent a lot of time helping her learn how to think about whether she wanted to do something or not. A wall in her mind kept her from considering that in a meaningful way, but there was another quagmire to it.

While she was constantly assured there was no longer any punishment if she didn't want to do something, she wasn't convinced. If the caring people in her life wanted something from her she couldn't give, the tangle of feelings about whether or not she'd let them down, disappointed them, failed them, would overcome her.

With Rory, there was something different about it. Her reasons for not wanting him to give her a choice on certain things, like answering his questions, had a different impulse. One she wasn't quite sure she understood. She just knew it felt right to feel that way. Less paralyzing.

She didn't want to talk to Dr. Taylor about it because she didn't want the psychiatrist to tell her a feeling was wrong that felt so deeply right.

"Okay." He didn't ask her more about that. Just held her hand, playing with her fingers, caressing her palm, and encouraged her to talk about other things. Like the last time she was here. What she, Elaine and Les had talked about, eaten. Where they'd gone after the meal, the little second-hand shops where Daralyn had found a dish drainer in a cheerful bright red color and a sink stopper with a red, yellow, blue and green rooster design on the handle.

He was easy to talk to. The way he watched her as she spoke had her tucking her hair behind her ear, smiling more than usual, and wanting to laugh. He also made her feel good about herself, just with his attention, and the more she seemed to feel good, the more absorbed he seemed to be in her. Since the table they were at was a good size, Rory had directed her to sit with just the corner between them, instead of across from one another. She had her legs crossed, and the side of her foot brushed his pants leg. Though she knew he couldn't feel it, she saw his gaze flick in that direction more than once, lingering on the contact.

When the food came, it was as if they'd been in a lavender-tinged bubble, and the waitress had stepped out of that concealing fog, bringing them back into their current surroundings.

"Here you go." She placed Daralyn's plate in front of her, a small portion of the chicken marsala with the equally modest-sized sides of garlic mashed potatoes and seasoned grilled vegetables. "Keep some room for that dessert, now."

Daralyn chewed every bite carefully, savoring the taste. Before coming to the Wilders, she ate the same staples every day. Plain oatmeal. Rice, potatoes, a small amount of meat or egg. Vegetables out of a can, or packaged fruit cups. The only seasoning in her father and uncle's house was salt and pepper, and she wasn't allowed to touch those. So when she'd first experienced Elaine's cooking, taken that first bite, flavor had exploded on her tongue. She'd put down her fork, too overwhelmed to do more than eat a few bites.

Elaine had quickly picked up on the issue and cooked her basics. Chicken and rice, with just a little salt added, but she'd give Daralyn a tiny portion of what everyone else was eating, so gradually her palate expanded. But taste was still something that amazed her, one of many things that was the norm for everyone else.

Rory had a different approach to food as well. Before his accident, he would have ordered a bigger, meatier steak, the kind Les would tease him about.

"As if there's not enough cow on the cow for you."

"That's what the potatoes are for," he'd retorted. "To fill in the empty spaces."

His diet now was consistently healthy. She'd picked up that it helped with his digestive system. His mother never pushed food on him the way she might with Thomas, Marcus or Les. And she didn't push it on Daralyn. It was odd sometimes, the similarities between her and Rory that had entirely different reasons.

Rory had good table manners, but so did she. Her father had instructed her how to act like other people in the ways that mattered. To blend enough, not stick out.

They hadn't counted on Elaine's sharp eyes, seeing more than the obvious.

She pulled herself out of her head. Another danger of the new was comparing it too much to the old. She focused on the present. Rory made her laugh seven times during the meal. When he chuckled, it was a masculine sound, one with a sensual undercurrent. He could make heat course through her so often from doing so very little.

They talked, the music played, and gradually everything settled into a low-level hum of contentment, with the right edge of simmering anxiety. An anxiety that connected to the look in his eyes when he gazed at her. It made her want him to touch her, kiss her again.

That could cause another problem, though—like what had happened last night. She couldn't let her mind go that way, because things would go bad again. Yet every time he looked toward her legs, she kept thinking about—wishing—he'd put his hand on her thigh. That possessive touch he sometimes had with her, that made everything in her universe still, point directly toward him. She imagined his fingers tightening, which would make her legs want to loosen, open...

No. She slammed the door shut as her body began that throb. No, no, *no.*

"You okay? You look tense all of a sudden."

She nodded. "I'm fine. I promise. Thought waves."

Thomas had helped her come up with that term. She had so many mood swings. Someone asking her about them, making her analyze each one, could be as stressful to her as having them. So the term had become a way to tell her guardians what was going on, while simultaneously indicating she didn't need any particular attention paid to them.

Rory caressed her face with his knuckles, then dropped that touch to the side of her throat. As he stroked her there, she forgot about food. She wanted to lift her chin, give him better access. Like a cat, but it wasn't the stroking alone she craved, but some kind of pressure. His hand circling her throat, holding her...

With a murmured sound that sounded part reverent, part oath, he reached down, gripped the seat of her chair, his fingers brushing her thigh and hip. He tugged it closer to him in one easy pull. "Move your table setting over," he said.

She did, him rearranging his so there was room for her to eat side by side with him. He cut his steak into bite-sized pieces so that one hand was free for him to drape his arm over her seat back. He stroked the round of her shoulder as he continued to eat, too, only with her in the shelter of his arm span.

Her body went on full alert when he eventually removed his arm and dropped it beneath the table, his hand resting on her leg. His fingers spread to cover her thigh, caress the fabric of her skirt and her beneath.

They were in a restaurant. He wasn't going to do more here, so she could maybe get away with what she was feeling. She'd have time to bring it back under control, so that when they were alone together later, if he wanted to do things like this, she wouldn't upset him. But now her body hovered as close as it dared to the bliss of those searing feelings. She was so aware of his hand there. Her thighs loosened on their own, it seemed, the one directly under his grasp shifting toward him.

Her body was going to betray her, she knew it, but she couldn't find it in her to stop charging toward that precipice. She felt slightly feverish, and she couldn't warn him they were headed into bad waters. He would be upset with her, maybe. He hadn't been yet. Maybe even if he saw how weak she was, he'd still be okay with her. Maybe he'd overlook it.

When her leg moved toward him, his dark eyes came her way. "Good girl," he murmured softly, and the flush that went through her was a tide of pure heat. "Eat your dinner, now," he said. "We have that dessert to look forward to."

CHAPTER SEVEN

*R*ory once again asked Lobelia to divvy up the dessert, so Daralyn had a small sample on her plate, while he took a portion of the rest, and had the rest boxed up. It worked out so well, she finished hers.

She was quiet on the way home, but Rory thought her reasons were the same as his. The good emotions and physical response tangled pleasantly together in the close quarters, providing enough in the way of conversation, all of it non-verbal.

When her knees had parted for him at dinner, he'd felt a jolt to his lower belly. He hadn't pushed it—hell, he wasn't sure what had taken him over, making him initiate the touch and then following it up with the praise, but both had felt as natural as breathing.

Before they went down that road, though, he reminded himself they had to figure out a way to talk about what had happened the other night with her. His gut told him that resolving it was vitally important.

Thinking about how she'd retreated from him, he considered pulling off to a side road to talk to her about it. She wouldn't have the option of jumping out of the van and running into her little house if things got uncomfortable.

He discarded the thought immediately, ashamed of even having it. It brought back the unpleasantly vivid post-accident recollection of the first time his buddies had taken him out on a Saturday. His friends had just been trying to help, trying to recreate their carefree cruising nights.

But he'd been in his total scared dickhead, bad attitude mode. When he wanted to go home, really wanted to go, they'd insisted on taking him by the liquor store and some of their old haunts. He'd become progressively more agitated, though he'd tried to conceal it. Then one of them had teased him, probably to help him relax.

"Not much you can do about it, can you? Just sit back and enjoy the ride."

He'd completely lost it. Opened the door and flung himself out of the fortunately parked vehicle. He had some insane idea that he was going to crawl around the back and open the trunk to get his folded-up chair. He barely had the strength to drag himself across the ground. When his buddies gathered over him, trying to figure out what was going on, he felt suffocated and started fighting them. Punching, screaming, telling them to take him home. A fucked-up reaction somewhere between PTSD and a kid having the worst tantrum of his life.

Take me home, take me home... Take me the fuck home.

It had been a serious setback on his physical therapy, because his still far too weak upper body hadn't been up for that kind of volatile reaction. But the mental setback had been worse. He'd been a simple guy, the kind who scoffed at psychobabble about depression and triggers. He still thought most people had the ability to pull themselves out of their own heads if they put effort into finding the handholds to do so. However, after coming face to face with what being in a pit of true, helpless despair felt like, he didn't scoff anymore. Pulling out of that feeling made climbing Mount Everest look easy in comparison.

He wouldn't be taking Daralyn anywhere she felt trapped. But the way she kept looking at him, pressing his hand whenever he could hold hers, made his desire to figure things out even stronger. Fortunately, when he reached her house, he could tell without a shadow of a doubt she wanted him to come in.

As they parked at her place, he noted Marcus and Thomas were home. The Mercedes was back, and the lights were on in the house.

After leaving the van and crossing the yard to her house, Rory held out his hand for her keys. He noted the coldness of Daralyn's fingers before he let her go and opened the door, gesturing her to go on in. She pushed back her fall of silky hair when she moved past him.

As he clicked the door shut, she was laying her purse on the table. He watched her transfer the flowers she'd brought in with her to a vase, and sit it on a side table. Then she stood before it, her gaze resting upon the blooms.

Her stillness, combined with her obvious heightened awareness of him, dictated his next actions. He killed the lights, letting what was coming in through the windows, thrown from the outdoor utility light and the moon, create a silver filter over everything.

She turned partly toward him, her head down, but her peripheral vision on him. Her lips were parted. Her hand had closed into a curl on the table. While her coldness was a warning sign of agitation, other signs showed the heat of attraction.

If he'd been able to walk, he would have come up right behind her, pressed himself against her, kissed her neck, held her close. Let her feel that all of him, his strength, his heart, every bit of his mind, was centered on her. That she didn't have to be afraid.

He could do the same thing a different way, following his gut down the road he knew they both wanted. His voice was rough but low as he glanced at the large living room window. "Close the blinds."

She'd worn a pair of white slip-on shoes with lace tops and rubber soles, so as she obeyed, she moved on nearly soundless feet. As she reached for the rod that would twist the blinds closed, she spoke. He heard the intriguing unsteadiness in her voice.

"There's usually just the occasional driver on the road, who only looks this way for a second. And Thomas and Marcus only have eyes for each other."

"I want only my eyes on you."

She finished the task. Then she turned toward him.

"Let's go into the bedroom," he said.

He followed her to the threshold. The back window overlooked a field, so he didn't tell her to close the blinds there, since it was providing some of the light he wanted to use to see her.

"I want the dress off." He almost said *take the dress off,* but for where he intended to go in these next few moments, he needed the important distinction. She needed the command, but him saying *I want* made it different, in the right way.

He had no intention of having sex with her. Hell, though it seemed they'd been headed on that track since that Christmas kiss, the reality was they'd only recently started pursuing this. A kiss, a spanking, a little petting. A hand on her thigh at dinner. This alone might be too soon, but it didn't feel that way. He wanted to see all of her. He ached to see her.

She gripped the dress, lifted it over her head. As she did, she showed him another simple cotton bra, but this one was pale yellow with a lace edge. She also revealed the curve of her rib cage and flat stomach, the shape of her hip bones, her thighs. She put the dress on a hanger and tucked it into her closet. She took care with everything given to her. He'd never seen her carelessly drop something over a chair, leave something out of place.

Don't dig into why that is. This is about the here and now, you and her.

Even so, as his gaze coursed over her exposed body, another stark memory invaded. During that summer when Daralyn had first come to live with them, and he could still walk, she never closed a door to give herself privacy. At first, they thought it was a claustrophobia thing. Then Elaine accompanied the sheriff to the now abandoned house to see if Daralyn had any personal items to pack. She discovered only the bedrooms that belonged to her uncle and father had doors. None on the small room with a twin bed that had been Daralyn's, or the one bathroom. Everything had been done in view of her male relatives. Modesty hadn't been an option.

So when the younger version of himself had been shuffling out of his room on a Saturday morning, he'd happened by the room Daralyn shared with Les. All that was in his head was the hope the girls hadn't beaten him to the upstairs bathroom, necessitating a grumbling descent to the one on the first floor. Then he'd glanced left into the open doorway and been brought to a halt.

He was a teenage boy. He had to look. But there were times since he'd wished he could unsee what he'd seen.

Daralyn had been standing in the middle of the floor, changing her shirt. She'd been turned toward the window, her back curled as she found the sleeves with her narrow hands. What came to mind instantly, disturbingly, was the skeleton in his biology class. Every vertebra was visible. Her ribs were painfully prominent. Until then he hadn't realized the extent of her malnourishment.

He should have, but he'd been an idiot high school kid, caught up in his head. At just over five feet tall, she'd weighed less than ninety pounds when the police took her out of her family home.

She'd filled out now, he reminded himself. Still thin, but not scary thin. Yet he could see it, the image of the past overlaying the present, as she faced away from him, smoothing invisible wrinkles out of the dress. There was nothing deliberately sexy about her pose, yet he couldn't take his eyes from the wave of her hair on her shoulders, the pull of the panties across one buttock, how the bra strap followed a horizontal line beneath her shoulder blades.

"Turn and face me."

She did, but he could tell something was unsettling her. He reached out, palm up. She came to him and laid her wrist in it, the way she'd done the other day. When he closed his grip over it, she settled. His surge of reaction, impossible to describe, was the exact right feeling for the moment.

"Bring me that throw pillow on your bed."

When he released her to do that, he bent and removed his feet from the foot plate, spreading them out to either side of it. She returned, holding the pillow before her midriff, and he nodded to the space between his feet, in front of the plate. "Put the pillow there, and kneel on it, facing me. Put your hands on my thighs."

Every time he doubted whether this was the right path or not, he'd get a reaction like the one she demonstrated now. The flush climbed higher on her chest and throat, and she moistened her lips, her fingers tightening on the pillow. As she obeyed, he noted something else, equally important. She settled once she was down there, her breathing evening out. He was about to disrupt that some, but they had to go down this path. He knew it.

Her eyes closed as he stroked her hair, threaded his fingers through it, over and over. It was nice just to do that, watch the way she swayed and moved with him. The dark and quiet held them, so when he spoke, his voice was husky. "Put your head on my leg."

She scooted in and did so with a little sigh, her arm curling around one of his calves. He kept stroking, following the smooth path between her shoulder blades, down to the strap of the bra, and back up again.

"I want to know what was happening the other night. When we stopped."

She tensed, as he expected. But instead of letting his own guilt about whatever had happened derail him, he sharpened his focus on her reactions. What she was struggling with, yes, there was shame, but it was balanced by those same elements of desire. He saw her knees tighten and would have bet money she was replaying it all in her head. He decided to confirm it.

"How much have you thought about it, Daralyn? What we did? How I took control of you?" And damn if saying those words didn't feel good.

"More than I should. I was bad, Rory. I couldn't...not feel the way I felt. I couldn't control it."

As the words sank in, a terrible realization filled his mind. Asking a question just the right way could solve a mystery, but if her answer meant what he thought, it was unthinkable. Since that made him wonder if he'd interpreted what she'd said correctly, he'd proceed with the assumption of what anyone else would think had gone wrong, and be ready to exit off that highway as soon as he was sure.

"That's okay," he said. "Whatever it is, we can work through it. Do you want to try? Do you trust me?"

She traced circles on his leg. "Of course I trust you. It's...not about that. It's about me. I can't...not feel the way I feel when you touch me. I don't know how."

"Okay. Tell me how it feels. Maybe I can help you with that."

"I start to feel things..."

"Between your legs?"

She went damn near rigid. Rory stroked her nape, massaged.

"Daralyn, we're adults. We know what parts we each have. And trust me, I consider all of yours lovely."

She swallowed, her head bobbing. "It gets so strong there, that feeling, when you touch me. And it...radiates out to other places. Radiate. That's a new word this week."

"It's a good one," he said. "And does something start to go wrong then?"

She lifted her head just long enough for him to see her anguish, the struggle in her features, before she ducked her head down again. "That *is* the wrong. The bad."

"What?"

She bit her lip. "It's wrong for me to react that way. Once, when I felt that way while my uncle was touching me, something happened I couldn't stop. It just kind of took over, and made me stiffen up. It felt good, in an overwhelming, shocking way. It was short, just a few seconds, but intense. I got really wet...between my legs. My uncle was so angry. He told me I was really bad. When I misbehaved, they punished me by putting me in the cellar without food or light, usually for a few hours or overnight. The punishment for that was a lot worse. Three days, I think. I lost track."

It took indescribable effort to keep stroking her the same way, not to haul her into his lap and hold her tight while emitting a stream of vile curses. Jesus fucking Christ.

He'd been right about something being off about her reaction. Sex didn't frighten her. Pleasure did. They'd taught her it was wrong for her to feel it, embedding the lesson so deeply that, when she'd started to get aroused by Rory's touch, she'd thought she was doing something bad. Something that would disappoint him.

As often as they'd used her, it was inevitable, especially during puberty, that an orgasm would sometimes happen. Inescapable biology, no shame.

"My uncle said...I was his brother's daughter." Her voice was a whisper. "That was one reason it was wrong for me to react that way to him touching me. But he also said a man is weak, and a woman is supposed to not encourage his weakness. She remains chaste in thought and deed, even when he's rutting upon her. Otherwise, she's encouraging his uncleanness."

She was reciting, and the hair rose on his neck as he heard the child behind the words, behind the woman at his feet. As he imagined a big-eyed adolescent, her too-thin arm held in a human monster's bruising grip as she was berated, the universe wasn't big enough to contain his rage. If Burton Moorfield had been where Rory could reach him, he'd have blown the bastard's brains out with his hunting rifle.

He also now knew that cellar door had been left in place for reasons other than preserving food.

There'd be shrinks who'd have lengthy discourses on whatever disorder her father and uncle suffered from, blah blah blah. Crazy was just crazy, and when it resulted in the abuse of a child, that kind of crazy needed to be put down, end of story for him.

He wasn't controlling his rage well enough. She looked a little pale. "I'm not mad at you," he said. "Not even slightly."

She started to get up, but he tightened his grip on her wrist.

"Stay here. I want you to stay here." When he reframed it, he felt that surge Marcus had talked about. He was doing this on his own terms. Following his gut. "Put your head back down on my leg. Be easy."

As she complied, he started to stroke her hair and between her shoulder blades again, light caresses that made her shiver and unconsciously press closer to him. While he did that, he calmed himself and thought about what he wanted. What she might want.

"I need to tell you something, Daralyn. I need you to believe me, even if everything in your life has told you different."

"Okay." Her voice was a whisper.

"Your uncle, what he told you? It's the exact opposite of what a man wants from the woman he desires. He wants to see her pleasure. When I see you're getting worked up by what I'm doing, *nothing* makes me happier. Because your pleasure is what increases mine. The more you're enjoying yourself, the better it feels to me."

As he watched her struggle with it, he drove down his anger, his impatience. Not with her, never with her, but with his aching wish that she didn't have to deal with this pain, this conflict within her, fifteen years of conditioning by sculless family members.

"Do you still brush your hair before you go to sleep?" he asked. "Like Les taught you?"

Surprise flitted across her face. "Usually, yes."

"Good. I'm going to do it tonight. I'm going to brush your hair, tuck you into bed, give you a good night kiss. A kiss that might go on about a half hour or so, but that's all I'm going to be after."

Pain fractured her features. "Because I'm too messed up to do what a woman could do for you," she said dully. "Like Amanda."

In a mere few words, she reminded him how much she noticed, as well as how complicated she was. Just like any other woman. Her face was filled with so many conflicting emotions it tore things apart inside him.

He brushed her cheek with his knuckles, did it slow, and she tipped her head into it, her lips resting against them. He ran his thumb over the dip of her chin. "One of your smiles does more for me than anything any other woman has. You make me want to give you the world. Don't say something like that to me again, or I'll give you another spanking. I may do it anyway, send you to bed with a smarting backside to help you remember."

The quick flick of her eyes up to his, her parted lips, said he'd distracted her. And that she wasn't exactly averse to his threat. It changed the direction of his reaction as well, but that direction was no less volatile than his fury.

"So," he persisted in a calm voice—with effort. "Go get ready for bed, except for the hair brushing part."

She rose, but at the bathroom door she stopped, fingered the jamb, her eyes on it. "Is there something you'd like me to wear, other than what I usually wear?"

Was it normal for new Doms and subs to have a whole other language happening underneath the spoken words? In the carefully posed question, he heard exactly what she was really asking.

What does my Master want me to wear?

"Yeah," he said. "I'm really glad you asked." Translation: *You pleased me. You please your Master, with every fucking thing you do and say.*

"A robe. Nothing else."

She bit her lip. "If...I get wet like that again, I won't be able to hide it."

"I don't want you to hide it." He sent her a direct look, and at her uncertainty, he spoke to her gently, but with firmness. "Go do what I've asked."

She nodded.

What he wanted to say was, *I hope you'll be so wet you can't hide it. Because I want to see it. Taste it. Smell it. Watch it bathe my cock, feel it on my tongue, have you rub it against my body.*

None of that would happen tonight. But he hoped he'd be able to get them closer to the moment and day it would.

As he shed his suit jacket and pulled off the tie, opened up the top couple buttons of his shirt, he was in an optimal position to watch her preparations, all the tempting views. Because though she now knew the appropriate times to close the bathroom door for privacy, she'd recognized, blissfully, that this was not one of those times.

She removed her bra. Hooked her underwear, took it down over her backside. A heart shape he wanted to cradle in both hands, knead that softness. She was killing him.

She put away the bra, rolled the panties into a neat ball and dropped them into a clothes hamper. She was standing in her bathroom naked. He noted a slight tension to her, but other than that, she didn't seem self-conscious. Les and Elaine had taught her what was socially appropriate, and that was what guided her when it came to nudity.

He wasn't going to think any more tonight about the why of that, because too big a part of his soul was still howling from her latest revelation, thinking her sexual pleasure was a punishable offense.

Modesty was one thing; a lover's regard was another. That tension, and how she had her back to him, suggested him looking at her naked had her a little unsettled. His gaze devoured every inch of pale skin. She was still too skinny. The doctor said she'd been malnourished for so long her metabolism might take years to right itself. And her indifferent appetite didn't help.

Well, he had it on good authority that sex stimulated the appetite.

Despite the thinness, the curve of hip and breast, the rounded shape of a buttock, was all woman. He wanted to press his mouth to her shoulders, her throat, every bump of her spine. He wanted his mouth between her legs. He imagined spreading her on her mattress and feasting on her sweet pussy as her hands tangled in his hair and she strained up to him.

Going down on a woman fascinated him. She became so helpless and full of passion at once, writhing, begging, clawing. Needing what he could give her with his mouth and tongue, the edge of his teeth.

He pulled himself out of that. One thing at a time. Brushing hair.

She'd retrieved her robe from the back hook of the bathroom door and was shrugging into it, the plush pink thing with hearts on it. Her shoulders disappeared under it, and the shape of her body reappeared as she tightened the sash, turned toward him.

"Brush." He nodded to the dresser "And the wooden foot stool from your kitchen."

When she brought those, he had put his feet back on his foot plate and adjusted his chair so he was square with her floor length mirror.

"Put the stool in front of me and sit on it, facing the mirror," he told her. "Tuck the skirt of the robe underneath you to give yourself a cushion." It would also keep it out of the way of his casters.

Curiosity in her gaze, she complied and settled on the stool, close enough his footplate was partly beneath it and she could lean back against his knees. He took the brush from her and left it in his lap.

"Untie the robe and shrug it off your shoulders. Let it fall to your waist. I want to see you."

Her gaze met his in the mirror. "Rory..."

"Nothing you feel is going to be wrong, Daralyn. Every reaction you have to what I'm doing is what I want you to feel. I want you to react this way. What your uncle told you was wrong." Repetition might not fix it, but it couldn't hurt.

"It was good to react that way when he touched me?" Clouds gathered in her expression.

A tricky question. Rory slid his fingers through her hair. As he did, he gripped and tugged. Tugged hard. Her body moved with his touch and her gaze went opaque, her lips parting.

"That's me, pulling your hair," he said huskily. "Now, imagine if someone came up to you and yanked on your hair to be mean. Would it feel the same inside?"

She shook her head.

"Both reactions are normal. But it's okay to like one more than the other. Our bodies don't know right or wrong, good or bad. That's our heads and our hearts. Our bodies react as bodies. Understand?"

Slowly, she nodded. He saw an intensity to her gaze, the way she looked when she was learning something, trying to fully grasp it. That gave him another idea. Daralyn often came to truths by a different path than most people took.

He leaned over to retrieve his phone from the jacket he'd laid on the bed. As he did an online search, he was aware of her eyes on him in the mirror. He extended the phone over her shoulder. "Read that. Aloud."

She looked at it, then looked up at him quickly. Back down. He molded his hands over her shoulders, the robe in the way, but his thumbs found her collar bones, rubbed. He noticed her breath rose and fell, a quick little response to the touch, as well as to draw in air to follow his direction.

"Arouse...to evoke or awaken, as in a feeling, emotion or response. Also...to awaken someone from sleep."

"What you're feeling when I touch you is arousal. And there's nothing I want more than to wake you up like that." He paused. "Didn't I tell you to do something?"

She jumped a little, remembering. He didn't smile, just kept looking at her in the mirror. She handed the phone back to him and he tossed it onto the bed, never taking his gaze from her as she loosened the sash and worked the robe off her shoulders. She didn't look at herself in the reflection; only him, so he made sure she saw what was in his expression as he dropped his attention to every inch of exposed skin. As the cloth tumbled to her waist, he gazed at her shoulders, her breasts. The nipples were tight little points that made saliva gather in his mouth. He wanted to suck on them, make her moan and cry out, get her even wetter.

Putting a choke hold on his desires, Rory lifted the brush, and started working it through her hair, those thick and strong locks that fell in captivating waves around her bare shoulders. He threaded his fingers through them, following the brush. On each round, he gripped her nape, stroked, kneaded.

Her fingers opened and closed on the pink terry cloth, her body swaying toward his. Her eyes were half closed, but he noted her breath was still shallow. "Daralyn," he said in that same steady voice, "I want you to cup your breasts. Run your fingers over your nipples. The better that feels, the more I want you to keep doing it."

Her cheeks stained red against too much white. She was trembling. "But...I'm not supposed to touch myself..."

He should have known the bastards would hit that one, too. No masturbating. No giving herself even a minute of pleasure.

He set aside the brush. "Let's do it together."

Sliding his arms in under hers, he cupped her hands and brought both sets to her small curves. When he molded her fingers over her breasts, his own were in between them. He felt the give of flesh, the different texture of the nipple graze his fingertips. She sucked in a breath when he did that. He had her fingers do it as well, playing them over herself. She shifted, her breath coming faster.

"I'm getting...excited. That's wrong."

"No. It's not wrong at all. You're waking up. Like opening your eyes and seeing the sun. Think of all the things you've realized are different since you came to be with us. Look at my face, Daralyn. Look at what *your* pleasure is doing for *me*."

Her wondrous expression went to his, and clung there as he kept his attention between that and her breasts, their overlapped hands there. She had her knees drawn up, pressed together, but the little shifts of her body told him it was time to change that up.

"You know how you opened your legs at the restaurant, when I touched your thigh? Do that now. Move the robe out of the way so I can see between your legs."

That internal conflict increased, but the dazed look in her eyes did too, a little moan slipping from her lips.

It was a precarious edge. She was aroused, but there was a struggle happening inside of her, past and present clashing. His own desire grew in leaps and bounds, the more she looked at him with that yearning expression, looking for him to take her down the path that had been denied her. He saw it in the increased trembling, and more of that heart-rending uncertainty in her eyes. He could almost feel the confused ache there.

Taking it slow and easy wasn't easy at all. She'd said she didn't always want choices when it came to him. While that might be the natural Dom and sub stuff, if she didn't understand she *could* choose, he was going to make extra sure he wasn't doing anything she didn't want, even if she couldn't express those wants.

"You don't have to question if what you're doing and feeling is right or wrong, Daralyn. If you're following my commands, it's my will you're obeying. Is my will wrong? What I want?"

She shook her head. "No. I don't think so. I feel better, when I listen to you. Your voice..."

He continued to knead her breasts, her fingers in between, so they squeezed together, teased her nipples. As he flicked over them with his stronger touch, she jerked, gasped. She was going to kill him.

"What about my voice?" he prodded.

"It's deep...it echoes...resonates. New word. Resonates, so when you're talking to customers, it fills the room. When you were here the other night, it filled the space, and stayed...like warmth from the space heater. Fire."

She could humble him. Fortunately, his desire was keeping him on point, its demands not letting the softer emotions take over before it was time.

"Rory..." The cry came as her body jerked. Her hands fluttered, turned and clasped his, his wrists. Her wide eyes went to his, and he realized her sex had spasmed with the beginning of an orgasm.

"Easy, girl. It's all good. I've got you. It gets better." He wouldn't let anything into this space with them. It was just him and her. Nothing connecting to the world beyond them, or the past. As her hands stayed hooked on his wrists, he cupped her breasts, full flesh-on-flesh, and began to play, knead, flick, lightly pinch. "You haven't done something I've asked. Spread your legs, Daralyn."

"I'm not supposed to feel..."

"You can feel anything you damn well want to feel," he told her, low, his eyes burning into hers in the mirror.

Too much. Too much anger. She shrank against him, and he reined it back, made a soothing note. "Spread your legs for me, baby."

She slowly did. Pushing the robe back, then parting her knees, adjusting her feet out. There. The lips of her sex, nestled in dark brown, silky hair that gleamed with moisture. Keeping one hand on her breast, he slid the other down, to the mouth of her sex. He had to lean forward to do that, which shifted his center of gravity, but he had the upper body control and strength to allow for it. Plus, he was leaning into her, a pleasant counterbalance of soft woman and the scent of jasmine.

He played his fingers over her and, as she shuddered and shook, his other hand slid upward, adjusted, closed over her throat. Her back was pressed to his legs, her shoulder blades against his knees. As she arched against his touch, her small breasts thrust out, the pink tips aching for a man's suckling mouth. His mouth.

There'd be time for that later. Now he just wanted this.

"Look at my eyes in the mirror, Daralyn."

She did, and when they skittered away, he made a harsh noise. They came back. "You'll keep your eyes on my face, no matter what happens in the next few minutes. Don't look away until I tell you that you can. See how much I enjoy watching you when you're feeling like this."

He'd delivered the command with the strength he'd felt it. More moisture slipped out of her, making her labia glisten, wetting his fingers. "You like it when I tell you what to do," he growled.

"It makes me feel safe." Her voice was strained as she delivered that gift to him. Her breath puffed along his skin because his head was bent close over hers. "Like everything's okay, when you say it is."

"It is." He massaged the wetness into her swollen flesh, flicked lightly over her clit.

"Feels like...butterfly. Dancing over a flower."

Male heat made his smile look almost dangerous, but that was because there was a glorious kind of pain fueling it. His striking girl, and her gift for words. Her love of using them in amazing ways.

"Rory...oh..."

Her back arched further, hips twitching. He tightened his grip on her throat, and the spasms grew stronger. "Is it okay...please...is it..."

"Yes. It is. It is *so* okay." He squeezed that slender column lightly even as he kept his other hand moving between her legs. He sensed the strength of the orgasm he might be summoning, and he wanted to see that. He wanted to see her completely shatter from the bliss of it. But intuition told him to reinforce who was in control. "But not until I say it is."

He put his burning gaze on her face in the mirror. "Hold your breasts in your hands like I was doing, Daralyn. Run your fingers over the nipples. Squeeze them, flick them."

She complied, even as she made a desperate little noise in her throat that became a chain of those kinds of sounds, needy moans. He answered with rough growls of approval, and words he offered back, in a hundred different versions. "Love seeing you excited like this. Want to push you over and make you scream..."

Her eyes stayed as wide as saucers throughout all of it, every act and sensation obviously new to her. So he saw the final wave coming in those hazel depths, even before her body's movements went from sinuous to hard jerks, deep shudders. Those wide eyes got wider, her mouth opening, seeking air.

"Now, baby. It's okay. Let it happen."

A cry of relief burst forth, but he saw the moment when the war started, inner defenses kicking in, a self-protection. She was trying to obey him, even as her body fought the climax like a drowning swimmer. He wouldn't let it win.

He let the movements of her body push his fingers inside her, his thumb firmly massaging the outside. At the same time, he pressed his face to the side of hers, his lips moving down to her collar bone, her throat, below his grip. He nipped her, then a stronger bite. With it, he demanded all her attention, inside and out, past and present, be on him, on what he was requiring of her. No one else.

She lost the battle. Or won it, from his fiercely satisfied perspective. A cry became a wail, and her body lifted and fell against his grip, a wild, strong, magnificent creature. Her hair rippled over his knuckles, cascading over her back, head tipped back against his shoulder.

At the height of it, the orgasm seemed to pull from something far deeper than the body. A good orgasm did, especially for women. Her eyes wheeled around as if she was lost at sea. He pressed his hand firmly against her cunt, a sealing in of that feeling, and she rode it, her hips pressing forward, pushing her sex into his touch, body still bucking.

She almost toppled the stool once or twice, but he was firmly planted in his chair now, his core drawn tight to hold her steady, even as he kept his hand moving on her wet, spasming sex.

Only when she seemed to have experienced all the aftershocks she could did he shift that hand. He banded his arm over her chest, moved the other hand from her throat to overlap it. He held her close, cocooned against him as she slowly came back to earth.

He'd never wanted to be inside a woman more, with full feeling in his cock and every inch of the body attached to it. But this was enough for now. More than enough.

"Rory," she whispered. Her voice was raspy. Hoarse. "Rory."

"Ssh. You're okay. I've got you." He hummed to her, one of the old country tunes from earlier in the evening, and pressed a kiss against her hair.

Her fingers were hooked over his forearms, nails digging in. She'd touched down like a feather, but now that slight sway to her body was becoming a more insistent rock against his hold. "Rory. I can't let go... I'm falling..."

Unease rippled through him, but he spoke soothingly. This was the flipside of the involuntary, pleasurable reaction she'd just experienced. A reaction she had no way to handle, no context, just his word. He had to make sure she could count on it, lean on it.

"You don't have to let go," he told her. "And I'm not letting go of you. Just hang on."

"Why...why...why..." He thought she was trying to ask him a question, the way she was struggling with the single word, but a blink later, there was no spare energy to figure it out.

Everything changed.

Yes, an orgasm could be a deeper-than-the-body experience, opening rooms in the heart that had been closed up for too long. But instead of turning the knob and pushing inward, her release had ripped them off the hinges, busting the frame.

Words disappeared, replaced by a raw, wailing cry. He was holding a wounded wild animal, not a woman. But she'd taken him at his word. She wasn't fighting to get away. She held onto as much of him as she could, with raking nails, pummeling fists, biting teeth.

His upper body was far stronger than hers, but she had the advantage of greater mobility. One of her thrashings tipped her over his arm, overbalancing him and the chair. Which, damn it all, broke his hold. She hit the floor on one knee as he grabbed onto her nearby bed, trying to catch himself. He missed, toppling out of the seat and onto the floor. The braked chair had tipped but it found the dresser, which sent it back to all wheels.

He'd been afraid he'd land on her, but she had rolled, was on her feet. She ran into everything in her path, as if what she was seeing wasn't this room. She knocked items off the dresser, then found the opening to the bedroom with flailing hands and was through it. She plowed into the sideboard in the kitchen. The flower vase rocked precariously, but didn't topple.

"No. Daralyn, stop." He bellowed it, but it was too late. She had slipped and stumbled through the kitchen and was at her front door. In the next breath she was out of it.

"Shit, shit, shit!"

He pushed himself to a sitting position, grabbed his phone off the end of the bed. Every part of him roared in protest, but he needed back up. He used voice control to try Marcus, then Thomas. Nothing.

While doing that, he was swearing, getting himself back into the chair, a process that required him to pull himself over to it, tuck his knees up against his body and use the leverage of that position and his core strength to haul himself back up into the seat. All of which took too much fucking time.

He shoved himself out of the bedroom, headed for the front door, standing wide open. Even as he went that way, his gaze was already darting over the limited rectangle of outdoor area he could see, trying to find her.

He couldn't hear her, which scared him worse than that wailing she'd been doing. The saying "sounded like a dying animal" was inaccurate, because a wounded animal, instinctually motivated not to draw the attention of predators, hid and became more silent if he or she could.

He came out the front door, his breath sobbing in his throat. If she'd run into the fields behind the house, he couldn't follow her. And what if she abruptly emerged from a field onto the road? At this time of night, she could be stepping in front of the car of a lightly buzzed neighbor, coming back from one of the local watering holes.

Fortunately, in the same blink of time that terrifying possibility and plenty more went through his mind, he also saw she was here. She was safe.

Marcus and Thomas hadn't answered their phones because they were with her. He suspected they'd seen her burst out the front door from their living room windows. She'd gone to ground in a nook formed by the rear corner of their house and the porch. She was backed in that alcove like a spider in a knot hole. Hunched into herself, down close to the ground, keening, rocking. Her robe was still off her shoulders, but she had it gathered around her like a blanket. It split open over her thigh practically to her hip, leaving no doubt she wore nothing under it.

He balanced on his back wheels to get off her front patio and manage the rough expanse of ground between it and her. His heart was in his throat, his head pounding. If he'd hurt her, set her back months on the progress she'd made in her day-to-day world, he'd never forgive himself.

He'd told her he wouldn't let her go. And she'd broken free, because he wasn't strong enough, whole enough, to be able to deliver on that promise.

He snarled at himself. *No time for this fucking self-pitying shit.* He was aware that Marcus said something to him, maybe Thomas, too, but he had one goal and he couldn't let anything interfere with it. He rolled right up to her, stopped where his feet were almost touching her folded-up legs. "Daralyn, look at me."

His faith in his gut was *not* bullshit. Though telling himself that and acting on it were different things, he wouldn't let himself back away from it. It sliced into his gut like knives, but he sharpened his tone. "Stop this shit and look at me. *Right now.*"

She cut off mid-keen. Her eyes snapped up to him, wheeled around, then came back to him. Rory didn't waste any time, making full use of the sudden attention. He put out his hand, keeping his tone brusque. "Come here."

She was staring at his hand. He could see her trying to make sense of it. He refused to doubt himself, even if the effort burned like acid in his chest.

"You make me wait, and you'll regret it," he said quietly. "I'll use your brush on your bare ass instead of my hand."

That flicker again. He sensed there was no real comprehension right now. Just feeling. He was banking she would move toward sanctuary on instinct, and she needed that sanctuary to be solid stone. It had to be able to handle the power of the storm within her. He'd be the still point at the center of that storm.

"I'm here, baby," he said. "Come here."

Slowly, she pushed herself up to her feet. Her legs were shaking, but she reached out and then he had her hand. He drew her in closer. Where she'd been sitting was where condensation from the roof fell and rarely dried out, since it stayed a shady spot through most of the day. As such, she had mud on her pretty robe, her bare legs.

She blinked, her gaze falling to it. "'I am clay that was never shaped.'"

The hollowness to her voice, that unnatural, hair-raising cadence, was the same as earlier, when she'd repeated what her uncle had said to her, about men's weakness. Why was it so many monsters twisted Bible quotes for their crazy shit?

Well, there were people who weren't monsters, who used it as well. His mother, for one. The designs of fate were a fucking mystery to him most days, but this was one of those moments when it made its intentions clear. A lifetime of Elaine making him go to church, study the Bible with her, offered him the important part of the quote, the part her uncle and father had left out when they'd used it against her.

"'You are fearfully and wonderfully made,'" he said, then reminded her she wasn't alone. "'Behold, I am toward God as you are; I too was pinched off from a piece of clay.'"

Tears gathered in her eyes. She swayed, her knees weakening, but he brought her to him with one hard yank just as they gave way. She crumpled over his lap. He lifted her, turned her in his arms with an effort that strained his back, because she was like a drunk, dead weight. He was aware of other hands helping him to position her, steadying him in the chair, but his full attention remained on her.

Her eyes held all the ancient sorrows of the world, from the very first time one soul had dealt pain to another. But he saw more, too. A flicker, as if she was trying to order things in her mind, get a grip. Giving her that breathing space was important. So were signs of normalcy.

He stroked her hair away from her face, reminding her of the brushing. She'd liked it, had leaned into it. She'd responded to it, physically and emotionally.

He kept doing that until he saw her remember that, use it to bring herself back, one painstaking thought at a time, a chain she was forming and linking together in her mind, like that bracelet he'd made for her. Watching that struggle happen, seeing how agonizingly hard it was for her, reminded him of another quote his mother used.

Do not lose heart. Though our outer self is wasting away, our inner self is being renewed day by day.

She'd used that quote to help him. At the time, he hadn't been that appreciative, grieving the loss of half his body. His inner strength hadn't meant shit to him. However, he could give Daralyn that quote, without the wasting away bit. As he spoke the words, her hands were on his chest, fingers twitching. Her head was against his shoulder, so he pressed his face to her forehead, then kissed it. "I'm here," he said quietly. "And you're amazing and wonderful. Don't lose heart."

His own was breaking. He might not be the right person for her, but fuck, he didn't know who was. So he'd make himself a vow, here and now and always, to stand by her, help her find what she needed. Give her whatever she needed, even if ultimately it meant she left him behind in the dust.

He'd taken offense when he'd thought his mother had implied he was a waystation. But truth? If that was what he ended up being, and he could help her heal enough that she found a lasting happiness, that was what he'd do.

Then he'd just push himself in front of a truck and die. If not happy, he'd at least be certain he'd done something worth doing.

She'd settled, simply resting in his arms, quiet. Her eyes had closed. Her body was doing little convulsive jerks from nerves, but her legs had relaxed against the hold of his arm around them.

His tunnel vision receded enough for him to realize that Thomas was at his elbow. Marcus was squatting by Rory's feet, his hand resting on Daralyn's back, adding to Rory's strength. When Rory looked into Marcus's face, he was startled to see something there he'd never seen before.

Nerves.

"I'm sorry, Rory," he said. "I told you to forge ahead. Maybe that wasn't the right thing."

For the past few days, a theory about Daralyn's state of mind had been playing in Rory's mind like a shy kid lurking in the shadows, afraid of being exposed to ridicule if it made itself known. But seeing the man who never doubted himself apologizing in the face of Daralyn's chaotic response clicked something into place.

Rory knew her. He stood in a spot in her soul they hadn't visited. His theory was right. Daralyn herself had given him the confirmation, with that biblical quote.

Those first couple weeks after his accident, there'd been some hope, that when the swelling went down, he'd get more mobility back. Even the possibility of walking again. Then they'd known for sure. There was no going back, no recovery. No walking again, even with braces. Not unless some major breakthrough happened in technology or spinal surgery.

Hearing that it wasn't a matter of being determined enough, willing to do enough exercises, that this was permanent, had been one of the hardest things in his life to hear. It was then he'd begun to realize the full scope of all he'd lost. He'd had to set fire to the house that was his life to rise from the ashes, create something new.

This had been that moment for her. That was why his gut refused to give in to his heart, let him think he'd fucked up. The surfeit of pleasure, of bliss in a lover's arms, ironically a good moment pointed toward the future, not the past, had brought the past flooding in. A reminder of all that had been lost, and taken from her. But also an indication of what possibilities lay ahead.

Grief was an ending, right before the door to the beginning. So, no. He wasn't going to do her the disservice of beating himself up, thinking he'd pushed her the wrong way, triggered something irreparable. He wasn't going to push her back into that box because of his own guilt.

He held her closer. She wasn't violent anymore, though she kept beating a light tattoo against his shoulder with her closed fist. Her head remained on the opposite shoulder, seeming like it was too heavy for her to hold it up. When he adjusted to obtain a better look at her face, tears were running down it like raindrops on glass, smooth and easy. Going the way of gravity, soaking into the earth of the past, but not salting it against the future. Just the opposite. He had to believe that.

And just like his family had for him, he had to believe it for her, too, no matter how dark and lost she felt right now.

He met Marcus's anguished look, and briefly moved his own hand to touch his brother-in-law's on Daralyn's back, a reassurance. Surprise passed through Marcus's gaze, reflected in Thomas's when they exchanged a look.

"It's okay," Rory murmured. "Everything's all right. Sometimes the world just makes you so mad, you have to lose it, and the closest thing to tear apart is yourself."

Thomas nodded, covering Marcus's hand so they all three had their hands on her, reassuring her. "Thanks for being here," Rory said.

Out of all of it, that was the hardest thing for him to say, since he wanted to always be the first one to protect her. But they'd had his back, as well as hers, and that was more important.

He glanced back across the driveway and yard to her house. Since the porch light next to the still-open door was on, he'd be chasing moths out of the house for the rest of the night. "If one of you can carry her over there, let's get her to bed."

He hated having to relinquish her, but he'd need both hands to cross the yard. He wouldn't let pride get her dumped on the ground.

"I'm okay," Daralyn said unexpectedly. She pushed slowly out of their hold and stood, swaying. Her fingers clung to his briefly, before her hand slipped away. She didn't look at any of them. Instead she tucked the robe around her, crossed her arms over her body and moved back toward the house at a tentative walk, her head down.

Rory didn't want to be far behind her, but he shot Thomas and Marcus an acknowledging glance. "I'm going to put her to bed, stay with her. She'll be all right. We're all right."

Thomas brushed a hand over Rory's shoulder, brotherly affection. "Check yourself over good. You've got some scratches on your arms."

Shit. The last thing he wanted tonight was an injury to his legs that would require tending. Hopefully he hadn't hit anything on his topple from the chair.

"I hear you, Mom," he said, amiable about it. "Stop looking so worried."

Thomas's faint smile didn't reach his eyes. "Tell yourself that. Your hands are shaking, and you look a little pale."

"You know where we are if you need us," Marcus added. Even as he put a reassuring hand on Thomas, his glance returned to the cottage, watching after Daralyn.

"It's good," Rory told him. He hoped Marcus understood, because he couldn't explain how he knew that. He just did.

After Rory followed Daralyn into the cottage and closed the door, Marcus and Thomas returned to their own porch. Marcus wasn't surprised when Thomas took a heavy seat on the front stoop. Marcus sat down next to him, putting a hand on his broad back. Thomas was understandably shaken up, but reassuring him helped Marcus settle down himself.

Daralyn's feral behavior had been startling, but the big shock had been Rory's comparative steadiness. Thinking about that put more confidence into the words Marcus spoke to Thomas now.

"He's okay. They both are."

Thomas ran a hand over his face. "Fuck, he was right for kidding me about acting like Mom. I was about to demand he take off his pants so I could check him myself."

"Good luck with that. He'd never strip around me."

Humor flitted through Thomas's gaze, but he remained serious. "He's strong, Marcus, but he's also vulnerable to infection. Plus a bunch of other stuff when he gets stressed, mentally or physically. Weaker immune system, and his heart and lungs are more at risk, because he's in a chair."

"He does the PT regularly," Marcus reminded him. "Which includes standing cardio. They strap him into that machine that I personally think could convert to some very interesting uses in the off hours. PT room by day, BDSM dungeon by night."

"Tell Rory that and he'll never go to PT again." Thomas sighed. "I know he's an adult now, and he takes care of himself, does all the things he should to keep himself healthy. Hell, he's grown up so much. Left behind a lot of the baggage. And out there, with her...who'd have thought he'd turn out to be that mature of a Dom, this soon?" He shot an amused look at Marcus. "Must be the mentor he has."

Marcus grunted. "Didn't feel that way when I saw her. It's different with your own sub. I thought I'd fucked up, given him advice based more on you than on her."

"No." Thomas touched his knee, leaned against him, drawing and giving strength at the same time. "Though I don't like to think about it much, you were a hell of an experienced Master, long before I met you. You knew Rory was going to figure this out. And he did."

Thomas gazed across the yard to the cottage. The blinds were still drawn, but the lights were on and all was quiet. "When he came out, he was as freaked out as we were, but then something clicked, kicked in, when he reached her."

Hearing Thomas confirm what he'd seen steadied him further, too. Marcus ran a hand down Thomas's back, hooked his thumb in the waistband of his jeans.

"And damn if she didn't respond to it, right in front of us." Thomas looked at him. "At that moment, I couldn't have raised my voice to her the way he did to save my life, or hers. I'm not even sure you could have."

"Hmm. When it comes to Daralyn, I think we both have a serious big brother, little sister complex. Rory doesn't." Marcus nudged Thomas. "And don't be too freaked out by his sudden onset of maturity. He'll have a snarky, angry moment tomorrow and remind you why he's your annoying little brother."

"Even the anger... It's still there, but he manages it better. It seems more targeted at the people who hurt her. Which is totally understandable."

"Yeah. A lot of that to go around." Marcus's expression clouded, his green eyes thoughtful. Thomas touched his leg, drawing his gaze.

"Hey. You okay?"

"Yeah." Marcus pulled himself out of his head, gripped Thomas's shoulder and gave it a hard squeeze. He had a sudden desire to be balls-deep in his sub. It would remind him that the bond between a Dom and sub could go to depths beyond the complete comprehension of anyone else. Even other Doms or subs.

"Let's head back in. For tonight, he's got it. He's got her."

CHAPTER EIGHT

*W*hen Rory closed the door behind him, Daralyn had stopped in the kitchen. She stood there shivering, the muddy robe drawn around her, one hand clutching and unclutching the thick fabric.

His certainty in the yard faltered. He stood witness to a battered soul, a person who'd lived a life directly opposite from what normal meant to him. The idea that he could guide her onto a shared path with him seemed ludicrous. But she couldn't afford his doubt, so he put it aside.

"Daralyn."

She turned to him. The aftermath had set in, her gaze filled with misery and regret. Self-flagellation. He wasn't going to allow that.

"Get me the hand towel by the sink."

She picked it up and padded across the kitchen to him, moving as if she carried a bag of boulders. After he took the towel from her hand, a whimsical thing with purple flowers printed on it, he draped it over his wheel. Reaching out, he uncurled her hands from the robe, pushed it off her shoulders, letting it fall to the floor with a damp weight.

Before she could shiver, he'd reclaimed her hand and brought her into his lap. He spoke softly. "Bring your legs up. Brace your feet against my push rim."

She did, and she was curled up against him, his arm around her back. He used his other hand to clasp the towel and wipe off her legs. Then he tossed it away and clasped her thigh, the one not pressed against him, to keep her in that folded up position. She'd knotted her hands against his shirt front, tucking her head under his chin. Since he'd unbuttoned the top two buttons of his shirt when he took off his tie, he felt her cheek against his skin.

"Hold onto me with both arms."

She slid them around him, and it freed his hands to push them back into her bedroom. Once there, he stopped by the bed, pulled back the covers. "Come get under the blankets."

"I had such a nice time tonight. I really did."

"I did, too. Still am. I'm right where I want to be, Daralyn. Get under the covers. You're cold, and I don't like that. Face the back window."

That last direction won him a puzzled look, but she reluctantly left his lap. She settled under the covers on her side, facing away from him.

"Stay like that. I'm going to get in the bed behind you, help you be warmer."

He unbuttoned his shirt, shrugged out of it. A peculiar stillness came over her, telling him she was aware of what he was doing. He pulled the undershirt over his head. Worked off the slacks and his shoes and socks. He didn't usually wear underwear, since it was another layer of material that could crease and cause a skin issue. However, since he'd worn the suit tonight, he'd donned dark boxer briefs, which he was glad for now. He'd leave those on, sending the message he wasn't going to ask for more from her.

He did a quick check with eyes and hands to confirm everything below the waist looked and felt good, no broken skin or blood.

"Can I look over my shoulder at you?" she asked.

"Yeah."

When she did, concern crossed her expression as she noted a red mark on his thigh. He'd already seen it himself, knew it was probably something he'd hit when he'd fallen out of his chair. "It's okay," he said. "The skin's not broken. It might bruise, but it's not a big deal. Hey."

Her face had creased like she was in pain. He leaned forward, bracing himself with one hand on the bed while he cupped her face. "Turn back toward the other way. I want to get you warm."

"I'm okay."

"I know that." He tightened his grip, looked her in the eye. "Do as I say."

She turned. He normally needed to rearrange his pillows to pad between his knees and other places susceptible to pressure sores, but this was fine for a short period. He didn't want any barriers between them. When he was finally in the right position to put his arm around her waist, and she scooted her butt into the cradle of his pelvis, it was more than worth the risk.

He could feel the give of her buttocks against those faint tingling spots in his thighs, her back against his chest, her side against his circling arm.

He pressed his face into her hair, inhaling her. He was holding her in his arms, naked and smooth, a bundle of sweet female scents. The little quivers he felt had to be stress, but maybe other things, too.

"I loved watching you climax," he murmured. "Did it feel good?"

A pause, then a slow nod. "I'm sorry about after."

He tightened his arm around her. "You don't apologize to me, not ever, unless I ask you for that. Got it?"

After a long moment, she nodded again.

"Good." He paused. "Did you ever talk to Les about sex?"

He steeled himself against the horror of the possibility, but since his sister was a grown woman, he'd get through it.

"No." She shook her head. "No one talks to me about this. Except you."

"Have you talked to the head doc about it? Particularly the way your uncle reacted to you getting worked up like that? Having an orgasm?"

Which made him recall her next appointment with Dr. Taylor was tomorrow morning. Good timing.

"We talk about other things. Until now...it wasn't a topic we needed to cover. She says I need to, but I haven't."

While she seemed to respond well to his commands, he wouldn't go that route on this. "Can you do me a favor? Can you bring it up with her?"

"I'll try. Yes. But I feel better...when you talk to me about it."

"I'm worried about fucking up, honey. Saying the wrong thing."

She tilted her head enough to look back at him. "Sometimes I think people are too careful around me. You know what I mean?"

Yeah, he did.

Her smile was tremulous around the edges. "It's like they think I'm carrying a bomb inside me, and if they say or do the wrong thing, I'll explode into a million pieces." Her expression sobered. "But I guess I proved that's what can happen."

"That's okay. You didn't do anything wrong. You're dealing with a lot. What I'm trying to say is that's why she's there. Like my example about the PT. She's someone trained to help you with anything I can't, or you can't figure out yourself. Just a suggestion, okay?"

Slow nod again. He had his hand over hers, and she moved it so his palm was over her breasts, his fingers resting in the hills and valleys, and then she cupped her other hand over that, pressed her hips deeper into the cradle of his. Anyone else, he'd say she was purpose-fully trying to tease him, but it was more like she was burrowing while trying to pull him around her like a blanket. He could do that.

He nudged her hair aside, put his lips to her neck, nuzzling her. "I liked watching you go over that edge, explode a whole different way."

He stroked her breast, fingers extending from where she held their hands tangled. "I want to do that to you again."

Her fingers quivered. "I'm afraid I'll...explode the other way again."

"Did it feel good to you, before that?"

She thought about it. "Yes," she said at last.

"Then don't worry about it. When you open a valve, the water pressure is intense. After that, it levels out, pours out in a smooth stream."

Her lips pressed together. He lifted his head enough to get a better look at her, and narrowed his eyes when he caught a smirk. "You're trying not to laugh at me."

The smile broke through, and she did chuckle a little. He gave her a reproving pinch on her buttock, then smoothed his hand over it, resisting the very strong urge to fondle, take a firmer grip and knead. "So you don't think I should pursue a career as a romance author? Or a poet?"

"I think you are a very good store manager."

He laughed out loud. Her head turned, her eyes roving over his face, her lips parting.

She obviously liked watching him laugh. When she lifted her fingers to touch his mouth, he kissed them, then cupped her face, running a caressing thumb over her cheek. Her eyes grew thoughtful again. She settled her head back onto the pillow, dipped her head over their hands.

"What are you thinking?" he said, putting his mouth back to her throat, teasing there, giving her a hint of teeth. She shivered at the edge.

"Can I do that for you?" she said. "What you did for me?"

It didn't surprise him that she'd thought of that. She was unfailingly generous, always thinking of ways she could help and serve others.

"You sure can. When I tell you it's okay. Right now, I want to take my time enjoying your body, your reactions. All that arousal that happens between your legs? Eventually I want to taste it. Put my mouth there, make you come that way."

She stilled. He wanted to ask her what she was thinking about that, but he decided to go another way. "You seemed to like the spanking the other night. It didn't seem to upset you."

"No...they didn't ever...not like that. He—"

"Don't," he said sharply. She flinched, and he cursed himself. Tried again, calmer.

"I said 'don't,' because I didn't want you to go there in your head." He took a breath. "But is it hard to do that? It's all right to tell me."

"No," she said after a long moment, confirming the truth he was having trouble accepting. "I like my life so much more now, Rory. But then, it was just different. Wrong or right, good or bad...it was just my life."

She shook her head, "It didn't happen often, but sometimes, when they praised me or were more kind, it made me feel..."

"Like you mattered."

"Yes. Dr. Taylor says that helped them keep me in a situation where I wouldn't reach out for help, and I understand that. But she also said it wasn't wrong for me to accept that kindness for what it was worth. Or see my life how I saw it then, the bad and not so bad. If it helped me survive it." She took a breath. "But when you get mad about it, it feels like I've said or done something wrong, bringing it up."

That made total sense. She had to be able to talk about this stuff, without him reacting. How the hell did he do that?

Same way he'd learned how to do plenty of other hard stuff. With practice.

He turned her over toward him, guiding her so she was curled in his arms, her head tucked under his chin. One of her arms crept under his, the other tucked between his chest and her body. Her bare breasts pressed against him. He stroked through her hair again, cradling her jaw and side of her throat. He didn't want to distress her, but he wasn't going to make a wrong assumption again, if he could avoid it by asking her the right questions.

"Whenever I touch you, Daralyn, if something doesn't feel right, or scares you the wrong way, can you tell me to stop? Truthfully."

She thought about it for a few heartbeats, then she shook her head against his chest. "No. I don't know if I can. When I think about doing it..."

In a heartbeat, she was a ball of quivering nerves, her breath rasping, a warning of a panic attack. He held her closer.

"Easy," he said. "You're fine. We're fine."

When she'd said no, they'd punished her.

Her reaction to anger was to draw inward, defuse. How was he going to get past that very male part of him that wanted to rage, tear apart anyone who'd hurt her?

"It's okay," he said, saying it to himself as much as her. All while holding her, rocking her. "It's okay."

"But I can't..." Despair drenched her tone. For fifteen years, she'd been told what she wanted wasn't an option. And they'd done such a good job that it was branded down to the unconscious level.

Telling her she could make choices didn't liberate her. It shattered her.

Until she could get there—and she would, he knew it—he would have to continue to determine, guess, or deduce her wants and needs, all while watching out for her well-being. And hope like hell the Dom part of him didn't get so used to it that he missed any attempts she made to start doing it for herself, such that he overrode her at the wrong moment.

It was a lot of responsibility, and he felt the weight of it, the fear of it. But he could handle it.

"I get it," he said, taking them away from the danger zone. "It's okay. Don't tell me what you want. Tell me what feels good."

A little bit of tension went out of her, though she spoke hesitantly. "I don't want to tell you what to do."

"Did I say that?" He made his tone firmer. Decisive. "Tell me what I said, Daralyn."

"You said to tell you what feels good."

"Right. It will be my decision, whether I do those things or not. Right?"

More relaxing of those tight muscles. It was a small miracle to him, discovering an avenue that might work. It seemed the Dominant side of his nature could read the submissive language of hers better than his conscious self.

"You holding me feels good."

"That's good, because that's what I want to do. What I'm going to keep doing."

Her fingers between them opened and closed against his chest. Her breathing was leveling out, but he decided a change of subject was in order.

"Hey, you know that guy in Florida with the specialty fixtures?"

"He sent us the picture of a spigot shaped like a dragon's head."

"Yeah, that's him. I was thinking about driving down and doing a face-to-face with him. See his stock in person. He's on the Gulf. I want you to go with me. I could go fishing, you could bring some books, hang out with me on the dock. School will be closed for the bank holiday in a couple weeks. You'd have a four-day weekend since you have no Friday classes. I can work out coverage for the store."

"Okay. Oh...sorry. I mean..."

He wasn't sure what she was apologizing for, then realized the arm she'd had threaded under his, hand resting on his waist, had shifted as she changed position. Now her palm was back on his side. He gave her a mock stern look.

"Did you just grab my ass?"

She colored three ways. "No...I just, my hand brushed..."

She came to a halt as he grinned at her, and she pushed lightly at him. Keeping her close in his arm span, he adjusted so he was lying on his back, her draped over his upper body, her arm on his chest, head up under his jaw. Her fingertips followed the curve of his pectoral, a small movement, just a couple inch span of skin. Shy, careful. She had no idea what that contact was doing to him.

He reached up, closed his hand on hers, flexed out her fingers to a wider reach. "Touch me however feels good, honey. Because all of it feels good to me."

When he met her gaze, confirming he meant it, they held that way for a long moment, humor dissipating in the face of a different set of emotions.

Slowly, she pushed herself up on an elbow, so she was gazing down at his body. The blanket was at her waist, so not only did he see the curves of her naked breasts, but the slope of her side, the shadowed juncture between her thighs, the fold of her legs as she rested on her hip. He made himself keep his hands where they were, one loosely curved over her hip, forearm pressed against her buttocks, fingers playing with the crease where thigh and hip met. His other arm was above his head, hand gripping the post of her headboard so he could dig into it for resolve if needed.

Laying her fingertips on his opposite shoulder, she drew her touch downward, over his biceps, the inside of his elbow, his forearm.

Heaven. Absolute bliss. Anyone who'd ever seen the way a simple breeze could turn a whole lake into a canvas of ripples was watching what it was like for a paraplegic, to be touched by a woman where he could *feel*.

She moved across, onto his abdomen, up around his nipple, toward his collar bone. She moved as carefully as a novice painter, afraid of taking a wrong stroke on that canvas. Or maybe an expert, knowing just where she wanted the brush to go.

Down from his neck and shoulder again, back over his pectoral, to his sternum. Her fingers threaded through the hair on his chest, over the bump of his nipple. A little extra exploration there. He'd been able to contain the reaction, until that moment. But when the pleasure rippled through him, capturing her attention, he realized he shouldn't be hiding it at all. The wave was strong enough to have him briefly closing his eyes, his hand tightening over her hip. Her gaze was intent and curious.

"Your hands feel good," he told her.

What an understatement. A normal guy his age had one major erogenous zone, between his legs. Yeah, other stuff felt good, but most guys he knew would agree. When an orgasm happened, it channeled through the cock and balls like a fire hose. But after losing sensation below the waist, he'd discovered the gods could be kind. Heightened sensation in the parts of his body above the level of his injury meant the whisper of a hand over his shoulders, his nipples, his abdomen, stirred the urgency that a woman's grip on his cock used to do.

Sex wasn't about genitalia, or only about fucking. He hadn't known that before. It was about *feeling*.

The movement of Daralyn's hands on his chest, his throat, his arms and shoulders, was something he fiercely enjoyed. He told her that, not letting himself avoid what it said about the parts that couldn't feel. Her eyes stayed wide, deep and thoughtful, her mouth moist. "So I can keep doing it?"

"Hell, yeah," he said, and the hoarseness in his voice made the gold in her hazel eyes deepen in color.

His plan for handling what had happened earlier had been to stay as long as he could determine she wanted him here. Maybe sleep in her bed, hold her through the night. But as they fed on the contact between them, her getting more absorbed in touching him, and him reacting to that contact, he realized that wasn't the only way to handle what had happened earlier.

He could show her how much power she had in those slim fingers of hers.

"You're so strong," she whispered, her hand moving over his biceps again. "You could carry me forever. I've dreamed that. You carrying me."

He tilted his head. "It wasn't a dream, baby. I did carry you once."

Surprise crossed her face. "When?"

"That first summer you stayed with us. You and Les were out doing chores. It was a really hot day, and you got overheated and passed out while feeding the chickens. She hollered and I came out with Mom. She was figuring out how to get you out of the heat and I picked you up, carried you inside."

His mother had called for Thomas, but Thomas was in the hay

barn, and Rory was right there. He remembered how astonishingly light she'd felt in his arms.

"I thought you opened your eyes once, but I didn't know if you remembered it or not."

"I thought it was a dream. I felt safe. You held me like you'd never drop me."

He'd never picked up a girl who'd passed out, who needed to be carried from point A to point B. The clammy feel of her skin, her paleness, the worry in his gut, reflected in Les and his mother's eyes, had made an impression. But his desire to protect her, and the realization of how much she'd needed his care in that moment, had made an even stronger one.

The illumination in the room, coming from the outside utility light, streaming through the bedroom window, shadowed and etched her thoughtful features. Her next question took him by surprise.

"Do you dream about it? When you could walk?"

"Yeah. Plenty of times. Sometimes, if it's a really vivid dream, when I wake up, I can't figure out why I'm trying to swing my legs to the floor and it's not working."

He used to hope that the mind would conquer the body in those vivid dreams, so when he was in that half-asleep state, things would kick in, just start working again.

Her fingertips drifted up, down. Following the arrow of hair toward the waistband of his boxers, then back up toward his navel. Her attention was on his face, the way he was pressing his lips together, the curl of his hand on the headboard as he stayed out of her path. "This feels really good to you?" she asked.

"Yeah. It does."

She moistened her lips. "You said it was okay for me to touch you. Does that mean...anywhere?"

"Mm-hmm."

"Where do you want me to touch you?"

"Everywhere."

She curled her hand around his waist. He felt the pressure and movement of her forearm against his side and glanced down to watch her trace the curve of his buttock over the fabric of his underwear. Even though he couldn't feel it, his memory could take over where his nerves couldn't.

He adjusted partially onto his side toward her, and she lay down to face him, scooting closer, cuddling into him. Her cheek rested on his chest as her fingertips glided up to the small of his back, his shoulder blades and back down again.

There'd been times, with a hand on his dick, working it, and his other hand running over his chest, his abdomen, playing around his navel, he'd brought himself to an orgasm, just to see what it would be like. But that was a pale shadow compared to how it felt when it was caused by Daralyn's hand trailing along his chest, teasing his nipples, her mouth high on his chest, moving up to his throat. He cupped her head as she nibbled the area beneath his ear, and when her fingers tightened on his side, digging into the layer of muscle over his rib cage, his stomach muscles contracted.

As she moved below his waist again, he watched the flex of her thin arm, imagined she was following the crease between his buttocks, then her fingers fanning out along the cheek again, to the back of his thigh. A quick shiver went up his spine.

She drew back, was watching his face. "Can you feel it there?"

He shook his head.

"Can you show me...where you stop feeling it?"

"It's fuzzy. Not a straight line, sensation on this side and nothing on the other side. It's kind of a gradual thing. But it mostly stops at the waist."

He gripped her wrist, and took her hand to the top of his buttocks, just below the waistband of his boxer briefs. "I can feel traces of things in this area. Not real strongly. It's kind of like phantom sensation. And here."

He brought her hand around, resting her fingers on the leg hem edge of his boxer briefs, high on his thighs, a couple inches away from the bulge of his testicles and cock under the stretched fabric.

He released her then, and reinforced his earlier instruction. "Everywhere, Daralyn. I'll tell you if I want you to stop."

She skated her fingers down his thigh, then back up. She moved her hand over his groin area, around his cock. When she at last gripped him through the fabric, stroked, he let her keep the driver's seat, decide how she wanted to go.

Reflexogenic hard-ons didn't result in a pile driver of an erection, but there were ways he could get it harder, keep it up. Watching her explore was pleasurable torment.

He'd given some thought to whether she'd even want to have sex. He was better equipped than most men, so to speak, to accept that. But her interest, her reaction, said that she was interested. And her pleasure meant a whole hell of a lot to him.

"I want to be inside you at some point, Daralyn."

"Okay." Her brief hesitation, her tone, the softening of her mouth and brightness of her eyes, told him she was greenlighting the idea, though he'd still ask a few more questions to be sure, when the time came.

She'd moved her touch up to his abdomen again. She seemed intensely interested in how it made his muscles tighten and his breath shorten, and he gripped her more urgently with the hand on her hip.

He let go of the headboard to bring her face back up, so they could meet gazes. "I'm not ever going to force you to tell me what you want, Daralyn. But if ever you do, it will be a gift to me. Every time you do it."

She pressed her lips together. "I... Sometimes I feel like you already know. That I don't have to say it."

"I'm not as smart as I might seem. Thomas and Les should have told you that."

A slight smile appeared on her lips. "Being inside me... Will it be tonight?"

"I think we need to think about it some. Take a breath."

She didn't say anything to that. Her eyes lowered, and her breathing was shallow. Her fingers curled into his stomach, little bites of her nails.

Signs of disappointment, which surprised the hell out of him. He needed to explain further, so she knew it wasn't a rejection. Not even close. Hand to God, if he was in the middle of church right now and she asked him to make love to her, he wouldn't hesitate even a second. God would understand. He'd created Daralyn, after all.

"I want to right now," he said. "But there's more to it than that."

He'd taken these steps with Amanda Brewster, and it had turned out all right. But truthfully, that had been about him, taking his first steps toward finding out he could still enjoy sex. Also toward something he'd been surprised to find was more important to his sense of his masculinity and pride as a lover: he could make it enjoyable for the woman he was with.

Having a woman willing to muddle through that with him had meant so much. His feelings for Amanda Brewster would forever dwell in the same room in his heart reserved for firsts—first loves, first kisses. His love for her wasn't an "in love" love, and it didn't come close to the intensity he felt about Daralyn. But with Amanda, he'd confirmed that sex, while forever different for him, could still be intense and satisfying. Fulfilling.

Even more vital, it could be intimate.

That said, explaining how sex worked for him wasn't such a common conversation that it came easily, particularly with a woman he wanted to be strong for, to care for. But being around other disabled guys who'd gone through it had helped him realize the stumbling points were often self-generated. If the person was worth talking to about it—and Daralyn was—it would ultimately turn out the way it should.

"You noticed when you touch me above the waist, I get pretty stirred up. Right?"

She nodded, her eyes serious. "It doesn't work the same way for every guy with an SCI, spinal cord injury," he said. "It depends on where our injury is, what kind of sensation we have left, but for me, when you're touching my chest, my throat, it feels to me the way it does to another guy, when his arousal shows itself in his cock. I'm just feeling that somewhere else, if that makes sense." Much like women could feel it in a lot of different places.

"When you were taking off your clothes," he said, "touching yourself, it felt like my skin, wherever I could feel it, was catching fire, sensitive to everything. And when you touched me in those places, it felt so good I didn't want you to stop."

Her lips parted, hazel eyes heating. He loved that she had moved her hand back up his chest, caressing him in reaction to his words, before she consciously thought of it. He closed his hand on hers, gave her a smile. "Don't distract me. I have to finish getting this out."

He glimpsed that little smile again, the one that hinted at the day, maybe closer to the near future than anticipated, where she might feel safe to tease him.

"You know how when I say certain things to you, or you imagine me touching you, you get aroused?" Before her past could yank her back to that automatic shame and anxiety, he reminded her how he felt about it. "Something I love to see happen. You've seen that, haven't you?"

Her brow creased, but she nodded again, her eyes clearing and body relaxing once more.

"Well, I can't do that." He tapped his head. "That's called a psychogenic reaction, when it comes from here. But I can get hard with direct contact. Like when you were touching me there just now. That's reflexogenic."

He brushed his knuckles over her cheek, smiled. "Stop trying to spell it in your head. I'll give it to you for your book. Later."

Her lips tipped up slightly. Time to get deeper into it. The stuff that was a pain in the ass, something else he doubted anyone would ever see in a romance novel.

"When I decide it's time to be inside you, there's a little more to it. There are things I have to do before sex to make sure it's good for both of us."

"Can I help with any of it?"

Why was he not surprised that was her first question? "I love that you asked that, but they're things I can handle. They just require a little bit of time beforehand. To keep an erection good enough for sex, I take a pill, which requires about fifteen minutes to kick in." He moved his touch to her neck and shoulder, caressed with purpose. "There are a lot of ways to occupy those fifteen minutes."

Her chin lifted, reacting to his touch, but he thought the way she pressed into it was also a reaction to the edge he put into his words, a sensual threat.

Once hard enough, he'd slide a well-lubricated, flexible silicone ring on the base of his cock, over a condom, to maintain his erection. He told her that, and lifted her hand, kissing her fingers. "That's something you can help me do, especially if I tell you to do it. Right?"

"Yes." She gave him that breathy syllable, while she watched his lips play over her fingers. The blanket was pulled up under her arm, but the tops of her breasts quivered with the lift and fall of her breath, and he could feel the tightening of her nipples against his side.

Now the last part of it. "I also have to do some things in the bathroom to prepare for sex, to keep other less romantic things from happening during."

Like empty his bladder, his bowels beforehand if needed, depending on the time of day. He was lucky enough not to have to wear a catheter bag, but he still had to cath himself to void his bladder. He wasn't going to go into detail on those things with her, though. Not if he didn't have to do so.

"So that's it. The high level." He stroked the tops of her breasts, moved up to the pocket at the base of her throat, logging every reaction, the glazing in her eyes as he teased her flesh. Maybe he would deep suckle those two pretty breasts she kept innocently flashing at him, or put his hand between her legs and bring her to climax again. Her arousal was a need he craved to satisfy, much as he wanted to keep driving it back up for his viewing pleasure, again and again.

"We don't have to take that step today, tomorrow, or anytime soon," he said. "We can give one another pleasure without it. But there's a caveman part of me that wants to do it as a claiming, Daralyn." He paused, his thumb resting on her neck pulse, stroking in a slow firm way that had her breath shortening. "I do want you to belong to me," he said.

Her dark eyes glowed with a fire that shot straight through his center. A neon sign in his book that she wasn't just accepting that statement with meek resignation. Then her words confirmed it. Her fingers curled over his hands, holding them. "Are you sure we can't do those things now?"

It was the closest she'd come to saying she wanted something with words. And it figured, that the first thing she straight out asked him for, no way to interpret it any other way, was something he wasn't so sure was a good idea for her yet.

Falling out of one's chair was one of the most important fears to overcome. The best way to do it was to learn how to get back into the chair when it happened. Because then that fear wouldn't stand in the way of anything you wanted.

She needed to know he wouldn't back off every time she had a breakdown. That he trusted her to decide whether she could get up, dust herself off and keep going, or if she needed to try another day.

She needed to know when he read those messages from her as clearly as he did right now, he wouldn't back away from them.

"No," he said. "We don't have to wait."

CHAPTER NINE

*N*ow it was his turn to prop himself on an elbow. He put his hand on her chest, exerting pressure to tell her he wanted her flat on her back. She obeyed, resting nervous hands on her abdomen. He moved his hand from her chest there, curling his fingers over her overlapped wrists, a light manacle that captured her attention. He felt the texture of the scar on the underside of her forearm as he ran his thumb over it.

"I'm going to go into your bathroom," he said. "I'll be a few minutes. While I'm in there, I want you to be warm." He reached over, lifted his dress shirt off the end of the bed. "Put this on."

He transferred himself back into his chair as she sat up to don the shirt. Going to her dresser, he found a drawer full of cotton underwear in a variety of pastel shades. He chose pink, and returned, laying it on one slender leg. "And these."

Surprise crossed her gaze, no doubt because he was having her put on clothes. But that was because he liked the look, a woman in his shirt and a simple pair of panties. When she complied, moving onto her knees to make it happen, her long hair fell forward over her shoulders. The neckline of his shirt revealed the curve of her breast. She'd only buttoned the two buttons in the middle. When she was done, she hesitated, then lay back again, the way he'd originally put her.

"Good," he said, warm approval in his voice. "Put your fingers inside the panties, on yourself." His gaze flicked meaningful in that direction. "Don't move those fingers. You just rest them there. Think about how I'm going to touch you, put my mouth on you, put my cock inside you, when I come back."

"Rory..." His name was a breath on her lips.

"You are so goddamn beautiful," he said. "Nothing you want is wrong, you know that? And if you could be inside my head, you'd know that, down to the soul."

He gestured before she could get uptight about his fierce tone. "Do it now. Put your hand where I told you to."

She wet her lips, that erotic anxiety that captivated him. Her hand slipped into the panties and he bit back a groan of pure want, seeing a tiny blot of moisture against the panel already. "Keep your fingers where I told you," he reminded her. "Don't move them. Tell me you understand."

"I do. Yes."

He felt her eyes on him as he turned and went into her small bathroom, which had just enough room for him to close the door. He took a long, steadying breath and turned his attention to what needed to happen.

While he'd had no intention of this date ending in sex, he thanked God he'd prepared for it. In the pack that hooked to the back of his chair, he carried extra catheters, but also a silicone cock ring in a small plastic lubricant pouch, ED meds, and condoms. He dry swallowed the pill first. When they reached the point where it was needed, he'd be ready. As he'd said, he could take his time, do a hell of a lot for her, and her for him, before she closed her wet heat around him.

Moving around in that small space was precarious, but he took care of what was needed, washed his hands. He removed the rest of his clothes and draped a towel over his lap.

Before he emerged from the bathroom, he took a look at himself in the small mirror over the sink. At first, he'd avoided looking at himself in mirrors, not able to handle what he was, what he looked like. Maybe that was why he'd noticed how rarely Daralyn looked at herself. Just furtive looks to ensure she looked presentable. Not a full-on meeting of one's eyes, facing the person in the mirror.

He could look at himself now, and that ability was an important self-care message. When he looked at himself, he was sending a message to his reflection.

Be what she needs, and be who you are. Deep down, soul level, both sides of that equation.

He left the bathroom. As he came back into the bedroom, he stopped at the foot of the bed to let himself look, because it was an incomparable view.

Any worries about whether this was the right course or not vanished. The instincts that had told him what instructions to give her had had better results than he'd expected.

She was trembling, and not from fear or cold. Having her put her hand on her sex, forbidding her to move it, meant the ripples of sensation had built and spread outward. Her body quivered with three hundred horsepower sexual urgency. Her gaze was back to that feverish heat, her face taut with it.

He moved to the side of the bed. "Give me your fingers."

She withdrew them from the panties, her arm shaking. He gripped her wrist, nuzzled her fingers, nostrils flaring at the scent of her arousal. As he licked the tips, teasing her, a little sound came from her throat. "Nice as that is," he said, "I want a taste straight from the source."

Keeping his grip on her wrist, he reached out with the other hand and molded it around her inner thigh. With the pressure of that touch, he guided her to slide in his direction, bringing her pretty backside to the edge of the mattress. He positioned her feet on his push rims, the chair locked in place. Then he slid his hands beneath her thighs, cupped his palms under her buttocks and lifted her up to bring his mouth to her cunt.

He answered an urgent mewl of female need with a pleased male growl. He played with her over the cotton of the panties, rubbing his tongue over the cushion of petals beneath, the swollen bud of her clit. Her buttocks tightened in his grip and he squeezed, hard enough to have her gasping.

"Unbutton my shirt," he said against her flesh, and reveled in how she fumbled to obey him in her dazed state. He attacked her cunt even more passionately, his tongue pushing against the cotton, lips sucking.

The shirt fell away from her, exposing her upper torso, the rise of her breasts as she twisted. Her toes gripped his push rims, her thighs locked against his shoulders. He paused to remove the panties, enjoying the way her ass pressed into his lap, her legs coming together and rising in front of him so he could kiss the backs of her knees before he spread her legs on either side of him again. He dropped the panties to the side and discovered her wetness up close and personal.

As he slid his tongue inside her, she didn't climax, but she did come apart, in all the right ways. A harsh, surprised noise came from her, a ripple that made her body undulate in his grip. He saw her eyes flash toward him, and she was clawing the covers.

They'd never done this to her. He'd bet his life on it. Because this was all about her pleasure.

"Rory..." made it past her lips, once, twice, and then she was moaning his name over and over as he took her up, closer to that pinnacle, but not quite there.

He'd pushed the towel off his lap when he brought her to the edge, and now he shifted his grip to her waist, let her hips ease down to his thighs. The opened shirt got left behind, falling off her shoulders and onto the edge of the mattress, so he held a fully naked woman in his hands.

She was already reaching for him with eagerness. He'd intended to get her lost in that desire she'd tasted earlier in the night. She now had the tentative confidence to grip it in both hands, and he wouldn't give her any breaks in those waves of pleasure to doubt herself, introduce all the worries about what her responses could and couldn't be.

Everything she saw and felt from him would confirm what he'd told her—nothing her body or mind or heart wanted was wrong. Not with him.

Unconditional acceptance. He'd never understood what that meant. Now he did. He knew her heart as well as his own in this moment.

He'd tucked the ring into a side pocket of his pack. After sheathing himself in the condom, he removed the ring from the lubricated pouch to slide it onto himself, all the way to the base. She watched, and he saw her fingers twitch with the desire to touch him. They were on the same damn page on that. He guided her hands down between them, her thighs straddling him. "Touch me," he murmured. "Stroke me in a way that tells me how much you want me inside."

He dipped his head to watch her hands close over him, explore, stroke in a jerky way that told him her desire was continuing to affect her coordination. Savage satisfaction speared through him.

He lifted her under the arms, let her feel that his strength was supporting her. "Put me inside you," he said, because he wasn't letting her go.

She bit her lip and he watched her fit the head of his cock into the mouth of her sex. As he slowly lowered her weight, she picked up on what was needed, her fingers sliding along him, helping to guide him deeper until he knew he was in position. He brought her all the way down to the hilt, so she was sitting snug on his lap. Her lips had parted, eyes glazing even more as she internalized the sensations. Though he couldn't feel it in his cock, the tightness in his lower belly, the hard pounding of his heart, the sheer amount of sensation in every part of him that he could register...it was indescribable.

When his father had the sex talk with him, years ago, Rory hadn't really paid attention to the things that weren't about the physical. Thank God all those undigested details had stayed in some corner of his mind, ready to be called when he was mature enough to hear them.

You might want to have sex with everything with a pretty face, son, but when it happens with someone you love...it won't matter how it goes, you'll remember it more than any other time If you continue to love one another, it will become the best that sex can be. Because the best sex comes from the heart. Not lower down.

Now he knew exactly what his dad had meant.

Daralyn's hands had landed on his shoulders, were gripping them hard. He had his on her hips, and he pushed her down even deeper, watching her face for any signs of the wrong kind of reaction. Her grip increased, and her head tipped back, her long hair flowing over her bare shoulders.

"You are fucking beautiful," he murmured again. "Ride me, Daralyn. I want to watch."

The feeling low in his gut built, getting tighter as she rose and fell, her small breasts quivering, neck arched, slim arm muscles flexing as she held onto him, scraping her nails over his shoulders. As she dipped forward, her lips pressed against his throat, below his ear. She'd remembered everything he'd said about being so sexually sensitive in his upper body and she was eager to give him pleasure, too.

He held on to her, letting her know he had her and she could get as wild as her body wanted. He loved watching her get lost in it, even as primal reaction surged in him, shoving away thought and leaving only the warrior desire of possession. Every live nerve ending caught fire so that he could move with her, follow that rhythm with his upper body.

He curled his hand in her hair, wrapped and tightened the grip so he kept her head tipped back, her throat exposed. Banding his arm around her waist, he brought her even closer, tighter, holding her down for a minute on his cock as he captured her breast in his mouth, suckling. She cried out, her nails digging in, scraping over his skin. That was it. He wanted her to lose herself enough to mark his flesh.

She quivered against his hold and he shifted his palm to her buttock, gripping with a bruising hold that told her without words that now he wanted her to stay still. She shuddered with the effort it took, a plea humming in her throat as he slowed himself down, leisurely suckling, making hungry, wet noises against her nipple before he moved to the other. When he took his time there, he heard the noisy swallowing in her throat. Her fingers were busy, making those scraping pathways across his back.

He knew her pussy was clamping down on him, because his coiled lower belly reaction was growing, a flush spreading across his chest and back. An orgasm was pending because something was stroking, holding his cock. Something hot and wet, and needing what he could give to it, and her.

He started moving her with the flex and release of his arm as he kept suckling. Pressure and gravity told him he was hitting her clit against his pelvis with every downward stroke. Breath left her, and he treasured that begging note in her voice as his name slipped out. "Rory..."

He stopped, holding her on him, and lifted his head long enough to meet her gaze, inches from his. "Not until I say. I want it to build for you until it takes you over, and you lose your mind. Got it?"

His voice was a harsh growl, and she responded just as he'd intended. Color hit two high spots in her cheeks, and her voice was an erratic whisper. "Yes, Rory."

"Good."

He went back to her breasts. They were perfect and small, the nipples so tight and sweet in his mouth. Her body kept jerking, little spasms, and when he kneaded her buttocks in one large hand, his fingers sliding along the seam, that jerking increased. Which increased the friction of her clit where they were fully locked on one another.

"Rory..." The bliss of desperation. Most women would enjoy fighting their natural reaction to obey his command, knowing there was no true downside to losing the battle.

But for Daralyn, there was a line past which sensual torment could become actual torment, a fear of failure. He was sure she knew he'd never hurt her, but she'd been taught that failure meant disappointment, bad things.

He wouldn't let her go there. Eventually, he'd show her the pleasurable kind of failure, the kind that meant good things, but not tonight.

He lifted his head, his mouth wet from teasing her nipples, and brought his hand back to her nape, pulling her in to kiss him. She was ravenous, frantically licking at his mouth, kissing his lips, tangling her tongue with his as he moved her up and down, up and down.

"Rory..." this one was nearly a cry for help.

He pulled her back, holding one hand in her hair, the other at her hip as he moved her on him in that inexorable rhythm. He locked gazes with her.

"Come for me. Don't hold anything back. I've got you. Say it. Say it, Daralyn."

"You've got me," she gasped. And then she started to climax.

It was still a struggle. This time, though, she won the fight, because he was in her corner, and he didn't give her a choice. His hands on her, demanding, squeezing, lifting and lowering her. He didn't let her fight it off. He savored that look in her eyes as everything turned internal and the body took over. She was spasming on his cock, because his reaction was getting more intense as well, building. Her nails raked him as a cry ripped from her throat. His hand on her hair kept her face turned in his direction and her gaze landed on his, held there as he showed her the demand in his expression. He let her hold onto it like a lifeline. She was doing what he'd commanded. She was pleasing him. In every way. He had her.

Another hard cry ripped from her throat, a flush climbing from her neck to her jaw and into her fair cheeks. He worked her on his cock, kept her going.

The fight was over and won. Shock gripped her expression as the full force of the orgasm took her, took any control at all. She was in his hands, with no decisions needing to be made. It swept her away in bliss, and he was right there in the clouds with her. The climax grabbed him, too, took him over. A harsh grunt ripped from him, his whole body tightening up, and the surprise that flashed through her gaze then became a type of joy, her hands upon him as they rode that wave of sensation together.

The way it should be.

~

When they came down, he made sure he had both arms around her, didn't ease their hold even when she went limp, her head resting on his shoulder, her arms loosely looped around him. He stroked her damp skin wherever he could reach it, murmured to her. "Good girl," he said softly. "Beautiful woman. I got you."

And things like that. Whatever came to mind that told her he was pleased with her, that she'd done nothing but please him. Including giving herself to her own pleasure, as he'd ordered.

She held onto him, shuddered. Sometimes those shudders became more powerful, and he stroked her, soothed her. Reminded her again she'd done as he'd commanded. Not a single thing wrong with that.

But he thought it needed more reinforcement. He wasn't going to take the chance that her mind would turn on her in the aftermath. At length, he eased her back, framed the side of her face with one hand. "I want you on the bed. On your hands and knees, facing away from me."

She gave him a curious look beneath her lashes, but didn't question. He helped her, guiding her to step down around his foot plate and turn away, toward the bed.

No matter that they'd just finished, he still wanted to groan at the sight of her obeying him, putting a knee up on the mattress, then the rest of her, waiting on hands and knees, her wet cunt and trembling thighs on display for him. Her toes hooked the edge of the mattress, the tender soles of her feet facing him.

He'd removed the ring and tucked it away. He'd handle clean up shortly, but he'd take care of this first. Putting a hand on her buttock, he splayed his fingers, let his thumb brush her sensitive pussy. It was flushed with her climax, the tissues swollen in the aftermath of taking him inside her. He was going on pure instinct here, and he hoped he wasn't wrong. He wasn't going to stop himself to overanalyze it.

She gasped when he slapped her ass with his open palm, making it a pretty forceful blow. "Down on your elbows," he said.

She didn't hesitate, and that tightness was back in his chest as the position lifted her ass higher. "I'm going to do that until I want to stop," he said. "And each time, I'm going to ask you a question, and you're going to answer it with the word 'yes.'" He slapped her again. "If you don't, I'll do it until you do. Understand?"

"Yes," she whispered.

"Did you please me?" *Slap.*

"Yes."

"Did you please me better than any woman ever has?" A harder slap, so she couldn't overthink it. She bit back a yelp.

"Yes."

He rubbed the smarting flesh, stroking her still wet pussy again. "Are you the most beautiful woman I've ever seen?"

She'd dipped her head, so he glimpsed a tiny, pained smile, swallowed by something more intense as he landed the blow.

"Y-Yes."

"Are you going to believe me when I tell you how much you pleased me?" *Slap.*

"Yes."

"I don't believe you. Say it again." A harder slap again, and this time it produced a different response, unexpected to both of them.

"Yes, sir."

He rubbed his hand over the offended area. *Yes, sir.* Wow. If he'd been capable of it, he had a feeling his cock would have sprung back to full, iron hard reaction to the address. It sure felt that way in his head.

"Good," he said, after a brief pause, not so long that she'd think she'd done something wrong. "Lie down now."

She lowered herself to her side facing him, though her head was down, her hair curtaining her face. "Will you stay with me?"

He grunted. "No choice. After sex that intense, I don't think I can walk. Oh, wait."

That tiny smile again. He'd go to the bathroom and handle that necessary clean up first, but before he did so, he leaned over the mattress, touched her face, pushed the curtain of hair away from her eyes. "I would love to go to sleep with you in my arms."

That smile disappeared from her lips, but only to move up into her eyes, mixed with a surfeit of emotion he recognized as what was in his own heart.

"I can make you breakfast in the morning," she said.

"Only if you wear my shirt while you do it," he said. "And nothing else."

Her lashes flicked up, and at last her gaze met his. It was only for a second, but when she looked back down, her voice held need and pleasure both. "Yes, sir," she murmured.

CHAPTER TEN

The next morning, those two syllables stayed in his head, along with every other detail of the night, there to revisit, consider, savor.

When he'd had his first sex as a teen, he'd been possessed by a goofy euphoria. During the next week or two, at random moments, three words would pop into his mind, laced with a wonder, satisfaction, and excitement for more.

I've had sex.

It had seemed like a major milestone at the time, and he supposed it had been, but in reflection, it was like getting his driver's license. It was a threshold. Once crossed, it opened him up to deeper opportunities.

Far deeper.

She'd made him breakfast as promised, and had worn his shirt. They'd sat at her small table, her turned sideways in her chair, her bare feet braced on the wheel of his as she worked on a piece of toast and the egg she'd scrambled for herself. She'd made him a ham and cheese omelet with cut up green peppers and garlic pepper seasoning.

The one thing his mother and sister hadn't had to teach Daralyn was how to cook. She'd told Les that Oscar or Burton would cook something they wanted her to make, and then she was supposed to remember how to do it. Though her reading skills had been poor, her memory was exceptional. And once she was cooking with Les and his mom, she'd shown she had an innate talent for it, improving the flavoring and textures when encouraged to do so.

Leaving her was difficult. He wanted to hang out with her all morning, but she had her appointment with Dr. Taylor, and he had his workout session with Red.

Rory didn't skip workouts, and it wasn't a vanity thing. Since a variety of uncontrollable things could muck up his physical regimen, he knew the dangers of voluntary lapses.

After that, he'd be relieving Johnny at the store, since Johnny was handling opening this morning.

Rory eased his impatience with the separation by reminding himself she'd be at the store in the afternoon. And by claiming a good lingering kiss from her. Which meant when he left her, she had a soft look to her mouth, a shine to her eyes.

His last, long look from the front seat of his van was a picture that could carry him through the day.

Through the picture window he saw her sitting at the kitchen table where he'd told her to stay and finish her breakfast. She had her knees pulled up, her bare toes curled over the seat edge. Since she wasn't wearing any panties, he could nicely torment himself by imagining what that looked like.

There'd been a schoolbook lying on the table. After he left, she'd probably open it up, lay a case knife on it to hold it open. Pick bits off the remaining piece of toast as she read.

But right now she was looking out the window at him. As he raised a hand in farewell, she did the same, giving him what he thought might be a bit of an uncertain smile. She'd be thinking about a lot of stuff today, he was sure. Hopefully those thoughts would be pleasant. When he saw her this afternoon, he'd make sure of it.

Red, short for Red Skull, the only name he'd ever offered, was a biker enthusiast, fitness trainer, and former PT who still filled in for vacationing therapists at the county rehab center. He also owned a gym within thirty minutes of where Rory lived.

Since many of his clients were service veterans in wheelchairs, the gym included some of the same equipment that was at the rehab center. Which meant Rory could do a lot of his conditioning in Red's more regular-feeling gym.

All of that, including the guy's personality, made Red the perfect adaptive fitness trainer for Rory.

"You're giving it extra effort today, my man," Red said, spotting him on the parallel bars. Rory had braces strapped on his legs to keep them straight and locked as he grunted through getting from one end of the bars to the other.

"Not that you're ever a slacker," the trainer continued. "Except at the beginning, when you were whining about some dumbass problem with your legs."

Rory shot the personal trainer a strained though amused look. "Let's see you do pull ups with a chair strapped to your ass."

Red spread his hands out with a grin, then smoothly reached for Rory's hips as he wobbled. "Nope, got it," he bit out.

"Know you do," Red said, while keeping close, his steel-grey eyes sharp. "Gotta look like you're paying me to do something."

Standing cardio was important for lower body circulation, internal organ function, as well as giving his hip and upper torso muscles a workout, but it was never fun. When he'd first started to do it, it was hell. And not just during the PT sessions. The lure of painkillers to ease the aftermath was a whole other battle. Most everyone in a chair dealt with certain levels of pain, but some days could be worse than others.

However, today's pain was a welcome reminder that he'd used some muscles last night he hadn't used in a while. Since Red didn't miss much, he caught the difference in Rory's attitude over it.

"Uh-oh. I know that look. Part caveman, hear me roar, part dork-in-love. Did you finally lay it out there for that sweet little girl you work with?"

Rory just shot him a grin, though the effort cost him his grip on the bar. Red was there, though, getting him back on track and focused. He saved further conversation until Rory made it to the end and got unstrapped, back in the chair.

"Take a breath." Red handed him a bottle of water, knowing Rory would need it before moving to the next station. The standing cardio machine was an automated contraption that would straighten his body, hold it upright with the aid of secure straps as Rory worked his arms and chest.

He wouldn't need a spotter for that, so Red excused himself a minute to check on several of his other clients. The rest of the gym looked like any other, though Red spaced out his equipment wider and everything here was disabled friendly. Rory hid a smile at the cat-eyed blonde who fastened her gaze hungrily on Red as he leaned over where she was stretched out on the weight bench. Guy got plenty of attention from his able-bodied clientele, but that was a given, the way he sported the shaved head biker look, all the tattoos and muscles. While Red wasn't married, he'd told Rory he was occasionally tempted to put on a cheap wedding ring, just to keep the come-ons to a minimum.

"Except I'm not sure I want to know which ones wouldn't consider that a dealbreaker," he'd said with a grimace. "I'd rather think the best of my customers, you know?"

Now he came back to Rory, giving him a narrow look at Rory's grin. "Shut up," he said. "And how about you spill?"

"What do you mean? You already know who I'm jacked up about."

Red snorted. "Not that. We've been working together a while, man. I know when you've got something on your mind. Any way I can help?"

Rory had been considering whether to broach it with Red, so he guessed there was no reason to put it off. "I need to get myself in shape for something new."

"Gotcha. What's the goal?"

When he hesitated, Red gave him a shrewd look. "First day, what'd I say were the two things that concern a guy the most about being in a chair?

"Taking a piss or dump on his own, and having sex that doesn't become a circus side show." Rory remembered it easily, because Red had said it to him a lot.

Red nodded. "I've heard both ends of that spectrum, and everything in between. So hit me with it. It's just between you and me and my three million social media followers."

"Yeah right." Rory chuckled, but met Red's gaze squarely. "I want to have sex on top. Beginning to end."

Red pursed his lips. "Doable. Especially if you do a man's job right, which means warming her up first, hot and ready as a Pop Tart."

Rory winced. "C'mon man. This woman is important."

"I get that. No guy in a chair is going to contemplate busting his ass for that level of conditioning unless he thinks she's worth it." Red put a hand on his shoulder, his expression serious. "I wasn't disrespecting her, man. Not a bit. A woman caught up in her passion is a thing of sacred beauty, and that's no lie."

"Yeah. Okay." Rory lifted a shoulder. "That was actually pretty poetic."

"Well, a good Pop Tart is a religious experience."

Red danced back from Rory's right jab, fast enough it still made glancing contact with his abdomen. Probably a good thing, since hitting Red's abs would be like bashing concrete.

"Whoa, boy's got mad fight skills. Let's get to it. Variety adds to the spice. Right, my man?"

~

Telling Red what he needed was a good thing. Rory reminded himself of that as he hiked himself from his chair into the driver's seat of the van with muscles that throbbed. He'd need to keep moving and stretching through the day, or in short order those muscles would feel like they'd been injected with acid. Even so, when his cell rang, he almost unmanfully wept with joy at the option of pressing the button on the steering wheel to activate the handsfree. Even lifting a phone to his ear sounded like too much effort.

"Just checking in," Thomas said. "Everything okay this morning? Daralyn waved at us when Mom picked her up to take her to Dr. Taylor's, but we didn't get a chance to talk to her. Wanted to make sure you're both okay."

"Better than," Rory said, and meant it. "How about you guys? I know that was a little over the top."

Thomas's voice reflected surprise that he'd asked. "Yeah, we're good. Mainly we were worried about her, and you. Marcus in particular."

"Tell him that it turned out good. She's even going with me to

Florida, for that trip to look at fixtures. I'm working on scheduling coverage at the store."

"Good." Thomas sounded pleased. "I can take a day if you need me to. Marcus has that thing in New York, but if it doesn't overlap, we can be here to help."

"If I can't get full coverage and it won't mess you up, I may take you up on that."

"No problem." Thomas paused. When he spoke next, he'd lowered his voice some. "Hey, can you do me a favor?"

Rory could count on one hand the number of times those words had come out of his brother's mouth, in the kind of tone that said the request was pretty important. "Depends. Does it involve being a back-roads tour guide for the Dallas Cowboy cheerleaders?"

Brother-speak for *sure, hit me with it.*

Thomas chuckled. "I think Daralyn would have something to say about that."

As Rory thought of her reaction to Amanda Brewster, a smile crossed his face. If he didn't watch himself, she might check with his mother for tips on how to use that skillet. His head was far too easy a target in his chair.

"You might be right. What did you need, bro?"

"Can you stop by here for a few minutes? Let Marcus know face-to-face things are okay with Daralyn and you."

"No problem." Rory was surprised it had rattled Marcus that much. "Is he all right?"

"Yeah." Thomas paused. In the ensuing silence, Rory wondered if Thomas was doing for Marcus what he himself had done, when Marcus had asked specific questions about Daralyn. Weighing what information was okay to share, against what would respect the privacy of someone you were worried about.

"Marcus has lost key people in his life, Rory," Thomas said at last, his voice still quiet. "When he was younger. To bad things. He's pretty protective of people he considers family, and Daralyn matters a lot to him. So do you, though I'd probably have to stick matchsticks under his nails to get him to admit it."

"Hide his hair mousse. That'd be a worse torture."

Thomas chuckled. "Believe it or not, he doesn't use any. His hair just looks that way. Straight out of bed."

"That's just sick."

"Tell me about it. But don't ever mention it to him, because he'll spend thirty minutes telling you how the right shampoos and conditioners make mousse unnecessary."

"Talk about torture. Okay, I'm close. I was headed back to the house for my shower. I'll stop by."

"Appreciate it."

"You want me to tell him you're mother-henning him?"

"You want me to paint your toenails in your sleep again?"

Rory snorted. "I keep telling Mom we need to take your key."

"Like I need one around here. When we bought this place, Marcus couldn't believe there were no locks on the doors. Total culture shock."

Rory chuckled as he pulled up in front of their house. "Okay. I'll make up some reason I'm here."

"No, don't bother. He'll know I called you. I wouldn't lie to him about it anyway. I just don't always give him advance warning when I'm looking out for him. You know the personality type, right? A controlling alpha you can't do anything for, unless you go through the backdoor."

"I have no idea who you mean, but now I know you're worried about him. You made the joke for that way too easy."

"Shithead." Thomas cut the connection, leaving Rory grinning ear to ear. Which fuck, somehow connected to his neck and shoulders, and sent another ripple of agony through the muscles he'd worked. He assumed honking the horn until Marcus came out so they could have a talk through the open window of the van wouldn't fly, so he reminded himself that movement was the friend of sore muscles.

After he rolled down his ramp, he saw Thomas in the barn loft, offering a wave and pointing downward, telling him Marcus was in the barn office. Rory gave him a thumbs up and Thomas turned back to whatever he was doing up there. Usually he had several easels set up with works in progress. If they were sketches, concepts, he kept the doors open to nature, like today. Final paintings meant the upper doors would be closed or he'd have a curtain of plastic strips pulled across the opening, so he could get the light but didn't have to worry about anything blowing in and sticking to the paint.

As Rory entered the lower level of the barn, he heard Marcus finishing up a phone call. Perfect timing. He also understood why Thomas had reached out to him—the faint smell of cigarette smoke.

Marcus didn't have a lot of tells, but that was one. The guy smoked when a bug had seriously crawled up his ass. Guilt twinged. He probably should have called last night or first thing this morning, confirmed everything was good. Like everyone else but Thomas, Rory always just assumed Marcus was fine. But that was why Thomas was Marcus's person and vice versa.

He pushed himself into the doorway of the office. Marcus had a desk in here, a chair and a couch. Pretty spare for the roomy space, but it gave him pacing room, like now. He was more casual today, in faded jeans that fit him like an action star's and a loose cotton shirt. The shirt was a deep purple with a graffiti style design of the New York skyline. Probably some designer label, since it had that casual yet fashionable look Marcus pulled off as effortlessly as the hair.

But when Rory glanced at his face, he nixed the mildly insulting volley that usually opened their conversations.

Marcus's command of himself and his surroundings could be as intimidating as hell. Even his pissed-off side was calculated. Rory should know, since he'd been on the receiving end. The guy had once thrown a hundred-pound sack of grain at him when he was in his unbraked chair. But at that time it had been a targeted move, to get Rory to wake up and stop adding to the straws that were making Thomas's life a nightmare.

Marcus not looking in control and smooth made the world feel out of balance. But no one was invincible; Rory knew that as well as anyone. What surprised the hell out of him was that Thomas thought he might be able to help Marcus feel better.

"Hey," he said. "Thought I'd stop in and let you know Daralyn is doing good this morning."

Marcus's attention had been on him as soon as he appeared in the doorway. Now his serious mouth tilted a little at the corner. It didn't make him look less tired, but it gave his expression a wryness that eased Rory's concerns. "Thomas."

"Can't blame him. You look a little rough."

Marcus sat down on the sofa, stretching his arm out along the back. "I'm all right."

Rory made a noncommittal noise. "Don't know if Thomas told you, but she's going with me to Florida."

"He did." Marcus tapped out a cigarette and lit it. It was a good thing most people didn't look like a black and white film star when they smoked, or everyone would be lining up to get lung cancer.

Marcus considered Rory a long moment. "The way you handled things by the barn last night. You were as calm as any Dom I've ever seen during a crisis with their sub. How did you know what to do? If I can ask without invading your privacy, or Daralyn's."

The compliment took him off guard, but it also reassured him. "Some of it...I just knew. Felt it. Does that sound crazy?"

Marcus shook his head. "Not for a natural Dom, one that has all the raw material and drive already in him. But you said that was only some of it. What's the other part?"

He weighed his answer, decided it was okay to discuss, since it was a memory Thomas knew, and Thomas said he didn't hide things from Marcus.

"When Daralyn first came to live with us, we all had some sit downs with the court-appointed shrink. The one before Dr. Taylor. And with Mom and Dad. It helped us get on the same page about how to deal with certain things. Particularly her panic attacks."

She'd had them almost daily when she first came to live with them. After a couple particularly bad ones, the psychiatrist had suggested meds as one of the alternatives.

"Mom and Dad decided against it." Rory recalled his mother's explanation.

"That girl has had to suppress so much of herself for so long. If she needs to yell and scream, cry and act out...well, she's overdue for it, isn't she? We help her, be there for her and protect her, and give her the space to work it out."

His mother and Daralyn had struck another deal. If things happened with Daralyn that worried Mom, Mom would talk to the shrink about them. Not tattling. Not that way. Mom had figured out early that Daralyn had a hard time telling the psychiatrist anything, but if the doctor already knew enough to ask Daralyn more targeted questions, she made better progress with her. A win-win, and a good safety net to head off more serious missteps.

"You'll have to trust me, honey. When I talk to Dr. Katz, it's not because you've done something wrong. Not ever."

Elaine had had that discussion with Daralyn at their kitchen table, while Rory had been in the living room, doing his homework. He'd heard Daralyn say "Yes, ma'am," in her quiet way, and Elaine's even quieter sigh after the girl asked to be excused to go to her room. There was no way to tell how Daralyn felt about any of it. Not in those first days, when she accepted everything with the same eerily blank face.

But no matter her personal doubts, Elaine had been firm on one point. *"If we get bogged down in second guessing ourselves or overreacting when she has a bad day, we'll never help her look forward. And whatever small steps she makes forward, we celebrate those moments with her, rather than dwelling on the darkness she's endured."*

He paraphrased that for Marcus. Marcus drew on the cigarette, tapping the ashes into an open paper cup. No ash tray, but Thomas didn't like him to smoke. Marcus was the unquestionable Dominant in their relationship, but there were other gives and takes between two people who loved each other.

"How do you think Elaine figured that out?" he asked.

That was easy to recall. Especially since every memory he had that involved Daralyn recently seemed to be tagged and transported to his frontal lobe, which made it easier to sift through the information, figure out how it fit with where he wanted to go with her.

"During that first summer Daralyn stayed with us, when the courts were trying to decide where to put her, she was helping Mom with a project in the attic, helping her clear out some things. She got sick. A bad flu bug. She hid it."

"How do you hide a bad flu bug?"

"Through a lifetime of learning to hide everything about yourself because you had to," Rory said flatly.

The hard spark of recognition in Marcus's gaze reminded Rory of one thing Thomas *had* let slip about Marcus. He'd spent his teen years on the New York City streets.

"So Daralyn's up in the hot attic, doing most of the up and down ladder work because of Mom's bad knee," Rory continued. "Her stomach is cramping, she's nauseous, but she carried some plastic bags up there and got sick in them, hid them behind some old suitcases. Mom assumed she would have taken them to the outside trash when no one was looking. But then on one of her trips down the ladder, she almost faints. When Mom grabs her, she realizes Daralyn is burning up with fever."

Elaine got Daralyn into bed and called the family doctor. Rory had been outside doing chores while the situation unfolded. When he'd come to the house to get some iced tea, he'd ended up standing outside the open screen door, listening. In those days, his parents had had a lot of kitchen pow-wows about how to handle things with Daralyn.

"The panic in her eyes tore me up," Elaine admitted to her husband, her voice strained. A quick glance inside showed Rory that his dad was gripping Elaine's shaking hands with one of his large ones, the other on her back, the strength of his wide palm supporting and reassuring her. His weathered face and dark brown eyes reflected concern for his wife, and pain for the damaged girl they'd decided to take in.

"Even as I'm holding her because she can't hold herself up, she kept saying 'I'm fine. Really, I can do it. It's all right.'" Elaine shook her head. "I called Dr. Katz after I got her settled the way Dr. Mourning said to do. He'll be here in about an hour. Dr. Katz said that Daralyn thinks if she can't do something we want her to do—anything at all—we'll send her away. Those monsters told her that getting sick, being useless, was what bad girls that nobody wanted did."

"Son of a bitch," his father had muttered, a sentiment that Rory emphatically agreed with. He hadn't been sick often in his life, just the occasional cold or flu, but the one thing he'd never doubted was his parents' care and patience about it. Evident when his dad made him stay in bed, not letting him help with chores or go to school until he was okay. Or his mom, fussing over him with fluids and blankets, checking his temperature with her cool, competent hands as he slept the sick away with bedrest.

He came back to the present and Marcus. "This all happened *before* Mom realized we couldn't overreact. The flu thing got to her, and for the next few days she had all of us tripping over ourselves to care for Daralyn, do a hundred things to tell her how much she was part of the family. We just about smothered her."

Rory grimaced. The more comfort and reassurance they tried to push on her, the more she shut down.

"That was when Mom realized coddling her made it worse. Ever since then, she's treated every stumble Daralyn has the same way she'd react to one of us falling when we were toddlers. Caring, but brisk, practical. Pick us up, brush us off and help us move forward."

It was at night, in her husband's arms, Elaine had wept over it. Or talked to him about how much it shredded her, to see Daralyn struggling with the simplest things, trying so hard to cope. Rory found that out from Les, since her bedroom shared a thin wall with theirs.

"So that was what helped you keep it together last night," Marcus observed. He'd stubbed out the cigarette and was studying Rory closely.

"She needed me to keep it together," Rory said, which was the answer that mattered. But he added, "Her childhood was a nightmare. But through some miracle, there were things happening that allowed Daralyn to become Daralyn, and she hasn't let that go. They didn't break her. When last night happened, I admit I had a bad *oh shit* moment, but I also stepped outside my own head and thought about how shattered she'd be if she thought she'd messed up what had happened between us inside her house. When I told her to come to me, when I didn't act like something had gotten really fucked up, I told her she hadn't."

The smile that crossed Marcus's face now was more genuine, though still serious. "I should have remembered that myself. A sub isn't trusting you to be perfect. They're trusting that you're putting their wellbeing at the top of your list. If a mistake happens, you're going to fix it. Which includes helping them make it right."

From last night's positive outcome, Rory agreed, but it relieved him to hear Marcus reinforce it. And led him to another topic, since he was here. "I've read the stuff you sent me. I think you were on to something the other night, what you said about my parents and how things were between them."

Rory lifted a shoulder. "In the beginning, I wasn't sure what freaked me out more, that I was going down this road, or that it was way more natural-feeling than I expected. But when it takes over between us, I don't feel like some guy wanting to tie her to a big cross or have her kneel naked beside me while I eat my dinner. It's more like...I'm taking control, and she's giving me that control."

He took a breath. "Not just the sex. It's like I'm pulling her under an umbrella I'm holding. And when I read stuff about domestic discipline, head of the household, that kind of thing, that connects to it, closest fit, but not perfect. There's this control, gentle-like most the time, but steady and firm, forming the center of our relationship. Fuck it, forget it. I can't figure out how to say it."

Marcus's gaze warmed. "You said it well enough. Better than. How you feel things is even more important than how you describe them. But if I had to guess? I'd say what you two have is a very deep psychological Dom/sub relationship."

Marcus tapped his head and chest. "All relationships exist in the head and heart, more than anywhere else. But for some people, the physical manifestation is going sky diving together, hiking Machu Picchu. For others, it's Friday night television and sharing the paper on Sunday morning. Neither one is wrong."

Marcus paused, considering. "Would you and Daralyn like the chance to see different Dom/sub relationships in action, in a lowkey environment? Not in a club. This is a private party happening around the time you were planning to go to Florida."

Rory raised a brow. "I don't know. Maybe. Where?"

"Outside of Tampa. Julie and Des would be there," Marcus added.

Julie was a close friend of Thomas and Marcus's. Over time, she'd practically adopted Rory's family as her own, such that she was present at most of their holiday get-togethers and weighed in on any family dramas. While she loved her own family, she compared them to a group of polite aliens, a total cosmic mismatch with her outgoing and affectionate personality.

Though Thomas had met her in New York, she currently ran a theater in Charlotte that specialized in erotic productions, an artsy community theater style thing. As a result, it wasn't surprising to hear she'd be at something like what Marcus was describing. "Is Julie recruiting for her next show?"

"Not exactly." Marcus met his gaze and what Rory saw jolted him. "No way."

Marcus chuckled. "Julie told me it was okay for you to know. I clued her into what was going on with you and Daralyn. High level only. I wasn't abusing your privacy, because she'd already picked up on it. It happens when you're deep in that world. You start to have a radar for it."

"So she and Des…"

Rory had a blink to imagine Julie as a flamboyant Mistress, complete with boots and whip. She was an outspoken person with a flair for drama, so that image worked.

"Yes. Des has been her Master for some time now. Before they got married."

Okay, got that wrong. He should have realized there were no assumptions with this stuff. While Daralyn being a submissive would surprise no one, Thomas wouldn't fit what most people would think about when they said the word. Yet that day on the back porch, it had been clear; not only did Marcus hold those reins in firm hands, Thomas needed that, down to the soul level.

Much like Rory felt about Daralyn, when she opened that part of herself to a deeper view.

On the flip side, imagining Julie's husband, Desmond Hayes, as a Dom was new ground. But when Rory considered it, framing the quiet yet resolute Des as a total take-charge, still-waters Dominant was spot-on. And he should have figured that out quicker, because while he could fleetingly imagine Julie with the stereotyped Dominatrix gear, he could not in any reality, even for a second, imagine Des as a sub.

Yeah, Marcus might be right about that radar.

"So is this where we cue the Joan Cusack moment from *In and Out?*" Rory asked.

"'Is *everybody* kinky?'" Marcus chuckled. "I'm still so proud of you for watching that movie. Your red neck is all but disappearing."

"Not in this lifetime. Fuck off, Light-Loafers. Go get a manicure."

"Ah, there it is, fresh as a sunburn after plowing a corn field. Anyhow, back to Florida. Do you remember Tyler Winterman from our wedding?"

"Vaguely. Isn't he the guy that pisses you off because he outbid you on some weird Japanese sculpture of a wave and a sword?" As Rory spoke, he sifted through the blur of faces in his head from his brother's wedding. "Though I admit, the samurai sword sounded sweet. You could detach it and melt the rest of it down for scrap."

"I'm going to ignore that," Marcus said. "How about the stunning woman with white-blond hair and blue eyes? Do you remember her?"

A light went off. "Yeah. Definitely remember her."

"Figured," Marcus said dryly. "That's Marguerite. She's his wife, so he would have been the guy sitting next to her. Anyhow, Tyler holds an annual fundraiser carnival on his property, a total kink fest, but he also hosts a couple smaller, quieter events during the year, with a closer group of friends. By special invitation only."

"So Julie knows him?"

"Yes, but the reason they received an invite has to do with Des. He's a well-known rope artist in the BDSM world, so he'll be doing a demo at the event. Plus, Tyler's interested in recruiting some of Julie's theater performers for future events, so they'll also do some networking."

Marcus waved a hand. "But business isn't the main purpose of the event. It's enjoying the pleasures of BDSM in an environment where people can attend openly as Dominants and submissives. You'd see a variety of things. The setting is also ideal. He has a fantastic place, a restored plantation house, with a handful of guest houses on the property."

"If it's by special invitation only, how do we get one? Do I reach out to Julie?"

Marcus grimaced. "Much as I hate to admit this much of a relationship with Tyler, if I request an invitation for you and Daralyn, it'd be a done deal. He'll send it directly to you. If your plans change, just politely decline, no problem."

"Good to know." Hearing that eased his concerns about locking them into something he or Daralyn might not ultimately feel good about. "If we go, wouldn't we be expected to...participate?"

"Absolutely not," Marcus said. "You can go simply to watch and learn, or participate at whatever level you wish. There are very structured rules at an event like this, and Tyler will be the first to explain them to you. They're not the kind of rules meant to steal the oxygen out of the room. They're intended to ensure the most comfortable experience possible for everyone attending."

When Marcus met Rory's gaze, there was a flintiness to his green eyes that reassured him. "Safety and respect are the two most important parts of a BDSM environment. If ever you find yourself in one where either of those things are missing, you should leave immediately."

"Got it."

"So, do you want me to have him send you the invite?"

Him and Daralyn at a Dom/sub event in Florida. Hearing him say it, even in his head, sounded a little out there. But Rory also couldn't deny the track he and Daralyn seemed to be on, or that he wanted to pursue it even deeper.

"Yeah, okay. Thanks. I better get going. I've got to clean up some before I head for the store." As he backed out the door, he nodded to the cup on the table. "Remember not to smoke around Daralyn. And air it out in here before she gets home. Maybe even change your clothes."

Marcus lifted a brow. "You worried about her inhaling secondhand smoke?"

Rory frowned. "Well, yeah, but no. She hates the smell of cigarette smoke. If she hangs around it too much, she gets sick to her stomach. You didn't know?"

"No. I didn't. She never..." Rory could see he was thinking it over. "I don't smoke often, but if I do, she leaves the porch. In that way she does. A quiet excuse, slipping away." His gaze came back to Rory. "Why?"

"If I had to guess, it's because Oscar and Burton were both smokers."

As he headed for his own house and the quick shower he really needed for the sake of anyone within ten feet of him, his cell rang again. He didn't recognize the number, but he often gave out his cell to customers, so he picked up. "Wilder General Store. Rory here."

"Mr. Wilder." The woman's voice was smooth and professional. "I'm Marjorie, Dr. Taylor's assistant. She wanted to talk to you. Is now a good time?"

Daralyn's session would have ended an hour ago. She and his mom usually went out for brunch afterward, followed by a walk in a nearby park. Rituals that helped Daralyn even out. The sessions, while far better than they used to be, still seemed to drain her emotionally. Being the center of attention, even for her own mental health, was never a comfortable experience for Daralyn. Long and short, she wasn't due back in town until after lunch, so getting a call from Dr. Taylor's office filled him with alarm.

"Is everything okay with Daralyn?"

"Oh, yes sir," Marjorie assured him. "Dr. Taylor just needs to talk to you a moment. Please hold."

A click and then another person spoke. With a rasp that added interest to the otherwise flowing, comfortable tone, Dr. Taylor sounded like she was in her thirties. He'd never met her, but he'd always imagined her older, like his mother's age.

"This is Susan Taylor, Daralyn's psychiatrist. First, my assistant said you were worried. No reason to be. I'm actually calling you because of good things that happened with today's session. Daralyn has discussed the changes in her relationship with you."

While he'd encouraged Daralyn to talk to Dr. Taylor about the sexual things happening between them, he hadn't expected to talk to Dr. Taylor directly about that. His embarrassed wince was followed by a not insignificant wonder at just how much Daralyn had told her.

Since the doc said good things had happened, at least it didn't sound like she was thinking of raking him over the coals for the Dom/sub stuff.

"The purpose of my call may seem a little unusual. However, since I've been counseling Daralyn and guiding your mother on her care for some time, it's not quite as off the path as you'd expect."

The psychiatrist paused. "I asked Daralyn if she thought it was a good idea if I talked to you sometimes, about things happening between the two of you. Give you the chance to ask me questions. She said she thought it was a good idea, and signed the waiver, allowing me to have discussions with you about her."

Good thing he was sitting down—a personal joke he indulged in his head sometimes—since that would have taken the floor out from beneath him. He pulled the van over to the side of the road, because the conversation had taken a turn that required his full attention. "No kidding."

"You sound relieved."

More than she knew. "I wouldn't hurt her for the world," he said. "I want to do everything I can to make sure I don't."

Though another part of him wondered what would happen if his gut and the psychiatrist's opinion took different paths on something. But no need to borrow trouble.

"That reflects what she's told me about you." Dr. Taylor's tone warmed. "She's a very special young woman, and you and your whole family have been her advocates from the beginning. I'm not understating it when I tell you that your family saved her life."

"You think her uncle or father would have gone that far?" Even knowing Daralyn was safe and sound now, the thought gave his stomach an unpleasant lurch.

"Always a possibility. But the greatest danger was that they ultimately would have destroyed the part of her that has miraculously survived, that has been able to find her own identity, get as far as she has under your family's care."

It was so eerily close to what he'd told Marcus, it came back to him now. *Through some miracle, there were things happening that allowed Daralyn to become Daralyn, and she hasn't let that go. They didn't break her.*

"For the most part," Dr. Taylor said, "I think we could handle things with the occasional five- or ten-minute phone call, initiated by either of us, depending on the situation. However, since we've never met face-to-face, would you like the chance to do so?"

"Yeah, absolutely." He pulled himself out of his head enough to remember his manners. "Yes, ma'am. I'd appreciate that a lot."

"I've had a cancellation, if you can make it here in about an hour. Or we can schedule another time."

He could make it if he pushed himself. And he would. "If the employee I have covering me at the store is good to stay a while, I'll be there. Thanks very much, Dr. Taylor."

"I'm looking forward to meeting you, Mr. Wilder. I believe you are a very special man, too.

After that remarkable statement, she disconnected the call.

Susan Taylor's office was located in the nearby town of Rockingham, in a two-story medical building by the hospital.

Rory took the elevator up to the second level to reach her suite. Marjorie, her assistant, was in her forties. She wore a navy-blue dress and dangling earrings that looked like sparkling blue dolphins. Rory waited for Dr. Taylor in a comfortable waiting room with a pale green couch, matching guest chairs, and a soothing picture of lemons on an old wood table. The framed work was positioned over the sofa.

He imagined Daralyn here earlier. He bet she'd chosen the chair with the best view of that picture.

Just beyond Marjorie's area, he could see Dr. Taylor's office. The door was half-open, revealing another cozy space with warm colors, pictures of rustic farm scenes. A trio of pillar candles flickered on a side table, while a big box of tissues was placed within reach of the guest chairs.

Had Daralyn left the doc's office crying? Or no reaction, just all closed in on herself? Did she feel unburdened, like going to confessional? Even knowing women had that peculiar habit of crying to help them feel better, Rory really didn't like to think of Daralyn doing that without him around to comfort her.

Maybe next time he'd volunteer to take her to the appointment, instead of his mother doing it.

"Rory." Susan Taylor stepped into the threshold. She was tall, had curly brown short hair, and wore gray slacks and a lavender blouse. The somewhat corporate business outfit was softened by the inviting expression on her face, and her choice of jewelry. A yin and yang pendant on a silver chain around her throat, and matching earrings. She also had a trio of chunky lavender and gray stone bracelets on one arm.

Surprise crossed her expression as her gaze coursed over him. She held out her hand. "Hello."

"Pleasure." He shook it, glanced down at himself. "Let me guess. You thought I was taller?"

She chuckled. "Come on in. Make yourself comfortable. Oh, wait a second." She held up her hand, disappeared in her office and then returned, rolling out one of the cushioned guest chairs. Marjorie rose and took it, wheeling it into her work area. "I don't want you to have to wedge yourself in here," Dr. Taylor said.

When he came in and she closed the door behind them, she turned to face him. "I didn't know you were in a wheelchair," she said. "Some time ago, Elaine mentioned one of her sons having an accident, but I didn't make the connection."

"Daralyn must not talk about me much, then."

"On the contrary. That's why I was surprised. She talks about you all the time. Particularly recently. She's never said a word about it."

"Oh." That was a hell of a realization. It called to mind what Will, one of his buddies in his adaptive challenge group, had told him.

They'd been on a bus, headed for Kitty Hawk and a day of hang gliding. Rory hadn't yet been up for that, but he'd gone along to watch. Will's able-bodied girlfriend Kate had been with them, and she and Will talked about how they met.

"I didn't notice the chair all that much," Kate said, in her broad Australian accent. "It was like noticing what kind of shirt or shoes he was wearing. His confidence and sense of humor made the biggest impression on me."

Will ran his palm up her upper arm, giving her a squeeze and a smile. "If it's not a problem that I let define me, then for the right girl, it's not going to be a problem either."

Rory was sure his face had reflected his *yeah, right* reaction, because Will had given him a knowing look. "If you want to get there bad enough, you'll get there, man. You have to work on yourself, on your view of yourself, before you're fit to be with anyone else. But that's the same for anyone, disabled or not. Right?"

Coming back to the present, Rory parked himself in the spot the guest chair had occupied while Dr. Taylor took a seat on the sofa across from him. She gestured to a K-cup maker. "I have coffee and tea," she said.

"No, thanks." Before he asked any questions, he wanted to make sure. This wasn't just about him, after all. "So on the phone, you said she was okay with this. If you don't mind, can you tell me a little more about that? I don't want to overstep."

"I'm pleased you're sensitive to her feelings. I'm clear on the parameters, so I'll ensure we stay within them. However, I don't mind explaining how it came about to reassure you of the same."

Dr. Taylor sat back and crossed her legs. Professional but relaxed, looking ready to take any topic in stride. He could see why Daralyn felt comfortable around her. He thought anyone would.

"You're aware that Daralyn never asks for anything for herself. Not for herself, not personally. Someone has to ask her first, and even then, what does she say, if someone asks if she needs more pie, more anything?"

"She says I'm fine, but thank you. Never outright no, but never a yes. Usually we read her cues and don't ask. We just decide what we think she wants. Which sounds bad when I say it out loud."

"It would, if the person listening didn't know how much care and focused attention your family puts into figuring out her non-verbal cues," Dr. Taylor reassured him. "So, you already know Daralyn didn't say 'Dr. Taylor, I want Rory to be able to talk to you about me, because it's too difficult for me to explain some things to him.' But I picked up that desire from her, and asked her the right questions to get to the same place."

She met Rory's gaze. "It's tricky ground. It always has been. But it's ground we all started walking a long time ago."

"She's made a lot of progress. You've been key to that."

She inclined her head. "Thank you, but I'm not being modest when I say your family is primarily responsible. Every forward step she has made has been the result of your love for her, your willingness to develop a partnership with me that is open and honest, all of us aligned in her best interest while attempting to give her room for self-determination."

She cocked her head. "That's a tricky path as well, isn't it? From what I've deduced, you are very protective of her. And now you are in a romantic relationship with her."

Had those Dom/sub vibes come up in conversation? Or, if they had, had Daralyn framed them as a more traditional or old-fashioned male/female relationship? Had Dr. Taylor been told about the spanking?

Those kinds of concerns were about his comfort levels, so he pushed that aside and asked his most pressing question. "Has following my gut caused her any problems?"

She mulled that over, which closed a cold fist around his heart for several uncomfortable moments. "No more than any attempt to fit two lives together more intimately does," she said at last. "It's important that relationships evolve naturally with Daralyn. From what I can tell so far, your instincts and knowledge of her are serving you both well."

"Okay." He took a breath, let it out. Dr. Taylor clasped her hands loosely over one knee.

"She told me what happened when she became sexually aroused, how she initially responded to it, and how you handled it. How you asked her to talk to me about it." Her expression tightened. "I thank you for that. Helping a person with such a prolonged history of abuse involves long term therapy for that very reason. The layers get peeled back over time, and when they do, they can reveal even more deeply buried things, things we cannot guess at, probably because so much of it is unimaginable. So, please, ask the question that you're hesitating over. Your honesty can only help her."

Fair enough. "I expected her to be afraid of sex. But she's not. Only her own reactions to it. It's made me wonder about how they... Doc, I can't even begin to tell you how much I don't want to think about it, see it in my head, talk about it. But I feel like I need to understand some of it."

Dr. Taylor nodded. "A very reasonable and intelligent conclusion. You may already know some of this, but it should help fill in some gaps. They started sharing her around the time she was six years old. Her mother died when she was five, so I assume that was the trigger. One woman left the home, so Daralyn became her replacement. Which suggests to me her father and uncle also shared her mother. Unlike Daralyn, she was severely beaten, on a regular basis. Ended up in the hospital multiple times. Never filed one charge against them. Social workers couldn't get her to even consider it."

Dr. Taylor's expression was grave. "I have that from police reports, not Daralyn herself. She has very little memory of her mother, except as a shadow who fed and bathed her for a short period of her life."

The psychiatrist rose, started herself a cup of tea. Rory shook his head when she offered him something again. He thought he might crush the cup in his hand. He didn't want to hear this. But if Daralyn had had to live it, he could damn well handle hearing it.

"I believe Oscar and Burton Moorfield found the abuse distasteful," Dr. Taylor said, taking in his expression. "Viewed it as 'necessary' only because Daralyn's mother was too old to be properly trained to obey them without question, serving them however they demanded. So after she died, Daralyn was the perfect answer to that. She could be trained from the very first."

She returned to the sofa, cup in hand. It was one of those photo mugs, with a Westie on it. Her dog, he assumed. "Pre-puberty, they made a moderate effort to choose methods of release less painful to a child of her age and physical development." She glanced his way. "An orifice less risky for their needs."

He was going to be sick. He swallowed, hard, and Dr. Taylor's eyes were on him.

"Okay?"

He inclined his head, jaw tight. "Keep going. Please."

"Her father had more control of his impulses than her uncle. When Burton was drinking or high, he was far less careful. Oscar appears to have intervened enough to keep her out of a hospital, which they would have avoided, for obvious reasons. He apparently had a friend who was a male pediatrics nurse—a fellow pedophile— who treated her several times for UTIs and other issues."

She rested a hand on her knee, her other hand on the cup she'd placed at her side. "Serving their sexual needs was merely one of the domestic functions they required of her. While they cared nothing for her responses, emotionally or physically, once they moved to sexual intercourse, when she was around eleven years old, a basic effort was made to ensure the act was not unbearably painful." Her mouth thinned. "Again, a functional decision, not a compassionate one. They weren't sadists. Her involuntary reaction to that level of pain would have been disruptive to their own release."

She took a breath. "So, to answer your question, other than those times with her uncle, she didn't fear sex any more or less than their other requirements of her. Denying them, or doing something they found objectionable, held a far greater terror for her."

Rory stared into space while she sipped her tea. He expected Dr. Taylor was giving him time to figure out what he wanted to say or ask next.

"I don't envy you your job, Doc. I have a punching bag that could file a domestic violence complaint against me. The more I learn about what they did to her, the more I have to beat the crap out of it."

"I'm glad you have that outlet. I expect you're smart enough to have realized your justified anger at them isn't something she can handle well."

"Yeah. Is *she* angry at them?"

Dr. Taylor's eyes filled with sadness. "I think she views them as a caged and abused animal does. Just glad to be free, even while always fearing she'll wake up and find herself in that cage again. Only this time, having found a life that is so much more than that, she'll have lost the coping skills to survive it."

"So the key is helping prove to her she'll never be in that cage again."

"Helping her prove it to herself," Dr. Taylor corrected. "Every positive change for Daralyn will come from inside her. That's what we focus upon, because it teaches her she has personal power. Your behavior and feelings toward her are very important, Rory, but it's vital for me to emphasize that. The only thing we can give her are tools. Not a solution. That has to come from her for it to be real."

"That makes sense." He went with a different question, honestly needing to back away from the other. "Food. Has she explained why she won't eat much? She said they were always on her about wasting food, but I think it's more than that."

"You're perceptive. Daralyn wasn't *allowed* to want things. If it looked like she had a desire for anything, and I do mean anything, she didn't get it. Which meant if she acted too hungry, they took the food away. To survive, she learned to eat indifferently, even as her body was starving. It's remarkable that she learned a complex adaptation like that at such a young age. After enough years of shutting it down in her head, it became a permanent thing, like it does for a severe anorexic. I'm not sure she even knows what genuine hunger is anymore."

Rory thought about Daralyn's cooking skills. What had it been like, cooking food for those two assholes to enjoy, while they denied her all but stingy bits of it?

But Dr. Taylor was wrong about one thing. Daralyn did know what genuine hunger was. He'd seen it, in her expression, in her body language, when he was touching her. Feeding that hunger, satisfying it, letting it open up until she felt free to consume everything in the world she wanted to taste, know, feel, learn, was something he welcomed, encouraged. Cherished.

He was tapping his push rim hard, alternating thumb and forefinger, a sign of agitation. He stopped when he saw the psychiatrist note the tell, but he met her gaze squarely, let her see his feelings. "When my punching bag is done for, do you have any good anger management techniques that will keep me from murdering her uncle?"

Dr. Taylor chuckled grimly. He appreciated the commiseration in her expression. "When Daralyn finally started to share more details on her family history, I kept a fifteen-minute block open after our sessions. I'd call my children, my husband, watch something on my computer that restored my faith in humanity. Because what can happen to the defenseless in this world is unimaginably horrific."

She paused. "The problem seems so simple. She's no longer under their control. She can simply say what she wants, do what she wants, and see there are no negative consequences. Over time, with repetition, she'll become more comfortable with it, right? But it doesn't work like that. It's more like being trapped in a cave, with multiple exits, all of them sealed by cave-ins, and having only what's in that cave with you to try and dig yourself out. Some things are going to work. Some aren't. Some will work for a while, then break. And just as you've chipped out a good section, it undermines another part of the cave so it collapses again, this time leaving you even less space, less hope for freeing yourself."

Christ. As a person watching Daralyn trying to claim happiness day by day, attempting to stretch her wings, the analogy was pretty much dead-on accurate. "Do you think she'll ever get there?"

"I believe in her. I believe she'll never stop trying."

The simple answer wrenched his heart, because it matched his own. He met Dr. Taylor's eyes. "Doc, tell me what I can do."

"Keep doing what you're doing. While Daralyn, your family, and I continue to do what we're doing. Do you have any phobias, Mr. Wilder?"

"Rory," he said.

She inclined her head. "Rory, then. While everyone else is armed with a million logical, verifiable reasons why the phobia is unfounded, it means nothing to the person with the fear. It is ingrained, a deep part of their makeup, usually tangled with many other issues. This is like that. It will take a lot of time, therapy and a mix of experiences to get her to the point she can express her own wants and needs. We won't know exactly what combination will work...until it does."

Her gaze met his. "Until then, she is a person who manages best on clear expectations and structure."

"Yeah." He cleared his throat. "I was thinking maybe that's why we're doing okay together. Not just because I know her history. I, uh... I have kind of an old school approach to our relationship. Kind of a calling the shots thing."

"You're the dominant in a romantic relationship." Her tone held no condemnation, which relieved him. A light smile played on her lips.

"You were braced for a feminist tirade, I see. Healthy relationships can take a variety of forms, and they have to be evaluated based on the people involved, not societal parameters."

He expected she'd meant dominant generically, not a capital D, but he could still work with it. "Yes, ma'am. She responds to it, really strongly. I don't know if that's an okay thing to encourage," he admitted. Though he wasn't sure how he could resist opening that door if he shouldn't, knowing Daralyn's response to that side of him seemed as well fitted as a key to a lock.

Dr. Taylor lifted a shoulder. "There's this idea that if you hand a million dollars and a mansion to someone born into poverty, that it will solve all their problems. On the rare occasion, you'll find someone who will make that work. Far more frequently, they will be unable to hold onto the money, or maintain the house, because they have no experience managing either of those things. That transition to prosperity requires time, guidance, a structure. It's not at all unusual that in her first romantic relationship, Daralyn needs more structure."

An assessment he didn't disagree with, though he didn't particularly care for the phrasing, which made him sound like the first stop on a much longer train ride, one that could take her from him. But he'd already acknowledged that possibility, so he wouldn't get bogged down in it.

"For people from a toxic family dynamic like Daralyn's," she continued, "it takes years of therapy for them to learn to assert themselves in a positive, healthy way. As we've discussed."

Her gaze met his. "Then there are people who are submissives from the beginning. In some ways, their road to recovery is... Easier is the wrong word, but they are the grasses that bend with the wind. They will always bend with the wind, because it's their nature." Her gaze sharpened. "She's not a doormat. That's not what I mean."

"She's a natural submissive," Rory said, relieved he'd been given the opening. "She feels better when someone else has the control. But does she understand that giving someone that control is a choice? That's the biggest worry I have, Doc."

"Yes," Dr. Taylor said, her finger stabbing her chair arm. The emphatic reaction, the strong approval in her expression, told him he'd passed an important test. "Thank you, Rory, for being the one to point it out yourself. The biggest danger a person like Daralyn will face in a relationship is having choices taken from her, purposefully or inadvertently, because she can't make them for herself. At least not in the usual way most people recognize or adjust to accommodate."

The woman leaned forward again, clasping her hands together on the top knee of her crossed legs. "I suspect your question connects to a specific situation. Would you like to discuss it?"

He hesitated. "I know she's given permission for you to answer my questions. But I'm wondering if me telling you the things that happen between us, if that's the same thing or something different. I don't want to betray her trust."

"Completely understandable. Perhaps you can find out her thoughts on it, in much the same roundabout way I have. If you feel like she is okay with it, you could save the questions in that problematic area for a future phone call."

Good thought. But his gut told him not to hold off on the Joe thing. As he described how Daralyn had reacted to her professor's attentions, with that adamant declaration to Rory about belonging to him, Dr. Taylor's mouth got straight and firm again.

"I want to think about that one," she said. "It's difficult for me to say if that's a destructive behavior, or just more of Daralyn's thought processes I don't fully understand. I made a couple mistakes early on, thinking I could match up what was going on in her head with other case studies. Every session with her is a maze. Sometimes I find myself in entirely new places, or wandering in circles. Other times I hit a wall, or she puts one up when I don't expect it."

Not much different from his experiences with Daralyn. In the doctor's intelligent blue eyes, pleasant by default, Rory nevertheless saw indications of when she'd hit those walls and been frustrated, or deeply concerned. "Daralyn feels things so vividly, so strongly," she said. "When I talk her through confusing feelings, she uses my advice as a sculpting knife, creating the path before her according to what works for her." A quick smile. "The way all of us live our lives, really."

She glanced at his chair. "I expect you have your own unique perspective on overcoming challenges."

He guessed every shrink knew the stages of grief a person with a disability handled to get back to living life the way it was meant to be lived. Rory gave her a wry look. "Yeah, except Daralyn doesn't seem to have the primary tool in her arsenal I had."

"Which was?"

"Anger. I was really good at it. It's a serious testament to my family's love that they didn't shoot me like Old Yeller and put me out of my misery. And theirs."

Dr. Taylor chuckled. "Everything I've learned about your family suggests they have an extraordinary amount of loyalty to one another. Which includes the person they took into their home. Daralyn is very lucky to have all of you."

"Maybe. Honestly, I feel kind of lucky that we have her."

Dr. Taylor's smile lit up the room. "Good answer."

CHAPTER ELEVEN

*I*t had been a busy morning. Rory checked the hay and grain inventory and knew he'd have to place an order this week. They were low on several other popular items as well, a good sign for the month's profits.

He'd always liked the idea of running the family business, but finding he was good at managing it had been an additional perk. Their profit margin had grown steadily the past couple years, thanks to repackaging the store as a yesteryear "nostalgia boutique," for God's sake.

It hadn't been that way at first. They'd been giving the idea a lukewarm try when his father was alive, but they were still a basic equipment repair and feed operation, in danger of becoming defunct from competition by nearby box stores, and due to fewer people operating functioning farms.

Then his Dad had passed, Rory had his accident, and Thomas came home to manage the store, as the eldest son. One day, Elaine had brought Thomas a magazine article about a store like theirs, up in Ohio. They'd revamped their look and inventory, but they hadn't stopped at more fully embracing the old-timey general store feel. They'd connected to other small hardware and community general stores doing the same, becoming a network that advertised itself as a road trip destination, like the big fall yard sale that spanned hundreds of miles, the locations dotted along the picturesque rural highways that the interstates had replaced as the most convenient thoroughfares.

In the margins of the article were carefully printed handwritten ideas about joining the network. Which included stocking the store with local crafts and foods, and hosting or sponsoring holiday events. Such as hayrides in the fall, a haunted corn maze at Halloween, carriage rides at Christmas. Creating a petting zoo with farm animals. The store would be the hub of all of it, thriving on nostalgia while simultaneously continuing its functional role as supplier of local farming needs.

"Mom, this might just work." Thomas's face, too creased with concerns in those days, had been briefly transformed by a spark of excitement. "We could talk to Mrs. Bluefield at that travel agency you and Dad used for your cruise. She could probably recommend how to get ourselves into some of the higher-end destination trip blogs and e-zines with these other stores. And she could spread the word to her network of travel agencies and tour companies."

Elaine nodded. "Daralyn brought me the article. The notes are hers."

Thomas's serious smile wreathed his handsome features. "Don't know why I'm surprised to hear that. Let's call her into this family meeting. If she's going to be the genius that planted the idea, she's going to help water it and help it grow."

And she had, her quiet enthusiasm inspiring all of them in various ways.

For instance, something as simple as the restroom. Rory had remodeled it last year, transforming it from an employees-only closet into a more spacious area for their tourist traffic. Daralyn had mentioned to Thomas that some kind of relevant interior design would make it an even more appealing space. Thomas soon after came up with the idea of mounting a few junk hardware pieces on the bathroom wall, with a trio of old four-inch wide paintbrushes in the center. He painted each set of bristles a different bright color, then sketched simple paintings over them. White clouds against the blue, a frog against the yellow, and a white church on the green one. He'd added dots of yellow around it, as if the church was in a field of sunflowers.

The online reviews of their place constantly mentioned the "quaint bathroom décor." Noticing that, Rory had local residents bring him their old paintbrushes, and he kept them in a bin, selling them for a buck apiece so the tourists could take them home and turn them into their own wall art.

Elaine had led the charge on the consigned consumables, stocking the store with community produced homemade jams, pies and salsas, as well as quilting and other needlecraft projects. Rory pursued the metal and woodworkers. Like John Tracer, who designed his wooden birdhouses to look like famous houses or movie icons, such as Tara and Twelve Oaks from *Gone With the Wind* or the Michelin man from *Ghostbusters*, his round mouth the perfect place for a bird to pop in and create a nest.

After taking over management of the store, Rory had also upped their social media presence by working out a deal with Forest, a tech geek he knew in high school, who ran a marketing business in Charlotte. Daralyn had shown an interest in maintaining the platforms, handling the online communication, posting pictures, notices of sales, that kind of thing.

His dad would have been pleased to see what they'd accomplished, even as he probably would have felt he'd lacked the current day savvy to make it happen. He was a farmer first, the store having originally been a way to supplement the flagging income from that. But that was okay. Rory was proud to have been a part of the family effort to take the idea his dad had started and make it work.

He glanced toward the painting mounted behind the cash register, and a faint smile touched his mouth. His brother had contributed to the consignment inventory with a few pastoral scenes, totally different from the erotic pieces he did for galleries. This one was just a picture of a clapboard farmhouse, backed by a field and the sun setting behind it, but there was something about the way his brother painted that caught the eye. The heart, too, since Rory was only admitting it to himself.

A tiny figure worked in the field, but even with that perspective, there was a sense of the farmer's focus, his hard work, evidence of a real person. Rory suspected Thomas had been imagining their dad when he'd painted it. Just looking at it made Rory miss him, the never-in-doubt love of their gruff-spoken father, the feel of his rough hand tousling his hair, on his shoulder. The earthy smell of his skin and clothes, the lingering scent of his aftershave on Sundays.

Dad had been a simple man, a lot like Rory. But now Rory knew even a simple man could be complicated in what he felt or desired, and how he shaped those feelings into action to reach goals, handle disappointments, or care for those people and principles that mattered most.

A deeper grin wreathed his face as he remembered the conflicting pricing advice Thomas and Marcus had given him about Thomas's handful of pictures for the store.

"If it's a neighbor, give it to them for what you think they can afford," Thomas had said. "No more than fifty dollars. For tourists, make your best call. Whatever's fair and will bring in good money for the store."

Marcus had rolled his eyes. "I'm selling your original work for four figures or more, and you want to price it like it's yard sale junk."

"What I'm selling in the store are local scenes and color," Thomas pointed out. "They're not gallery-level stuff."

While Rory agreed with his brother's logic on pricing, when he looked at that painting on the wall—hell, any of his brother's work— he wasn't so sure about Thomas's downplay of its quality. But Rory liked that Thomas never let his success as an artist get away with him. And the bug up Marcus's ass about selling it like "yard sale junk" only added to Rory's pleasure in hinting that he might do so.

He looked up from the computer as the screen door slammed. Johnny muscled in another couple bags of weed and feed, restocking the few they kept on the inside shelves. Rory had given him the chance to hang around and earn some extra hours as they reorganized the landscape inventory outside. They were putting the lawn ornamentation and fall foliage in a more prominent viewing display with the road. A good percentage of their October beach traffic would be empty nesters who liked to do a lot of fall decorating, inside and out.

Daralyn was planting weather hardy ornamentals and native plants in different colored pots to arrange around the display. She'd even talked about having a fairy garden area, since those had been getting real popular.

Rory wasn't so sure they should diversify that much, since the fairy garden stuff wasn't cheap, even at cost. One of his mom's friends was into fairy gardens, though, and had offered to do a free class here afterhours, with the attendees covering the cost of their initial supplies. Daralyn had suggested having catalogs available in the store so once they got their projects off the ground, they would order more things for them, without the store having to keep a lot of it in stock.

Daralyn had also told him she'd handle closing on the night of the class, because she was thinking of starting her own fairy garden in front of her cottage. In short, she liked the fairy garden stuff, which automatically made him more open to the idea.

And speaking of which, they'd finally gotten a lull, no one else in the store. When Daralyn had arrived after lunch, he'd been busy with customers, and then more had come in, needing her attention. They hadn't had a moment together alone, but when she met his eyes in that first moment, she'd smiled her shy smile. She was obviously okay after her Dr. Taylor appointment, and the things in her gaze suggested she had more on her mind than that. Good things, the kind occupying his own thoughts.

He'd been inside her, his mouth on her, her hands on him. And she seemed more than okay with that.

He thought of her sitting at her kitchen table in his shirt, and knew he'd want to see her again tonight. Maybe do it all over again. But right now he wanted to see her, period, while they could steal a moment.

"Johnny, is Daralyn still outside?" He called out the question as he swept the cursor across his screen to put the computer to sleep.

"Yeah, man." Johnny straightened. Built husky, as a former high school linebacker would be, he had a face full of dark whiskers and looked like a younger cousin of the Duck Dynasty crew. "She was going to move that load of pine straw over to the west side of the building, to make room for more of the girly stuff up front."

"What?" Rory's head snapped up. "How is she moving it?"

"The smaller tractor, what else? The trailer was already hooked up to it and last week, I showed her how to—"

He was already around the counter, pushing toward the front door. As he heard the tractor start up, that roar of sound, he went out the door fast, kicking up the front of his chair with a jerk of his upper body so the casters didn't catch on the stoop. The screen door bounced off the siding.

"Daralyn."

He was downwind, and there was a good breeze. Plus that engine noise swallowed all other sound. She was trundling toward the section Johnny had described, her hands carefully placed on the wheel, her expression focused, attentive on her goal.

As he turned her way, he pivoted too sharply, a wheel leaving the ground, but he shifted his weight to slam it back down before the chair could tip. His shoulders flexed like rubber bands as he headed her way. It only took moments, but it felt like hours.

She was making the turn to back the trailer up. When she looked over her opposite shoulder, she saw him. He made a sharp slicing motion with his hand.

A puzzled look crossed her face. She brought the tractor to a halt and put it on idle, leaning down as he rolled up to her. She obviously thought he was there to give her additional instruction. He sure as hell was.

"Get off of that thing," he shouted over the noise. "Right now."

Her expression was curious, but still relaxed. "It's okay," she called back. "Johnny told me how to use it. It's just a--"

"Shut it down. Get the fuck off of it." He needed her off it, right now, and he banged his chair against the side. When he closed his hand around her arm, her startled glance jumped up to his face.

Of all times for her to get stubborn with him, to trust that fragile thing between them, the promise he'd made her, she went with now. Her chin set.

"I know how to do this. I can do this."

"No, you can't. If you don't get your ass off that thing this instant, I swear to God I will blister it so you can't walk for a week."

Red stained her cheeks as the rest of her flesh around it went pale. He'd tightened his grip, and he realized he was hurting her. With an oath, he let her go, but he dipped down, going for the keys. Since they were just out of his reach, he shoved himself half out of the chair to lunge at them.

Goddamn it, he hadn't braked the chair. It rolled back as he moved forward.

He was falling.

He heard her startled cry as the chair spun off and his elbow slammed into the floor near the brake pedal. The tractor wasn't going anywhere, but that didn't matter. The noise this close...

A fist closed around his whole upper body, driving the rage away and leaving oxygen-deprived terror, her face sucked away as he was left only a pinpoint of light.

"Shut it off," he said, but he couldn't get the words out. His chest had seized up, his throat closing as the rest of his body hit the ground. Everything below the waist collapsed in a disordered heap, the weight of it yanking at his rigid upper body, but his arm kept him hooked against the tractor floor. As she turned off the equipment, everything should have gone silent. But it couldn't stop the roaring noise of that engine in his head.

She'd jumped off next to him and he heard Johnny's feet pounding across the parking lot. *Fuck, don't let anyone come, don't...*

Too late. A vehicle was entering the parking lot, a pickup. Mac Dublin was calling out the open window, asking if he could help, what had happened...

Rory's eyes met Daralyn's. He had latched onto her again, physically confirming she was off the tractor. He was most definitely not hanging onto her because the thunder in his chest was painful, and clammy sweat covered his shaking body. All he saw were her hazel eyes. Then he heard her voice.

Not panic stricken by his craziness. Not upset with him. Instead, it was calm and easy as a steady blowing wind over the fields, rustling through the corn just before harvest.

"He's just fine, Mr. Dublin. You're here for your order, aren't you? Johnny, will you go in and take care of Mr. Dublin? The tools he ordered are labeled in the back. He already paid for them. We're okay. Please go take care of that."

He could only see her, but whatever she'd said, however she'd delivered it, had both men backing off. Whether reluctantly or not, he didn't know. All he knew was relief that they were gone. And that the roaring was dying away, leaving the quiet of her breath, her voice. A world without that tractor engine noise.

When it had rolled on him, the engine had stayed on. He'd been pinned under a screaming, hot-breathed monster.

Her hands were on his shoulders, one slipping down to tuck under his arm. "Can you turn, so we can prop you against a wheel? Is that okay?"

He wanted to be three counties away from the thing, but he needed to act like a sane person again. Tractor was off, he reminded himself. It was on level, stable ground. He helped her, hauling his weight around to put himself on the cushion of grass next to the back wheel. She helped adjust his legs out in front of him, since his hands were shaking. Then she was squatting on her heels, her eyes worried. He reclaimed her hand, held it too tightly.

"I don't want you on a tractor," he said. "Ever. Understand?"

She cupped his face, her fingers moving over his jaw, the hammer of his pulse in his throat. She stayed there, stroking, soothing it.

"Yes, Rory."

His gaze moved to the track she'd taken across the lot. Nothing tricky to it, not on its face. But parallel to the area where she had planned to put the pine straw was a drainage ditch. Not a big, deep wide thing, but turn the tractor too far out to back the trailer, and it could dip into that ditch. The whole thing could go over in a somersault that could pitch the driver, land on him. The damn things were so susceptible to rolling if you didn't pay attention. Like the pond embankment that had flanked the field he'd been tilling, the ground unstable from recent rains...

"Rory. You're hurting me."

He let out an oath at her quiet words and released her hand. She didn't try to reassure him with things that wouldn't have made any difference. She just sat down next to him, shoulder to shoulder, her knees drawn up, her sneaker pressed against his thigh. He dropped his hand so he could cover it. She wasn't wearing socks, so he could rub his thumb over her ankle, the visible top of her foot, feel her soft flesh.

"You can feel this, right?"

When she nodded, it swamped him. It didn't so much anymore, but in moments like this, it did. The words came out choked.

"I sure wish I could."

Her arms slipped around his shoulders, his head, drawing him down as he used his own arms to hold her hard to him, his forehead and nose pressed to her shoulder and breast. She was breathing slow and even, with little hitches. When moisture hit his temple, he realized she was crying. For him.

It made him get hold of himself, which meant the embarrassment hit hard. There was a time he would have lashed out because of it, driven everyone away while he pulled his ass together. But he'd learned that wasn't the way to deal with it. He raised his head, cleared his throat as he brushed a tendril of hair away from her serious face. "Sorry," he said. "Sorry I yelled at you."

"It's okay. I understand why now. I thought... I thought you didn't think I could do it."

"No. It wasn't that. You can do anything." If she told him she could fly, he'd believe it. It was why he worried that, once she figured out how to use those wings, she'd go far beyond where he could reach her.

He'd had enough of dealing with his fears for one day, though. It was amazing how exhausting five minutes could be. He felt like he needed a three-hour nap. Maybe in that hammock behind his house. Maybe with her lying in his arms. He liked the idea more than the thought of Heaven. Maybe because it sounded like one and the same.

"I owe you dinner," he said.

She slanted him a glance. "Oh?"

He liked that she didn't assure him he didn't. In fact, he thought he caught a glimpse of the kind of look a woman gave a man when she knew she had him on the hook, in the right kind of way.

Dr. Taylor was right. Today's session must have gone really well.

"I could cook for you," he said.

She lifted a brow. "You can't cook."

"That is not true. I make a hell of a fried peanut butter and jelly sandwich."

When she smiled, he tightened his hand on her foot. "So what's your preference? A nice dinner out, or fried PB and J at my place? Mom has a church thing tonight. She won't see what a mess I make in the kitchen."

He said it as a joke, knowing she'd leave it to him to choose. But she surprised him.

"PB and J of course." Her gaze flicked away, then came back to him, and he was lost in those mix of green and gold colors, the hints of blue-grey on the edges, the flecks of black. "Can I kiss you?"

"Yeah," he said, his voice thick. "Anytime."

Anytime you want.

She leaned in, her hand sliding along his chest, to his neck, then up, to cradle his jaw again. Did she take that leisurely track because now she knew how much he liked feeling her hands on his upper body? Or did she do it because she liked to do it for her own pleasure? Maybe both. He liked that idea best.

She shifted, so she was pressed against him as her mouth moved over his. Though she'd asked to kiss him, when their lips met, he felt the giving on her part, the invitation, the craving for him to take. He didn't need to be invited twice. His hand was on her shoulder and throat, then up to her jaw and covering the rabbiting pulse beneath the heel of his hand as he pulled her across his lap. He held her close as he kissed her, parting her lips, diving deep, teasing her with his tongue.

His shaking turned into a deep shudder that leveled out, brought him back to himself. From her murmur against his lips, the shift of her body, he was pretty sure he'd started to get an erection. He didn't know if the life-or-death adrenaline thing could be contributing to that, but he knew holding her on his lap sure did.

At length, Rory lifted his head. Mac's truck was gone, and he hadn't even noticed. Johnny was still in the store. Probably watching them through the windows and snickering, but that was okay. Way better than him worrying about having to come to Rory's rescue like a guy scooping a flapping, injured bird off the ground.

Daralyn was fully limp in his arms, her eyes on his, her expression satisfyingly flushed and dazed at once. "Thanks," he said. "Thanks for always seeing me as a man. No matter what's happening."

Her eyes darkened, and her hand covered his on her face. "I've never seen you as anything else."

He was ready to get his day back on track, but his body had other ideas. He could push himself through a grueling workout, do a full day at the store, no problem. Yet when something happened like what had gone down with the tractor, no more than freaking ten minutes of his life, the mental exhaustion became a full body clamp. He needed to recharge, and Daralyn and Johnny both noticed. They were shooting him concerned looks, and ping-ponging the same with one another. Like he couldn't see that.

Daralyn sidled up to him behind the counter. "It's been pretty quiet this afternoon," she said carefully. "You could probably take off if you have other stuff you need to do before dinner."

Like a nap. She wouldn't say it, even if it was as clear in her face as the yearning for it in his head.

"Like prepping for the NASA summit and curing cancer?" He spoke tightly, so her half-smile in response was nervous. "I'm good. I mean it. It's okay."

She nodded and went back to what she was doing, but he knew he was struggling. He felt warm, a light perspiration on his upper lip. Shit. If he got a fever, that could fuck their plans to head to Florida in the near future.

A car pulling in drew his attention, but it wasn't a customer. It was his mother. Goddamn it.

When he glanced toward Daralyn and saw her and Johnny exchange a significant look, his temper went from spark to full flame.

"I told you I was fine," he said sharply.

Daralyn froze in place where she'd been stocking boxes of nails. Johnny, sharpening a brace of knives, paused and looked his way.

"When I say I'm fine, I'm fine," Rory said. "I don't need either of you texting my mom."

Johnny gave him a puzzled look. "I didn't, man."

Rory turned his searing gaze back toward Daralyn, but one glance at her stricken face told him she hadn't, either.

For the past week or two, Elaine had been busy with a church bazaar thing. However, on a normal week it wasn't unusual for her to stop by at least once a day. She'd helped his dad run the place for years, and she liked to keep her hand in, a reminder to them she was available to help.

So her arriving right now was just plain old Murphy's Law— nothing more.

"Crap," Rory muttered, and ran a hand over his face.

Elaine breezed in, the store bells announcing her entrance. Johnny had merely shrugged and returned to what he was doing, Rory's crankiness dismissed in typical male fashion. Daralyn's expression was carefully closed, though, and he wanted to fix that now. His asshole meter with her today was beyond the max.

His mom put a tote bag on the counter next to him. "Sally Wilson gave me some more of her preserves. Said you were low when she stopped in the other day."

He was summoning a casual response when she glanced at him and took a second, harder look. "You look flushed, son. Are you running a fever?"

She reached out with curled fingers to brush them against his brow. He drew back. "I'm fine."

Johnny was smirking at him. What he would normally do when Rory's mom was being a mom. When Johnny's mom stopped into the store, it was no different. Rory knew that, knew his mother hadn't done a single thing different from usual to warrant Rory getting his hackles up.

"Maybe you should take a couple hours off," Elaine said, and turned to Johnny and Daralyn. "You two could handle closing if he—"

"Mom," he snapped. "That's my call, not yours. I run the store. I said I was fine."

When Elaine's startled gaze flicked to him, he couldn't help his involuntary glance toward Daralyn.

While his mother needed reading glasses for almost everything now, she still managed to see like a hawk when it came to her kids. Her gaze became thoughtful, then faintly amused. As if he was twelve, and she thought it adorable that he didn't want to be babied in front of a girl.

Him not wanting to be treated like a kid in front of a woman he was in a relationship with was true enough. But he was a grown man who had a short fuse with people talking over and around him. As if his physical handicap automatically came with debilitating brain damage. Hell, the first few months he'd been in a chair, he remembered going to a restaurant with his family where the waitress asked them what he wanted to eat, instead of Rory directly. For fuck's sake.

The rational part of him knew his mother would have reacted to Les or Thomas looking like crap the same way. Yet it also wasn't the same, because she'd been with him every painful step of the way, from the time of his accident to him learning how to live as a paraplegic. Including all the horrible, undignified steps that went along with that. She knew as much about his health as he did.

Her lips had set in a firm little line that said she might take him to task about his attitude later, but thankfully she said nothing further. "All right son." She touched his hand. "But do take care, hmm?"

"I will, Mom. I promise." He softened his tone, gave her a look that said he knew he was being an ass. Then he teased her, an interim apology. "You're such a mom."

Her gaze warmed. "Yes, I am. Remember, I have church tonight. We're going to work on pricing the bazaar items afterward, so I may run late."

She waved to Daralyn and Johnny and then she was back in the parking lot, getting in her car and heading out. Rory returned to what he was doing at the counter, but he was conscious of Daralyn, working only a few feet away, her shoulders tense.

Dealing with the bad things that had shaped her into what she was now didn't make her less in his eyes. Far from it. He could tell her that all day, but the best way to do that was by example.

Being an adult could be such a pain in the ass.

He turned toward Daralyn, drawing her attention. "I'm sorry," he said. He included Johnny in his glance. "Neither of you deserved the attitude. And, if you're okay with it still, I'm going to head out early."

The words tried to stick in his throat, but he shoved them out, a rough throat clearing. "I'll be at the house, so if things get busy, call me and I'll come back in."

"You got it, man."

Rory shifted his gaze back to Daralyn. "When you get done, if you want, you could come by. I'll be in the hammock in the backyard."

"That's so sweet of you, dude, but only if it's a double wide so we can snuggle."

Rory shot Johnny a look as Daralyn bit back a smile. "Shut up, asshole."

Johnny grinned and fortunately headed off toward storage. Rory moved out from behind the counter, drawing closer to Daralyn. "If you want to bring your school stuff, it's a nice spot for studying. I promise not to be an ogre."

"First time for everything," Johnny called over his shoulder.

"I'm going to replace you with Brenda Lee," Rory said, referencing Johnny's border collie. "She's smarter, and I can pay her in sausage balls."

Johnny's chuckle drifted back before he disappeared entirely.

Daralyn gave him another little smile and Rory extended his hand. "Come here."

She'd lowered her gaze, but now it snapped back up. "Rory. You're bleeding."

He followed her glance down. He didn't see it, not until she closed the distance and squatted by the chair, pointing. He shifted his weight, bracing himself on his push rim so he could lift his hip. It was an awkward angle, so he still had to reach down to feel. There was a rip in his jeans, and the back of his right thigh was wet. Fucking hell. When he'd fallen out of the chair and rolled, he must have caught himself on something, like the metal step plate. The old tractor had plenty of rough edges.

A deeper probe said it wasn't something he could clean up and band-aid. Shit. He should have checked himself right away. He knew better. But he'd been so knotted up over how he'd acted around Daralyn—and privately relieved as hell he hadn't soiled himself from the stress. All he'd wanted was to move as fast as possible back to "normal" around her. Which meant he hadn't done the self-care he normally would have done.

He *had* acted like a fucking twelve-year-old trying to impress a girl.

Well, no worries about that anymore. Now he had to deal with this, even if it knocked his pride down lower than an ant's knees. "Crap," he said, trying to keep it light. "Tell Johnny I need a ride to the urgent care."

"I'll go with you."

"No." He shook his head. "I need you to run the store. I'll have Johnny give Amanda a shout and ask if she can come back you up. Hey." He touched her tense face. "I just need to have it cleaned and looked at. It's okay. I'm okay." Though he was betting he was going to need a couple stitches, since the blood was still seeping, despite him putting pressure on it from his seated position.

"Okay," she said, but he could tell it didn't make her happy.

"It's all good," he told her. "Promise."

After Rory and Johnny left, taking Rory's van, Daralyn couldn't stop thinking about him, worrying.

He'd been upset when he thought they'd called Elaine. She under-stood Rory didn't want to be treated like a child, but knowing her presence contributed to that embarrassment, that her opinion of him mattered, was something she found stunning.

Witnessing anyone demonstrating care and love, whether it was between mother and son, friends, siblings, husbands and wives... Even after five years away from the way her life had been, she still found it a special miracle that people not only cared about one another, but would offer it so openly.

She kept glancing at her phone, though he'd barely had time to get to the urgent care, let alone check in and be seen. Since his jeans had been stained but he'd been sitting in a smear of blood, not a puddle, maybe it was in a spot that just kept breaking open if he shifted. She'd noticed he did that frequently during the day, something he told her helped prevent pressure sores.

Johnny texted Daralyn that Amanda was on her way and, sure enough, she arrived in a few minutes. Amanda also worked at the drugstore in town, which was why she was studying to be a pharmacy tech, to earn more money and take on greater responsibilities.

Rory had teased her about Amanda, and Daralyn guessed she did have mixed feelings about the girl. Amanda had been a cheerleader. She was still pretty, always put together, her hair and makeup perfect. She possessed a curvy body that made every man, young or old, take a look.

All that was fine, but it wasn't why she bugged Daralyn. Rory had dated Amanda in high school. He'd liked her, been attracted her, but what he had with her now was different. Deeper. Amanda had gone out with Rory *after* his accident.

Even though they weren't dating now, and Amanda had no obvious designs on Rory, being around the girl made Daralyn feel small and uncertain, unexpectedly resentful at times. Since Daralyn picked up a lot of town gossip from the comings and goings of customers, she knew Amanda had been dating Marty French for some time now. He ran the town jewelry store, and everyone said it was getting serious between them.

Knowing Amanda was with someone helped Daralyn deal with her confusing mix of feelings toward the girl. Plus, Amanda was nothing but nice toward her, even if there was a stiff formality to it, as if they both seemed unable to figure out what to say to one another.

It also wasn't the first time she'd worked with Amanda in the store, though usually Rory, Elaine or Johnny were here as a buffer. Thankfully, Amanda didn't ask her to talk much. They handled the flow of customers, and in between those moments, Amanda pitched in without complaint to help Daralyn price a new shipment of tools.

When her phone beeped, Amanda pulled it out of the back pocket of her snug jeans and glanced at it. "Hey, Johnny said he's headed to Rory's to drop him off. He had to have three stitches, but he's all good."

Three stitches. Daralyn's hands shook and she put down the drill bits she'd been measuring. But it was okay. He was okay. She really wished she'd gone with him. But she managed to say the proper thing in an even enough tone.

"Oh. That's good, then." Her phone had remained dark. That made sense. Rory was the patient and he likely hadn't had a chance to text, and Johnny knew Amanda was here. It still made Daralyn feel left out.

"Hey, how about when Johnny gets here, you head on over to check on him? The two of us can cover things. And tell Rory he's not paying me. This definitely falls under the friends-helping-friends category."

At Daralyn's undecided look, Amanda drew closer, and her expression was kind. "I can tell you're really worried about him. Really, I don't mind covering. And if anything comes up tonight where he needs something from the pharmacy, tell him he can call me. I can access the over-the-counter stuff after hours."

"That's really nice. Thanks." Daralyn struggled to smile, but it failed.

"Aw, sweetie, you're really gone over him, aren't you?" Amanda continued before Daralyn could decide if she needed to flee the conversation. "I'm so glad. He's one of the really good ones, you know? Like Marty. Some of the girls I went to school with, all they could think about was getting out of here, going to bigger cities and meeting these guys who they thought had seen and done so much more than the guys around here. And doing things like that themselves."

Amanda shrugged. "That's cool, and okay, and probably pretty true. But to my way of thinking, building a nest where you're happy is more important than building it somewhere that impresses other people. Gotta follow your heart. That's the most important thing."

Amanda grimaced. "Sorry, I'm just rambling, but you look really worried. Sometimes you're like being around a deer. Not sure if what I say will spook you or not."

It was the most straightforward thing she'd ever said to Daralyn, and there was no meanness in the observation. Maybe because she was worried about Rory, really wanting to be with him, Daralyn's ability to make appropriate small talk, never her best skill, failed her.

"I don't know how to feel about you," she said abruptly. "I don't know...how to deal with some things the way other people do."

Amanda sent her a shrewd look. "Like me and Rory having been together."

Daralyn bit her lip. "Um...that's none of my business. That's between you and Rory, and I respect his privacy. As well as yours. It's okay."

"I have a feeling it *is* your business. And this is between us girls." Amanda gave her a conspiratorial smile. "Rory and I had our time, and it was good. Really good. But we never connected heart to heart, if that makes sense. When we were teens, we had a good time and enjoyed one another, and we thought about more, the way teenagers will, but we're not meant for the long haul together."

Daralyn thought about that. "How are your studies going?" she ventured shyly. "For the pharmacy tech job?"

"Oh, really good." Amanda brightened, reminding Daralyn of how she felt about her own classes. "I've been learning so much, and Bill, our pharmacist, is so encouraging. He's been helping me by..."

As Amanda's enthusiasm for her career path broke through, any tension Daralyn had about her and Rory's connection ebbed away. The woman's kindness was genuine.

Even after five years, that too was unexpected. Though dutifully followed Dr. Taylor's suggestions, Daralyn could never shake the uneasiness that said the people she trusted the most could decide she wasn't worth their time, because she was too damaged. Not connected to them by blood, not really belonging.

She wondered what it would be like, to go to bed at night without the fear she would wake in the morning and find it had all been a dream. She'd still be in a tiny room, every thought she had competing with the incessant drone of her father's television, the stale smell of cigarettes, and the dull edge of an empty belly. The futile hope underneath it all, that something new would happen to change the colorless routine of her bleak waking hours.

Her phone buzzed and she stole a look at it.

Hammock offer stands. I'm good. You worry too much.

"He just texted you," Amanda said, grinning. "I could tell. You got all doe-eyed. Want to talk about how dreamy our guys are? Marty gets this intense look when he's fixing jewelry that makes my knees weak. I know just how stupid that sounds, so quick, tell me something equally dumb so I won't feel like a lovesick idiot."

A slow smile crossed Daralyn's face. "When Rory's doing the financials for the store, he gets very focused. He'll prop his hand on the counter and stroke his beard. The computer light will catch his eyes. They're brown, but when that happens, they have touches of gold. He has a lock of hair that falls over his forehead here," she passed her fingers over her own, "And I always want to brush it back, just so it will fall back down and I can do it again."

Amanda blinked. "Wow. You need to talk more often, Daralyn."

Les and Julie had on occasion set up impromptu "slumber parties" for the three of them in Les's room, during holidays when they were both here. That was when Daralyn had learned about Rory and Amanda's past together. She'd often listened to giggling exchanges like this about men. But she'd never had someone, not part of Rory's family or their inner circle, engage her in such a conversation. It made her nervous and happy at once, especially when Amanda's grin widened.

"Okay, so let's move on to arms. Who knew a jeweler would have biceps like creek rock? When we go out to a restaurant, I like curling my hand over Marty's, leaning against him, while we're reading the menu."

Rory's arms were incredibly strong. Daralyn loved the feel of them around her. She nodded, an agreement that Amanda apparently realized was about Rory, not Marty. A conversation where the subject was a matter of the heart, so they both understood it.

Throughout her journey away from that small, dark room, people had told her a lot of things about how things would get better. However, it was in moments like these, where she saw it could actually happen, that she made a noticeable step forward, away from that uneasiness.

Nothing more than a lack of understanding and unfounded fears had stood between her and a friendship with Amanda. Her first friendship made on her own.

Johnny's truck was pulling back in. "I think I will go check on him," Daralyn told her new friend. "Thank you."

CHAPTER TWELVE

She found him in the wide rope hammock in his backyard, just like he'd said. He'd brought a couple pillows out and had his head on one, his knee propped up on the other. Thanks to a loose pair of shorts, the bandaged wound on his thigh had air between it and the ropes.

He wasn't wearing anything else, the sculpted beauty of his upper body, all muscular, smooth curves and masculine angles, available to her appreciative gaze. Autumn in their part of North Carolina was often sprinkled with warmer days, remnants of the past summer season. She was very grateful this was one of those days.

It was more than Amanda's influence that made her especially notice. It was last night, too. She'd thought about it a hundred different ways today, him touching her, being inside her. She'd lingered over the moments when he'd let her touch him, her fingertips trailing over the same terrain she was looking at now. He'd reacted in such a memorable way when she put her mouth on his throat, his shoulders, explored his upper body.

It made her want to do more of it. Like when she kissed him at the tractor, and she'd felt the energy gather beneath her touch, just from caressing his chest and shoulders.

Her gaze slid to his legs. In addition to PT, he did what he called passive range of motion exercises to help their circulation and keep the muscle in them from atrophying. Though they lacked the obvious strength and vibrancy of his upper body, the skin was healthy, a light layer of dark hair on his shins and thighs matching the gleaming mat on his chest. The five o'clock shadow above his neatly trimmed beard gave him a rakish look.

His brown eyes had locked upon her the moment she emerged around the corner of the house. The way he watched her come toward him put butterflies in her stomach. He wanted to touch her, too, something that made her skin tingle all the places he'd touched her last night. Which had been basically everywhere.

"Hey," he said. "Teach me to overreact next time, right?"

"I'm glad you're all right," she responded. In that moment by the tractor, her own calmness had taken her by surprise, summoning a person inside herself she hadn't expected. One capable of directing Johnny and Mac back in the store and caring for Rory in the way needed. Protecting him had been more important to her than anything, even her own fears or the grip of her own weaknesses.

There was a pair of outdoor chairs close to the hammock and a table between them. She put her backpack on it as he extended a hand to her.

"I'll let you do your schoolwork, promise, but come lie here with me first."

She put her hips on the edge and, as he gripped her hand and tugged, the demands of gravity helped her bring her legs up and then roll her against him. It made her smile, and then feel other, deeper things, because he was ready, curling a possessive arm around her to bring her right up against him. It seemed natural to drape over him, her leg over his uninjured one, her arm across his chest, hand cupped over his shoulder.

He'd said she could kiss him anytime, and she thought that also applied to her touch on his upper body. So she flattened her palm over his heart, moving her fingers in slow strokes over his warm flesh, down to his nipple and combing through the chest hair. He brushed his lips over her temple as she explored, nuzzled her, teased her, moving down her cheekbone as she lifted her face to his. His hand slid over her chin and throat, thumb tracing her collar bone. Her whole body wanted to melt against the strength of his, her thigh tightening over him. When his arm around her shifted, his palm cupping her buttock, squeezing, she pressed closer.

He broke the kiss after a lingering moment, but kept his hand where it was, making slow circles, caresses, that had tingles shooting through her thighs and up between them, all the way up to her throat and mouth. How his eyes lingered on her lips enhanced the feeling. Exacerbated it. New word.

"I don't need to do schoolwork," she said. "I finished most of it last night."

His lips curved. "Then what's in the bag?"

"My notebook, and a book from the library. It's one that Dr. Taylor recommended to me, about Irish immigrant children who were transported out west in the late 1800s and early 1900s." When she'd started reading it last night, she knew why Dr. Taylor had recommended *Orphan Train* to her. The life of the orphans, their feelings about how unpredictable life was, how they could never plan or count on anything, was familiar. As was their inability to trust, even when it seemed life had stabilized, improved. And they'd been real people, struggling with some of the same things Daralyn was, only about a hundred years ago.

"Dr. Taylor seems like good people. I met with her today." Rory's gaze held hers. "She said you were okay with that."

"Yes." Talking about it more than that would make her uncomfortable. She didn't want this moment to be about Dr. Taylor, or anything but how wonderful and anxious in the right kind of way it felt to be lying in the hammock with him.

She glanced over her shoulder at his chair, positioned on the other side of the hammock. Getting into the hammock couldn't have been an easy feat. "You never seem to worry about falling."

He shrugged. "You get past it. You have to. The first time I fell and figured out how to get myself back into the chair on my own, without it taking days, I honest-to-God felt like I'd won the winning touchdown for a state championship."

They lay in silence a few moments, the hammock swaying slightly from their combined weights and the fall breeze. The tree canopies above them were starting to turn yellow. In full fall plumage, they would look like the sun in leaf form.

She remembered when he was on the football team. She'd never been to one of his games—far too noisy, too much activity. But she'd heard the recap when his family came home afterward, when she saw the light in his eyes, the flush of victory and excitement.

It made her think of earlier today, that startling, heartbreaking moment when he'd touched her ankle.

You can feel this, right? I sure wish I could.

"Do you miss it a lot, playing football?" she asked softly. Then she shook her head. "I'm sorry. I shouldn't have asked that."

He brushed his lips over her forehead again. "You can ask me whatever you want, remember? Quid pro quo. And it's okay. I'm okay with what my life is now. I miss it sometimes, but mostly I miss being able to move like that. I wouldn't have done anything with football after high school, because being great there doesn't necessarily mean you'll be picked up by a college team. And now, I'm glad it wasn't going in that direction. Because to lose that, in addition to the ability to walk...not sure if I could have handled that."

He grimaced. "But knowing that I can still have ninety percent of what I figured my life would look like, working my family's store, living in my hometown? I think that's what really helped me deal with it, if that makes sense."

She nodded. She liked lying here, listening to him talk. His deep voice had the effect she'd mentioned to him, surrounding her, steadying her. All throughout the day, even when he was with customers, as long as she was within hearing distance, it did that.

But here, with her head on his chest, that was the best, because it vibrated against her, filling her mind, her body.

He'd moved his hand to her hip, his fingers wrapped at her waist. "You have any other questions for me?"

She did, this one inspired by the playful moment with Amanda. "Les told me your mother named you after the hero of a romance novel."

He groaned. "I knew I should have drowned her as a baby. Yeah. It was a Viking romance called *Tara's Song*, and the hero's name was Rorik. She still has it on that shelf of books down in the basement storage room. Dad said she named me that because I came out looking ready to raid and pillage. Mom said she just liked the name."

"Rorik," she murmured, trying it out. She slid her hand over his chest, back, forth, tracing the skin some more, threading through the curling hair. She spread her fingers out wide, so she could caress his upper abdomen, follow the slope of his rib cage, how it framed his muscled upper abdomen.

She wondered if he would tell her to stop. Instead, his hand slid from her hip up her side, passing over her upper arm until he reached the side of her neck. His fingers caught in her hair, loose on her shoulders because she'd taken out the ponytail before she came to see him. He gripped her hair, tightened his hold in that way that made things in her stomach flutter as the rest of her stilled.

He used that grip to tilt her head back, make her meet his gaze. "I want that gorgeous mouth of yours on me," he said. "Everywhere I can feel it."

The switch from relaxed banter, his rueful self-deprecation, to this, a sudden dominant intensity coupled with a sentence that felt undeniably like an order, had shivers running through her.

She adjusted so she was propped up against his side, and then leaned over him, bringing her mouth to his chest. He kept his hand in her hair, guiding her as she tasted, nuzzled his warm, firm skin, brushed her nose and then her cheek against his chest hair. His abdomen contracted under her palm, resting against it.

A quick glance upward showed his fiery gaze fixed on her face. She moved her mouth over his nipple, licked it delicately with the tip of her tongue, kissed and sucked lightly. The response was breathtaking. He arched up, his other hand falling on her shoulder, while his grip on her scalp became even stronger, holding her there as she teased. Until he hauled her up to his mouth in a breathtakingly demanding way.

She made a needy sound into it as he devoured, playing with her tongue, her lips, moving his other hand down so he was gripping her ass again, pulling her over him so she was stretched out almost fully upon him, her thighs open over his propped thigh so it pressed between her legs.

He eased her back enough to pin her with that unrelenting stare. "Take off everything but your panties. Then turn around, face toward my feet, and thread your legs through here." He reached above him, past the straight frame piece over their heads, where the strung hammock ropes narrowed into a V-shape leading to the part that was tied around the tree. "Ask me why I want you to do that."

"Why?" she whispered.

"I want to put my mouth between your legs. Feel you writhe and squirm and come apart while I play with what's mine as long as I want. It's a nice afternoon. A lot of time to do stuff in a leisurely, long way. Mom won't be home until late, and no one can see us back here."

Her heartbeat had moved up into her throat. She moved as if through a warm, strong wind, tipping herself off the hammock to remove everything but her pink cotton underwear. He held on to her when she removed the jeans, steadying her. His gaze didn't leave her as she followed his orders.

Moving on a hammock wasn't easy, and his desires were already making her unsteady, but as always, she was able to rely on his strength, the guidance of his hands. Her body felt like it was vibrating to a dancing rhythm she could feel in her blood, as he helped her back onto the hammock, straddling him backward. He moved her with sure hands so she could thread her feet and ankles through the ropes past that cross piece. Her knees spread out and pressed into his shoulders, her shins resting on the pillow that extended out on either side of his head.

Threading her feet through those ropes kept her legs apart, she realized, spread open the width of his shoulders. He added to the sense of restraint by wrapping his arms over her thighs and waist, bringing her farther up his chest as the pillows gave his head the angle to put his mouth exactly where he'd described.

It was still a shock, having his mouth between her thighs. She'd only been allowed to serve her uncle and father's pleasure. None of it was for her. Whereas everything Rory did seemed intended to take her to this place of mindless ecstasy.

Even more amazing, he'd made it clear doing so, watching her get lost in it, gave him enormous pleasure.

In this position, she was lying on his abdomen, her head resting on his thighs. She could feel the nest of his cock and testicles against her throat and upper chest, so she reached beneath her to find him under the shorts, explore. He wasn't wearing any underwear. Though his cock responded to her touch, hardening, and she really liked touching him so intimately, she knew he couldn't feel it, not right there. Still, from what he'd said, the reaction would build elsewhere, in deep parts of himself the way his touch did to her.

From his pleased growl against her, he really liked watching her body arch and writhe as his mouth made her dance. His strong hands tightened on her and the ropes bit into her legs, creating an additional jolt to the spiraling reaction within her.

She didn't have to question it. Dr. Taylor worked with her on expressing herself. Rory did the same, in a very different way.

She was shuddering, and he lifted his mouth enough to speak against her. "Am I hard, Daralyn?"

"Yes," she breathed. Then she gasped as he gripped her panties at the hip and ripped the seam there. When he shifted his grip to her waist, exerted pressure, she followed his guidance to slip her feet from between the ropes, turn around and straddle him. It took some time, especially with her current lack of coordination, but his hands were on her the whole time, steadying her, helping her.

She'd praised his upper body strength to Amanda, but when driven by his desire to have her the way he commanded, the ripple of muscle across his shoulders and chest, the tightening of his stomach muscles, was riveting.

As she completed the turn and settled back on his hips, the fabric of the torn panties slipped forward, over her mound, exposing it, the garment now only held by one leg. His brown eyes sparked with heat as he gazed at that, then he slid his attention upward, lingering on the tight points of her nipples.

"Put me inside you," he said.

Her hands had only been off of him for a matter of seconds, and her body had been shifting and sliding over his groin throughout the turning process. Which meant he was still rigid enough she could put him inside her. As she tugged his loose shorts to his upper thighs, lifting the waistband over his erection, he closed his hand over her neck, the heel of his hand against her sternum to help her stay upright.

At that pressure against her throat, another wave of sensations went through her, while everything else in her went still. He saw it, the grip tightening. It was a way of speaking to one another without words, without full understanding, but with full feeling. "Use your muscles inside," he said. "Keep squeezing down on me. It will keep me hard enough, like the grip of your hand, and it will feel good to you."

It all felt good to her, but she obeyed, and discovered a new level of pleasure. His cock did respond to the internal stroking, and as he began to raise and lower her, that feeling expanded, so she was gasping with every downward stroke, the firm resilience of his body rubbing and pressing against the sensitive outside of her sex.

"So beautiful," he muttered. The hammock was moving with them, not always in sync, but that added to the sensations, the pinnacle staying just out of reach so the pleasure just kept building. He moved one hand on her hip, the other still on her throat, while she kept her inner muscles clutching him, over and over, her hips jerking against his pelvis, rubbing herself there.

When she'd had that first orgasm with him, she'd fought it, afraid of it. Now, everything he did summoned those overwhelming intense surges, and the fire in his eyes wouldn't let her fight it. If she had any doubt about that, his words confirmed it.

"Now," he growled. "Let go, Daralyn. I've got you."

"Oh..." As the cry burst from her, his face reflected male triumph. She felt like a conquest. Like treasure. The world swam in sunlight, green and yellow trees, and the rough hemp of the hammock. In the center of it all was him, his brown eyes locked upon her, carrying her through that swirl of colors.

His expression became more rigid, his hand convulsed on her hip, and she knew he'd released as well. That knowledge drove her further, shuddering through her, little ripples that kept the pleasure going. And when her climax finally ebbed, he brought her down full upon him for another deep kiss. She reveled in it, splaying her hands out on his bare chest, feeling the coarse hair of his legs against her sensitive inner thighs. Her sex kept pulsing with final aftershocks against his cock and testicles.

He had his hand deep in her hair. The kiss eased apart, reluctantly, and she rested her face against his shoulder and throat, the rope of the hammock. Her breath was fast and heavy, and his was the same, lifting and lowering her body as his chest expanded. Combined with the sway of the hammock, she felt like she was in a cradle. Of his arms, of the hammock, of nature, of bliss.

They stayed that way for a while. She opened her mouth to ask if she was too heavy, if he needed her to move, but he made a quelling noise before she could speak and she subsided. He reached down, found the side of her panties where the seam was still holding, but he fixed that, tore it too and pulled the ruined garment away, tossed it over on top of her folded clothes. She looked at it there, evidence of his impatient desire for her, and her heart beat a little harder.

"Sorry about that," he murmured. "I'll buy you a new pair."

She nodded against him, not because she cared about that, but because she didn't have any words that matched all the feelings she had right now. She spoke to him through touch, her fingers tracing patterns along his biceps, his chest, exploring every inch of his tanned skin. His hands were running slow, caressing lines down her back, the upper rise of her buttocks. Then back up, tracing her vertebrae.

Her body responded with a low-level aroused attention that followed his touch wherever it went, while her mind entered a drifting, dreamlike peace as she rode those sensations. She could stay balanced on that edge forever.

"Shit," he said abruptly. "I didn't use a condom. The way I come, my swimmers mainly end up in my bladder, but still. There's a chance..."

"It's okay," she said drowsily. "I can't get pregnant."

"What?"

The dreamlike feeling vanished, replaced by tension at the sharp surprise in his voice. She cursed herself for speaking without thought. People wanted children. Rory would make a wonderful father. She shouldn't have told him...

No. Maybe she should have told him sooner.

She started to push away, figuring he'd want her to get off him now. He did let her move, but only to guide her to lie next to him again so they could look at one another more easily. He adjusted his shorts back over himself, then guided her leg back over him, her arm too, not letting her withdraw or curl her arms defensively against herself. He gave her the warmth of his body for her suddenly much colder one.

"Oh Daralyn, I'm so sorry."

She saw he was gazing down at her, his eyes full of pain. He cupped her face, stroking her cheek. "Had you thought about having kids?" he asked.

His distress and concern were for her, not him. As she swallowed an aching lump in her throat, she wondered if he'd shut down any thoughts of having kids himself because of the chair. "I don't know. Maybe. There's so much I've only just started to think about. I know that seems strange, after five years."

"Doesn't seem strange at all." He paused. "I want to ask more about it, but I don't want to upset you. So how about you tell me what you can, and if that's nothing, we'll leave it alone for now. All right?"

She wet her lips. "You could ask Dr. Taylor. Could you ask her?"

"Yeah. I can do that."

He seemed okay with it, but the knot in her belly wouldn't go away, a peculiar feeling after everything else being loosened from the orgasm. He helped by wrapping his arms around her and kissing the top of her head. "It's all right," he said. "But I bet you're going to be a mother someday, like by adopting. You just have so much love in you."

How could she be a mother when she couldn't handle normal things, like going to a movie or simply offering an opinion? How could she raise a baby, protect it?

"Do you want them?" she asked, fearful of the answer.

The broad shoulder under her hand lifted. "If it happens, I'll be happy about it. If it doesn't, my life can be full without them." His arm tightened around her. "Especially if I have the right person to spend it with."

He hadn't answered the question directly, but her awareness of that was pushed aside by the significance of that last sentence. She didn't breathe. She couldn't.

"I'm not saying something like that to lock you into being with me, Daralyn. You've got a lot of living to do before you make that kind of choice."

Her head snapped up and her lips parted, but he touched her chin and gave her that look that kept the words from being spoken. "I know you've said you belong to me," he said evenly. "I love hearing that. But when I know for sure that you chose me, that you believe it down to your soul—that's when I'll tell you you're mine for good."

She wanted to argue with that, but she knew she couldn't. Which left her feeling out of sorts and strange. Fortunately, he shifted the topic. "If I didn't mess things up with this cut on my leg, we've been invited to a party when we go to Florida."

"A party?" She didn't handle crowds well, but she trusted his knowledge of that. Maybe she could handle it with him by her side. Even enjoy it. She'd be willing to try, for him.

"Yeah. It's a special kind of party." When she glanced up at him, she was surprised to see he looked a little uncomfortable. "How much do you know about Domination and submission? BDSM?"

During those pajama parties with Les, Julie had talked about the performances at her erotic theater. The topic of BDSM had come up. Les had asked Julie a *lot* of surprisingly in-depth questions about it.

As Julie explained the basics of Dominance/submission relationships and BDSM play, Daralyn had absorbed the details the way she gathered information on anything new that crossed her path. But she'd also felt an unsettling recognition of it. When Julie went into the more emotional parts of being Dominant or submissive, it was as if she were describing something Daralyn knew, deep inside. Something already part of who she was.

Other things Julie talked about had brought Rory right out front in Daralyn's mind, which made her feel warm and prickly, needing him then and there, his strength and support beside her. It also made her think of how often during a family get-together, like when they had finished a meal and were hanging out in the living room at Elaine's, or Marcus and Thomas's, she ended up choosing to sit, not just near Rory, but at his feet, her shoulder propped against his shins. She couldn't exactly remember when it had started, but it was habit now, a place of comfort and security for her.

The day Rory had put the chain on her wrist, the one she was still wearing for school nights and keeping in her pocket or by her bed other times, her mind had shot right to those discussions. Apparently, the seeds Julie had planted had been doing some serious growing since then.

"Some. Julie has talked about it," she said. "I really don't know much about it except what I've heard from her." *And felt.*

"This is a private party of that sort." He ran a hand up and down her back. "Daralyn, what you and I have been doing...exploring. A lot of it has to do with that. I don't know if you realize that. I didn't really, until I did, if that makes sense. And then Marcus..."

He bit that off, but she nodded. "That makes sense, talking to Marcus. Since he and Thomas are that way."

He tipped up her chin, his eyes on hers. "You knew that? How did you know that?"

She colored a little, but was glad he was aware. She wasn't forced to choose between Thomas and Marcus's privacy and answering his question. "I clean their house, share meals with them. I'm around them...a lot, and I've noticed things."

Things that had clicked into place when she heard Julie discuss the structure of a Dom/sub relationship.

"They don't do things in front of you." He shot her an ominous look, which she was hasty to answer.

"No, of course not. It's just...it's there. Like finding something because you know where to look."

His eyes flickered, and he slid his fingers along her cheek, then down to her throat, her collarbone. As he stroked, the pressure of his fingers had her chin lifting, her breath shortening. He watched every reaction passing over her face, and his lips curved in a sensual way that sent butterflies through her lower belly. "Yeah. I can see that. You're always surprising me, you know that?"

Before she could answer, he kissed her again, in his wonderfully lingering way, his mouth playing over hers, stroking, caressing. She leaned into it, her own breath feathering out. He'd never kissed her with his hand still around her throat. As he increased the grip, a tiny noise came from her. He drew back, their eyes still so close. "You like that. I can tell. When I collar you with my hand. Hold you still in my palm."

She didn't have to speak, because he saw the answer. "We'll go to that party," he said. "It might give us other good ideas to explore."

He released her with a playful smile the right side of dangerous, but brought her back close to his side, letting her rest her head on his chest again. He slid his touch down to the curve of her hip, fingers stroking her buttock.

"Will it be lots of people?" she asked after another pause.

"Marcus said it'd be a few dozen couples, spread out on the grounds of this big plantation house." He squeezed her. "We're not going to do anything you don't want to do. If you're worried about how to tell me that, don't. I'll be paying attention, so I'll know what those things are, even if you don't tell me. I expect we'll mostly be watching. I'm learning about this stuff, too."

But images kept swirling in her head, strong ones. The chain around her wrist, the way Rory took her over...the bite of the hammock ropes against her legs. She wanted to go. She opened her mouth to say it, but nothing came out.

That was okay. He'd said they were going.

"So," he said, after another few minutes of gently rocking in the hammock, listening to the breeze and the birds. "That book you brought. How about you read it to me? Does it have pictures?"

She smiled. "It doesn't. But the words create some pretty powerful ones."

"Words will do that."

CHAPTER THIRTEEN

*H*is diligent care of the wound had done its job. The threat of a fever vanished, and by the time the day to leave for Florida came, the possibility that they'd have to cancel their trip had passed. The stitches had only recently been removed, meaning he'd still have to take extra care with the area, but he could handle that.

So here they were, Daralyn in the passenger seat of his van, on a sunny day perfect for traveling and adventure.

She'd brought books she could read to him, and snacks. They'd made a stop at the roadside stand of a Gullah basket weaver outside Charleston, because his mother had asked them to buy her a couple baskets. Then on to Georgia, where he pulled off at Huerta's, a produce place Mrs. Beatrice had recommended from her frequent trips to Florida to see her daughter.

The proprietors also operated the landscaping business next door, which included retail plant sales and a veritable field of lawn ornamentation. As Rory talked to Huerta, a fellow family businessman whose employees were his wife and adult kids, he watched Daralyn move through concrete statues of whimsical pigs and naked Grecian figures. When she discovered the fairy garden Huerta's wife had created among an arrangement of potted ferns, she squatted on her heels and studied it, a delighted smile on her face.

Her excitement about the trip, her pleasure now, had eased a concern inside him, raised by his mother and Thomas. They'd reminded him this was the first time Daralyn had traveled this far from home, since she'd come to live with them.

During the first couple hours on the road, he'd asked her about it. "Are you okay? You don't seem nervous."

"No." She smiled at him. "I'm with you."

When he saw Huerta watching him with a knowing grin on his face, he offered a wry smile and paid for the peaches he'd picked out.

"She's a pretty girl," Huerta said. "You're a fortunate man."

"In every way," Rory responded.

He guessed some men might get embarrassed about being so caught up in a woman, but he wouldn't be one of them. He'd be far more of an idiot for denying himself the pleasure of getting lost in her, the expressiveness of her face, the messages her body language sent. He was conscious of everything around her, too, from a crack in the pavement that could cause her to stumble, to each person who crossed her path. Dr. Taylor was right. He was protective, but he was conscious enough of it not to get carried away. Mostly.

He thought about what Will had said, about working on himself first, making sure he was someone worth being in a relationship with. Today he had even more reasons to be glad he had taken the steps that led to his comfort with this trip, being able to watch over Daralyn, help reinforce that she could count on him while she was with him.

On his first trip with the adaptive challenge group, Bud, a quadriplegic, had been driving the ten-passenger van. When he pulled up in front of the store, all the passengers had been carrying on like his football team going to an away game. They hung out the windows and hollered at him, as if Rory coming with them was the highlight of the trip.

Everyone on the bus had some kind of SCI. Not one of them had been scared or soaked with sweat over it, though, while he'd been both, enough he couldn't hide it.

But it had been okay. Instead of making a big deal of it, once they got him settled, they started talking to each other, recounting their first forays into independence, the missteps, embarrassments, the stuff that could happen. They joked about it the way he might have when he was way younger and doing the craziest shit on his dirt bike with his buddies, all of them trying to outdo one another on wipeouts and stunts.

Somewhere during that trip, he'd started to relax. Even more importantly, he'd started looking beyond merely coping to actually living again.

Being around the others had told him he didn't have to plow that road by himself, or even plow the road at all. Others, including the members of that group, had plowed, surfaced and paved it. They'd made the journey way smoother for him—and a lot less frightening and lonely. He loved his family more than anything, but they couldn't give him that. Which finally had him understanding why all those people in his court—family, friends, medical team— had pushed so hard for him to get involved with the disabled community.

Before he'd taken that step, he'd resisted, accused them of terrible stuff like not wanting him around, wanting to unload the burden that he'd become. The shame he often felt about his behavior back then made him wish he could think of some way to make it up to his family, even as he knew that him finally getting past that bullshit had been the best way to do it.

Eventually, he'd been confident enough to make a trip on his own. The group had been headed to West Virginia for a weekend of paddle boarding. He hadn't been able to get away from the store on the day they departed, but he could join them a day later. So with the van he'd acquired only a few months before, he'd driven himself up there on his own.

Yeah, he'd been scared, but with every mile that passed beneath the van's wheels, fear slipped away, replaced by sheer fucking joy. It was the first time since the accident he'd been away from home, on his own, without anyone to watch over him. The freedom of that was indescribable.

He loved being home, at the store, but since then, he took his travel times as a vital reaffirmation. He could be on his own and be okay.

He hoped this trip was giving Daralyn some of the same gifts. As he watched her pick up a tiny figurine, two hedgehogs on a seesaw, placed under a garden of colorful ceramic mushrooms, he wondered if she felt some of the same ebullience. She wasn't on her own, but she was traveling, seeing new things, and absolutely safe to spread her wings as far as she wanted. He'd make sure of it.

He asked Huerta how much the hedgehog and a half dozen of the mushrooms were, and paid for them. When she came back to him empty-handed and he told her to go back and get them, she'd bounded away like a deer.

"These will go over so well in the store," she said as they returned to the van, the figurines carefully wrapped and tucked into a store bag. "I bet people will snap them right up."

"They probably will," he agreed. "But those are yours."

"Oh, you didn't have to...I could have bought them with my money."

"Yeah, you could have. But I wanted to buy them for you. So hush up about it and get in the van."

His mock stern look made her smile and look away. Which meant after he held her door for her, he pushed himself closer, tugged her down by her ponytail to kiss her mouth. Her hazel eyes were bright.

"I'm having a really good day," she said impulsively.

"Me too." He gave her hair an additional tug and then closed the door.

Once they were back on the road, his phone rang. Seeing the name on the display, he shot Daralyn a smile and clicked the button on his steering wheel to answer. "Hey, Julie."

"Oh my God, I'm so excited." Her vivacious voice, her fast New York way of talking, filled every available space in the van in a heart-beat. He and Daralyn exchanged another twinkling look. "It's total fate, you know it is. What are the chances you guys would be in Florida at the same time Des and I are down here? Hey, there's a street festival tomorrow. Tyler says if we go first thing in the morning, about ten o'clock, it's not really crowded. We can wander around, then grab lunch. He also says there's a food truck that sells the best organic stuff you've ever tasted. Party's not until the evening, so there'll be plenty of time for you to recuperate."

She paused. "Are you still there?"

"Just waiting for you to run out of oxygen," Rory said. "No wonder Des is such a quiet guy."

She laughed. "On the things that matter, he's very good at making himself heard. I can't apologize for being excited. I am so jazzed about you two being there. Daralyn, is he behaving himself and being a good travel companion? Allowing bathroom breaks rather than making you hold it for the entire drive?"

"Yes," Daralyn responded, sending Rory a smile. "He's been wonderful. We bought baskets outside Charleston and just left a produce stand. He got me ice cream."

"Our Rory? The cranky guy? Are you sure? You must be traveling with someone else."

"I'm hanging up on you," Rory informed the caller. "I don't have to take this abuse in my own vehicle."

Julie laughed, then her tone became more serious. "Really, I'm tickled you two will be at the party. Will you be staying at one of Tyler's guesthouses?"

"He offered, but Brick has a fishing cottage down that way. Thought I'd do some fishing while I was there."

"Brick," Julie mused. "Isn't that your old high school teammate? The seriously built guy who helped you with the Christmas tree shipment last year, when he was visiting his mom? Ooh, the fireman?"

"He did help. I wouldn't call him built. Those muscles are all show." He glanced over to see Daralyn's smile. "What? You got something to say?"

The smile vanished, but the sparkle in her eyes remained. "No, Rory," she said solemnly.

"Yeah, right."

Julie laughed. "Don't let him bully you, Daralyn. Des is giving me the stink eye right now. The Powers That Be gave women eyes to notice these things. Not men, though. Our men are only supposed to have eyes for us. Oh, gotta go. My stage manager is calling, and I better see what the crisis is about. I'll shoot you the deets on the street fair and you can text me if you want to go. Love you both. Drive safe."

She clicked off, leaving Rory chuckling. "How many words did we get in there?"

Daralyn's smile returned, but her eyes were thoughtful.

"What?" he asked.

"She said 'our men.' It made me think of Amanda."

"What about her?"

"She's been a good friend to you. I didn't really realize that, until recently."

He wasn't sure where she was headed with the comment, but that appeared to be it. She subsided, returned to watching the passing scenery. At the next stop light, he re-captured her hand and rubbed a thumb over her palm, drawing her attention. "Daralyn?"

"Yes?"

"I am your man. A hundred percent."

Her hand tightened over his and she nodded, gazing down at it. He didn't say any more. Even though it was sometimes difficult to tell with her, she looked okay with that declaration, not troubled.

He'd learned to wait her out. Watching and listening often told him what she needed. Time. It was usually all that was needed to prove to her the words meant something real.

Brick had assured him the place was a cottage, not a stinky fishing shack only suitable for male friends wanting a weekend of beer swilling, fishing and peeing off the back porch.

"I have a property manager," he'd told Rory. "Preps it before I have guests or am coming myself. No ramps though, bro. I'll look into fixing that before your next visit."

"How many girls have you brought there? Do I need to hose the place down?"

"Naw. Property manager handles that, too. Probably has to wear a haz-mat suit, but..."

"Ass wipe."

The conversation had satisfied him that Daralyn would be comfortable there. As for the ramp, all he'd needed was a heads up. Rory had brought a portable aluminum one Brick had said would be long enough to ascend the three short steps to the porch. He'd told Rory not to hesitate to screw it to the boards if he wanted to do so.

The cottage was as Brick had described it, a smallish place with neat blue wood siding, a tin roof and wraparound porch. There were a couple flower boxes in front. Sago palms and a scattering of begonias populated the natural areas clustered around the base of mature palm trees. The place looked welcoming to a woman, but not too fussy for a man with Brick's tastes.

The marsh area out back was at high tide, the sun starting to set, creating a mellow gold and silver sky, reflected in the water. After he and Daralyn put their few items inside, they sat on the back screened porch and watched the sun crack on the horizon. She moved her chair closer to him so he could put an arm around her. With her leaning against him, he couldn't help but think what it would be like to have this experience forever, the two of them in their own home. Being a family.

The only shadow on that thought came from his recollection of the brief call he'd made to Dr. Taylor, after the hammock afternoon. He'd learned the truth about Daralyn's statement about children.

"Childhood stress and trauma, particularly chronic sexual abuse, can have a very strong impact on fertility," the doctor had told him. "And as we discussed, there were times her uncle wasn't as restrained as her father was. Daralyn has some physical damage to the reproductive system that may have been from that."

She'd paused. "As far as adoption, until she demonstrates a far higher degree of socialization than she currently does, she wouldn't be approved as a prospective parent, even with my recommendation, which I would certainly give when I feel she's ready for that step. Now, if she marries someone who meets their requirements, that could help things. But..."

He'd smoothly filled in the blank. "I'm paralyzed, and whether or not they'll admit it, the two sets of factors added together wouldn't put us at the top of the list."

Even a healthy paraplegic who took care of himself knew the biases, which unfortunately were fed by the facts associated with the passage of time. He'd likely need a power chair at some point, because he'd have degeneration in his shoulder joints. He could also develop complications related to the simple fact the internal organs and systems were not designed for a human to spend his life sitting on his ass.

All of which were potential risks, not certain ones, and even if they happened, they could be managed. He was just as capable of being a parent as anyone else. He'd just have to educate the right people and agencies when and if the time came.

"It's a surmountable obstacle," he said. "And it's not anything we're looking at right this minute."

"Of course," she said. "I just want you to be prepared, if it comes to that. But Rory, when and if it happens, you can count on me to be in your corner and Daralyn's."

That was good to know. Because he loved what his parents had, what they'd built. He wanted it, too. And it was more on his radar than he'd admit to anyone except himself.

"I love it here." Daralyn put her head on his shoulder, her hand inside the grip of his. "It's so peaceful."

"Yeah." He put his head down on hers. "I'm in love with you. You know that, right?"

He hadn't meant to say it straight out like that. Hell, not so long ago, he'd reminded her she had the right to make choices about being with him. She had enough trouble with that idea without him throwing out something like him being in love with her. But his heart was so full, with her here like this, with everything that had happened with them so far, he had to say it. He didn't know how not to say it.

She'd gone really still, and she gripped his hand with both of hers. "I feel like you're inside me all the time," she said softly. "Helping me breathe, and smile, and see the world the way you do. Bravely."

It was so unexpected, he went as still as she did. Then she moved. She slid off her chair, moving down beside his feet, leaning against his leg. She'd kept hold of his hand, and now laid her head against his knee. "And right here," she said. "I can't explain it, but this is where I feel the most at peace."

He stroked her hair, wound her ponytail around his knuckles, let his fingertips graze her cheek. "Me, too," he said.

They met Julie and Des at the festival the next morning. Julie's suggestion of arriving early served a couple purposes. It was easier navigation for him, and she also knew about Daralyn's problem with crowds.

Since Daralyn had become more comfortable attending her classes, Rory anticipated her handling it better than Julie probably expected. Daralyn had looked a little nervous on the way over, but it had been balanced with an eagerness about the festival that would have been notably absent just a short time ago.

Julie was a curvy forty-something with endless energy and a creative mind that never stopped working. The combination had made her a successful community theater manager in the Big Apple, and with the erotic theater she now operated outside the Charlotte city limits. Her decision to accept her friend Madison's invitation to get that theater running had brought Desmond Hayes across her path.

Though a roofer by trade, Des looked like the roadie for a successful Southern rock band, with long brown hair, a body lean as beef jerky and roped with wiry muscle. He had a quietness to him that steadied Julie's more erratic moments, whereas she brought out his dry humor.

She and Des were waiting for them at the park entrance, and when she spotted them coming toward them, she bounced forward and engulfed Daralyn in a hug. A pivot on her toe and she'd squeezed Rory in a bosom-suffusing embrace, not a bad thing, since Julie was nicely endowed.

Not that he had any thoughts about her like that, but great breasts were great breasts, and always deserved to be acknowledged.

From the glint in Des's eyes after she let him go, Rory suspected the thought reflected in his eyes, but Des knew Rory saw Julie only as family. A guy in love couldn't help the surge of possessiveness, though. Rory knew that himself, watching the way Des's long, strong fingers molded over Daralyn's hip and back when they exchanged a hug.

It was a natural thing in their family, everyone greeting one another with a hug, but Rory noted that Daralyn was more shy about it with Des. Just like with Rory and Marcus, her gaze skittered away from a direct meet of his. She apparently picked up on the Dom vibe subconsciously, like animal instinct.

He was picking up the cues himself, the Dom/sub body language between Des and Julie. Once one knew where to look, it was clear. It was in the way Des touched Julie and how she immediately looked to him, plus Rory's awareness of a hard-to-explain feeling about the energy between them. Rory wondered if it was as pronounced between him and Daralyn. If it was, he liked the idea.

"You have to see the potter's booth we found," Julie was telling Daralyn. "He has some gorgeous pieces. Des is thinking about buying one for Elaine for her birthday. Come see what you think. He also makes these little animals out of bits of leftover clay, and they are so cute. Far more affordable, too. I thought you might want one or two for your window ledge in the kitchen."

Julie clasped Daralyn's hand and was pulling her forward. Daralyn looked back at him, checking, and Rory gave her a nod. Her face brightened and she joined Julie in trotting ahead.

Des slid his hands into the pockets of his well-worn jeans as he ambled beside Rory. They checked out a booth selling pocketknives, Des picking up a couple to examine them. Rory offered his opinion before they nodded to the vendor and continued the companionable stroll.

Not surprising, the girls had stopped at a jewelry booth instead of making a straight line for the potter. Rory watched Julie hold a cuff to Daralyn's ear, brushing her hair back onto her shoulder. The cuff looked like a delicate vine with blooming flowers that sparkled in the morning light along the curve of her ear. When Daralyn glanced his way, he nodded. He liked it. Pretty and sexy. Like his girl.

"Happy to answer anything on your mind, if you have questions about the party tonight."

Rory glanced at Des. He must have been logging the byplay between him and Daralyn, same as Rory had between him and Julie. Well, he wasn't going to say no to the offer. He trusted Marcus, but a second opinion never hurt.

"Have you ever been to one?"

"Plenty. I've done rope demo all over the country."

After learning Des was a "rope artist," Rory had looked up some of that. He'd thought about it even more after threading Daralyn's legs through the hammock ropes and seeing the light impressions of the hemp on her limbs afterward.

"Marcus said you're doing one at the party tonight," Rory ventured.

Des nodded. "It's kind of like that in the BDSM community. We're there as guests, but if my skills help others, or if it adds to the atmosphere, I'm always open to doing a demo to pay my way." Des slanted him a grin. "And don't worry. Tyler's old money, richer than Lucifer, but he isn't stuck up and he doesn't suffer assholes."

"Good to know. What can I do to make sure she feels good there?"

Des gave him an approving look. "Best first question ever. You're going to be fine."

As they discussed some of the finer points of what Rory could expect at the party, as well as some deeper questions, he found Des was as good as Marcus at breaking it down, making him feel like there were no stupid questions.

While they talked, he was pleased to see that, except for quick glances to make sure she knew where Rory was, Daralyn seemed more comfortable among the flow of people than he'd ever seen her. Even when people pressed closer in the small space under the vendor tents.

When Julie swung back to tell Des the price of the piece he was considering for Elaine, she confirmed it. "I can't believe it," she said. "What a difference. Last time Les and I took her shopping, back several months ago, she was better—she's always improving—but she was still sticking right with us."

"Going to school has helped a lot," Rory said. "And I think she's been getting more comfortable ever since she started helping in the store."

"No question. But Les said you helped make the school thing finally happen. Just look at her," Julie said. "It's you, Rory."

Rory glanced toward Daralyn as she laughed at something one of the vendors said. She was so enchanting, he expected she'd be offered the biggest discounts anyone else would see today. The store suppliers were always cutting her breaks when she called in orders. Breaks even Jesus couldn't get from those guys.

She looked his way again, smiled. His hand curled over his push rim. He was glad to see her comfort level, glad he had helped with it. But the openness of his conversation with Des prompted his next question.

"Do you think she's too dependent on me?"

Julie sent him a surprised look. "No way. You're helping her to be more *independent*." She gave him a feline smile. "Besides, from what I can tell, she's not orbiting around you. You're orbiting around her."

He sighed, tapped the wheel. "No question, but still. You know what I mean."

"I do. Rory, she has your family. She has all of you. She always will. You know it."

Maybe he'd stop worrying if his own feelings weren't so strong. When it came to her, his every heartbeat pounded out one word.

Mine, mine, mine.

Des slid a hand around Julie's waist, then moved it up her back, fondling her neck beneath her thick tail of hair. The familiar gesture had her leaning against him, looking up into his face. A quietness gripped her that was rare for Julie, a peacefulness that increased as Des brushed a kiss over her forehead. She closed her eyes, pressing her face against his tanned throat as he looked toward Rory.

"Having a woman belong to you, one who wants to belong to a Master, can be the best thing for her," Des said quietly. "Every Dom worth his salt knows that. And questions himself constantly to make sure he's looking out for her best interests. Not that he lets her see that," he added, sending a twinkling look to Julie, who opened her eyes and smiled at him. "Can't have our women knowing we ever doubt our absolute rule of law over them."

"Yeah, right." She punched him playfully in the side. "I know just when to call you Sir Asshole. Sir."

She was teasing him, but when he grasped her fist and raised it to his lips, spreading out her fingers before he kissed her palm, that last *Sir* came out a little less taunting. A lot more breathless.

Then her gaze cleared as she noted a festival schedule displayed on a sandwich board sign. "Ooh, there's a music performance at the top of the hour, over at the pavilion. Let's go check it out. We can come back to the booths."

Julie hurried forward to collect Daralyn and then waved imperiously at them to follow her toward the pavilion. Des shot Rory an amused look. "Are you familiar with the term power sub?"

Rory chuckled. "Only recently, but after I learned it, imagining Julie as a submissive was a lot easier."

As they willingly followed the two women, Rory saw the seating under the large tent was a semi-circle of benches, on a slope so those in back could see as well as those in the front. Though things weren't crowded yet, there were festival workers wandering through the gathering audience, handing out programs.

"Des, why don't we go grab a couple drinks?" Julie said. "They have an acai lemonade that Daralyn and I want to try. Rory, you want a beer?"

"Yeah, if they've got Bud Lite."

Des gave him a thumbs up and he and Julie headed for the food vendors. Daralyn returned to Rory's side, resting her hand on his shoulder. When he glanced up at her, he saw she was wearing the ear cuff. He reached up and traced it, making her smile, lower her eyes in the way that inspired him to kiss her senseless.

Before he could do that, one of the festival workers, a middle-aged guy with thinning hair and an amiable expression, approached. "Sir, there's a great spot for people in wheelchairs down in front," he said. He stuffed the programs back into a sling around his front. "I'll show it to you."

"That's all right. I'll—"

The man had already stepped forward, put his hands on the bar on the back of Rory's chair. With a friendly nod to Daralyn, he started to push Rory briskly in that direction. "I'll just get you there. You'll—"

He about pitched over Rory's shoulder as Rory engaged the brake and the chair skidded.

It had been a kneejerk reaction, and not a good one, since the collision between opposing forces on a slope toward the stage tipped him forward. The guy jerked back, still holding onto the back bar, which kept the chair upright, but that wasn't the problem. Rory was almost thrown out of the seat, though a death grip on his push rims and locking his upper body, no matter the pain that speared through his lower back, kept him in it.

But as non-ideal as ending up on the ground would have been, Rory preferred it to the alternative.

He hit the brake release and spun the chair around to face the guy head on. "Do *not* touch my chair," he said.

Though he was trying to keep his voice even, the man's startled look said he'd conveyed cold and pissed.

"We're just trying to keep things moving along," the man said in a placating voice. "Keeping the aisle clear. I was trying to help—"

"You can help by listening, and without putting your hands on me," Rory said.

Daralyn's eyes were wide, and she looked uncertain of the situation. His heart was hammering up in his ears, and he told himself to stay calm.

Something like this brought back those times when he'd been all but helpless. He'd projected that so obviously that often no one thought to ask if something was okay with him before they did it.

He wasn't helpless anymore, and goddamn it, no matter what condition he was in, it pissed him off when people assumed this shit was okay. He was here with a woman, with friends.

"I..." The man's color was high, and he was about to commit the mistake of being resentful, which could turn this ugly, unless Rory could call back the temper spiking hard in his chest.

But Daralyn was here, and fortunately Des's words were fresh in his mind. Her well-being was the most important thing. Then Daralyn herself reminded him of it, in the best way possible.

"Where would you like me to sit, Rory?" She drew close to his side again, and rested her hand on his shoulder, fingers curling into the cotton of his shirt.

Yeah, the volatility of the situation unsettled her, but not as much as he'd expected. She didn't acknowledge the man. Her gaze and attention were on Rory, waiting for his lead. That sole focus calmed him just the way it needed to do.

She moved with him, hand still on his shoulder, as he guided her to the back row. He settled her on the aluminum bench and then moved his chair behind her, where he could see and not block the aisle. It would also allow him easy egress if they decided not to stay for the whole concert.

The guy had trailed after them. A glance told Rory he was waffling on whether he'd been dismissed, or if he needed to offer a stiff apology. He also looked like he was warring with ill feeling at being treated like the bad guy. Rory quelled the urge to tell him to *fuck off* by considering the next person in a chair who might cross his path. He sighed and made eye contact with the guy, drawing him closer.

"It's like being in a car," Rory said. "You don't take the wheel unless the driver invites you to do it. Sorry I got pissed, but if I need help, I'll tell you. Same as any person who walked in here on two legs. Make sense?"

He made sure to show the man he was willing to be okay with it if he was. And added to it by extending a hand. "I'm Rory."

The volunteer studied him, then gave a short nod, shook the hand. "Milton. Apologies, sir."

"Accepted. Thanks for being willing to help."

As Milton moved away, Daralyn remained quiet. She had her hands curled on the edge of the bleacher and was leaning forward, her spine straight as a hypotenuse.

When she straightened, he put a hand on her shoulder. She touched her chin to it, a quick nuzzle. He held that position, steadying himself.

"People make decisions for me a lot," she said. Her tone was neutral. "I understand why it bothers you so much."

He realized, like him, she had to find the balance between accepting people's help, asking for it when it was needed, and helping them understand when it wasn't. It was an ongoing thing. Plus she had the added challenge of not being able to clearly express it as a want or desire.

She had her head tilted, him in her peripheral vision as he stroked her cheek, the decorated curve of her ear. He let his hand come to a rest on the back of her neck, stroking under the neckline of the knit shirt she was wearing. A little sigh lifted and lowered her shoulders.

"But you..." she said quietly. "When you do it...it always feels right to me."

He understood why Dr. Taylor needed to work with Daralyn about expressing her wants and needs. But for someone paying close enough attention—someone to whom her wants and needs mattered more than anything—her desires were as obvious as if she'd shouted them out loud, let them echo through the universe.

The way they echoed through his heart.

CHAPTER FOURTEEN

ulie and Des had to be at Tyler's early, so when they parted at the festival, they told Rory they'd meet them there. Rory and Daralyn returned to the fishing cottage.

Daralyn set herself up on the cushioned porch swing, reading a book. Rory checked out a couple of Brick's fishing magazines and put his gear in order so he could look forward to a day of casting off the dock tomorrow. A tin roof shelter built over the end of it provided shade, with another wooden swing hanging from the rafters. With those features in place, he expected Daralyn would be comfortable hanging out with him by the water, doing some more reading.

The girl never seemed to tire of books. The first time Les had taken Daralyn with her to the town library, his sister had come home with a look on her face Rory had never forgotten. It was the kind of look a person had when they realized how different someone else's life could be from their own.

"I wasn't sure I was going to get her out before closing time," Les had told Elaine, after Daralyn went up to her room, carrying one book against her chest. "She just walked up and down the rows, trailing her fingers along the spines. When I told her she could check books out, take them home, bring them back and get more, that that's the way libraries worked…"

Les's eyes had welled with tears, and she'd broken down, cried. Elaine had wept with her. Even Rory had felt a lump in his throat. It was probably a good thing Daralyn had missed that part, because at that point in their relationship with her, seeing Rory's mom and sister crying might have freaked her out.

When his sister finally found her voice, she added, "That saying, about one small effort on my part might change someone's life in a far bigger way? I saw that in her face, Mom. It was like I'd given her Heaven, and all I did was help her get a library card."

When Rory shifted his gaze to the person filling his mind, a light smile touched his lips. Between a full week of work, school, and then yesterday's drive, followed by this morning's festival, it wasn't surprising to see Daralyn had nodded off on the swing.

Since it was likely to be a late night, he probably should talk himself into a nap, too. But having her here all to himself, total privacy and no interruptions from family or the store, his mind went another way.

He pushed over to her and removed the book from her limp hands before it fell to the boards. As she opened her eyes and blinked sleepily at him, the trust in her face stirred him.

"Take off all your clothes," he said. "I want you to take a nap that way."

A woven throw was spread over her legs. Despite it being a comfortable fall afternoon in Florida, she'd needed it for the breeze off the marsh. The girl had zero body fat. In a few minutes, he'd retrieve the quilt folded over the couch to replace the throw, to ensure she stayed warm. But first he waited for her to follow his command.

She rose, standing before him as she removed her clothes. Her dark lashes fanned her cheeks in that tempting gesture of submission. When she stood before him in nothing, he molded a hand over her hip, thumb stroking the soft area of her belly near her navel. He watched her sway into his touch as he lifted that touch to her breast, caressed the side of it with his knuckles. Her nipple changed shape, a call for attention. She was his to play with for hours, do so many things to give her pleasure. The flush in her cheeks, the tense curl of her fingers, the erratic sound of her breath, only made him more interested in the idea.

"I have a question for you, Daralyn," he said. "And there's only one answer to it. It's one syllable, starts with a y and ends with an s."

Her lips curved and he smiled, too, though if she'd looked up, he knew his eyes would have been dead serious. "Anything else and you'll be in trouble. Understand me?"

"Yes."

"Do you please me?"

"Yes."

"Better than any woman ever has?"

"Yes."

"Good," he said. "Lie back down and sleep. I'll wake you when it's time to get ready."

The furtive look from beneath her lashes pleased him even more. It suggested she wasn't entirely happy that he wasn't going to pursue more. He wanted her desire to build, wanted her anticipation to grow stronger. He was figuring that would be the best way to keep any worries she might have about tonight from taking the upper hand.

She was lying back down on the porch swing. As she adjusted, he went into the house and brought the quilt out, tucking it over her. Her gaze was on him as he put himself to the right of the swing, at an angle so he was gazing down on her head and one bared shoulder, the fingers curled up under her chin.

He rested his hand on the chains holding the swing and began moving it in a slow rock while he started looking through another fishing magazine. He didn't read much, mostly listening to her breathing and watching her profile. He didn't need anything more than that to occupy him. His woman was naked at his command, lying under a blanket he'd tucked around her, and she slept because she trusted him to watch over her.

When his gaze slid to the chains holding the chair up, his mind went back to those rope sites he'd visited, attractive submissives bound in elaborate designs.

What was in his mind was a little more straightforward, but no less appealing. Brick had several coils of rope in his boat shed. Rory imagined Daralyn sitting in the center of the swing, her arms tied and stretched out to either side of her, the ropes bound to the chains holding the swing off the ground. Another loop of rope could be hooked around each knee and attached to the arms of the swing, keeping her legs spread open.

He imagined positioning himself square with the swing, but a few feet back, using something like the broom in the kitchen to push the chair, keep it moving in a steady slow rock rhythm like he was doing now. All while he kept her on display for him alone, naked and beautiful. He'd ask her to look at him with her hazel eyes, watch them grow needy and desperate with desire. He'd watch the dampness of her cunt turn into a glistening temptation to his mouth and fingers.

In his head, that was how she'd respond to that, but how about in reality? Maybe he shouldn't have looked at so much of that stuff. It had put ideas in his head far beyond the simple liking of how she followed his orders and wanted to kneel at his feet. But since that seemed to arouse her deeply, it couldn't help but make him wonder how much further they could take it.

Well, that was one of the reasons they'd talked about going to the party tonight, right? He just didn't want to set off any bad memories. Her father and uncle might have forced her to walk around naked, but she hadn't reacted badly to Rory's command to remove her clothes, now or in the past. Each time, he'd gone slow, gauged her reaction, and seen nothing but a willingness to follow his direction, reinforced by physical desire.

Trust the gut but take it slow. So far it had proven itself a workable strategy. Because she trusted him. A gift he had no intention of losing.

He had his phone in his shirt pocket. Though he didn't have to stay religiously on call with the store, during operating hours he liked to keep a weather eye on it. It was always possible a customer might come in for an order with special instructions, and Johnny, Amanda or his mom wouldn't know the details. However, he kept the system pretty up to date.

He smiled, remembering when Les and Thomas had talked them into automating. He'd grumbled about it and his mom had fussed about losing her notebook full of scribbled notes and paper files. Now he knew just how much time the computer saved them. Even Mom routinely talked about how nice it was to not have the back room full of file cabinets, and how much quicker it made tax preparation. She might not be tech savvy, but she had a great head for business.

As if thinking about it had summoned a call, the phone began to vibrate. He bit back a sigh, hoping it was a telemarketer he could ignore.

It wasn't, but the name on the display was a welcome one.

He went into the house as he answered, pitching his voice low until he was in the kitchen. From here, he could still see Daralyn through the window. "Hey, man, this place is a real dump," he said by way of a greeting. "Can't believe it hasn't been bull-dozed."

Brick chuckled. His deep, gravelly voice could make Vin Diesel sound like he was snorting helium. In high school, his nickname had been Deep Throat, though that had also been because of how hard he hammered the opposing team. He'd been a formidable middle line-backer to Johnny's strong side position.

"You must have taken a wrong turn and ended up back in our locker room," Brick retorted. Which really had been a dump. It hadn't been renovated since the fifties. They could have drip irrigated a field with the holes in the roof.

"Seriously, man, this is nice," Rory told him. "Daralyn loves it. I meant to text you. Sorry I made you have to check in on us."

"Naw, that's not why I'm calling. You know our high school reunion is coming up. First one for our class."

"Yeah. I got the invite."

He was going, he wasn't chickenshit, but he had mixed feelings about it. His local high school friends knew he'd ended up in a chair, but those who'd headed off to college or other places, that was another story.

"The first part of the night they're going to have an awards cere-mony for those graduates who've done things worth mentioning."

"Like Sammy Jo giving up weed and settling down to become a married accountant? That should have hit the front page." Feeling the stirrings of hunger, Rory decided to make a sandwich. Maybe he could get Daralyn to eat one when she woke. As he laid out the bread and cold cuts they'd bought at the nearby grocery, he heard Brick chuckle again.

"No lie. Wonder if she ever had that marijuana leaf tattoo removed from her ass? Anyway, you're on the award list."

"Say what?" Rory stopped spreading mayo on the wheat bread. "Right. Good one."

"Serious, man." Brick sobered, sounding like the adult they somehow miraculously both were now. "You've done more than your share to help the local economy, keeping a respect for the small-town feel while helping people feed their families. It's been noticed."

Rory frowned. "This sounds like some guy-in-a-wheelchair dick stroke. I didn't do that on my own, Brick. This is my parents' store. My mom and dad, Thomas, Daralyn, they have every bit as much to do with the store's success as I do."

"No question, but you've become the guy in charge. The nominating committee already talked to your mom and Thomas, and they both agree. You not only took over that role, you did it when you could have sat on your ass—literally. The store's become an economic anchor for our hometown, and the increased outreach to the community you've driven has made that happen."

Rory shifted. He wasn't comfortable with this. "You know, there's this guy I see at PT every once in a while, Manfred Jones. He lives over in Rockingham. He ended up in a chair a decade ago because he was in a gang and got shot in the back. No family, no health insurance beyond Medicaid, and he's still managed to become a small business owner in his neighborhood, and a big volunteer at a local rec center, trying to keep kids from following in his footsteps."

"The city of Rockingham should give him an award."

"Yeah. He deserves it. Not some guy who had every bit of family support to help him get where he was now."

Brick sighed. "I get what you're saying, man. But there's no reason you can't accept the award on behalf of your family."

Rory put the sandwich together, tapped the case knife on the counter. "Fran Potts is heading up the reunion committee. Why isn't she calling me about this?"

"Because she knew you wouldn't accept it unless a friend leaned on you."

Rory shook his head, ran a hand over his face. "I'm not trying to be a dick. Really."

"I know that." Brick's voice registered understanding. "Seriously, think about it. I do think this would mean a whole lot to your family. Particularly your mom. But you really do deserve this award, as much as any member of your family. You ended up being a lot tougher than I would have expected, often as I had to keep your skinny ass from getting sacked."

"My speed kept me from getting sacked. You were slower than a lumbering bear out there."

Not true, of course. Brick had been a hell of a player. "I don't know, man." Rory cleared his throat. "I'm going to have to think about it. I have time, right?"

"Some. They'll get the final program printed and up on the website in a couple weeks. Oh and hey, I shouldn't tell you this, because it will surefire make you turn it down, but Hayworth said if they give it to you, he might make the trip."

"No shit." Rory smiled, but it came with a spurt of regret. "How's he doing?"

"Eh. You know him." Brick paused. "He gets on the wagon a while, then falls off. He's hanging on to that car salesman job by the skin of his teeth. Last time I saw him, he'd gotten into coke, too. I want to bash his fucking brains in. Being up in Raleigh isn't helping him. The only friends he hangs with are ones with habits as bad or worse than his. If he means it, about coming to see you accept this award, it'll be the first time he's been home to the family farm since he got kicked off the team at State. Might do him some good. Maybe we can chain him in the barn for a couple years and detox him."

Rory snorted. "Yeah."

They didn't say anything for a moment, the silence expressing their combined frustration. "Well, we'll see," Brick said at last. "Talk to your mom and brother, get their sense on it, before you reject it outright. I for one would be proud as hell to see you accept it."

Rory gave a half-laugh. "You're just kissing up to me because you like my sister."

"Has the fiancé boyfriend stayed good and gone?"

"He has. Ever since she told him she wanted to graduate before she got married and he asked for his ring back."

"Douchebag. I'll shed tears over it."

"I'm sure. Stay away from my sister, you perv."

"Make me, Wheels."

"I'll cut off your dick, and you won't have any thoughts about girls ever again."

Brick chuckled. "Have to cut off the big lump above my shoulders and carve out my heart for that, my man. The way I feel about Les is about way more than my dick."

Rory understood that, for sure. "Then one of these days you should tell her."

"Let her get that medical degree first, put the doctor plaque on her door, then I'll make my move. Be the kept man of a rich doctor."

"Yeah, yeah. Wait too long and she'll be in Africa somewhere, working out of a tent, thousands of miles away from you. She'll have fallen for some bearded mission doctor who wears Birkenstocks."

"Best place to make my play. Well beyond the reach of her protective brothers."

"It's not us you're scared of. It's my mother."

"Can you blame me?"

"Not a bit."

A few more seconds of back and forth, and then they ended the call. Rory sat for a couple contemplative moments, looking at the counter without seeing the sandwich resting there.

Would they have offered the award to him if he wasn't disabled? That apprehension would dog him, make him reluctant to accept it at face value. Yet another part of himself he wanted to despise remembered being on the team, getting congratulated for the wins. The cheers of the students, the energy of the pep rallies, being at the center of that...

"What do you think?" he asked.

He turned the chair in her direction. Daralyn was standing in the doorway, barefoot, shoulders exposed by the loose hold of the quilt she had gathered around her. The corners trailed the ground around her ankles. The triangle of skin across her sternum was a deeper golden color, thanks to the V-neck shirts she most often wore. Her hair was down, tousled around her delicate features.

"I think it's wonderful," she said.

"Do you think they're giving it to me because I'm in a wheelchair?"

"Yes," she said simply, surprising him. "Because you didn't let it stop you from being who you wanted to be."

"It changed who I wanted to be."

"Is that person better than who you used to want to be?"

He cut the sandwich in half and brought it to the table, nodding to one of the chairs so she'd join him. "It's difficult for me to be cranky about it if you're going to be sensible, ask the right questions."

A small smile. She slipped into the chair and studied the sandwich.

He pulled a peach out of the Huerta's bag on the table, and cut it up with his pocketknife. As she watched, he put a few slices on her plate. Picking up one, she cradled it in her palm and inhaled it. She liked smelling her food before she ate it, as if she was drawing nourishment just from that. But her gaze went to him, noted his attention lingering on her bare shoulders. She was still holding the throw clutched around her, one hand in front of her breasts.

Slowly, she straightened her back, loosened her grip so the blanket slid away, pooled around her hips. Her chin was up. She knew he wanted to look, and she'd responded to his desires without him saying a word.

"Christ, you floor me," he said, low. "And you have such perfect breasts."

She pinkened like the softer colors of the peach. Picking up a slice, he brushed it over her nipple. It stiffened as he squeezed the fruit, made the juice drip over it. Then he used it like a brush, painting her skin with the peach's flesh.

Her head was tilted down so she could watch what he was doing. Then he murmured again.

"Chin up and eyes forward."

When she complied, he put a palm on the table, leaned in and put his mouth on the curve of her breast, tasted the juice on her skin. A trembling hand touched the back of his neck, fingers sliding up into his hair. She moved against him as he captured her nipple and started to suckle. Her soft moan gave him a jolt of pleasure, as did the tightening of her fingers, the caress of them against his nape.

When at last he drew back, he looked down the slope of her abdomen to her thighs. He gripped the blanket, pulled it away. As he did, her thighs shifted, parting.

He brought his attention back to her face, finding her mouth soft and eyes uncertain but needy. He dropped his hand down, let his knuckles brush her clit, once, twice, play over the petals of her cunt. She swallowed noisily, and he liked the way it showed him the moistness of her mouth.

Slowly, he took his hand away, sat back. "Eat," he said.

That same subtle look of dissatisfaction, and this time he answered it, reaching out and tapping her chin, drawing her gaze to his direct one. "Yeah, I'm denying you. Keeping you excited, a little on edge. I want your mind centered on what I want from you, instead of caught up in things you don't need to worry about. Okay?"

"Yes, sir. I mean, Rory."

He gave her an unsmiling look. "Sir works when you feel it."

He loved when her pupils got large, expressing her wonder at what was going on in her body, in her responses to what he was doing to her. "I...what should I wear tonight, sir?"

"Did you bring something specific for the party?"

"I did, but I wasn't sure. There was something Les and Julie bought with me a long time ago. I've never worn it. Would you like to see it?"

Rory shook his head. "Not until you're wearing it." He gave her a heated smile. "Surprise me. And stay just like that while we eat. It increases my appetite."

~

She'd been in the bathroom for about a half hour after her shower. He'd knocked and checked on her at least once, and she'd hesitantly indicated she was fine, it was just taking a little while. In her voice, he didn't hear any of the usual alarm flags, particularly that strained note that told him she was getting into crisis mode. But he did wonder what the hold-up was.

He'd chosen black jeans and a blue dress shirt, sleeves rolled up and open at the throat. He'd belted the jeans with a new black belt, and wore his black cowboy boots under the denim. It was dressy enough for a party at a fancy house, but would leave him more comfortable than a suit for whatever the night would hold.

When the doorknob turned on the bathroom, he wasn't sure what to expect. If Les and Julie had helped her pick it out, then he expected it to be pretty, classy. When she stepped out, it was both those things. But it was also something that took his breath away, because of what he'd said—she was wearing it.

He'd dated cheerleaders and girls who liked looking hot. Not trashy, but a short skirt and a snug top showing off a fine figure looked damn good on them.

This was...he couldn't explain why her outfit struck him as so incredibly sexy. It was more than her looking beautiful, fuckable. It was because of what the dress said about the woman wearing it.

The deep wine color enhanced the rich shade of her shiny brown hair, which she'd curled and clipped back with a long flat barrette. The bodice of the dress was silky, with an embroidered pattern like feathers. It fit her upper body perfectly, molding the sweet lines of her small breasts, the nip of her waist. The skirt flowed over her hips and fell to mid-calf, the fabric so light it swirled around her legs and hips as she moved.

A wide sash outlined her waist, a bow embellishing the hip. Overlapped cap-like short sleeves showed the bare lengths of her graceful arms. The dress's sculpted neckline wasn't low, but it did expose her collar bones and a wide crescent of skin beneath. She wore a silver necklace with a tiny wine-colored rose as the pendant. Wisps of hair curled around her brow and forehead, framing her face.

She'd put on makeup. Lightly, thickening the already thick lashes and making her luminous hazel eyes capable of piercing a man to the bone when she lifted them to look at him. Her lips were a delicate pink that picked up the wine color of the dress.

He'd rarely seen her in anything but sneakers or flat sandals. The silver strappy shoes she wore were wedges, a couple inches high. He motioned and she did a slow full turn for him, so he viewed the contours of her waist from the back, the outline of her shoulder blades against the thin fabric. The skirt flowed like water, highlighting the flare of her hips, giving him glimpses of shapely calves and ankles. She wore filmy silver-gray stockings.

Her underwear might be her usual practical cottons, but if Julie and Les had bought her something to coordinate with the dress, he might owe them a fervent thank you. He'd let himself find out later. Right now, he wanted to tell her in a million different ways how damn humbled and amazed he was to be her escort. Yet babbling like that at a woman wouldn't really reassure her that he was a Dominant in control of his own emotions, as well as her well-being.

So he held out an astoundingly steady hand. Everything in him tightened up at the way she immediately came to him. He kissed her knuckles, found her hand cold. Just like that, his uncertainty melted away, as it often did when he could focus on making sure she was okay, rather than his own confidence, or lack thereof.

"You are beautiful," he told her. "The most beautiful woman I've ever seen."

Now she flushed and her lips parted, but he cut across her. "Think carefully before you tell me I'm wrong. I'm dying to know what you've got on under that dress, and a good spanking would answer that. Plus make us late."

She pressed her lips together, her hazel eyes flashing with a mix of emotions. He squeezed her hand. "Let's go."

The sun was setting, offering some pretty scenery as he drove them out of their rural location to the main highway. It would connect them to another lush area of marshlands and maritime forest outside the city. Tyler's place was more northwest of Tampa.

She was quiet on the drive, and he didn't talk a lot either, staying closely attuned to her body language. Some tension, her hands curled in her lap. Fingers twitching. Back straight. He noted each time she swallowed, the movements of her lips.

It was that which finally clued him into what was going on. It punched him hard in the center of his own desires for her. So far, he'd seen it at this level only when they were fully into a moment intended for that, like in the hammock or in her room.

She was really aroused.

He'd gotten her hot and bothered at the kitchen table and deliberately left her that way. Then she'd fixed herself up in an outfit intended to be attractive, to appeal to him. They were both hyperaware they were headed for a party attended solely by Dominants and submissives.

And she would be at the party as his.

When Rory saw a pull off with a good view over the marshes, he took it, putting the van in park. He unlocked the driver's seat so he could turn it toward her, which put him closer, his knee brushing the side of her leg.

"Look at me, Daralyn," he said.

She did. The sun was fast disappearing over the horizon, making her pupils even darker, her face shadowed, but he could see the tense set of her glossy lips. When he extended his hand, she laid hers in it. He rested their clasped hands on her thigh, and locked gazes with her.

"Put my hand where you know I want it to be," he said.

Where he knew *she* wanted it to be.

The changes in her expression, in her body, all of her responses when he used that tone, were enough to make him want to do nothing more than keep her naked in his bed. She was staring at him with such raw hunger and unvoiced need. A hard shiver ran through her, particularly her thighs.

She adjusted their grips so that she was holding his wrist, but he saw the struggle in her. Some snarl of emotions was hampering her. He refused to let her past tamper with her reaction, dilute the truth of it, derail her. Not tonight.

"Don't make me tell you twice," he said, low. "You better be dripping wet for me, because you know that's what I want. If you're not, I'll be making sure that I fix that, right here and now."

She was barely breathing, and he put his free hand on her face. "Do it," he breathed, and there was literally nothing in the universe but the two of them.

Slowly, she guided his hand under the flowing skirt, her thighs parting for him. He felt the brush of the lace tops of her stockings. When she brought his fingers to her sex, her labia were swollen into a plump cushion against the silk and lace of a very impractical, non-cotton pair of panties. The crotch was damp and sleek under his caressing touch. As he feathered his fingers over it, her hand tightened on his wrist.

"Now take your hand away. Reach around the seat on either side of you, as if I'd tied your wrists back around it."

She complied, which lifted her upper body. He fervently hoped she was wearing a bra that matched the panties. He thought she was, because the thinness of the dress's fabric showed the points of aroused nipples. He rested his gaze there as he stroked her. A tiny moan caught in her throat, firing his own desires.

"Are you close to having an orgasm, Daralyn? Use words."

"I—I think so."

"If you get too close, tell me. I don't want you to have one yet."

He saw the delightful flash of exasperation, and let it go unremarked, especially when he saw a chaser of panic, a darting glance toward him. She was afraid he'd seen it, the involuntary rebellious feeling. He'd love her to trust him enough to one day beg him, and beg him hard, for what she wanted. Let him punish her for that rebelliousness, but in a way that wasn't a punishment for it at all.

"Easy. Relax for me." It was a warning to keep her from jerking at the wrong moment. He curled his free hand around the side of her seat to steady himself as he leaned further forward and found his way beneath lace and silk, working his fingers in at the right angle. Two fingers, sliding into that wetness, stroking the swollen, veined tissues that spasmed against him, clutching his fingers.

Her breath left her, her shoulders flexing in reaction. As he rubbed his thumb with slow purpose over her clit, he brought the other hand back to cup her cheek. Her gaze shifted to his face, then away, feral, needy. Propping his forearm against the side of her seat, he closed his hand over her throat, which snapped her gaze back to him. She might not hold it for more than a blink unless ordered, but her attention dropped to his mouth and clung there, telling him he had her full attention.

"I love watching you come apart like this. Love touching you. You like it when my fingers are inside you, don't you? Nod for me."

She did, and though he'd told her to do it, she meant it. "Oh..." Another sound escaped her as he changed his rhythm, and suddenly there was panic. "Rory, I can't..."

"It's all right, baby. I changed my mind. I want to watch you come. Do it now." If tonight went as intended, she'd be built back up to that same level of arousal in no time.

Every part of him was right there with her as she lost herself to it, body arching and pulling against the hold she had on the seat back. As he worked her clit and thrust within her, easily now, thanks to the drenched heat of her cunt, the moans increased in strength. Her head rocked back and forth, then thrashed as she hit that peak, her cry echoing through the van, resounding in his chest. Her spread legs convulsed hard as she kept them open for him, despite the strong wave of sensations. He felt like he could absorb the shudders in her body through his own.

He kept it going until she came down from that edge, floating like a feather back to the van and to him. She was mumbling, and he dipped his head to her mouth. "What?"

"So...new. Didn't know it could feel like that, and be...okay."

Like most teenage boys, he'd been jerking off practically since the moment he'd learned how good it felt. He couldn't imagine what it was like to her, to be discovering at twenty years old that a climax was something to be enjoyed, not suppressed, not feared or something to feel shame about.

He had been the one to give her that gift. And he would keep giving it to her, as creatively and as often as he could make it happen. He kissed her, making it strong, possessive, how he was feeling it, the way she was needing it. When he was done, he pulled back enough to stare into her confused, dazed eyes.

"Who do you belong to, Daralyn?"

"You," she whispered.

"Why did you come?"

"B-because you told me to."

"Exactly. Good girl." He pressed his lips back on hers, kissed her with his fingers resting inside her, until she settled into it, until he knew nothing else was competing with what he was telling her, trying to make her believe different. But he wasn't going to leave it that open-ended.

"Daralyn, nothing you feel tonight will be wrong. Okay?" He eased his fingers even deeper, watched her twitch, tremble. "Anything that worries you, you'll tell me, and I'll make it better. At this kind of party, I'm totally in charge. Not a single step, not a single thought you have, will be made without that safety net there. Tell me you understand."

She stared at him. That limitless mix of emotions was back in her gaze. He needed her to believe him, and he put it in the edge of his voice, the sternness. An extra little thrust. That last one seemed to be the defining moment.

"Yes." The first syllable went up a couple octaves, in breathy response to the penetration. "I understand."

"Good."

He withdrew his hand, tasted his fingers while she watched and trembled. "Guess we are going to be late now," he observed. "I'll tell Des and Julie it's all your fault."

Flashing her a grin, he started up the van again.

He was glad he told her all that when he was feeling a hundred percent sure of himself, because soon after, they turned onto Tyler's property, and a whole lot of unsettling variables came into play.

Tyler Winterman's driveway was practically a mile long, through old growth maritime forest. When the house finally came into view, Rory was sure if John Cooper saw it, it would become his next bird house.

The restored antebellum mansion was a graceful vision of tall windows, Grecian columns, a hipped roof that expanded into a half circle with blocked molding over the front entranceway. The grand double doors were accessible up eight marble steps, carved in a giant crescent around the two weight-bearing main pillars.

The property matched the house, the structure sitting on a spit of land bordered on two sides by a wide, winding tributary of the Intra-coastal Waterway. The current ran steady and strong. Since a wide balcony ran around all the sides of the house he could see, he expected there were no bad views from any part of the house.

He reminded himself of what Des had said about Tyler, and pushed aside his kneejerk wariness of someone far outside his income bracket. Logistics were less easy to overlook. He wasn't seeing a way up those steps, short of getting himself out of the chair and hauling himself up, dragging the chair with him. He might be able to find a more graceful way of getting inside from another entrance. Walkways flowed from the steps and disappeared around the corners of the house behind mature azaleas, magnolias and an array of rose bushes that probably bloomed their heads off in spring and summer.

While a practical necessity, looking for an alternative entrance always made him feel like a burglar looking for an unlocked window. The alternative, sending Daralyn up to knock on the door and find out how he could get in, wasn't much more appealing.

As he circled around and opened her door, she was staring at the place while sitting still as a mouse. Except her hands, which were tangling and untangling in her lap.

"I bet he has dust bunnies under his couch, just like everyone else."

That surprised a little smile out of her, which made him feel more at ease, too. He gently tugged her out to stand next to him.

"Do you think Marcus and Thomas have been to this kind of party before?" she asked.

"Much as I'd prefer not to imagine that, yeah, I'm sure they have." As they moved toward the front door, between pushes, he kept touching her hand on his shoulder. It helped him get his act together, not worry about shit that didn't matter. If they had to go around the house, they would. She'd follow his lead, so he'd make damn sure it was a relaxed one. This was an adventure, like Disneyland.

They also didn't have to rush inside. He could take all the time in the world and just talk to her, settle them both down. He stopped at the base of the stairs, gazing up at the door. The bronze knockers were a pair of lion heads. He squinted. Or maybe tigers.

He glanced at her. "Thomas said this would remind us of one of his fancy gallery shindigs."

"Pretty clothes, drinking fruity wine out of sparkling long-stemmed glasses, wandering past all the pictures, saying smart things about them." She managed another ghost of a smile. "That's how he describes it."

"Exactly. The people who can't think of anything just stand there and look thoughtfully at them. Praying that no one asks them to say anything smart."

"If they do," a deep, cultured voice came from behind them, "you say—quite solemnly, but with a particularly jaded air—'I'm still processing the author's intent.'"

Still holding Daralyn's hand, Rory turned to see a man standing on the paved walkway. He was framed by a pair of hydrangea bushes heavy with purple-blue blooms. With that background and in belted charcoal grey slacks and an open-necked black dress shirt, he exuded a mix of Southern gentleman, old money and urban sophisticate.

His dark hair was touched with silver, and his broad shoulders and fit body reminded Rory of Ben Affleck's version of Bruce Wayne. Meeting the man's vaguely familiar gaze, he found the amber-colored eyes steady and warm. Friendly. The man closed the distance between them and extended a hand to Rory. "Tyler Winterman, your host. We met briefly at the wedding, but I'm not sure we ever had the chance to speak."

As Rory accepted the hand, he liked the grip. Strong, but nothing to prove. Also not too purposefully weak, like Daralyn's professor had done.

Tyler turned his attention to Daralyn. "And you're Daralyn," he said. "You belong to Rory."

Her eyes widened slightly, her lips parting. "I...yes, sir."

When Tyler spoke to her, Rory put his hand back over hers on his shoulder. Tyler's gaze grew even kinder, registering the cue of her nervousness. It made Rory like him more. It also prompted him to add his own two cents.

"It's a privilege and a gift I'm working to earn," he said.

Tyler's expression reflected approval. "Which is part of why you're here tonight. As a good host, my intent is to ensure you have the experience you're seeking. Even if you're not entirely sure what that is."

Marcus had said he'd respect their privacy as much as possible, but Tyler would have to be told some things about them, in order for their host to vet Rory and Daralyn properly for this kind of party. While that had admittedly made Rory a little uneasy, he understood the need. Marcus had offered additional reassurance.

"He's an arrogant dick. But Tyler's also the best kind of Dom, through and through. He's one of the most respected in the BDSM scene, which is a pretty close-knit community."

Tyler gestured toward the marble stairs, taking a few steps in that direction so Rory followed and saw what one of the pillars had concealed. There was a ramp. And not one tacked in as an afterthought. It was an integrated feature of the entranceway, the strip between the ramp and the adjacent stairs a sunken planter with blue-green ornamental grass, the feathery tops bobbing in the breeze. Another reason he'd missed the ramp's presence.

"The exit to our gardens in the back are ground level, so no obstacles there," Tyler said. "I'd like to bring you into the house first, though, so we can talk privately about the protocols in place tonight."

Rory took the ramp, Daralyn next to him on the steps. She passed her hand over the tops of the ornamental grasses between them, smiling when the feathery tops tickled her wrist. She spread out her fingers to enjoy the sensation, sending Rory a pleased look.

"Is your wife here tonight?" Rory asked Tyler.

"Most definitely." The flicker in Tyler's gaze, the trace of heat and pleasure in his voice, reflected his feelings for his spouse, even in her absence. "She's handling other hostess duties while I greet you."

His attention moved briefly to Daralyn as he opened one of the double doors. "She's particularly looking forward to meeting you, Daralyn. Julie's told her a lot about you."

That surprised Daralyn. Rory, too. But Julie loved Daralyn as much as the rest of his family, and was equally protective of her. So maybe Marguerite and Daralyn had some common interests, though Rory wasn't sure what those would be. He didn't know a lot about Marguerite. He remembered a woman who had a unique kind of beauty combined with a strangely goddess-like vibe, for lack of a better word.

No. There was a better word. A Domme vibe.

Now that he had a different context in which to frame it, that was what he remembered about her. Since Tyler was obviously a hundred percent Dom, it created a puzzle with no ready answer in Rory's mind.

Well, Marcus had said seeing Dom/sub relationships playing out in real life, versus in a book or on a screen, might give him a whole different perspective on what the possibilities were. Not only how wide an area there was to explore, but the freedom to choose what corners of it fit him and Daralyn. Tyler and Marguerite's relationship might be a case in point.

Tyler gestured Daralyn in before him and stepped back so Rory could maneuver over the short stoop.

Once inside, he counted himself fortunate that Daralyn took a long, jaw-drop moment to gaze at the foyer, because it let him do the same.

A double staircase curved along the walls on either side to meet on a wide landing bordered with painted white iron balustrades. The window in the backdrop was the shape of a half moon, nearly ten feet in diameter. A glittering chandelier hung in the foreground, descending from a domed ceiling that showed a blue sky punctuated with soft clouds. On one of his mother's trips to Vegas, she'd brought back pictures of the Venetian shopping mall ceiling, which looked a lot like it.

They could hear the murmur of conversation somewhere, the faint notes of music. Pleasing scents filled the air. Fragrant and teasing, not overpowering. Though Rory couldn't separate it out enough to figure if it was food or floral, something about the scent spoke of the erotic, sharpening his senses and making him want to slide his fingers along the lengths of Daralyn's, stroke and play. She felt it too, her own fingers curling into his shirt.

"Please take a seat here." Tyler gestured Daralyn to a divan placed in the foyer, lots of gold velvet and dark wood. It had space next to it for Rory's chair. Rory noted her eyes were everywhere, digesting the personal photos and colorful art on the walls, the flower arrangements, the French doors that led to a sunken living room where they could see a horseshoe of deep sofas and a giant flatscreen. Though their surroundings obviously said money, there were plenty of personal touches that projected a welcoming and inclusive atmosphere. This place was a home, not a showpiece.

Reinforcing it, Tyler had sat down on the other end of the divan, one knee up on it to face Daralyn and Rory. He looked as relaxed as Rory would in his own home. Just beyond his shoulder, Rory could see beneath the right side of the curving staircase. A large oak door was flanked by the sculpture of a nude, dancing woman with long flowing hair. A vibration seemed to be affecting the door, as if the music they were hearing might be playing behind it.

"That leads to the inside dungeon play area," Tyler said, following Rory's attention. At Daralyn's startled look, he smiled. "That's a common term in our world, but it doesn't mean anything scary. Not that way. When I'm not holding one of these events, it's a recreation area, including an indoor saltwater pool."

Except for their very brief discussion about her awareness of the D/s world, Rory realized he had no idea how much terminology or mechanics Daralyn knew about all this. Should he have shared some of the stuff Marcus had loaned him to read, discussed his own Internet searches? He'd figured those kinds of things would just unsettle her, but Tyler's glance his way made him wonder if the guy was thinking the same thing. What kind of Dom brought his sub to this kind of party and didn't tell her what to expect?

The kind of Dom who didn't know much himself. Who thought it might be good to see it unfold together. Except as the Dom, he was supposed to stay a couple steps ahead. He'd focused on the front end safety, like confirming this guy was okay through Marcus and Thomas. But maybe staying ahead was also about prepping her for what he was going to see, as much as he could. Christ, had he fucked up?

"People who prefer to ease into play, who are still figuring out their preferences, usually like to start in the garden," Tyler said, holding his gaze. "It's a more open-feeling environment. There are also several socializing areas, so the intensity of the things you might see are tempered by that."

Rory nodded. Message received, and he didn't feel judged, which helped. Tyler inclined his head, then included them both in the sweep of his gaze again. "We only have a few rules, but they are inviolate."

Rory saw Daralyn roll the word around on her tongue. *Inviolate.*

"If these rules are broken, depending on the circumstances, you'll be asked to leave. They're simple rules, easy to understand, such that breaking them would be interpreted as a willful act."

Daralyn's expression became wary, uncertain. Tyler reached out, took her hand. "Don't worry, little one. I have no doubt you and your Master will be fine, but it's best to be clear about these. They keep all of us safe, and ensure our enjoyment of our time together."

The way Daralyn looked toward Rory when Tyler called him her Master rolled a lot of powerful things through Rory. A stronger echo of when she'd called him "*sir.*"

Tyler's words also seemed to ease Daralyn's tension, which was good. But with his serious Dom vibes and authoritative voice, Rory assumed Tyler could reassure a woman hanging off the edge of a cliff by her fingernails.

"While you're here, you'll see people engaged in play they enjoy or are experimenting with," their host continued, withdrawing his hand from Daralyn's. "Don't disrupt them with questions, or physically insert yourself into the scene without invitation. If they want you to participate, they will initiate that."

Tyler rested his elbow on the sofa arm, his hands clasped as he braced his long legs. "If you're invited to play and don't wish to do so, polite honesty is all that is needed. There are no egos to negotiate here. If you're more comfortable with not being approached at all, we have a wrist band you can wear that tells people you are here to watch and learn only, not participate. You may take the band off if you get more comfortable."

That appealed to Rory. He'd likely go that route and see how things unfolded from there. Less pressure on both of them.

"We do have alcohol," Tyler continued. "But we expect everyone to be responsible with it. If you are playing and your level of play discourages alcohol use, we expect you to self-regulate.

"Finally, there are no judgments here, except by our Dungeon

Masters. They're wearing black shirts and brown khakis, and a lit lanyard that says Dungeon Master on the tag. If they deem a scene is out of hand, they will intervene."

His gaze sharpened. "If you see something that concerns you, approach them, discuss it quietly, and they will handle it. They have in-depth information on those playing here tonight, their preferences and level of play. Since you don't have that information, you may not know all the facts that make seemingly edgy play acceptable. But be assured, keeping everyone safe is the top priority. Some things are not everyone's kink, so if you feel that way, keep the opinion to yourself. We don't tolerate any discourteous treatment of our guests."

His pleasant tone returned. "If you want to use any of our equipment, and you're not sure how it works, don't hesitate to ask a DM. We also have plenty of Doms and subs willing to provide guidance. This is a big playground, and there's always room for more people on the monkey bars."

That surprised a smile out of Daralyn, and Tyler answered it with one of his own. "That's another important thing to remember. What happens here is serious, but it can also be about play, joy and laughter. It is a party, after all."

He kept his gaze on Daralyn now. "For almost everything else tonight, I would defer to your Dom and let him answer for you both, or wait until he's given you permission to answer me. However, for this question, I need your direct answer. Have you understood the rules, and do you have any questions about them?"

Daralyn shook her head. "Yes sir. And no, I don't have any questions. Thank you."

Tyler glanced at Rory, and Rory gave him the same nod of acceptance. "Good. I'll give you a brief tour of the garden area, and then you can decide how you want to enjoy the amenities. If and when you're ready for the Dungeon, it's a fairly self-guided space, and there's sufficient room to navigate in there." His gaze touched the chair. "I'm going to go ahead and give you the non-player bracelets, so you can decide whether to don them or not. Sound good?"

"Yes, sir," Rory responded. "Are Des and Julie here yet?"

"Yes." The pleasure in Tyler's expression told Rory that the couple were well-liked by the host. "Their demonstration will start in about a half hour, so they're off getting ready for that. They'll join the party afterwards. I know they'll be delighted to see you. They're staying on my property tonight, so if you want to linger and visit them when the party officially concludes, you're welcome to stay as long as you wish."

After another pause, during which Rory sensed Tyler was giving them one more chance to consider any further questions, he at last rose and gave them a smile.

"Ready to go down the rabbit hole?"

CHAPTER FIFTEEN

*W*ith some wandering time before Des and Julie's demo, Rory decided the several acres of impressive landscaping out back would be the best space to explore. With Daralyn's love of gardening, he expected it would be a better environment for them both.

In contrast to the festival, where she'd seemed more comfortable wandering, Daralyn stayed right with him. That was probably because there were plenty of distracting things on display in the gardens that had nothing to do with flowers.

The scenes were similar to what he'd seen online, except there they sometimes came off more tawdry, off-putting and porno-like. In this setting, they called more to mind one of the movies he'd watched that Marcus had loaned him, something by the Andrew Blake guy. Graceful garden settings, bubbling fountains sparkling from the torches. Doms dressed in their best. Some of the subs weren't wearing any clothes, but they were still formal, hair gleaming, skin smooth or oiled, displaying a collar that might be rich leather or studded with metal and diamonds.

A sharp whooshing slap noise drew his attention to a woman who was tied on a giant spoked wheel. She had short dark hair and wore a pink thong. A tattoo of a tree followed the valley of her spine, with tiny purple flowers on the branch tips. They shuddered with the movement of her shoulders. The man flogging her looked like a charismatic Ichabod Crane, thin and bony but with piercing dark eyes. The fall of straps had made the whooshing noise. He wasn't hitting her particularly hard, Rory thought, though her skin was red from the impact.

She had a vibrator locked against her sex with the help of an adjustable bracket attached to the wheel. She was moaning against the gag. As he and Daralyn moved around to see her from the other side of the wheel, her body had that flush that said she was really close to...

She climaxed. As she screamed against the gag, her juices bathed the bulbous head of the vibrator, making it glisten. The Dom traded out the flogger for a cane when she was right in the middle of it, and landed several far harder, quick strikes with it, which elevated those screams, made her buck harder.

Daralyn's grip dug into his shoulder. He quickly glanced up at her, concerned she might be upset. Instead, her reaction startled him. She looked almost hypnotized.

They'd come to a halt to watch and Daralyn was leaning forward slightly, matching each breath the climaxing woman took. He moved his fingers on hers, a reassuring caress, and the spell broke, her glance flitting to his. He lifted his hand, brushed a warm cheek. She ducked her head, but he thought she was embarrassed the right way.

It made him curious. He brought her around in front of him so he could put his hands on her hips, guide her down to sit in his lap, her feet braced out on either side of his. He wrapped an arm around her waist, put his head next to her shoulder. "Just watch," he murmured.

She gripped his forearm as the Dom circled his sub. She'd sagged against her bonds, then arched back as he took the vibrator up a notch. Her cunt had to be sensitive after that kind of climax. Her incoherent pleas confirmed she was uncomfortable, and yet as he told her how good she was, how she pleased him, Rory could see her struggling to bear it without complaint. As they watched, she passed that discomfort level and began to get aroused again. Her Dom bit at her thighs with light touches of the cane, which seemed to only increase the reaction. Pleading cries were replaced by soft moans.

He picked up the flogger, and what ensued was a ballet of movement, the flogger straps falling against her breasts, her swollen nipples, her back, alternating with short strikes of the cane against her thighs and ass.

When she was obviously close to coming again, he notched the flogger and cane, crossed in his grip, under her chin. He used that pressure to bring her mouth up to his for his kiss. "My sweet slave," he murmured, and tears were on her cheeks, her trembling lips. "Come for me."

She obeyed, her body bucking in hard jerks, as he watched her with those piercing eyes, his lips so close to hers, brushing over them in teasing sips as she moaned, as her body strained, wanting more...

It was mesmerizing to Rory, too. And it wasn't the flogger and cane, not exactly. He liked the mental give and take, what the sub was giving her Dom, the way she was aroused by his command of her. How the Dom was goaded to take her to higher and higher levels of arousal because of her submission, her devotion. Because it was what they both wanted, to push those limits for each other.

He had Daralyn's waist banded in a hard grip. Suddenly the things he'd read or looked at online had become real, giving more scope to what he was feeling inside.

"Ready to go look at something else?" he said in her ear.

When she nodded, he eased her back to her feet and they moved onward. Next stop was a chess game. Two Dommes were the players, a guy on his hands and knees holding up the table. And he had a...holy crap. Some kind of machine had a dildo pushing in and out of his ass while he tried to hold that table still. It was a good thing the chess pieces were plastic, because Rory would bet good money they were going to end up on the ground.

As they circled the tableau, he realized the guy's dick was trussed up in straps that might make it impossible for him to come. Or really, really difficult, even as that dildo would be insisting. No wonder his face was contorted with the strain. The Dommes looked totally unconcerned, contemplating their next move and exchanging comments about mundane stuff, chatting and laughing like women at a coffee shop. One wore a little black dress, the other in sleek denim jeans with sparkles shot through them and a purple tunic top. A small audience sitting on nearby chairs watched the tableau as if it was theater, and he guessed it was.

He figured out which Domme the sub belonged to within seconds. Though she was chatting and acting all casual, she had her hand resting on his hip, fingers stroking the upper curve of his ass. The calf of one of her crossed legs was pressed against his shoulder. He had his cheek against it, as if drawing strength from that contact she was allowing.

It was interesting, thought-provoking, but Rory didn't really care much about watching some guy take it up the ass. Daralyn seemed okay with proceeding. Nearby, one man lay on a table while a woman coated her hands in alcohol and set them on fire. The chemical reaction created a barrier that allowed her to move her hands gracefully over him without burning either of them. From the bliss on the recipient's face, he was feeling the heat in the right way. The woman did the fire play so easily, Rory expected she might be another demo performer, like Des.

The candle wax scene they found next kept their attention. Rory guided Daralyn to put a hip on his thigh, giving her a place to rest herself. He had his arm loosely around her hips, hers around his shoulders as they watched. The male Dom was finishing up a design on a woman's back, the wax patterned like a cheetah's pelt. Every drizzle of the hot paraffin had her twitching. She wore a tail in a plug up her backside and had on kitten ears, plus an eye mask with whiskers alongside the nose piece. She was on a table on all fours. As the Dom finished, she rubbed her head against his shoulder, just like a cat would.

While a lot of this might not necessarily be his thing, watching it... that was a different matter, because the sexual energy swirling high around each tableau affected the audience. Every scene projected the absorbing connection between Dom and sub. Whether the scene was someone's kink or not, from the rapt attention of each observer, including Daralyn and him, Rory deduced that connection was everyone's thing.

The two of them were moving through these sights like kids in a somewhat intimidating candy store. As the Dom, he wasn't sure if he was supposed to be acting a certain way about this stuff. Nonchalant? Casual? Was he supposed to be telling her to pay closer attention to some things than others?

It would be like offering direction when they were both uncertain of the map, where it would take them, what it would show them. He decided the way they were doing it was the best way. Whatever he felt, like putting her on his lap, holding her close while they watched the flogging, seemed to be the right thing. Just staying connected to her, tuned in to her reactions, making her aware he was here with her, for every part of the journey. For now, he thought that was enough. If questions or discussions were needed, they would happen when they happened.

Daralyn's hand was on his shoulder, and he touched her frequently. He noted the grip of her hand, the strength of it, varied from scene to scene, indications of her focus on one type of play versus another. And what specific aspects seemed to most absorb her.

The way a sub reacted when a restraint was tightened, and his Dom whispered to him. Or how another Master's eyes held his female sub's gaze with such absolute control... The arch of her body at the strike of his whip, his hand over her throat, the tug at her collar.

Rory realized it was the same for Daralyn as it was for him. It wasn't so much the mechanics or tools holding their attention. It was what messages they drew out of the sub, out of the Dom, that grabbed them both.

They had worked their way over to the curtain-backed dais where Des and Julie's demo would be held. He found a spot just off the nearby paved path, pushing his chair halfway onto the grass, in case Daralyn wanted to sink down at his feet. He had a towel in his pack to protect her dress, but for now he put her on his lap, facing the stage. He liked that position, her back against his chest, his arms looped around her.

By the time the curtain rustled and Des and Julie emerged, a couple dozen people were watching, sitting on the grass or utilizing an arranged group of folding chairs.

Julie wore a sports bra and dark clingy shorts. Rory found himself grateful for that. Julie definitely wasn't his sister, but she was family. It would be easier to watch and get lost in this if she wasn't naked. Though if this ended up with Des bringing her to climax in front of everyone, that comfort zone was out the window.

Julie positioned herself in the center of the dais, her eyes down. Rory could see her breath making her breasts rise and fall. She seemed calm and expectant both, focused on Des. He stepped up behind her and put a blindfold over her eyes, lacing it in back so it molded to her face. Then he ran his hands up and down her arms, a reminder of his presence.

He trailed a rope across her shoulders, along her neck, her face. She nuzzled it, showing her pleasure at having it near her. He guided her arms behind her, boxed beneath her shoulder blades, and then he began to wrap the rope over them, holding them in place.

It was like watching a ballet. In a matter of several moments, Des had a twisted braid of rope between her ample breasts, framed by a line of ropes above and below that went over and under to tie at her elbows and armpits. It held the boxed arms close to her back and lifted her posture, so her breasts were thrust out. Her nipples had hardened, showing her arousal at what he was doing, restraining her.

Rory glanced at Daralyn. She was in the trance she'd seemed to be in for the first scene, only it was deepening. The more Des restrained Julie, the more absorbed Daralyn became. Not wanting to disrupt the flow of it, Rory ran a slow hand down her back, over her hip, over the curve of her buttock. All while he watched every change in her face.

Daralyn's gaze stayed locked on Des and Julie, but she moved back into him, pressing her body to his with an urgency that told him arousal and the environment were taking away her normal self-consciousness.

Out of the many different clues he'd picked up about her childhood, she'd never once indicated her uncle or father had restrained her. So like oral sex, this might be entirely new territory, her reactions unfettered by the past.

Des turned Julie in a graceful twirl, taking her down to her knees in a quick movement. A hand to the back of the neck pushed her forward, held her body in a C-curve on her knees. She had her thick hair in a ponytail, and he bound it in rope, attaching the end to one of the tall poles driven into the ground around the front edge of the small dais.

It was only the first attachment point. When he was done, she was tied up with an elaborate design of ropes over her upper torso and spread thighs. Then, in another dramatic movement, he'd taken her off the ground, turned her so she was in a side stroke position, like in water. Her face and upper torso were angled toward the night sky, her hip and side of her thigh parallel to the stage. She was helpless, completely in his hands and ropes as he caressed her, all the while murmuring to her. When he tipped her head back, sipped from her mouth, she shuddered. Rory doubted she was aware of anything else.

He didn't think Daralyn was, either.

How someone who'd had all control taken from her for so long could be stimulated by seeing the same was an intriguing puzzle. Was it because Julie projected no worry, no fear at all, being helpless in Des's hands?

In every movement Des made that Julie submitted to, melting into him, it reminded Rory of each time Daralyn had submitted to him, in ways large and small. A back and forth message that said, *I trust you. I feel safe with you.*

A gift he wanted to give and receive, all at the same time.

The grassy area had given the audience room to form a loose semi-circle around the dais, not crowd one another. He saw a variety of reactions, some like his and Daralyn's. Other people he guessed liked doing the rope stuff, too, because they seemed to be carefully watching Des's technique.

He'd said he'd done this all over the country, suggesting he was a big deal for this kind of thing. If Rory hadn't deduced it from that comment, he could do so merely from watching him. It was like looking at Thomas's paintings, the artistry practically leaping off the canvas and grabbing the viewer by the throat. Such a creation made a person look at it, feel like there was something there worth seeing, even if they couldn't describe why it was so absorbing.

They were done. Des sketched a brief bow to the crowd, a signal the demo was over, and then began to unwrap Julie from the ropes, removing her blindfold.

Some people wandered off, but others stayed, watching him do what Rory knew would be called aftercare. Des loosened the ropes with as much sensual attention as he'd put them on, taking his time, caressing Julie's skin with the loosened twine, bending down to press his lips to the red marks he'd left there.

When he was done removing all the bindings, he tilted her face toward him, kissed her mouth. Rory glimpsed Julie's eyes, focused on her Dom, aware of nothing else. Floating and calm. He would have expected some part of her drama-loving soul to stay conscious of her audience. But Rory suspected Julie had been as wrapped up in her Master's attention as securely as in his ropes.

Des's attention had a different shape from Thomas's painting process. Rory had watched his brother completely lost in it, such that a gas explosion a hundred feet away would barely have registered. There was some of that all-encompassing focus to Des while doing the rope, but there was a vital difference as well. Not once had Rory felt he'd lost the intense connection with Julie, his awareness of her mental and physical state. He'd stayed locked into everything she'd been feeling, how she'd been reacting. Though nothing had seemed to go amiss during the demo, if it had, Rory had no doubt Des would have been a step ahead of it.

Seeing the place such experience and time could take a Dom and sub, spawned something in Rory's gut he could only call yearning. To be and do the same for Daralyn. To learn how to be that kind of Master for her.

Daralyn had eased from his lap, sunk to her knees next to his chair, her hand fluttering down to rest on his leg. As he looked at her, that yearning sharpened and cut something open in him. It bled into his upper body, made it ache.

Somewhere along the way, he'd turned away from the idea that he could be all that for someone. Not that he couldn't be in love or be a good partner. But he'd wanted to be someone's hero, the person they could believe would be there for them, no matter what.

Maybe he'd thought being in a chair made that a pipe dream. But when she looked up at him, need and desire in her gaze, and sought the clasp of his hand, he saw that somewhere in her, she believed he could be that for her.

It was a dream that could maybe come true for them both.

After Des untied Julie fully, he'd picked her up and carried her back behind the curtain. Figuring they'd join the party after she emerged from that floating state, Rory took Daralyn exploring some more. A pavilion tent had been set up providing food and drinks. The tent also featured a performance dais, where they appeared to be setting up for another demo.

"What do you think they'll be doing?" Daralyn asked.

"Food." The answer came from a young woman moving past them. She was about their age and had brown curly hair, somewhat tamed by a silk scarf that picked up the blue hues in her tie-dyed skirt. A necklace of blue stones with a silver pentagram as a pendant broke up the solid tone of her sleeveless black tank. She was barefoot. Even so, from the brisk air about her, Rory thought she might be a volunteer helping out.

"They'll be doing an erotic food display," she explained. "Ways to turn your submissive into a centerpiece for a meal. Or a dessert." She beamed. "Most importantly, there will be cupcakes for everyone at the end."

She pointed to a wooden sign mounted next to the pavilion opening. "That tells you the demo schedule for the tent. You can find them next to any of the places where platforms are set up, so you can plan for what you're interested in." She smiled at them again. "I'm Chloe. I work with Marguerite at Tea Leaves, and I usually volunteer to help out at these things with my husband, Brendan. When we're not playing ourselves. We take shifts so everyone can have fun. He's around here somewhere. You're Rory, aren't you? Which makes you Daralyn."

At their surprised looks, she chuckled. "This event's a pretty small one, so those of us helping know most the guests." She twinkled at Rory. "Your names stuck in my brain. I was hoping to get the chance to say hello."

"Can't imagine what made it easy to remember us," Rory said with a wry smile.

Chloe glanced at his chair and shrugged, easy with it in a way he liked. "Can't deny that it did help with the name-to- face association, but that wasn't what cinched it. You look like your brother. Not the same hair style or anything. It's in the face, the way you hold yourself. Only you have the seriously sexy Dom vibe, whereas Thomas rocks the seriously sexy sub vibe."

Her phone buzzed, and she glanced down at it. "Whoops, got to run. Another batch of cupcakes have cooled enough to be frosted, and I am the frost minion. But I hope to see you guys later. If you stay late, things get really mellow and fun during the wee hours." She winked. "And sometimes some really intense things happen, too, if that's also something you'd like. Nice to meet you. Tell Thomas he still owes me that dance he promised me at my wedding reception. Full on tango."

"I'm better at it," Rory said.

Chloe laughed. "I bet. Talk to you guys soon."

As she hurried away, Daralyn looked at him. "Thomas agrees."

"Agrees with what?"

"He says you used to be a way better dancer than him, before you joined the football team and decided you had to be cool." A light smile flirted over her lips.

Rory snorted. "I'm still a better dancer than him. Chloe only thinks I was joking. I'll take you dancing one night."

Her eyes lit with a mix of anticipation and mild terror at the thought. Then her gaze traveled beyond him and she made a pleased noise. Following her glance, Rory saw Julie and Des headed in their direction.

While more in tune with her surroundings, Julie still looked way more mellow than her usual self, walking with a dreamy tranquility in the curve of Des's sure arm. Chloe, who'd headed in their direction, paused to give Julie a hug and Des a brief touch on his arm before she kept moving toward her cupcake frosting task.

Then Julie saw them. Her eyes lit with joy, and she gripped Des's arm, a non-verbal way of telling him she was all right, and hurried forward to hug Daralyn.

"You both look great," Julie said. "But no offense, Rory, Daralyn looks *so* incredible."

"None taken and I couldn't agree more," he responded. Daralyn did her shy, pleased smile as he tightened his grip on her hand. Could the girl do anything that didn't squeeze his heart into pulp?

"I have to take your picture tonight to send to Les," Julie told Daralyn. "Proof of how awesome your personal shoppers are."

Rory offered Des a hand to shake. "That demo was incredible."

"Really," Daralyn echoed, shooting a glance at Des before coming back to Julie. "It was...well, incredible. I couldn't look away."

"She couldn't." Rory slid an arm around her waist, tugging her to lean against him as he stroked her hip. "She was pretty caught up in it."

He noticed Julie's dreamy look. "What?"

She gusted a happy sigh. "I love seeing the two of you together. Makes me feel all gooey."

Des sent Rory the male patented *women* look, but it was followed up by a glance toward Julie as full of feeling as what Rory felt for

Daralyn. Proving it, Des circled Julie's waist, much as Rory had Daralyn's, and drew her to his lean hip. "I'll take a picture of both of our gorgeous women to send to Les. She'll like that."

"And one of Rory and Daralyn. So she can get gooey over them, too."

Des nodded with a smile, then looked toward Rory. "Would you like to try it? The rope stuff?"

The question was directed solely to him. Tyler had pointed it out during the review of the rules. In this environment, Doms were asked what their subs might want. The subs weren't asked directly. Rory had noted everything in their environment fit with that. Like whenever waitstaff had come by with food and drink, the offer had been, "Would you or your sub like one?"

Daralyn seemed entirely at ease with that. Earlier in the day, when she'd expressed, in her roundabout way, that she wasn't always thrilled when people made decisions for her, she'd also made a point of saying she didn't have that problem with him.

It came back to what lay between the two of them, no one else, not even someone in her past or what problems she had expressing her feelings.

So yeah, he was interested in the rope stuff. But he did a check on Daralyn's body language. An interesting kind of tension had gripped her, like how she reacted when he gripped her wrist or throat.

During Des and Julie's demo, Rory had watched Daralyn forget everything, get lost in it. How often did she get to let down every guard, relinquish every worry, and give herself to pure feeling?

He kept a peripheral eye on her as he answered the rope artist. "Yeah, but I'm not sure I'm up for doing the whole elaborate suspension thing."

"I had something easy in mind. Ropework 101, an introduction to the possibilities. That stretch of grass on the west side of the house is a nice spot, with a breeze off the water."

Daralyn had pressed her lips together at the more specific suggestion, and her fingers curled against her thighs. It gave him all the go-ahead he needed.

"Sounds good," Rory said. "Long as you're not going to need me to do a lot of maneuvering on the grass." The lawn was trimmed short enough to push across without having to lift his casters, but it wasn't ideal ground for smooth pivots and swift turns.

"Nope. You'll be pretty stationary."

"Lead the way, then."

On the way, they stopped at the dais where Julie and Des had done their demo, and Des came out from behind the curtain with a coil of blue rope. Then they headed toward the place he'd indicated.

A stone bench, angled to view both the garden area and the water, was available near the spot. Des pressed Julie down on it. As he did, he brushed a knuckle along her cheek and murmured something. She gazed up at him, a slight smile on her face, and a lot of feeling in her eyes.

When Des came toward them, Julie shifted her attention toward Rory and Daralyn, and her lively eyes narrowed. "What?"

Rory affected her mannerisms, throwing up his hands. "You two just make me feel so gooey."

"Shut up."

Daralyn chuckled as Rory grinned. Des gave them an indulgent, patient look that Rory thought would work well on squabbling offspring, when and if he and Julie took that step. Then he squared off with Rory and Daralyn, and his manner shifted to a more serious mien. For Julie, too. Despite her usual effusiveness, she subsided into a quiet, unobtrusive observer, much as Rory suspected she did when watching theater rehearsals.

As Rory locked the brakes on his chair, Daralyn shifted closer to his side. "Have her face you," Des said.

Daralyn obediently did so while Rory took her hands. "Breathe," he told her, with a smile. A reminder it was all okay. Her color was high and eyes a little bright. Nervous but excited too, so that was all good.

"State of mind is important," Des said, moving around them. "Both of you take a breath. Focus on one another." He stopped behind Daralyn, a couple feet back and to the side, so she couldn't see him, but Rory had a direct view.

"Daralyn," Des continued, his even timbre suggesting, reassuringly, that he knew everything about what he was talking about, "there's nothing more important than your Master's direction, his will. And nothing is more important to him than your protection and well-being."

"Absolutely," Rory said, meeting her eyes. The torch light turned them a fascinating mixture of pewter and green, with glints of gold.

So now he took a breath, and Daralyn copied the gesture, showing she was following Des's direction and focusing on Rory's lead. It changed the atmosphere further. Their circle of the world evolved into something separate from everything outside of it.

Des made a gesture toward Rory's feet, nodded to Daralyn and pantomimed a lifting of his hands. Rory got it. "Kneel at my feet, Daralyn," he said. "Still facing me."

When she did, his heart tilted in the usual way when she assumed that position. "Lift your hands up to me," he said. "Palms down."

She did it almost exactly as Des had demonstrated, her wrists side by side, the fingers open like a bird's wings. She kept her eyes lowered, her lips parted. He watched the rise and fall of her breasts beneath the wine-colored fabric of her dress. The skirt had floated down around her so she looked like a wild primrose.

Des brought the blue rope to Rory. "Wrap it twice around her wrists and then one wrap in the middle, between her wrists. Do it slow, and tighten it. Watch her."

Curious at his emphasis on the last, Rory complied, looping the rope around her slim wrists, held up for him. He didn't have to watch too closely; the reaction was noticeable the second he made the wrap. Her breath shortened, and her body stilled. When he did the wrap in the middle, tightening the hold of the ropes on either wrist, she swayed toward him.

He glanced at Des, and the spark in the man's gaze needed no words, since the feeling echoed in Rory's gut. It was the kind of response a Dom wanted to see, to know he was on the right track.

"May I?" Des asked.

Rory nodded. Des dropped to one knee behind Daralyn, moving her skirt out of the way so he didn't plant his thick-tread black shoe on it. He reached beneath her arms and took the ends of the rope Rory was holding. There was a good amount of it; Rory estimated about twenty-five feet. Des threaded the ends under either of her arms, did something against her back to hold their position and then came back, pulling the two ropes over her upper arms, so her bound wrists were pulled in against her breasts. He did it slow, so Rory could watch what he was doing.

From the fluid way he did it, Rory expected Des to keep going. Instead, the rope artist immediately stopped. He left the rope tied loosely in front of her bound wrists, the trailing ends in Rory's grasp before he rose to his feet and backed off two clear strides, putting distance between him and Daralyn.

"Rory." Des's sharp tone and pointed gaze held a clear warning.

Rory had been watching what Des was doing. When Des said "watch her," he should have stuck with that for the duration.

The transfer of the rope to Des and back to Rory again had taken less than a few seconds. Des's touch upon her had been firm and functional, gentle, nothing inappropriate. When he'd leaned forward to pass the rope back around her upper arms, his chest had brushed Daralyn's shoulder blades.

Perhaps that was how Des had noticed she'd gone rigid as a corpse. Her face had lost all color.

Rory dropped the ends of the rope over his knee and clasped her bound wrists in his hand. "Daralyn."

Christ, she had become like ice. No wonder she looked whiter than snow. Even resting on her knees, she was starting to wobble. Afraid her eyes were going to roll up into her head, he pulled the rope loose from around her torso. Des moved back in to help, unwrapping them in a blink, trying to touch her as little possible.

That left just her bound wrists resting in Rory's lap and a pool of rope on the ground by her knee. However, when Rory started to take the rope off her wrists, one-handed because he was keeping one arm wrapped around her, she made a noise of protest, curling her fingers up against her chest and hunching into herself, her head tucked over them.

He paused, undecided, his gaze shooting to Des. The rope artist, resting on his heels a couple feet away, was watching her as closely as Rory was now.

"The wrists should be okay," Des said in a calm voice. "The ropes aren't tight enough to restrict blood flow." He paused, gave Rory a significant look. "You tied that part."

Rory digested that. Nodded. "Can you give us a second, but not go too far?"

"You got it. I'll be over here with Julie. I'll deal with that."

Rory hadn't noticed the approach of one of the Dungeon Masters. Though it got his back up, he discarded the feeling in the next breath, glad there were experienced, sharp eyes detecting something was amiss when the Dom didn't. Being new to this shit didn't change his desire to kick his own ass. But him being pissed at himself, embarrassed that others were witnessing his missteps, didn't do anyone any good, especially Daralyn.

He'd rely on Des's experience to handle the conversation with the Dungeon Master while Rory focused on her. She was still so cold. Since it was a warmish autumn night, typical for Florida, neither one of them had extra layers. A coat wasn't what she needed, though.

Rory opened the front of his shirt and brought her to a standing position on her knees. When he pulled her up against him, her hip pressed to his legs, she was against the heat of his body. Her bound arms were between them, her forearms pressed to his chest and abdomen, but the heat would transfer through her limbs and into the rest of her.

She dropped her forehead against his chest and shuddered, but it was a gesture of relief, telling him she was drawing strength from him, steadying herself.

"Talk to me," he ordered. "What's going on?"

She shook her head. "I—I'm fine. I just...I'm so sorry..."

He could deal with this a couple ways. Coddle her, not make her talk. Take her home. That didn't feel right.

"That's not what I asked you," he said, touching her chin. She nestled her hand into his palm, and he resisted the urge to let her hide her face against him. He resisted the even greater desire to fold every part of himself around her, protect her. He couldn't let his protective instincts take choices from her. He had to channel his decisions toward her right to choose and express herself, even when she was way too willing to give up that right.

He pulled her face back up so she was meeting his gaze. "Not what I asked," he repeated. "I want to know what just happened."

She pressed her lips together, and her eyes got an odd light to them. "I...I didn't...I wasn't ready, but... If... Are you going to share me with Des?"

"What?" His involuntary shock made her more apologetic.

"I'm sorry. I shouldn't have hesitated. I...My father, he...said my uncle...that a good girl will do what her father says...family... Des is part of your family..."

Jesus Christ. She was sinking like a ship before his eyes, and for a second his stunned reaction pulled him down in the same vortex. They'd done this way too soon. What the hell had he been thinking? This could be major trauma shit, far beyond his layperson ability to deal with it.

"I told...Dr. Taylor we were doing this... She said..." Daralyn closed her eyes, took a breath. "She said to trust you...to know what I..."

She couldn't say it, but he took it from her. "To know what you want."

Dr. Taylor had told her to trust him. And she could, damn it. He pulled free of the sucking panic, gave himself a fierce mental shake. Though she was teetering on the edge of a panic attack, her expression shut down in that way that said they'd hit a really bad bump, none of it was unfamiliar ground, even if being at this party was.

Des had noticed how she wanted the bindings Rory had tied upon her left alone. It wasn't that which had derailed her. It was the touch of someone else, being bound by someone else. Testing it, praying he wasn't wrong and about to take her deeper into the abyss, Rory wrapped his hand in the trailing ends of the rope, close to her wrists. He also slid his other hand to her nape, putting firm pressure there, holding her still.

Her gaze flitted to his rope-wrapped hand, noted how it held her to him. One breath, two, and he saw the nature of the stillness gripping her change. It moved ponderously from that darkness and back toward him.

"Look at me. Unh-uh. You keep your eyes on mine."

Her hazel eyes had lifted to his with effort, and then tried to shift away. Not this time. His fingers flexed on her and her gaze came back to his relentless one.

"You know what the most important thing in the whole world is to me?" he asked

"To walk again," she whispered.

Wow. Another gut punch, because the seemingly obvious answer hadn't even crossed his mind.

"No," he said. "Any other guesses?"

Her gaze slid to his chest, and this time he allowed it, though he rubbed the back of her neck with his fingers, a tender stroke. "No," she said. "But I'd give it to you if I could."

Was this the way it was with love? Just when you thought there was no room in your heart to love someone more, a simple declaration doubled the size of the organ, made it press into every corner of his chest, squeezing the air from his lungs.

"I'm really glad to hear that," he managed. "One more time. Look into my eyes, Daralyn. I want you to see this one come straight from my soul. So you'll know how absolutely and totally it's the truth."

It took some doing, but she eventually lifted her chin and met his gaze. He made her do that part on her own, but once she obeyed, he helped by adjusting his touch to cup her face, stroke her chin, the line of her throat. He heard the little sob of her breath. She was balanced on the edge of despair and hope, confusion and fear, but she was giving herself into his hands, trusting him to pull her out of darkness.

"Your happiness is the most important thing in the whole world to me." The raw feeling in his heart made his voice rough.

Her eyes got a little wet. So much pain. He kept touching her face, her mouth. "When I turned those ropes over to Des, you thought I was planning to share you with him, because your father"—the rat bastard cocksucker—"told you the person you belong to gets to make that call. Yes or no?"

A little jerk of her head. He pressed onward. "And that upset you so badly, thinking I was about to do that, that you nearly passed out."

"I'm sorry. I should—"

"It's not a good idea to apologize to me for that," he said mildly. "If I put out a collection jar at the store to pay someone to kill your uncle, we'd not only have enough money by closing time to hire a top of the line hitman, we'd have enough left over to fund the annual town Fourth of July picnic."

Her eyes snapped up to him. He stroked her face some more. She didn't want to talk about this, he knew it, so he wouldn't push it much further. But he wanted to try one more thing. Even if it went badly, maybe he'd dug up the ground enough a seed would finally take root, despite how many others kept getting washed away by the storms that this subject caused within her.

"When someone has branded it to your core that you don't have the right to want things, it's hard to shake that. I get it. But I want you to say one thing to me. Even if you're just mimicking my words, even if you don't feel it yet."

"Rory."

He took a tighter hold on her. "Say, 'I don't want you to share me with another man.'"

Her gaze darted around, came back to him, jumped away again. "I..."

"You can do it," he said. "I know you can. You can do anything."

"I...please." She shuddered. "I don't want...please don't..."

She convulsed, and then she bolted, scrambling away, stumbling to her feet, her hands still tied.

His heart leaped into his throat. He was chasing after her in an instant, but with the grass he couldn't move as fast as she could run. Which she was doing, in a panicked, mindless kind of way.

The tributary, with its fast current and deep waters, was just beyond the light of those tiki torches. If she stumbled over the bulkhead, fell into the water and darkness and hit her head...

He aged ten years in ten heartbeats, which was when she collapsed to her knees and hunched forward, bracing herself on the ground with one hand as she began to heave.

That was why she'd been scrambling away. To deposit the contents of her stomach in the grass, instead of on him.

He tuned into his surroundings enough to notice he wasn't alone. Des was between her and the water, poised alertly a few feet ahead of the track she'd been taking. Julie and the Dungeon Master were also just now catching up, keeping a distance, but still forming a loose four-point circle around her.

Rory had no idea how Des had moved that fast, but he felt nothing but gratitude. He could only manage a nod though, since all of his current energy was devoted to settling his heart rate so he didn't go into cardiac arrest.

He didn't let that stop him from closing the distance between him and Daralyn, though. He rested a hand on her back, gave her a soothing touch. Since she was shaking, hopefully she'd miss the tremor in his own hand.

She needed his strength, so he pulled it together. He couldn't worry about what his audience was thinking, or if he was about to be thrown out of this place. His only focus was the woman he'd protect with every resource he had. He'd have to rely on Des and Julie to keep handling whatever was going on around them.

She seemed to be finished throwing up, so he kept stroking her, murmuring, doing the quiet things to tell her he was here and it was okay. His heart cracked over the struggle he felt going on within her. Jesus, he couldn't imagine how exhausting it must be for her. Would she ever be able to break free of the hold the past had on her, to say what she wanted for her own self, her own life?

Fuck, Dr. Taylor had warned him, told him that expressing what she wanted wasn't as simple as saying it out loud. But he'd felt so close to it.

So he'd pushed. Okay. He'd fucked up. But she was here, she was okay, it was okay. And he'd keep doing what he was already doing. Read her desires from her body language, get as close to what she wanted as anyone could. He wouldn't let their damage to her keep her from it.

She'd sat back on her heels, but she was rocking back and forth, curled over her bound hands, her back rounded. "Please don't say we have to go home," she whispered. "I wanted to do...the ropes. I just couldn't...when he touched me..."

It was so unexpected, at first he thought he'd misheard her. While he recognized it had been unconscious, driven by the erratic tangle of her emotions, the physical stress of her nervous stomach, it took an act of will not to react with a fist pump.

I wanted to do the ropes.

He held that in and kept stroking her, feeling the bumps of her vertebrae. He wanted to tell her he was sorry for not paying better attention, but she'd keep trying to take the blame. He needed to change the focus for both of them.

"Come on up here. Let me see you."

She adjusted onto her knees, then put a foot under her. He took it from there, using her momentum and his strength to slide her up and onto his lap, adjusting her so she was leaning on her hip against him, cradled in his one arm. He reclaimed the trailing lengths of rope, a considerable amount of it, drawing it into a pile in her lap.

Julie approached, left a bottle of water next to his wheel, but withdrew without a word, just a reassuring look. Daralyn had her face pressed into his throat, so only he saw her.

Julie and Daralyn were friends, but this, what was happening right now, it was a Dom/sub thing. And Tyler had said no one disrupted a moment between a Dom and sub unless invited.

Everything rested with Rory now, as long as the DM didn't disagree, and apparently he didn't. He was still nearby, but he was sticking to the peripherals.

Rory opened the water and offered it to Daralyn. She took it, swishing the water around her mouth. With a furtive look toward him, she spat it out in the grass and then took a few more swallows, clearing out the taste of her being sick. Then she handed it back to him with a nod. He recapped it and set it down next to them.

He sent a pointed look at the front of her dress, pinched up folds of her skirt as if looking for something. Her brow creased. "What are you doing?" she asked thickly.

"I've hung out with football players who partied and drank too much. Not a one of them could vomit without getting it all over themselves. You could give them lessons."

Her weak attempt at a smile came with a little glistening in her eyes, a quivering of her chin. "Hey." He tightened his arm around her. "Easy. I've got you."

She let out a little sigh, her body melting more into his, her head back on his shoulder. He rested his hand on the pile of rope in her lap while clasping the ends close to the wrist bindings. A little tug caused a flicker in her gaze, one he noted as he pulled back enough to look at her face. "So," he said casually. "You did it."

"What...did I do?" Her voice was still rusty.

"You said you wanted to do the rope stuff."

She blinked. When a million conflicting emotions crossed her face, he interlaced his fingers with her tense ones, stroked her wrists around the hold of the rope.

"You feel up to doing a little more?"

CHAPTER SIXTEEN

*H*e waited a beat. She'd agree to it, whether she did or didn't want to do more, but when he detected relief and an easing of her features, he had his true answer.

His gut might be as clueless as the rest of him, but he wasn't Dr. Taylor. Words weren't going to get them where they needed to go. Neither was going home and giving up on this. She'd asked him not to do that, which in his book was expressing something she wanted.

She nodded.

"Good." He gestured to Des. As Julie's Dom came toward him, Rory turned his attention to the Dungeon Master, standing a little farther away. He had steady blue-gray eyes that looked a little dangerous, short cropped hair and a tribal tattoo around one of the biceps exposed by his short-sleeved shirt. He had the compact build and previously broken nose of a fighter.

His eyes also held the concern that Des's had, suggesting he was here to be in Rory's corner as much as Daralyn's, especially if Rory was doing everything he could to keep his sub safe.

Rory nodded to him, acknowledging it, and returned his attention to Des. "Two things. First, I don't want to put her down quite yet. Will you help me get my chair over there?"

He tilted his head toward another section of grass, the right distance away from where she'd thrown up.

"Sure," Des said. "Just tell me what to do."

Rory tilted his chair back into Des's capable hands, and helped push so the two of them were able to put the chair where it needed to be without taking Daralyn out of his lap.

"That's one thing," Des said as Rory settled. "What's the second?"

"Will you walk me through the rest of it?" Rory asked.

"Sure thing." Des's eyes gleamed. He squeezed Rory's shoulder a subtle, strong gesture expressing full understanding of both what Rory was feeling and trying to do for his sub.

"I'm going to finish what Des was showing us," Rory told her. "But it will only be my hands on you. All right? I need to hear words."

"Okay. Yes. Yes, Rory."

He touched her face. "Why don't we make that a little more formal?"

He'd surprised her that time. Her gaze flicked up, then back down. "Yes, sir."

"Good." He gently guided Daralyn back down on her knees before him. He ran a thumb over the scar on the underside of her forearm, where the rope overlapped it. No redness.

"Does this chafe here?"

She shook her head. "No, sir."

"Good. It's important you tell me if anything is uncomfortable, because that interferes with what I want to happen. Understand?"

She nodded, her shoulders easing further. He repeated what Des had done, working the double wrap over her upper arms, drawing her wrists to her chest. Des walked him through how to do the smooth-lying twist in the back. It held the rope in position without putting an uncomfortable knot against her spine. When he did that part, he had to press Daralyn forward, her head briefly resting against his chest, her hands in his lap, then he eased her back to her heels to continue the rope tying in front.

Her eyes were full of confusion, some apprehension, and yet also a longing that told him whatever was going on right now, she didn't want him to stop. A new tension was back in her shoulders and upper body. The right kind.

Since he'd caught up to where they were before, he looked toward Des. "What was next?" he asked.

The loose way Des kept his long dark hair tied back framed his lean face, emphasizing the intent expression. "Pass the two ends of the rope between her legs, on the outside of the labia, and then run them between her buttocks. You'll be fastening the ropes to the double wrap high on her back. The skirt's thin enough it should be able to just fold down beneath the rope's hold at her waist and lower back."

Rory did it, finding his way beneath the filmy layers of her skirt to her panties. He caressed her there, the silk and lace, before he passed the rope on either side of her labia.

Though not as smooth and practiced as Des, that was okay. The pleasure of this wasn't about getting caught up in technique or the complexity of the design. It was about taking his time, letting his hands slide intimately over her, registering her every reaction to him binding her, including the way she leaned into his touch as he did it.

Since he'd left his shirt open, her breath fluttered against his chest. When he had to press her further forward toward him to reach behind her, her lips brushed his chest, sending tendrils of sensation through him, all the way from waist to earlobes.

His hands tightened on her, and that possessive response caused her to nuzzle him, taste him with the tip of her tongue. Her behavior told him she was headed back toward that trancelike state she'd demonstrated when she'd been watching the scenes...or when he'd first wrapped her hands. A hazy zone of desire and need. She was back on track, and he was right there with her, watching her reaction grow with everything he did to her.

Des was moving around them, a wide circle, giving him further direction and tips in an unobtrusive tone. "Make it snug. Let her feel her Master's hold, his ownership, on her hands, her body, between her legs."

A good cue. As he did it, Rory kissed the back of her neck. "That rope is the same as my hold on you," he murmured. "Only mine. Everywhere on your body. Do you feel it?"

She nodded. She was doing that shallow breathing thing, the right kind. It was only then he noticed the Dungeon Master had moved on, another vote of confidence. Whether that confidence was in Des or Rory, Rory would take it.

Rory hooked his fingers in the double wrap beneath her shoulder blades to make space to thread the two ropes through. Mindful of Des's instruction, he took up all the slack, aware of when that pressure compressed against her sex, against the rim of her backside, even with the thin folds of cloth between them. This time the tiny sound that came from her was unmistakably desire. Her hands curled in their bindings, meeting knuckle to knuckle, like furled flowers. He could see them against his lap, because her chin shifted to the left, her cheek pressing against them.

Des moved back to Julie. She'd left the bench to sit in the grass, her legs folded to one side as she braced herself on her hip. When Des stood beside her, his knee was pressed against her shoulder. His hand fell to it to play with her hair, brush his knuckles over her cheek. Partly a reassurance, because this had probably been as stressful to her as it had been to Rory. They were all invested in the well-being of the incomparable woman he was wrapping in rope. But she was his responsibility, and that was the way he wanted it.

"Have her straighten up on her knees, and wrap the remaining rope around her calves," Des said. "Down to her ankles and around the soles of her shoes."

Rory spoke that direction to her and Daralyn lifted her upper body off his lap, straightening her back. Her position meant he could press his shoulder against her torso, curl an arm around her waist and use her to brace himself as he leaned down and worked the ropes around her calves and shoes one-handed to finish it off.

Her bound hands gripped his shirt, the pressure of her hold containing not only the urgency of her arousal, but also a steadying grip. He wasn't the only one watching out for the person he was with. It invoked a powerful mix of feelings in him, too.

He sat back to look upon his handiwork. She was tied from shoulders to her ankles. If she really struggled, the ropes would give enough to let her get free, but there wasn't much chance of that. Except for the brief flex of her fingers, releasing him as he straightened, she was as still as he'd ever seen her.

Rory glanced at Des. He pointed to his own eyes, Rory's. "Look at me, Daralyn," Rory said.

Her lashes fluttered and lifted, and he was looking into the eyes of a wild animal. One who'd suddenly become tame, not through being broken, but from finding the hand of the Master she craved.

Maybe before coming here and being immersed in a world where people spoke in those terms so easily, he wouldn't have put it that way in his head, but now he couldn't call it anything else. When he ran a finger over her mouth, she kissed and nuzzled it eagerly. He slid the hand into her hair, holding tight as he brought her closer, dipped his head to put his mouth on her throat. Then he bit her.

A savagery he hadn't experienced before rose within him. As he tightened the clamp of his jaw, she was pressed against him, curled fists gripping his open shirt again, latched on as fiercely as he was to her flesh.

It took a big effort to recall himself enough to realize they were doing this in front of Des and Julie, but then he realized they weren't. Des had helped Julie to her feet, and they were already a distance away, wandering off toward the gardens.

Now he'd say what was in his gut. What he felt. And he'd say it, not as some gentle reassurance, but the way the kind of man he was would. The kind of Master he was would.

"I will never, ever share you with another man, Daralyn. Not ever."

Her hazel eyes flared with brilliant emotion, but he didn't stop. "Reason one? I'm a *very* possessive, *very* monogamous kind of guy."

He held her fast, letting her feel the strength behind the statement. The pure ownership. It might not be Dr. Taylor-approved, but in this environment, this moment, it was what was true, and what he felt they both needed.

"Reason two. You don't want to be shared. I don't need to hear it to know I'm right." He touched her chin, reinforcing the lock between their gazes. "Even if you can't ever tell me with words what you want and need, I will spend every moment we have together figuring it out, so I can care for you, respect you, love you."

She swallowed, and the physical and emotional responses tangled in her expression. It made her look even more eternally beautiful, fragile and precious to him. Enough that his primal resolve was mixed with a kind of awe, a sacred respect, for what she meant to him. As he'd told Marcus, when he'd asked Rory how much he loved her.

Like whatever God is. More than I understand or know, but want to spend a lifetime finding out.

"Remember what I told you, back when we started down this road? When the day comes that you can tell me what you want, about anything, whether it's what you want for dessert or how you want to do this"—he tugged on the ropes—"that will be the greatest gift you can give me."

He brought her up to him for another full on, deep kiss. He took his own damn sweet time with it, reinforcing his words with an undeniable claim as he played with her tongue, her provocative lips. She responded just as he knew she would, unconsciously pushing and pulling against him with an urgency that had him sliding his hands down, cupping her sides, his palms against the give of her breasts, fingers firm against her rib cage.

He backed off only to indulge a good long look at the ropes outlining her curves as she trembled and strained in their grip. How the bindings rumpled and molded the wine-colored fabric over her body. The flutter of her tousled hair around her face emphasized the swollen lips, her feverish look of pure need.

When she pressed her lips together to wet them, he could easily imagine them on his flesh. Then her eyes traveled down his torso, to his lap.

"It made me feel so good, when you put your mouth between my legs," she said hesitantly. "Can it feel that way...for you?"

"Yeah." In a different way, but watching her do it would create all sorts of reactions in the places he could feel. So he let the needs in them both guide him.

He wasn't the exhibitionist type. This was a quiet stretch of lawn, but the party was happening just a stone's throw away. However, it was an environment where people were matter of fact about being naked and doing sexual things in front of everyone else. The rules put a cocoon around them that wouldn't be disturbed. No interruptions.

It made his next decision feel more natural. Under her gaze, he unbuckled his belt, opened his jeans. Since he'd already opened his shirt, it wasn't in the way. He brought himself out, stroking to give himself a start on an erection. "Put your mouth on me, Daralyn," he ordered.

She inched forward, bending over his lap. It put her hands close enough to his cock that she could take over the grip on it even with her bonds. As she angled it to her mouth, he tilted his head to the side so he could watch her lips touch his crown. She nuzzled it, kissed it, teased him with the tip of her tongue as his cock responded further, stretching to a greater length and thickness. Then her lips opened to take him in, slide down.

She lightly circled his girth, rubbing him even as she sucked on him, her cheeks hollowing and lips shifting in a way that told him she was running her tongue over his length.

If he had a hundred percent feeling in that area, he'd be fighting not to spew. She not only knew what she was doing, she was good at it.

He understood why that was, and that knowledge wanted to invade his mind with images and thoughts that would tear away anything good about this moment. But as he focused on her, the truth threw up an impenetrable wall and those disruptive thoughts died behind it.

He was a sexually experienced man, a generous and considerate lover. So he knew Daralyn was serving him with obvious need, a deep desire to give him pleasure, because it gave her pleasure. Even if she didn't acknowledge that in words, he could be her witness, take the victory, hold it for her, knowing that it was a hundred percent *her* wants that were driving this.

Her fingers curled tight on his base, anchoring his dick so she could go all the way down, come back up, suck on him. What she was doing with her tongue and mouth was keeping him stiff, and he wanted to be inside her. But for that, he'd wait until they had full privacy. For now, he had all he needed.

He curled his fingers in her hair, holding her, pushing her down deeper, bringing her back up, controlling her movements. Her hands convulsed on him, telling him she liked that reminder that he was in charge, that she was serving him. Watching the set of her shoulders under the thin fabric, the way the ropes were tied over her legs and the soles of her shoes, brought up a mix of the caveman and protector both. He'd tied her up, but he'd make sure she'd feel safe when she was that vulnerable. He'd protect her from anything.

He tipped his head back, taking a long shuddering breath as her mouth brought him to peak, making the starry sky above blur and then slowly, pleasurably come back into focus. During that wave, he let his hand tighten almost to the point of pain, and then he eased it, a light tug telling her he wanted her to lift her head.

As she watched him, her lips wet and hair mussed, he tucked

himself back into his jeans, then backed his chair the distance needed to shift to the edge of his seat, lower himself to the grass with her. He adjusted the chair so that when he put an arm around her, he had his back braced against a locked wheel. Then he removed the rope from her legs and shoes but left the body harness that kept her hands and arms bound, ropes pressing into her sex and the cleft of her buttocks. He eased her down to her side on the grass and stretched out next to her. They were face to face, his arm bent under his head as he ran a hand over her upper arm, her side, her hip. Here they were, the two of them lying in soft grass, by the water, on a beautiful fall night.

He found his way beneath her skirt to the top of her thigh, and back further, caressing the crescent curve along the point where the cloth was held by the rope running between her buttocks.

Then he came around to the front, where the two lines of rope framed her sex. When he feathered a finger over her clit through the fabric of her panties, she gasped. Her bound hands rested on top of his forearm, so her fingers, while not impeding him, were digging into his skin, that sweet involuntary reaction as he kept playing, teasing. Light brushes over her swollen clitoris, the wet petals of her sex that had drenched the crotch of the panties.

"Keep looking at my face," he ordered her. "I want you to see just what your arousal means to me. How much it pleases me."

She kept doing that little licking her lips thing, and knowing she'd had her mouth on him minutes ago only helped his intent now. His body might have released, but there were other parts of him where the need had only doubled.

"I think you like the restraint part of things. No choices to make, just trusting me to do whatever I want to you...because it feels good, doesn't it?"

A quick nod.

"Words, Daralyn," he prompted.

"Yes...yes, sir."

Light brush. Brush. Brush. He was barely touching her, yet he could feel her climax building, see it in the increased desperation in her face.

"I'd like to be inside you right now, because I know your sweet cunt would be squeezing down on my cock. Even though my nerves can't tell my brain you're doing it, my cock knows, and fucking loves it. Loves being inside you."

"Rory..." It was a raw plea, not a question, but he made it one, to keep her attention on him.

"Yeah, baby?"

"I..."

"Tell me what's going on. You're about to come, aren't you? Soon as you say it, you have my permission to do it."

"Yes...I am...I...oh..."

She went over, shuddering as he curled his other arm around her head, drew her to his shoulder so her cries were muffled by his body. She rocked hard against him, strained against the ropes. From the way she writhed, he expected the rope between her buttocks, even with the dress and underwear in the way, had provided more intriguing friction.

Her panties had gone from damp to soaked, and he drew patterns in it over her sex, relishing her tiny little noises of sensual discomfort as he teased hyper-sensitive nerves.

"Sshh," he murmured. "I like touching you right after. I like how you squirm."

She let out a half gasp that might have been a laugh if she wasn't still riding those aftershocks. He pushed her to her back and leaned over her, loving the way that felt, to lean down upon her, feel her breasts against his chest as he kissed her. Her mouth moved against his erratically as her body quivered from the climax he'd given it.

In between the kisses, he kept speaking soothing words to her, rocking her, stroking her body. Did she realize how far she'd come in a handful of weeks? To his way of thinking, she'd done herself a disservice, that night she'd despaired about having trouble with her first day of school. Every day of the past five years had been moving her toward breakthrough moments like these, where she could claim joy and happiness for herself.

He was the lucky one, blessed to be in the right moment and place to be able to share it with her, help her make those steps. Maybe they'd been on a side-by-side journey all along, and some merciful power had decided on the optimal moment for those paths to turn toward one another, link.

He cupped her backside, spreading his fingers out over her cheeks and then squeezing, so she'd feel the rope between them more acutely, rubbing against her rim.

"Did you know you can wear a rope harness under your clothes? Ropes around your breasts and between your legs, like this? We have a lot of nice soft and silky nylon at the store. I think I'll learn how to do that, make you wear it under your clothes at the store one day. I like the idea of no one else but me knowing it's there, and that I tied you up in it."

His eyes burned into her glazed ones. "At the end of the day, I'll have you take everything off but the ropes, straddle me, put me inside. I'll watch you ride me, the ropes holding you, your breasts quivering. You'll get that sweet, feminine mist of perspiration on your neck that makes your hair curl there. I love the way you look at me when you're like this. So needy, so past any worries..."

She made a little moan, tipping up her face. Asking for a kiss, his hungry girl. Her wants were there, so close. Behind a wall, yes, but every day they were building higher, getting closer to the top, wanting to spill over and break that damn wall down. He was happy to help make it happen. Every kiss, every moment they spent together, was another sledgehammer strike against that barrier.

The kiss he gave her this time conveyed all that and more. They'd both just climaxed, but the act felt like a starting gate. He wanted to do more, give her more, see her come a million different ways. He wanted to give her every sensual torment, take her head way past this world and into one where she didn't have to worry about anything, except the next thing he'd demand of her to give her a universe-shattering orgasm.

"What do you think?" he asked huskily. "Would I be cruel, to make you wear ropes under your clothes?"

She shook her head, then remembered. "No sir. No...I'd like that. I mean—"

Before she could backtrack, startled by the second time tonight she'd slipped, he captured her mouth again. As Dr. Taylor had said, there were a lot of things that went into a healing potion.

He could add his own unique ingredients to it.

~

When he finally removed the ropes, he rubbed the lightly chafed area of her wrists. As he did that, they were sitting up again, his back once more against the wheel of his chair. She put her forehead on his shoulder, sank back fully against him. He slid his arm around her, his brow creasing at the impulsive movement, even as it pleased him, her looking for that contact.

More aftercare. That was what she needed, so he took his time, holding her, gazing at the water and night sky. They shared more of the bottled water, watched the distant party-goers, highlighted by the strung lights, the flutter of torch flame, and the graceful lines of the plantation house behind them. The way the pool house was lit up made it look like a wedding cake.

As he'd removed the ropes, he'd noted a look on her face that told him she missed their hold. He'd get on that harness idea soon. In the meantime, her reaction gave him an idea for the next place he wanted to check out. So when he thought she was ready, he suggested they rejoin the party around the pavilion tent, check the booths behind it. On their earlier circuit, they'd discovered a small handful of craftspeople were set up back there, offering goods related to the evening's events.

She was amenable to the idea. After he lifted himself back into the chair and she straightened and smoothed her clothing, they made their way back to the walkway and toward the populated area of the grounds again. On the way, Rory dropped the neatly re-coiled rope on the dais next to the curtained area where Des had retrieved it. Rory had no doubt it was part of the rope artist's personal stash. He couldn't see Des trusting his sub to any rope he hadn't chosen and conditioned himself.

The craftspeople selectively chosen for this event offered leather goods, jewelry, clothing and BDSM toys. There was also a corset seller. It was to that booth that Rory took Daralyn.

The corsetier was a middle-aged stout woman who, in her corset and white ruffled blouse with a gathered skirt, looked like a tavern maid in a Robin Hood film. She had sky blue eyes and a blunt-edged crop of short hair the color of maple syrup.

"I'm Callie, and you'll look amazing in a corset," she told Daralyn. "As for these," she cupped her own ample breasts, "It doesn't matter how small they are. In a corset, your Master's gaze won't be able to leave them."

When Daralyn sent Rory a glance, he responded with a grin. "I love yours. I'm open to any new way to show them off." He nodded to a light gray corset with pale green flowers on it. He thought it would be a good match for her hazel eyes. "Try that one."

"Do you want it over her dress, or would you like to see how it looks on under it?" Callie asked.

"Under it," Rory decided.

The vendor nodded. "Out here, or behind the changing curtain? There's room behind it if you want to join us."

He was on board with that. "Behind the curtain. I'll follow you."

"Very good, sir." Callie proceeded them, holding open the curtain for Daralyn. The vendor booths had temporary event flooring, just like the pavilion tent, so his chair rolled easily. He parked himself in a corner where he had a good view, but the two women had room to maneuver.

"This dress is so lovely," Callie said. "May I help her remove it?"

Daralyn's gaze had remained upon him. Holding her attention, Rory nodded. As the woman moved behind Daralyn and untied the sash, then slid the zipper down, he saw a light shiver course through his sub. When the corsetier pushed the dress off her shoulders, Rory managed, barely, to bite back a groan. He'd already known she wasn't wearing her usual underwear, but now he saw it in its full glory. A matching wine-colored set, the panties and bra were all sheer lace and satin. Which worked fucking fabulously with the shimmering thigh highs, the lace tops a dove gray color.

Bless Julie and Les. Not that he'd ever tell his sister she'd picked out some seriously cock-stirring underwear for the woman who'd captured his heart.

"May I remove the bra?" Callie asked. Again, Daralyn looked to him, and Rory gestured his assent to the woman.

As the cups slipped away, Daralyn stood before him in only the panties, thigh-highs and the low heels. Damn.

Daralyn lowered her lashes, as if seeing what was in his eyes was too powerful for her to hold his gaze. That only increased the possessive feeling inside his chest, the hard thump of his heart. The corsetier knew her business, because she remained quiet, recognizing what was happening between her client and his sub was a private matter, desiring as little outside intrusion on the experience as possible.

She fitted the corset around Daralyn, hooking it in front and moving to the back to begin the tightening process. She reached forward once to adjust the garment, ensure it was placed properly beneath her breasts. Rory noted Daralyn had no tension about being touched by a woman. Even though her gaze remained lowered, he sensed her attention hadn't shifted from him even once.

"Don't lock your knees, dearie," Callie said. "My breath would be shallow too, if a man was looking at me the way he's looking at you, but I don't want you passing out on me."

Daralyn's gaze flicked back up to him, then back down. "How am I looking at you, Daralyn?" Rory asked. "Tell me."

The faint stain on her cheeks that could enthrall him showed up. "Like…like you want to swallow me whole."

"I think I'd rather take small bites. Make the meal last even longer."

That tiny smile again, which always made him feel like she was right there with him, that he wasn't losing her down some dark hole.

Callie tightened the corset once more, and Rory's brow rose. Double damn. Daralyn's figure became more defined, her breasts swelling over the lace edge, just as promised. He couldn't take his eyes away.

"My apologies, sir," Callie said, her gaze on the slit in the curtain. "I have another customer. If you don't mind, I'll let them know I'm in a fitting and tell them how long I'll be."

"Take your time," Rory murmured. The woman shot him a playful smile as she passed him.

The moment Callie stepped out of the curtained space, he was moving forward. Like a dancer anticipating her partner, Daralyn came to the center of the space so he could circle her, study how the corset framed her heart-shaped ass, making it even more noticeable. He brushed his knuckles over that area, and the satin of her panties creased from the reactive flex of her buttocks. Coming back to the front, he trailed fingertips over the tops of her breasts. "Makes them more sensitive, doesn't it?"

"Yes, sir."

He feathered his touch over them several more times, and her pulse rabbited in her throat. "Are you afraid of me, Daralyn?"

Her gaze slipped to his and then away. "Yes. And no."

"Explain that to me."

She moistened her lips. "I know you'd never try to hurt me in a mean way, or scare me. But when you look at me like that...like the devouring thing, there's this fear low in my belly. But it feels like a good fear. Like...I want to be a little afraid of you."

He was sure any Dom liked hearing that kind of thing. But they fed a part of him that, even with his current confidence in himself, in who he was, still had some vital empty space. A man liked knowing his desire could make a woman feel a little nervous, in the good ways they all understood without putting it into words. Daralyn had just given him that acknowledgment, and it filled that empty space right up.

Sliding a finger under the top hook of the corset, he pulled her forward until she was bent toward him and he could put his mouth on the top of one pillowed breast. He tasted it, traced it with his tongue, curled inside the edge to her nipple and played with it against the hold of the brocade. He relished her jolt, the little mewl of need that told him that mix of frictions had sent a shot of desire right to her core.

"I intend to keep you feeling that way," he said. "And I'm not going to be the least bit sorry for it."

He guided her to straighten and then put his hands on her hips, stroking the line of the corset to her upper thighs. "You look stunning," he told her.

Her face lit up with pleasure, a look he liked a lot. As he heard Callie returning, he pushed himself back into his spot to give her room to return to Daralyn's side.

"This style has a very smooth profile," Callie continued, as if she hadn't left. "And this panel over the hooks keeps it from snagging delicate cloth. Would you like her to keep it on beneath her dress? She looks perfect in her dress, but this will give her shape and her movements a different look."

"Yes, ma'am. I'd like that a lot."

Her eyes twinkled at him and she retrieved the dress from the rack where she'd hung it. As she put it over Daralyn's head, Rory saw she was right. The additional layer of clothing padded Daralyn's underweight body and sculpted the upper and lower areas, making both far more noticeable.

"Thank you," he said. He retrieved his wallet from the side pocket of the pack fastened behind his chair and handed his card over to Callie. He hadn't asked the price, but he'd glanced at a couple tags and knew he could cover the three figures on it.

After it was processed and they'd bid Callie good-bye, Daralyn tucking her discarded bra into his pack, he pointed her toward another booth. "We're not done shopping yet," he said.

Apparently, he wasn't the only one who'd seen the price tags. "Oh, that was so expensive," Daralyn protested. "I know you're saving up for that all-terrain chair. I don't need..."

When he gave her a deliberate look, she stopped mid-sentence. He decided to translate the expression straight out, see how it worked for them both. "That's my decision, isn't it?"

She bit her lip. "Yes, sir."

"But I appreciate you being considerate of my money." He took her hand, squeezed it. "That chair is a nice-to-have. You, in a corset? That's a must-have."

She glowed at the comment, which just underlined it twice to him. He stopped before the jewelry booth. "Take a look at some of these," he told her.

The artisan had a wide variety of silver jewelry, with simple to more elaborate spiral designs. He was in the process of making more at a metal crafting station, allowing people to see his process. Despite his wares being delicate pieces of jewelry, he looked like a seventeenth century muscle-bound blacksmith, with a grizzled jaw and a head of bushy gray hair.

Rory browsed the pieces on display, but he was really watching Daralyn. She went back twice to a mouse pendant, his tail curled through one link of necklace chain, his paw gripping another. He'd get that one for her, in addition to the one that had originally drawn his attention to the booth.

It was a bracelet, intended to look like a chain, but the silver links were far more feminine than what he'd used to make her bracelet on the fly. The connecting piece was a heart whose point blossomed into a spiral that circled the heart shape, threaded through the chain links, and reconnected with the heart. When he picked it up and brought

Daralyn to him with a gesture, he put it around her wrist. Since it fit just right, despite the thinness of her wrist, he figured it was meant to be.

"I like this one," he said. "You're the heart, and the spirals are all the things you're reaching for. The things that can come back to your heart, feed it. That's what I hope you'll keep doing."

She trailed her fingers over the chain links. "And these are you," she said. "Holding my heart, giving it a place to rest."

She'd caught the jeweler's attention with the quiet observation, but he discreetly returned to his craft while Rory acted casual about a comment that had punched him right in the solar plexus. "Sounds like a good combination," he said.

When they left the booth, he'd purchased both items. Since the rose and silver pendant she'd worn with the dress was longer than the little mouse, she put the mouse necklace on above it, the tiny creature resting in the hollow of her throat. The bracelet was on her left wrist, that hand resting on his shoulder when they were in motion, or in his clasp, when they stopped to watch the other things happening around them.

Formal demos had given way to individual, impromptu scenes. At a gazebo, a woman on her knees serviced her bald-headed tattooed Dom, who wore biker leathers and stroked her head with gentle hands. He leaned against a column of the gazebo. Amid a grove of dwarf blooming azaleas, the blooms a delicate white-pink, another woman did rope work like Des. While she was less fluid and practiced, she was just as intently involved with her subject matter, tying three subs in an erotic pose, two men and one woman. It looked like they were locked together in the biblical sense, and fighting the desire to move, thrust, grind.

As they circled around the pool house to the open lawn on the other side, they found a game in progress, the applause and laughter drawing him and Daralyn to the entertainment. Fun, silly stuff, subs racing one another through an obstacle course carrying a stack of three teacups.

The subs started the race with vibrators inserted or strapped to their bodies. Remote controls were auctioned off to members of the audience so they could turn them on or off at random moments. But the challenge didn't stop with that. There were stations along the course, like spanking benches where the sub had to stop, bend over and get spanked by the Doms waiting there, with a choice of implements at their fingertips.

At another station, they had to kneel, service impressively sized and colorful candy phalluses. All of this while still holding the teacups. The next challenge station reversed it, the competitors becoming the recipients of the oral treatment, only this time from the mouths of other eagerly volunteering subs. Some were brought so close to climax the teacups were rattling precariously.

Rory was as fascinated as Daralyn, watching the competitors, two women and three men. All the money for the remotes, or the betting on the race winners, would go to the charities of the audience winners' choice.

The finish line involved putting the teacups down on a table, pouring tea in them and serving them to a table of the Masters and Mistresses, the ones to whom the competing subs belonged.

One of the female submissives won, a curvy thirty-something with green eyes, and highlighted brown hair. She wore a tropically patterned mint green and chocolate brown bikini, suggesting she'd taken advantage of the pool earlier in the evening. A transparent green scarf with tiny tassels and little bells was hooked jauntily around her hips.

After she completed the task, her Mistress had her kneel next to her while she sipped the tea thoughtfully. After an approving nod, she bent to kiss her woman's lips. Then she turned to the audience and gestured at the man who'd bid for the remote that controlled her sub's vibrator. He was a slim but muscular male, his long dark hair braided down his back. Since he was shirtless and wearing only a pair of jeans, a tattoo was visible under the tail of hair. The Celtic heart was overlaid by a triquetra and a pair of handcuffs. *Conditionally Yours* was written in script beneath, though a scar made it look as if the first word had been altered.

The Mistress met the man's gaze. "Reward her, Noah," she said.

Daralyn's hand gripped Rory's as Noah inclined his head and pressed a button on the remote, turning up the intensity so the woman immediately swayed and began to moan, her gaze latched on her Domme.

"That's my sweet rabbit," she said. "But you know you still don't get to come without my permission, Gen."

"Damn," Rory muttered, with admiration for the woman's stroke of deviltry. The Domme glanced his way. She had long red hair and a brilliant, glass-shard type gaze that told him she could be a lot tougher than this. But there was a tenderness there, too, as she returned her attention to the struggle happening at her feet.

When Gen was making pleading noises, her buttocks noticeably quivering even under the sheer gauze scarf, the woman nodded. "Now."

She let Gen rest her forehead on her latex clad thigh as her body convulsed, her hands clutching her Mistress's legs for an anchor as she screamed at the force of the climax that went through her. The Domme leaned over her, pressed her lips to her shoulder, her hands stroking the curve of her back.

She didn't tell Noah to turn off the vibrator until Gen was all done and jerking from the over stimulation. But then, as Gen slowly recovered, Noah drew close to them. He knelt next to the quivering submissive, slipping an arm around her as he kissed the Domme's thigh.

"Lyda handles two subs better than most of us handle one." The comment came from a man behind Rory, punctuated by an admiring chuckle and response from his male companion.

"That's because she's Type A enough to need two subs. She'd be bored otherwise."

Definitely another couple of Doms. Rory didn't turn to get a visual on the two men, because his attention had been pulled toward Daralyn's reaction.

"Oh..." She sounded breathless. "They're all three together." She was leaning against his chair. As he put his arm around her waist, supporting her, he stroked the line of the corset he could feel beneath her dress. He thought about how she'd look later tonight when it was just the two of them, her wearing only the form-fitting garment and her stockings. "Feeling a little weak, baby?" he asked solicitously. "Maybe you need some food. Or I could loosen a couple laces."

Her eyes glinted at him, her lips twisting in a rueful response he answered with a grin and a less suggestive idea.

"Let's go get one of those cupcakes."

CHAPTER SEVENTEEN

*T*hey were in time for another food demo, where they had the chance to watch a Dom decorate his female sub with several dessert options. Then he and Daralyn shared a cupcake, her laughing as she helped him get frosting out of his beard. He licked hers off her top lip.

It was getting close to time to call it a night. They were country people with a normal ten o'clock bedtime, up with the sunrise, and it was past midnight. They'd made a good accounting of themselves though, since the other guests had begun to thin out. Some he suspected would retire to the guest cottages, while others would head back into the city or to area hotels to continue their activities in private.

The evening had had some of everything. He'd seen a few scary things, but watching those things get other people off had undeniably affected him, and he thought Daralyn felt the same. He was also considering alternative uses for his store inventory, sure he'd never look at certain items the same way again.

They'd had that one scary moment when Daralyn had freaked out about Des touching her. But it had been more than balanced out with laughter, smiles, arousal, and a strengthened sense that the two of them were in this together. They were discovering new stuff, and comfortable being with one another while they did it.

As they swung back toward the pavilion for what he figured would be their last lap, he noted an informal gathering of people at several round tables, cozily spotlighted with strings of paper lanterns. The servers had consolidated the remaining food on a nearby smaller buffet table, next to a drink station still well stocked with an ample beer and wine selection. A pretty woman in a black dress and white collar with a heart lock was serving as bartender.

Julie and Des were sitting at one of the tables with Tyler, and gestured at Rory to join them. Daralyn looked pleased at the chance to visit, so he decided they'd stay a while longer. He guided her over to a chair next to Julie and ordered himself a light beer and Daralyn a soda from the attendant. Des moved the empty chair from beside Daralyn so Rory could slide in next to her.

Tyler, Des and Julie were sharing the table with two men and a woman, twenty-somethings like Rory and Daralyn. One of the men was a polished-looking kind of handsome, like a lawyer. The other man looked like a cross between Brick and Johnny. His callused hands suggested his job was some sort of manual labor. The woman between them was willowy, with straight dark hair and clear eyes. Both men had an arm along the back of her chair, a message of intimacy and belonging.

The lawyer-looking guy's hand overlapped the big man's, and he was stroking his forearm and her shoulder with an equal intimate ease. A possessive one. The bigger man's hand was cupped in the same way around the woman's shoulder, teasing a line up and down her upper arm.

Another threesome. In this world, that kind of grouping apparently wasn't all that unusual. And the touches between the men said it was a full three-way, not just two guys sharing a girl.

Polyamory. The term had come up while he was reading Marcus's recommendations. While he'd only recently wrapped his mind around men getting married, seeing relationships that weren't just one boy, one girl crop up in the BDSM research stuff made sense. He assumed most non-traditional relationships would find a comfortable overlap with other kinds.

The lawyer definitely had the Dom-vibe, but the gaze the bigger man periodically sent his way was harder to define. As if they might both be Doms to her, but to each other, it was more fluid, even as the lawyer probably still held the reins most of the time.

Rory told himself he wouldn't stare like a country bumpkin, but he did notice Daralyn studying and taking in the nuances, same as him.

"This is Geoff, Sam and Chris,' Julie told them. She'd started with the lawyer and proceeded in order to the right. Sam might be short for Samantha, Rory deduced. "They're from North Carolina, too, and made the trip with us for the party. I've been trying to get them interested in doing performances at the theater. Sam in particular." She winked. "Because if I get Sam, I'll get the two of them."

Geoff chuckled. "Yeah, I'm sure the city would be thrilled to discover one of their ADAs is doing erotic stage work on weekends."

Yep, had the attorney part right.

"You can wear a mask." Julie shrugged. "Several of our regulars do that. One of our writers drafted a skit for the next show that could have been written for you three specifically."

"It probably was." Sam leaned against Geoff's side and had her thigh pressed against Chris's. "You're just innocently saying it 'could have been written' for us."

"They know you too well, love." Des tugged Julie's hair. She was relaxed against him, her hand lying loosely on his thigh. They looked content, but Rory suspected Des was about as tired as he and Daralyn were.

Des had a couple challenging health issues, with insulin-resistant Type I diabetes at the center of it. Though he and Des never talked about it much, Rory suspected that commonality had helped them warm up to each other quicker than they probably already would have, since Rory was all good with someone who made Julie this happy. But Des knew what it was to have his life revolve around his health choices, not just as a look-good-for-the-girls or keep-the-doctor-off-your-back thing.

Tired they might be, but never tired enough to give family a hard time. "Run while you can," Rory advised Sam. "Julie's like a cute and fluffy pit bull."

"Cretin," Julie said.

Rory made a show of scratching his head. "What's a cretin? Itn't that them things you put on top of a salad? They's good when they have cheese in 'em."

Julie snorted as the others chuckled. "Just you wait," she told Rory. "I'll get *you* up on a stage one of these days."

"Only if you're thinking of doing something over my dead body, and I think there are laws about that."

Tyler was leaning back in his chair. While he listened to the banter with a light smile, Rory noted his attention wasn't fully on them. He was waiting for someone, and Rory had a good idea who it was. When the light in his eyes became focused heat, he knew she was headed for the table.

Since he didn't expect anything about Marguerite Winterman had changed since he'd seen her at his brother's wedding, Rory made sure he didn't take a swallow of beer before turning to follow Tyler's gaze. He'd probably choke on it.

Though the small handful of people hanging out in the tent likely saw her more often than he did, he wasn't surprised to see their attention drawn to her as she moved into the tent, headed toward her husband.

With a lithe body, silky, thick white-blond hair and pale blue eyes, Marguerite was stunning, but not in a cover model kind of way. It was a quality, not a group of physical features.

He'd remembered her correctly. She walked like a goddess touched down to earth. And after a night of being around Doms and subs, now he was certain she fell in the Domme category. Her attitude projected it, how she measured and appraised those around her.

But the way her eyes met and held Tyler's as she crossed the space between them, how she put her hand in his once she was within reach, sent another kind of message.

She was a Domme, yes. But not with him. She belonged to him. Rory guessed the right term was switch, but that submissive side was exclusively for Tyler. As soon as she looked away from her husband, the Domme was a hundred percent back.

Flowing white pants draped her hips while a gray sleeveless velvet top hugged her slim upper body. The fabric coaxed the fingers to stroke, if the owner of them didn't mind having the digits broken into little pieces by Tyler. Or, as he shot a second look at that Domme expression, by Marguerite herself.

On her swan neck was a twisted double strand of seed pearls, interspersed with tiny silver pieces that looked like icicles. A silver angel pendant had wings shaped to look like the icicles. The pendant rested just below the hollow of her throat. It was the only jewelry she wore.

"Ma'am," Rory said. Though he knew around here "ma'am" had a whole different meaning, for him the address was automatic manners.

Her gaze rested on him, and then moved to Daralyn. Yeah, he remembered that about her too. She didn't say much until she was darn good and ready. He wouldn't say she was unschooled in social cues, the way Daralyn had been and still struggled with. Marguerite Winterman simply discarded them as unnecessary.

Daralyn had been stealing looks at her, but when Marguerite's regard came directly to her, Daralyn was looking at her beverage again. His girl offered her polite smile in Marguerite's general direction. However, her hand on Rory's knee curled up in that way it did when she wasn't sure of a new person. He covered it with his, a reassurance.

"We're so glad you two could be here tonight." Marguerite spoke at last. She had a quiet voice. He didn't expect she raised it often, but it had a clarity that commanded attention.

"I worried we might not be fancy enough to get into the party," Rory admitted. "Well, me. I can't imagine Daralyn would be turned away from any get-together."

"Not by a host with any sense," Tyler reached over to tap his beer to the neck of Rory's before he brought his own to his lips, took a generous swallow. "The only person I ban from my property is Marcus."

Rory managed his own swallow without a sputter, but it was a close thing. Tyler's amber eyes twinkled. "It's to protect my art collection. He'll drool on it, ruin its value."

"I knew there was a reason I liked you," Rory said.

Marguerite leaned against the side of Tyler's chair rather than sitting. Her hand rested on his shoulder while his arm hooked around her waist, thumb sliding back and forth over her hip bone.

Though her body relaxed into his touch, Marguerite's pale blue gaze stayed on Daralyn. "Have you been enjoying the party, Daralyn?" she asked.

Yeah, definitely Domme. Marguerite had that direct way of asking a question that commanded an answer.

"Yes, ma'am." Daralyn knew the difference between someone

trying to get her to express her preferences and someone making polite conversation. But then Marguerite took it to a different level.

"What have you enjoyed the most about it?" Marguerite asked.

Shit. Daralyn was suddenly staring a hole in the table. Still, as he watched her wet her lips, Rory realized she had an answer, so he held his breath, waiting. "Being here with Rory," she said slowly. "And seeing everything...with him."

A nice thing to hear, and matched his own feelings on it. The others at the table were watching the interplay. It wasn't hard to recognize that Daralyn didn't like being the center of attention and was struggling with it. Rory picked up the thread to draw it away from her.

"I appreciated the invitation," he said. "It's given us the chance to learn new things in a comfortable way." He slanted a look toward Des. "Learning that rope thing in the store might have been awkward."

"At least during opening hours," Julie interjected. She sent Rory a meaningful wink, one that told him she was doing her part to help with the shift. "Though I think some of your customers already know the pervertible uses for your inventory. Like Mrs. Mueller..."

"Nnn-nh." Rory shook his head and made a show of sticking his fingers in his ears. "You are not putting images of Reverend Mueller's wife in my head I can't remove."

"She's a Baptist," Julie told the table.

"Definitely a kinkster, then," Geoff observed. Rory pointed a warning finger at him.

"I've just met you, but I will hurt you. Don't let the chair fool you."

"Fair warning, he's hard to beat up," Chris said. "He's thin but slippery. Being a lawyer, he has that oil coating on his skin."

Rory grinned, but beneath the genial expression, he was still watching Marguerite. She hadn't smiled during the exchange, and her gaze didn't move from Daralyn. She seemed to be divided between an internal focus on her own thoughts, and an external one, revolving around Daralyn.

She wasn't asking Daralyn anything directly, but Daralyn was keenly aware of the attention. Probably because Marguerite's focus didn't feel like the casual courtesy of a host. When he caught Julie's puzzled, concerned look, he had reinforcement that he wasn't imagining it. She didn't know what the fuck was going on here, either.

Daralyn's back was unusually straight, which could be because of the posture the corset's hold demanded, but the hand under his was quivering, and that trembling was moving up her arm. No matter what the deal was with Marguerite, he wasn't going to let Daralyn suffer another moment of discomfort under that unsettling stare. As his dad used to say when he and his siblings were squabbling: *You may not have started it, but I'm going to finish it.*

"Mrs. Winterman." He spoke at the tail end of another round of chuckles, over something he hadn't paid attention to. "Is there something I can help you with?"

Tyler's gaze came his way, the tiger eyes assessing. Under Rory's grasp, Daralyn's hand tensed at the edge in his polite tone. He wasn't pissed, though. Just protective. A lot of Masters and Mistresses had looked at Daralyn tonight, a casual assessment. Of him, too. But no judgment to it. The party had been everything Thomas had promised. No one putting on airs or going out of their way to make them feel uncomfortable.

This was something different.

Marguerite's attention finally shifted to him, held. Then her head dipped, a courtesy. "When you meet another person in a wheelchair, you feel a familiarity, because you have a better understanding than most of the paths you've each walked. Wouldn't you say?"

He didn't sense she was doing the stranger in the grocery line thing, the one who thought asking him how he'd ended up paralyzed fell in the same category as asking him about the frozen peas he was buying. She had a serious purpose, and it involved Daralyn.

"Maybe," he said. "But we're all different. Like you sub for him," he nodded in Tyler's direction, "but you're definitely not a sub. Not like Daralyn."

Tyler's amber gaze went from assessment to gun sight lock. He was ready to intervene if Rory became too forward, but that was warning for warning. Rory sent him a look that said he wasn't backing down from it. Not while his own sub was in the firing line.

Fortunately, Marguerite's lips curved in a small smile, her fingers molding over Tyler's broad shoulder. Half the tension hovering over the table dissipated.

"Very insightful, Mr. Wilder. May I address your submissive directly? I can speak to you instead, if you wish."

Rory glanced at Daralyn. She seemed to be doing her own internal conversation, because her chin had set and her back straightened a little. He saw her lips move silently, then she looked his way, managed a faint smile. She was unsettled, but okay.

He thought she'd said *"just like a customer"* to herself. He wasn't sure if that method was going to hack it for whatever Marguerite intended, but he was here. He could help.

"Long as I don't feel you're upsetting her. She's had a very good night tonight. I'd like to keep it that way."

Marguerite's pale blue eyes flickered. They were like pieces of the sky, just as vast. "I can understand that. Having someone willing to protect your soul with every bit of his own is a gift impossible to measure."

That last part had been sent right past him to Daralyn. Daralyn's gaze came up, slowly, and then met Marguerite's.

Rory noted Tyler was watching Marguerite, too, in a manner too familiar for Rory to miss. He watched Daralyn like that when he knew she was balanced on a precarious edge. If he hadn't been so closely locked into it with Daralyn, Rory might not have seen past Marguerite's strength as a Mistress to note it, see it in Tyler's protectiveness of her.

As the significance of that took shape in Rory's mind, Marguerite bent and spoke in Tyler's ear. His gaze softened, though his mouth remained firm. He brushed a knuckle over her cheek, tucked a lock of her silky hair behind her ear. Then he touched the pearl necklace, hooked it, a reminder, as their eyes held.

Rory's gaze slid to the angel pendant resting just below the tender pocket of Marguerite's throat, and that was when he understood. Or thought he did.

Tyler had intimate knowledge of where his goddess's vulnerabilities lay. But it was more than the Domme goddess thing that drew people's attention to Marguerite. It was the same quality that Daralyn had. They projected a spirit that was remarkably eternal and yet ephemerally fragile, in ways that could be so easily, terrifyingly missed. Which meant they weren't as resilient to the world's blows. Their souls had already absorbed more than a lifetime's worth of them.

Marguerite and Daralyn had a kinship in their past that no one should have to share, but they did.

Marguerite straightened and looked at Rory again. The Domme look was back, but there was no threat here. This was a reaching out, an attempt at an important connection. He noticed Daralyn's hand was no longer trembling in his grasp, and she was quietly looking at Marguerite.

"I'd like to show Daralyn a sculpture we keep in a private part of our gardens," Marguerite said. "I think she'll like it. You have my word. She'll be safe with me in every way."

Daralyn appeared curious but not unsettled in the wrong way. Even so, it was still an effort to consent to having her out of his sight, but Julie's reassuring look told him these were people who could be trusted.

He saw it in Tyler's expression as well.

"All right," Rory said.

～

With the noticeably strong magnetic field of energy around her, the white-haired Marguerite reminded Daralyn of the fairy queen Galadriel, one of the characters in the *Lord of the Rings* movies. Les had shown her the trilogy in small portions, until they made it through them all. When she told Daralyn the movies were based on books, Daralyn had checked the series out from the library. It had been her first experience in realizing how movies and books could tell stories in different but sometimes equally interesting ways. Different mediums. That's how Helga, the town librarian, had described it.

Daralyn was anxious that Marguerite would want to talk, but as they strolled in the gardens, away from the others, Marguerite didn't say anything. She stayed side by side with Daralyn, though, and the silence wasn't uncomfortable. The lack of conversation helped Daralyn relax some.

It also allowed her to give this section of the gardens her undivided attention. Like all the landscaping, it looked untamed without being unruly, the plantings layered and complementing one another. Their gardener knew what he or she was doing. Cell phones weren't allowed, for obvious reasons, but Daralyn wished she could photograph the plantings to show Elaine. But she'd remember and describe them to her. She was already fashioning a new display area in her head for their landscape inventory at the store, as well as developing a couple ideas for her own small yard.

Sculptures and small statuary tucked here and there added interest to the design. A bench and a stump provided spots for contemplation. That sense of sanctuary expanded when they reached what Daralyn thought might be their destination. This section was influenced by Japanese gardening styles, with a mix of small conifers and low growing flowering mosses. The mosses covered the large angular rocks, which had cool green border plants like variegated hosta tucked in between them. The rich burgundy color of several cut leaf Japanese maples was highlighted by artfully placed landscape lights, and the shade-loving plants of the glade were protected by the arms of two large live oaks.

Water plants floated in a koi pond. A trio of small black horses were leaping out of the depths of the small waterfall pouring into the pond, keeping the water moving.

"Shall we sit?"

Marguerite sank down on the wall built around the pond. Daralyn took a mirrored pose, the two of them sideways on the wall so they could watch the koi circle. It put her almost knee to knee with Marguerite. The corset's hold didn't let her sit as casually as she normally would, but she liked the way it felt, a restraint much like the ropes Rory put on her. A reminder of his presence, like the bracelet.

"We have a couple koi ponds on the property. The other one has a statue of Aphrodite, but this one was designed specifically for the horse sculpture."

"I saw the Aphrodite one earlier." It had been in the more public part of the gardens. "It's amazing. But this...this is so quiet."

"Yes." They sat for some minutes in that same companionable silence. When Marguerite trailed her fingers in the water, playing with the koi, Daralyn did the same, smiling at the way the fish nibbled at her fingertips. It was peaceful here, and the feeling that emanated from Marguerite was part of that ease.

Daralyn hadn't felt comfortable at the table with her. Not until Marguerite met her gaze that last time, and then something Daralyn couldn't describe had changed. Well, maybe she could. A door had opened in Marguerite's mind and Daralyn stepped in, at the exact moment that Marguerite did the same with her. So they didn't have to say anything. They were already inside, and knew what things looked like.

"It's nice, isn't it?" Marguerite mused. "To have a space where nothing is needed or expected. You can simply be, because you're all you need to be in this moment."

Managing the expectations, the intentions of others, could be overwhelming. Sometimes it seemed it was all Daralyn could do, just to keep an eye on the precarious balance of what was inside her. A tree, a garden, a square of blue—when she looked at them, those were things that could be managed, that could give without taking.

The square of blue was in Dr. Taylor's office, a painting mounted directly behind her desk. A blurry-edged shape against a washed-out field of watercolor blues and greens.

Marguerite's gaze lifted and took in their surroundings. "Gardeners seem to understand the importance of creating quiet spaces, for meditation, for simply being. The first time I saw the grounds here, I thought how overwhelming it must have been, to design and create it. But Robert, our gardener, told me a garden starts with one feeling. A plant put next to another plant that feels right there. He said it can start with a group of pots on an apartment balcony."

Daralyn's growing group of flowers and plants around her home had started with a couple pots Elaine had given her. Now three sides of the house had blooms, ornamental grasses and small shrubs.

"I've found that, too," she said.

Marguerite's gaze slid over hers, returned to the waterfall, and the trio of horses. "A horse is a thousand pounds of muscle, teeth and hooves," she said, "and yet their legs are absurdly fragile. I visited an equine rescue earlier this year. Those who have histories of severe abuse or neglect have a wariness in their eyes. But what breaks the heart is the hope, like a fluttering candle flame next to an open window."

Marguerite lifted her wet hand out of the water and extended it. Scar tissue formed a starburst across the top, from wrist to knuckles.

"That was done to me when I was a child. Along with many other things." The gaze that met Daralyn's was straightforward, no pity for herself, yet not casual nor dismissive either.

Before uneasiness could steal into Daralyn's lower belly, Marguerite made a calming gesture. When she continued to speak, her words seemed to move at the same cadence as the breeze that rustled the grasses around them and the live oak leaves above. It reminded Daralyn of the way it felt to read a book. The words offered for her own thoughts, no response required.

"For so many years, I existed," Marguerite said. "Succeeded because I needed to move forward. At first, that's a victory, an accomplishment so momentous the effort can't be measured. But if it remains the goal too long, it loses its value. I was at that point when I met Tyler."

Her pale blue eyes moved to Daralyn's, then went back to studying the world around them. When she'd first arrived at the table, Marguerite had shown the Mistress side of herself, her ability to pierce a person to the soul with her gaze. But now Daralyn wondered if there'd been a time when Marguerite hadn't looked at anyone directly, either.

Marguerite rose, gesturing, and Daralyn followed her around a sumptuous grove of fatsia. Here she found another sequestered space, still in the Japanese garden style, including a rock garden with a tiny bamboo rake and a wisteria arbor. Just beyond it was an open-air structure made of golden wood with a hipped roof. A tea house. She'd seen them in the garden supply magazines they received from their vendors.

Then Marguerite pivoted away from that section, drawing Daralyn's attention to a sculpture that, once turned in the right direction, was impossible to miss.

It was a bronze angel. Nearly life-sized and male, with half spread wings, every feather defined. An expression of warrior alertness was captured on his etched face, but there was also a light smile on his lips that spoke of generosity and a depth of spirit. His eyes seemed to penetrate the watcher, call to them.

Dark green ferns clustered around his pedestal, and another, smaller waterfall murmured near the statue. Marguerite drew her to a nearby bench, both of them sinking down to face the angel.

"Tyler had this commissioned to honor my brother," Marguerite said. "He died when we were very young. I was with him when it happened."

"Oh. I'm so sorry."

"At the time, they said I survived, but it wasn't true. We can't say that any part of us survives what happens to us. Not until we know how to live." Marguerite's eyes met Daralyn's. "How is that going for you, Daralyn?"

What do you want for dinner? Do you want to do this...or that? Even such casual questions could spawn anxiety. But this targeted question, aimed right at her center, stilled her. She was locked into a moment with Marguerite that reminded her of those times with Rory when everything fell away but what mattered.

"Some days better than others," she said honestly. "This is one of them."

"Good." Marguerite smiled. It wasn't an open or easy gesture. "For most people," she said, "life is about coming out of the womb into a world of possibilities. For others, it's about crawling out of a grave and discovering we are no longer dead."

A fierce look crossed her face. "They couldn't kill us. We are alive, and have so much living to do. But they will always be calling, because their darkness is something we can't leave behind. At times, it seems those shadows won't be satisfied until we're pulled back into those memories, those feelings, and trapped there forever. Each morning, we start the fight anew, and wonder when our strength to resist will falter."

Things rose up, wanted to choke her, but Marguerite's other arm slid around her, held her shoulders, steadied her.

"It's all right," Marguerite said, and now Daralyn heard the Domme side surface. "You're all right. Breathe. Relax. Don't fight it. Let it wash through."

Marguerite's reassurance, the strength in her hold, weren't Rory, but the method and tone were so much like him she could reach for him through Marguerite, hold onto that mental lifeline, steady herself, though the breathing part took extra effort with the corset. She didn't want the panic attack to require its removal, so she summoned the force of will to even her breathing and stave off any lightheadedness.

Fortunately, Marguerite didn't rush the process. They sat that way for a while, Marguerite demonstrating no urgency at all. Not until Daralyn herself had calmed did Marguerite eventually ease back. "All right?"

Daralyn nodded. "Yes, ma'am."

Marguerite pursed her lips. "Do you think about power, Daralyn? Having it?"

Daralyn frowned at the unexpected question. "I...I'm not sure what you mean."

"Rory loves you, and that gives you so much power. Not just over him, but over the world. Your world." Marguerite gave her a steady look. "He doesn't want anything to hurt you or cause you pain. Including him. But you have your own power to survive that. You proved it, didn't you? And now you're learning you not only had the power to survive, but to thrive. Live. Love."

Marguerite's white hair blew forward over her shoulder. The lustrous strands were such an unusual color. Daralyn lifted a hand toward it before she thought. She froze, her usual apprehension surging forth to counter the impulsive gesture.

"It's fine," Marguerite said. "I would like it if you touched my hair, Daralyn."

Daralyn stroked the thick silk of it with tentative fingers. Marguerite returned the favor, brushing Daralyn's hair from her brow. The gesture was neither sexual nor sisterly. It had a hint of something maternal to it, but not motherly. More on the warrior-teacher side of things.

"It wasn't until Tyler found a way to break through that I knew why I'd survived," Marguerite continued. "I'd lived before I met him, found ways to thrive, but I couldn't find my way back to what love was truly supposed to be until I met him."

Daralyn thought about Rory. Since that first kiss, she'd struggled with so many things between them. Those things hadn't been a straight line. Instead they were more like a spiral, touching past, present and future at the same time as they rotated around what the two of them were building between them. She suspected that was close to what Marguerite was talking about.

"At some point, you'll have to come face to face with that power to love, figure out how to take it inside you," Marguerite said. "Only you can do that. No one can force it on you, and no one who loves you will. But they will hope for it for you. Because they're standing on the other side of that choice, already knowing what we have to teach ourselves, because it was never taught to us the way it was to them."

"What's that?"

"That finding the bravery to love fully, with every cell of who we are, is the only answer to all of it. Don't be afraid of the power that comes from it, Daralyn. Whether it's used to rule or serve, it's a gift we should never turn down."

Daralyn turned Marguerite's hair over her fingers, watching it slide free, drift back to her shoulder. Marguerite offered that serious smile.

"Love isn't something you expect, let alone that it will have the strength to stand at your back. Even more than that, once you take it inside you, it will become the weapon, the home, the permanent place of stillness that transcends everything."

Marguerite gestured around them. "And that's when you make the true leap. You'll know you can rest in his arms, simply be, and it's all right. You are finally safe. No question, no act of yours or his, or anyone else's, will change your awareness of it. Love has made sure you can never be imprisoned in that place of fear again. You have changed forever. Broken free."

Her eyes came back to Daralyn's. "It's the hardest thing we have to learn. But we have the strength. It just takes time."

The mask dropped fully, and now Daralyn saw more than just a grown woman like herself. They were two young girls who would never forget what it was to live in unimaginable darkness, would never lose their wonder that somehow they'd stumbled through the darkness to the light.

This time she didn't have to ask. She reached out, closed her hand over Marguerite's, over the starburst scar. Marguerite's hand turned, and they gripped, held fast. Their gazes turned to the angel, to the gardens around him. "It's enough," Marguerite said softly. "Every moment like this is enough."

Daralyn's mind was so full of those words, all the possibilities of them, she had nothing else to say. But it wasn't needed. The energy changed, became easier, lighter, as did the look Marguerite turned her way. "Come see my tea house?" the woman asked.

"Yes, certainly."

As they rose, Daralyn's gaze fell on the necklace on Marguerite's throat. Marguerite saw it, and closed her fingers over the heart bracelet on Daralyn's arm. "Our Masters find ways to tell us they are with us, even when they aren't. That's a weapon, too." A feline smile crossed her lips. "A weapon they will wield on our behalf, even if it's to tear down the walls we build against them."

"Did you do that with Tyler?" Daralyn ventured.

Marguerite's gaze sparkled with unexpected humor. "Over and over again."

Daralyn thought of the handsome, silver-haired man with a tiger's eyes. He looked at Marguerite with a surfeit of emotions that all amounted to one thing.

She belonged to him, and he to her.

"But he didn't give up."

"No, he didn't. Thank the Goddess. I didn't make it easy. The greatest of understatements. But Tyler has told me in so many ways, mostly without words"—her gaze swept the tea house, the rock garden, angel and waterfall—"that none of that matters. Nothing could change how he felt about me. Everything I did only made his feelings grow stronger. Our bond was something that existed no matter what forces came against it. Like the peace of this glade."

Her attention came back to Daralyn. "Having that knowledge inside me...it's everything. It doesn't solve all problems; it simply tells me I will never face them alone. Not ever again."

CHAPTER EIGHTEEN

*G*oing to Florida had changed things, in a lot of good ways. It wasn't just one thing, but the way they all mixed together. Traveling together. Spending time at the cabin relaxing, reading, watching Rory fish. The amazing things they'd seen and done together at Tyler's party. Visiting Arnold Simms, the fixture vendor, on their last day in Florida, looking through his stock together, deciding what items would be most appealing to their customer base.

Looking back over the past few weeks, Daralyn thought she might be the most content she'd ever been in her life. Every day she could look forward to *more*. Learning more at school, helping more at the store, doing more in her garden, decorating her house.

Best of all was how much of that involved being with Rory. Their days were spent working side by side in the store, and their evenings... well, just thinking about some of the things they did could stop her in the middle of whatever she was doing to get lost in the memories. And the result? She'd emerge flushed and hungry for *more*.

One night they'd gone out for pizza with Marty and Amanda. Daralyn had the new experience of hanging out with friends...for fun. When Amanda and Marty had visited the juke box to choose some music, she'd tried Rory's beer, made a face.

"I didn't think you liked alcohol," he said.

"I just wanted to put my lips on the glass where yours have been."

Around him, her fear of saying things that didn't really fit into normal conversation had all but disappeared. Probably because of reactions like what had happened next. He'd moved his arm from the back of her chair, used the wrap of it to draw her up close and put his mouth on hers. His breath had been fragrant with the hops and warm with desire. When he'd broken the kiss, he'd cocked his brow and given her a smile that had curled her toes. "Always best to go to the source," he advised.

His seemingly limitless desire to give her pleasure left her only one choice—to embrace it. He drove her to the edge of ecstasy and beyond as often as possible. He could also be very demanding about the when and where of it, keeping her body humming, anticipating.

Her favorite way so far was when he had her straddle him in his chair, his hands on her hips, him inside her. His gaze would lock upon her like nothing else in the whole world was more important than watching the climax take her over. When he pulled raw screams of crazed pleasure from her, his avid brown gaze would devour her every reaction. Those responses only goaded him to do more things to tear helpless cries from her. When she finally came down, he would band both arms around her, suckle her breasts, sending hard aftershocks through her as strong as the climax itself.

He let her pleasure him too. While she eagerly embraced the ways he taught her to do it, she watched his reactions to her touch just as closely as he watched hers. She learned to take it even deeper, give him more than he expected. Though his cock would harden in her hands, it was the ways she used her mouth and touch on him above the waist that intensified his own response. When his body shuddered in the grip of his own release, his brown eyes flashing with fire and loss of focus, she cherished it, exulted in what felt like a victory. It reminded her of what Marguerite had said about power, and all the possible things she could have meant.

Afterward, after he did the necessary things to clean up, he'd return to her bed and usually spend the night there, holding her. He left her just before dawn to go home to shower and get ready for work. When Elaine went on her church trips, she'd stay at his house. Rory explained that while Elaine knew they were adults, and accepted they'd share a bed in the house when she wasn't home, she was tradi-tional enough to discourage that arrangement when she was there. Not when they weren't married.

Daralyn understood that. With all the care Elaine had shown Daralyn, she'd never want to do anything to disrespect her feelings. She also liked that Rory had that kind of respect and love for his mother.

Before she and Rory had become involved, when Marcus and Thomas were in New York, Daralyn would often join Rory and Elaine for an evening meal. That hadn't changed, either. Though she and Rory would go back to Daralyn's house afterward, Daralyn still came over for dinner at least every couple of days.

Sometimes they'd stay to watch a favorite TV program or movie with Rory's mother. Or Daralyn would help Elaine with a quilting project. They might go through garden magazines and discuss potential projects.

While he channel-surfed, Rory would put in his two cents. Other times he tinkered with his wheelchair in the shop adjacent to the house, making adjustments to it. After Daralyn helped Elaine, she'd go perch on a stool in the shop, reading, watching him work with his hands, secretly stealing glimpses of that intent look on his face she had mentioned to Amanda.

During one of those nights they stayed after dinner, Elaine's position on the two of them spending the night together under her roof unexpectedly changed.

It was during one of Elaine's favorite programs. The day at work had been a really busy one, such that Daralyn found herself nodding off while on the couch. Rory had transferred there from his chair so Daralyn could lie against his side. He'd nudged her to a more comfortable lying down position so she had her head on his thigh, fingers curled underneath it. As he rested his hand on her hip and back, stroking, she dozed. She was vaguely aware of Elaine in her recliner while she and Rory exchanged comments about the program.

Elaine's preference was to turn on the subtitles and keep the volume low. That worked better for Daralyn, too, but even as she drifted off, she knew she shouldn't fall asleep.

Never with the TV on. Even low.

Next thing she knew, it was blaring, so loud it seemed to make the walls vibrate. Stale cigarette smoke, old sweat. *Bad. You've been bad. Into the hole.* Hands were reaching for her, her father's breath on her face.

She floundered out of the dream like a marathon runner with no breath left, the TV screaming an alarm in her head.

"Daralyn, hey. You're okay. You're here. It's all right."

The TV sound disappeared, and she found Rory's hands on her, his brown eyes close and concerned.

Not real. Not there. You're no longer there.

She'd jerked up to a sitting position, her heart pounding painfully in her chest. She could barely speak, and he stroked her, continuing to soothe.

"It's okay. You're here, baby."

She was clutching his thigh, his jeans fortunately protecting his leg from her nails. She needed to say, "I'm fine," but she couldn't get it out yet.

Elaine was still sitting quietly in her chair. She understood Daralyn's panic attacks, so Daralyn didn't need to look her way or apologize. Not yet.

Instead, Daralyn just looked at Rory. Not at his eyes. His hands on her, his chest before her gaze, and then she'd moved back close, had buried her nose against him, inhaling deep. Not a trace of the dream lingered in his scent, and the TV's low murmur was no longer disruptive.

Rory coaxed her even closer, up against his side, fully under the shelter of his arm, where he continued to rub her upper arm. She rested her forehead on his shoulder, breathing. Just breathing.

After a time, he asked his mother another question about the show. A pause, and Elaine answered. They returned to normal conversation, helping her tension slip away like water under a bridge. Normal. They didn't treat her like glass. Didn't make a big deal of it.

A half hour later, when Elaine stood up to go to bed, she came to them. She leaned over, brushed a kiss over Rory's forehead. Then she did the same to Daralyn. She cupped Daralyn's face a brief second, her mother's gaze reviewing what she saw there, before she straightened with a decisive nod and turned toward the kitchen.

"Turn off the TV and lights when you head for bed," she said. "No sense in taking Daralyn home this late. I'll fix a ham and egg casserole in the morning before the two of you head to the store."

That was that. From that moment forward, Daralyn knew, whenever they were together at the end of the day, they could go to sleep together. Nightmares might chase her out of her dreams, but they wouldn't follow her once his arms closed around her, reminding her he was there.

The high school reunion was coming up. Daralyn knew from Elaine that Rory was getting an award, but Rory's take on it was he was accepting it on behalf of his family. Thomas and Marcus had already planned to fly back in for the event. Though a disappointed Les couldn't get away from school, she called to find out what Daralyn was going to wear.

"I thought the wine-colored dress," Daralyn told her. "Rory really likes that one."

"Unh-unh," Les said. "This reunion requires a new dress, trust me. Ask Amanda to take you shopping."

When Daralyn hesitantly did so at the store, next time Amanda stopped in, she was startled and then amused by Amanda's squeal of pleasure. "This is going to be so much fun," Amanda told her. "And don't worry. The secondhand place I'm thinking of will have something great, but nothing there is hugely expensive. You'll get a great dress and accessories for under fifty dollars. And it'll give me an excuse to get one, too. Something slinky that will steam up Marty's wire-rimmed glasses."

When Daralyn sent Rory a helpless look, he just grinned and made a "hands off" gesture. "No sane man gets in between women and their shopping."

"Ain't that the God's truth," Johnny said from the back.

"Oh shut up, both of you," Amanda told them tartly. "Like you aren't just as bad about hunting rifles and fishing poles."

"That's because those are useful," Johnny pointed out.

Amanda rolled her eyes. "Just ignore them, Daralyn."

Daralyn's only concern about the proposed outing was that she'd never successfully gone anywhere without a member of Rory's family being with her in some way. Like Elaine taking her to Dr. Taylor's, or Rory going to community college with her. But she had improved enough about going to school that Rory could drop her off and come back for her. She'd even considered—for half a second—learning how to drive.

Amanda had asked Johnny about his date for the reunion and was now teasing him about his vague response. "Oh yeah. You're fixing to get ready to start thinking about it," she said. "That'll work."

Sometimes, that was the way Daralyn felt about a lot of things she still couldn't tackle. It shamed her to know some part of her was already considering backing out of the dress shopping, or seeing if Elaine would go with them.

But after Amanda had left, telling Daralyn she'd be back tomorrow morning to pick her up at the house, Rory reminded her just how attuned he was to her moods.

"Hey." He came around the counter, took her hand and drew her close. He gripped her above the heart bracelet she rarely took off. During working hours, when she'd kept touching her arm, feeling as if something was missing, he'd told her she could wear it at the store, as long as she always remembered to take it off before operating any of the equipment.

Now he rubbed her flesh beneath the delicate links. "This says I'm with you, no matter where you are," he said. "You've got this. You'll have fun, pick out a pretty dress. Amanda will help you."

He flashed her a smile. "You know I have my road trip to Tabor City this weekend with my challenge group. I like the idea of you having fun while I'm gone."

So she'd gone and it had been...fun. She'd found a dress Amanda had raved over when Daralyn tried it on, and insisted that she buy it. So Daralyn had, and Amanda picked out a pretty purse to match. Her silver wedge sandals would work with the dress, so new shoes hadn't been necessary. Then she and Amanda ate an early lunch together. She was a good companion, carrying a lot of the conversation but coaxing Daralyn to talk, so that she found herself contributing to the conversation far more than she usually did. When they parted ways, Amanda gave her a quick hug that felt...good. Natural.

"Hey, let's go to the movies one afternoon," Amanda said as she headed back out Daralyn's door. "One of those sappy chick flicks Rory and Marty would rather be shot in the head than go see. Your mom might enjoy going, too. Sorry. I meant Elaine." Amanda flashed her an apologetic smile.

"Okay." Daralyn waved as Amanda drove away. She held her dress over her arm in its clear plastic covering, gazed out at the stretch of field behind the house, and absorbed the feelings of the day, realizing how few of them had been anxious or unpleasant. Like a good meal where each bite tasted good. Not just the first one or only some of them.

She went into the cottage and sat down on the bed, laying out the dress next to her. Putting her hand under the plastic, she caressed the fabric. It would need a couple tucks to make it fit properly. Daralyn was a decent seamstress, thanks to Elaine, but for this, she'd likely need her help.

It made her think of Amanda's apology. Elaine *was* Daralyn's mother, the closest to one she'd ever had. In all the ways that mattered.

She picked up her phone and called, Elaine picking up on the third ring. "Hey, honey, did you find a nice dress?"

Daralyn's throat got tight. Elaine sounded the same way she did when she talked to Rory, Les or Thomas. Any of her children. It had always been there, hadn't it? Just waiting to be noticed. She managed to push the words out, asking for Elaine's help to alter the dress.

"Oh, honey, I'd be thrilled to help. Why don't you come over for dinner around four and we'll do it after? Since Rory is off with those adrenaline junkie friends of his, we can have a girls' night."

Daralyn agreed. After a little more conversation, they ended the call, but then Daralyn sat another few minutes, thinking about all of it. She was juggling a schedule. School, friends, social events. Like...a normal person.

She had a family. A life. A job. A man she loved.

She smiled, thinking of him. Missing him. Her smile got bigger as she remembered how, during a recent phone call with Thomas, he'd mentioned, as she had, how he'd likely just wear something he already had to the reunion.

He only had the one casual suit, the one he'd worn to their dinner at the Purple Swan. It had worked for her, but she loved him in anything. Or nothing. All his long fine limbs, the intriguing curves and valleys of his body, his rougher hair and firm muscles.

Marcus had confiscated the phone, his tone of horror sharp enough to reach Daralyn, sitting next to Rory at the time. She'd been studying at her kitchen table and had to hide a smile at Rory's scowl. She was sure Thomas was on the other end with a similarly amused look.

"If you want to accept an award looking like a gap-toothed hillbilly who wears the same suit for a decade—"

"I don't need to look like some Abercrombie & Fitch nancy boy without hair on his balls..."

And so on.

She didn't know what they'd worked out, but it had involved Rory getting measured by a local tailor Marcus recommended. Rory was handsome in anything, but the idea of him in a new suit and tie, dressed up...

She recalled the night of Tyler's party, when they'd returned to Brick's cottage. As Rory made himself a cup of decaf coffee in the kitchen, he'd had the blue dress shirt open, the sleeves rolled up. She'd found herself staring at the movement of his hands, how the shirt lay against his bare chest. The heavy-lidded brown eyes had turned her way, saw her watching him...

She was moving her fingers along her thigh, back and forth, a slow glide, creating a low-level throb between her legs. She jumped up from the bed, her heartbeat accelerating as her gaze darted to all corners of the cottage. As if she expected someone to charge out at her, snapping like an angry dog.

Bad girl. Only bad girls act that way.

As she swayed there, indecisive, her eyes closed, pulling her back to the memory of Rory in that kitchen. He'd spoken to her low, brought her to him. Then he had her remove the dress, sit in his lap in only her stockings, panties and the corset. He'd held her while he made the coffee, added cream and sugar. She'd listened to his heartbeat, tipped her head up when he'd wanted to kiss her mouth, slow and long. He'd dropped his hand between her legs and stroked...

She tentatively cupped her breast, imagining his hand on it, the long, strong fingers. A few months ago, Elsa Pride had brought in a half-dozen chicks that had hatched when one of her hens managed to hide a set of eggs from her. Rory had offered to find someone in the community looking to add to their hen house. Daralyn remembered him holding one of the chicks in his hand, cradling it, his fingers moving over the soft down, the way he touched her flesh.

When she brushed her nipple, it was in a taut peak. The wave of sensation that shot through her startled her into another guilty survey of her surroundings. Nerves came in behind it, a strong uneasiness that bordered on nausea. She swallowed it down, just as her phone began to buzz.

With relief, she saw it was him.

"Hi," she said. "How did the ATV'ing go?"

"Way more fun than grown men should be allowed to have." He sounded tired, but his voice had that light quality she'd heard when men were off together, doing sports, so she knew he was having a good time. He also sounded really pleased to talk to her. The feeling was mutual. "How about shopping? How did that go?"

"We found a dress. Amanda says it's really pretty, and your mom is going to help me alter it tonight so it will fit right."

"I don't know why Marcus is worried about me having a new suit. Nobody's going to be looking at me with you there. Course, I'd better look my best, so no one thinks they can steal you away from this gap-toothed hillbilly."

"Not a possibility," she said staunchly. "Will you tell me more about your day?"

"Only if you spend at least five minutes telling me about yours."

She made it to ten, largely because he kept prompting her with questions. Then he launched into a summary of their cross-country outing on ATVs. She paid attention, but she also closed her eyes, let herself get carried away on his voice, that deep resonance that vibrated through her body. Her thighs, her lower belly, up through her breasts and throat...

She curled her fingers into a fist on her leg. What was the matter with her? While they didn't have actual sex every time they were together, Rory was pretty demanding about bringing her to orgasm. Maybe her body had gotten addicted to that. Spending a day with Amanda, who'd coaxed her into talking about the many things Daralyn liked about Rory, while reciprocating with some outrageously blatant things about Marty, had only increased her desires.

"So that was my day," he concluded. "A bunch of sweaty guys playing on Big Wheels. So tell me more about what you and Amanda talked about while dress shopping."

"You. And Marty."

"Oh yeah? Care to elaborate?"

He was teasing her, but she wasn't sure how he would feel about her thoughts, her wandering hands. She remembered that first time, in front of the mirror, when he'd had her touch herself. But that had been while he was watching.

"I may have done something bad. Or been about to do something bad. I'm not sure."

"I don't think that's possible," he said. "But tell me what it is."

"I...I was thinking about you. In Florida. And here. And listening to your voice, and...I wanted to touch myself, like you do. I started to...Rory, I'm sorry. I didn't mean to."

A pause, protracted enough to alarm her. She rushed to fill in the gap. "I'm so, so sorry. I know I shouldn't have—"

"Stop." When he used that tone, he was capable of bringing every thought to a halt, all of her centered on him. But she was shivering, abruptly cold and miserable, feeling like she'd failed him. "Hold on," he said shortly.

From the receding sound of voices and activity, she realized he was moving. He'd likely been in or close to the cabin he was sharing at the Tabor City campground.

"Okay, I'm somewhere private now. Are you at your place?"

"Yes. Rory—"

"I'm talking now. Are you in your bedroom?"

"Yes."

"Good. You know what a guy loves almost as much as a woman wanting to share a bed with him?"

"What?"

"A woman that puts him front and center in her mind when she's pleasuring herself." His voice got husky and thick. "And if you'll lie on your bed and touch yourself while I'm on the phone with you, this might just be the most perfect fucking day ever."

She swallowed. "So you're not mad."

"Oh, baby." The heat in his voice was almost as good as him putting his arms around her, because that tone said he'd be doing exactly that if he was there. "I don't think I could get mad at you about anything. But you touching yourself? That one doesn't come anywhere close to making that non-existent list. It gets me worked up. In fact..." he paused, and then that huskiness became a growl. "I might just like the idea of telling you that you can't touch yourself without calling me for permission first."

Her body liked that too, responding with a strong throb.

"Was that you? That little breath?"

"Yes."

He muttered a curse that sounded reverent. "I want you in your underwear on the bed. If it's cold, you can get under the covers."

She obeyed, leaving her jeans and short sleeved shirt on the side chair as she slid under the blanket and sheet.

"Tell me when you're there."

"I am."

"Put your hand in your panties. Start rubbing yourself. Imagine that I'm sitting by the bed, watching you. Spread your legs out, so I can see better."

As she complied, more of those erratic breaths slid from her. When he murmured encouragement, she let all those images crowd back in. He seemed to know it.

"Tell me what you're seeing in your head while doing this."

"You...watching me. Touching me. Telling me to spread my legs... oh..." A moan caught in her throat.

"You like it when I tell you what to do. I want you to slide two fingers inside yourself. Slide them in and out of that wetness, real slow. Push the heel of your hand against your clit, and use your thumb to stroke it. Lift your hips into the motion."

"Rory..."

"I'm here with you. I can feel it through my skin, seeing you do this in my head. There's no way I would ever be mad at you for embracing your pleasure, Daralyn. Not ever. Do you understand?"

"Yes. Thank you." Maybe he thought her gratitude was odd, but everything good he made her feel made her want to express it. Tears stabbed her eyes, made her voice shaky. He heard it, his voice becoming more soothing, while not losing an iota of its rough demand.

"I'm right here. Take your other hand and stroke your stomach, your sides, up to your throat and around, slow. Caress the tops of your breasts and slowly slide your hand into the bra, pushing the cup back with your knuckles so you can grip your breast like I do."

"Your hands are so much bigger. I like that, though I know my breasts are small."

"They're beautiful. Perfect and beautiful, just like all of you. Don't put yourself down, or I'll make you spank yourself."

She choked on a startled chuckle, and she heard the smile in his voice. "Don't think I won't. Keep stroking yourself. Touch yourself the way I would. Let me hear you think it out loud. I like how your voice is starting to shake."

He'd just given her the go-ahead to follow her imaginings, so she took him through it, how she saw him stroking her breasts, teasing her nipples. Sliding his hands down to cup her buttocks, squeeze as he lifted her to his mouth. He had the most adept mouth, playing over her wet flesh and drawing forth noises that didn't sound like they came from her, or if they did, from some primal place that connected to a time and a world when humans embraced their animal side.

"I like that," he mused, his voice thick. "Chasing you down in the forest, grabbing you around the waist. Or rolling us to the ground in a field of soft grass where I can have you in the sunshine or by moonlight, it doesn't matter. You're beautiful in every kind of light. You are the light."

"Rory..." Her voice lifted as her fingers pressed deep, the heel of her hand and thumb alternating on that bundle of nerves on the outside.

"Yeah, baby. I think you should come for your Master. Let him hear how much you miss him."

It was the word *Master* that did it, shoved her fully over the edge. He didn't use it often, but he'd used it more since Tyler's party. Ever since realizing how she responded to it, at just the right moment.

She climaxed around her fingers, feeling the clamp and ripple of those responsive tissues as her body bucked and her thumb rubbed over her clit, absorbing all the spasms. Her legs kicked, her back arched, and cool air touched her nipples as the blanket fell to her waist. She tried to tell him all that even as she came, knowing he'd want to hear her struggle to form words.

She missed him, missed him so much...

"Right here with me," he was saying in that rough tone as she came down. His stream of words filled her. "I've got you. You're all good. I'm so proud of you. I so wish I was with you, too. I'd put my mouth on you, taste that climax you just gave me, rub my face in your scent. I love that smell of you wanting me. First thing I'm going to do when I get back is push you down over whatever solid surface I can find, pull down your panties and taste that scent. Then I'm giving you a spanking for thinking this is something you needed to be sorry for. I might just use my push gloves for it. The leather palms will deliver a nice sting. Understand?"

"I understand," she whispered, shivering at the idea. And at everything else coursing through her. She'd seen him wear those gloves for his workouts, the way the leather molded to his palms oddly intriguing. "Rory..."

She wanted to say it so badly. Three words. It didn't matter what it attached to, how all the wants and needs that went with it could shred her. But he'd just told her yet another wondrous thing she'd always thought was wrong wasn't.

Day by day, experience by experience, he was dismantling the world that had formed her prison for so long. And he never stopped assuring her that whatever that world looked like, he would be there.

Like Marguerite had said. Though there was a gap between words and belief, she so wanted to believe. Enough that she yearned to form the words, force them past all those fears.

She could hear someone calling to him, but he shushed them and spoke into the phone. "What, baby?"

"I'm...glad you're having fun."

"All right." He paused. "Stop worrying. You're everything to me. Always."

Now the tears did spill forth. "Okay. Thank you. I...I'll see you when you get back."

She disconnected the call.

"I love you, Rory."

It echoed in the room, bounced back and hit her like a slap in the face. Curling up tight on the bed, she covered her head with her arms, hiding from the fallout, the wave of terror that came, even though she'd said it to no one but herself. The horrible blast of foreboding made her stomach heave. But she held fast against it. And eventually it receded.

She loved him. The feelings scared her. Thrilled her. He'd said he loved her, several times. He didn't seem to mind that she didn't say it back, but he understood so many things about her, without her having to give them voice.

Dr. Taylor kept inserting warnings about that in their conversations, but as long as Rory knew what was going on in her heart, she

307

didn't know why she had to rip herself apart, trying to pull what was inside out and express those feelings with words. The last time she'd tried had been at Tyler's party. She'd almost thrown herself blindly into the marsh and attracted the attention of a Dungeon Master. Most damning, she'd worried Rory, Des and Julie.

She wasn't obtuse, her word of the week. She knew Dr. Taylor was right, and so was Marguerite. Lately both women's words came at her so often she felt like she was hearing voices.

But life was so good now. And she'd worked so hard to get here. So very hard. Didn't she deserve to just...*be* for a while?

When she brushed up against those times where words might be needed and she didn't have them, the anxiety would set in. And underneath the anxiety was a slumbering dragon that slept far too lightly.

When it woke, it told her she would fall short and lose it all because she couldn't hold onto the things that mattered in the ways other people could. When she tried, she kept hitting the wall, and it was just too much, too big.

Why should she tear herself apart when things were going so well? Rory was happy with her, and his pleasure and approval balanced her world.

She was standing in bright sunlight by staying away from the shadows. If the clouds came, they would have to come looking for her. She wouldn't go looking for them.

CHAPTER NINETEEN

$\mathcal{T}$he day of the reunion, Elaine stopped by the store and suggested Daralyn come to their house to get dressed that night.

After his mother bustled back to the parking lot, Rory tossed Daralyn an amused look. "You know she's going to take a million pictures."

Daralyn was glad to be going to Elaine's, though. It minimized the chance she would cut and run. As the week progressed, she'd been getting more and more nervous about the night, making her wonder if she really was as ready for this as she believed she was. But she'd handled Tyler's party, school, going out on a double date. She had to be ready for this. She *was* ready for this.

A few hours later, she was in the upstairs guest room at Elaine and Rory's house, sitting in a chair in front of a mirror, letting Elaine work on her hair. Earlier, Daralyn had showered in the bathroom she'd once shared with Les and Rory. When she'd come into this room to unzip the garment bag that had held her dress all week, a whole new group of butterflies took off in her chest. Amanda had said it was perfect. She'd sent a picture of it to Les, and Rory's sister had gushed over it. "Oh God, Daralyn. Rory is going to be blown away."

Daralyn worried it was too much. But surely Elaine would have said if it was, when helping her with alterations. Instead, she'd only echoed what Les and Amanda had said. She'd also said she was going to help Daralyn do an upswept hair style that would go well with the formal style of the dress.

Daralyn had planned to leave it down, since Rory liked it that way, but Elaine insisted he would be pleased. Once Daralyn was dressed, Elaine had joined her to fix it up. Rory's mother winked as she tucked a hair comb embellished with a small rhinestone dragonfly into Daralyn's gleaming brown tresses. "Sometimes a man likes taking a woman's hair down. Don't tell him I was the one who said it, though. It will traumatize him, his mother knowing things like that."

It helped to listen to Elaine, whose flow of words was like a calm, gurgling brook. Daralyn also wore Rory's heart bracelet on one wrist. Elaine was loaning her a necklace for the night that was so pretty Daralyn had tried to give it back, afraid she'd lose it.

"Don't be silly," Elaine had chided, tapping her arm. "You won't lose it, and it's not a terribly expensive necklace. Robert and I didn't have money to spend on nonsense like that. I loved it for no other reason than he gave it to me, and he put real thought into it. I like swans."

The pendant was a silver swan with a Swarovski crystal for its body. It was strung on a black ribbon choker Elaine now tied around Daralyn's throat. "There. You look amazing, honey. Don't forget to breathe."

The dress was the kind of silver gray that seemed to have a touch of blue to it in certain lights. The bodice was an overlapped design of tiny gathered folds that molded to the upper body, while giving Daralyn's thin shape more substance. The strapless bra beneath was necessary because the dress was off the shoulder, a decorative wide gray ribbon of fabric looped loosely over her upper arms on either side.

It was the bareness of her shoulders that made her feel self-conscious, but when she'd been in the dressing room of the store, she'd imagined Rory's mouth there, his hands. She loved when he touched her shoulders and throat especially.

The knee-length skirt was light, flowing fabric, a couple layers of it, so there was no need for a slip.

Elaine glanced at her watch. Despite her amused comment about traumatizing her son, Daralyn thought Elaine's appearance tonight was a reminder she wasn't only a mother, but also a woman who'd fallen in love with a man and made a life with him. Her blue evening gown shot with silver sparkles hugged her lush curves, her dark dyed hair in a sweeping style similar to Daralyn's.

"Oh, almost forgot." Elaine clipped a pair of crystal tear drop earrings on Daralyn's lobes. "There you go. If you ever decide you want to get your ears pierced, we can do that up the road at the mall."

"Maybe," Daralyn said. Her heart thudded up into her throat when they heard Rory's chair bump into the base of the stairs. His deep voice drifted up to them.

"Are we going for fashionably late, Mom, or are we skipping this award BS and headed for the Barbecue Pit? It's kids-eat-free night. They don't specify that the kids have to be under a certain age, you know."

"I believe it's implied," Elaine called back, giving Daralyn a smile. "And you're not getting out of this, Rorik Andrew Wilder. I'm sending Daralyn down now."

She squeezed Daralyn's bare shoulders, beamed at her in the mirror. "You two go ahead and go. Marcus and Thomas are bringing me, so I'll meet you there." Her voice softened. "You look so wonderful, honey. Don't be afraid of anything tonight. You're surrounded by a whole community of people who care about you."

Daralyn wet her lips and gave her a little nod. But when she'd moved toward the door, she stopped and looked back at Elaine, who was giving herself a once over in the mirror.

Maybe it was because of how many things had been going right lately, but suddenly, a million emotions swamped Daralyn. She was looking at the woman who'd changed her life simply by noticing something no one else had. The words that came to her lips now had to be said.

"Thank you. For all of it. For everything. For...saving me. There's nothing...I can't say it right, but every day, every moment...I'm so grateful..."

Elaine's absent look sharpened as she turned around to meet Daralyn's expression, and registered the shaky note in her voice.

"I am so...honored that your son loves me," Daralyn managed, putting every bit of resolve she could find into the words. "And I will do everything I can to be...everything he needs..."

Elaine's eyes darkened. "Oh, honey." She closed the distance between them, clucking gently as she put her arms around Daralyn.

"My sweet girl. Even now, you don't realize how much you've given all of us. We love you so very much."

She eased back, gave Daralyn a forthright look. "If you and Rory do end up making a life together, he will be a very, very lucky man. And I will not hesitate to let him know that, whenever he needs reminding."

From the determined light in her eyes, Daralyn could see Elaine meant every word. "I want to give him so much, give all of you so much..."

Elaine sobered, touched her face. "I know you do. But I want you to remember that being who you are, living your life with generosity and love in your heart, however you feel that...that's the only thing I'll ever ask of you. Don't you *ever* think you owe us anything but the respect and love all family should give one another."

She gave Daralyn a playful nudge. "Now enough of this. Go show my son how beautiful you are, so he can get tongue-tied, like he was the very first time he realized girls were something he might like."

She winked, but she also ushered Daralyn quickly from the room. Daralyn noted the older woman's eyes were suspiciously wet as she closed the door.

Daralyn took a shaky breath. She hadn't meant to get all emotional —or do the same to Elaine—but it had just come to the top, how much of a miracle her life was, compared to what it had once been.

Yes, she was worried about tonight. But it was as Elaine said. She had people in her life who loved her, would stand by her. It was *not* something temporary that would disappear if she made a misstep. She would keep saying it to herself, over and over, until she believed it. They had earned that kind of loyalty from her. Their love was transforming her into someone who could finally believe like most people did, that her family—Elaine, Rory, Les, Thomas, all of them—*were* her family.

Nothing could take that from her.

Nothing could take that from her.

Please, please let nothing take that from me.

She started down the steps, holding the rail as she went so she didn't tumble from the heels. Rory was still at the bottom of the stairs, as if he'd been listening for the sound of her descent. So she saw how he took her in inch by inch, gaze lingering as he made his way from her legs, to her waist, the curves of her breasts and bare shoulders, absorbing every detail of the dress and the woman wearing it.

Daralyn was hyperaware of that regard, but at the sight of him, she had to take a tighter grip on the banister herself. She needed to thank Marcus for browbeating Rory into getting a tailored suit.

The gray jacket was a lightweight wool fabric that fit and accented his broad shoulders perfectly. His gray striped tie was a bold stroke against the white dress shirt that molded to his chest, coaxing her fingers to touch. The fit of the slacks on his thighs and hips was equally inspiring, but the corsage in a plastic container resting in his lap distracted her from a more thorough perusal. A spray of tiny white roses and baby's breath.

"You've never been to a prom," he said, as she lifted her gaze back to his intent brown eyes. "You deserve the full treatment. And you look...incredible."

He crooked his finger at her, a clear Master's command that centered her. The shakiness of her outburst to Elaine melted away. She came to him and he glanced pointedly toward his feet, at the carpet runner. There was no danger to her thigh-high stockings, something she was sure he'd taken into account.

It wouldn't matter to her anyway. She didn't worry about it, or Elaine, or anything at all but what he wanted from her. When she sank to her knees, he reached out and trailed a finger over her bare shoulder, making her shiver, her lips part. Then he cupped the side of her face, pulling her closer to him while also tilting her chin away from him. The position allowed him to rest his mouth on her frantically beating pulse.

"Later tonight, I'm going to put you on your back and make you touch yourself in that dress. Bring yourself to climax while I watch."

His fingers slipped away but he murmured to her to stay in that position, her head tilted away, chin pointed to her shoulder, as he fixed the corsage to the straight neckline of the dress. He caressed the curve of her breast beneath the fabric, exploring the edge of the strapless bra. As her lips parted at the stimulation, she felt his eyes on her. "I love how you respond when I touch you," he said.

He guided her face back to him so she could meet his eyes. When he took her hand to lift her to her feet, he kept her next to his chair.

Sending a pointed glance upstairs, he winked at her, a reassurance that he was staying conscious of Elaine's whereabouts. He slid a hand under the light skirt, up the length of her thigh to trace the lace top of the thigh high, then the elastic of her panties. With him leaning close, his scent, a clean masculine aftershave, filled her senses. She bit her lip as he found the satin-covered point of her sex.

"Widen your legs," he said, and she did, eyes fastened to him as he caressed her between them, a fingertip sliding over her clitoris as she bit back a little sound. "Thin bra," he said, eyeing her. "I can see your nipples becoming little points." He lifted his other hand to cup a breast, run a thumb over that area. "I like how you submit to my commands, Daralyn. I like it very much."

He'd taken things up a notch tonight, she realized. He was fully embracing the Dominance and submission between them with no apologies, no worries that she wouldn't trust his lead. She liked that very much, too, and wanted to tell him how it helped steady her. So she did, in the way she could and that he understood, with her eyes, the sway of her body toward him, her trust.

Maybe he was also being so assertive to help steady her. He seemed to have a sixth sense for knowing when she needed additional structure. But even if that was true, he was also doing it because it met a need and desire of his own, exercising that kind of control toward her, observing how it aroused her. That was something she particularly liked.

Drawing his hand from beneath the skirt, he claimed one of her hands, lifting it to his mouth to kiss her knuckles.

"You're with me," he said. "Don't worry about a thing tonight." His free hand caressed her face. "Are you going to worry?"

"I'm going to try not to."

"Good. Are you going to trust me?"

"Always. It's me I..."

She stopped. They both knew it was herself she didn't trust, but she wished she hadn't started to say it.

Rory brought her down onto his lap so he could brush his lips against her temple, her cheek, then moved to her mouth. He tasted her there before easing back, his eyes dominating her vision.

"One day, I hope you'll know that they're one and the same. Trusting yourself with me."

The organizers had debated having the reunion at a fancy hotel ballroom, but ultimately had decided on the nostalgic locale of the high school auditorium. With a bigger budget than school functions had, they'd impressively decorated the space with a creative array of drapes, standing pole lights, strung lanterns and other glittering decorations. It looked like a ballroom.

When Rory and Daralyn arrived, they'd been greeted warmly by neighbors, by friends, by his former classmates. Daralyn stayed close to his chair, slightly behind it, her hand on his shoulder.

Rory knew she was spun up about tonight, and not just because his mother had told him so earlier in the evening. Elaine had brought Rory the shirt she'd insisted on ironing for him. "She's extremely nervous, son, but trying to hide it."

He'd watched that anxiety build over the past several days. With Daralyn, there was a delicate balance between addressing an issue and not giving it too much attention. But seeing her suffer bothered him intensely, so he'd made a call to touch base with Dr. Taylor. The doc had given him a less than satisfying answer, even if it made sense.

"Daralyn is in a very good place right now, Rory," the psychiatrist had said. "She's built a lot of positive things to keep her from regressing, but for someone like her, the temptation is to completely enclose herself in that space, which also keeps her from going forward, addressing the hardest things of all, those buried the deepest inside her. Following you into new situations is going to take her toward possible confrontations with those things. Which she needs if she's ever going to break them open, heal them."

She paused. "You love her deeply. When she seems happy, the idea of exposing her to experiences that could make her unhappy is difficult. But that's when you have to question what love truly is. Is it keeping that person cocooned from the world, or standing beside her, living through the good and bad together?"

"Doc, anyone tell you that your ability to make good sense is annoying as hell?"

He'd startled a laugh out of her. "All the time. Usually from my husband. If he ever murders me, it will be right after I say something that makes perfect sense."

After that conversation, a resolve had grown inside him. All the Dom stuff he'd been learning these past few weeks, including the party in Florida and talks with Marcus, were all good. But there came a moment, just like with what Daralyn was facing, when a person decided to be all-in on what he knew he was, what he wanted to be, and how he wanted to express it.

When she'd come down the stairs with that pale face and the slight tremor to her hand on the banister, that resolve went into full lock. So, though a few weeks ago it might have felt like a shirt he'd just tried on and was figuring out the fit, tonight it had fit as perfectly as the suit Marcus had made him get.

These past few weeks had been the measuring, the trying on. Tonight he wore the mantle of a Master, and he wasn't backing away from it.

Daralyn was his heart and soul, his submissive, his woman, his best reason for being his best self. As he introduced her to people she didn't know, he met her gaze frequently, and whenever he was stationary, he kept his hand firmly upon hers on his shoulder.

There were things he didn't have as much power over, because he was in a chair. But with his voice, his will, when he fully embraced the power of being a Dom, it was something true and real a submissive recognized, that didn't have a damn thing to do with his mobility. He knew it in his heart, and it was reinforced by how Daralyn reacted to him.

She knew he was with her, every step of the journey.

As Rory had to introduce her to too many people she didn't know, Daralyn reminded herself there were a good many she did.

Like the one in front of them now.

"Well, look at that. When you hose the horse manure and turkey feed off him, he manages to clean up right nice."

Brick had extricated himself from a gaggle of women Daralyn assumed might be former female classmates, eager to reacquaint themselves with him, and made his way over to Rory and Daralyn. He swallowed Daralyn in a warm, easy hug before pumping Rory's free hand.

"I'm betting you still had to pay a woman to be your date," Brick observed, shooting Daralyn a wink. "Charge him double, Daralyn. I know what a pain in the ass he is."

Though Rory had grumbled it defied the laws of anatomy, Brick had filled out even more since he'd been the high school team line-backer. His friend had steady gray eyes, dark hair he kept short, and a close-cropped beard. Before he'd gone away to college to major in fire science and engineering, he'd been a town volunteer firefighter. He was currently working in Richmond as a deputy fire chief and arson investigator.

Les said he'd traveled to California and Australia to help fight fires as well. Rory's sister always claimed to have no interest in him, that her crush on him had been short-lived, a schoolgirl thing over one of her brother's idiot friends. However, she always seemed to know what Brick was up to, something the irrepressible Julie never failed to point out.

Rory made a show of looking around Brick's large bulk. "Apparently there wasn't enough money in the world to convince a woman to put up with you, even for one night."

"The spot on my arm stays open for one very special woman. I'm sad she couldn't make it tonight."

"Yeah, she was, too." Rory shot him a look. "But that was because of missing the award thing. Had nothing to do with you."

"Keep telling yourself that."

As the men teased one another, they moved toward the table that had been assigned to Rory and his family, close to the awards stage. Daralyn was relieved to take a seat next to Rory that backed up to the wall, while he flanked her on the outside. She could listen but not have to constantly engage as she managed all the stimuli around her. Fortunately, Marcus and Thomas arrived with Elaine shortly there-after, and Thomas sat on her other side, completing the reassuring sense of being enclosed by family.

As usual, Marcus made women, servers and guests alike, turn to stare, risking tripping over their feet or running into tables. Especially tonight, when he wore a tailored suit, his dress shirt open at the throat.

Thomas was a good-looking man himself, just like his brother. With Elaine in her blue evening gown, they made a handsome group.

But as Daralyn looked at all of them, she saw family. And the man who could make her trip over her own feet was sitting by her side. Ready to catch her if she stumbled.

The awards ceremony would kick off the evening. Older community members attending primarily for that reason could depart before the more boisterous schedule for the high school reunion began, which would include music and dancing. So as the time came for the ceremony to commence, the remaining chairs at their eight-person table were filled by Brick, Amanda and Marty. Johnny and his date, as well as more of Rory's school friends and teammates, were at nearby tables.

As Fran Potts, the reunion organizer, took the podium and began an introduction, Daralyn noted Rory studying the stage. The relaxed set of his shoulders had tightened. When he felt her regard, he sent her a slight smile, reassuring her.

But she noticed Thomas looking at the stage, too, and then he murmured something to Marcus. A frown creased his husband's brow. When Thomas leaned forward, catching Rory's eye, Rory shook his head, lifted a shoulder. "Not a big deal," he murmured. "I'll figure it out."

The opening remarks were done, and the handful of awards began to be introduced. From a glance at the program that had been given out, Daralyn knew Rory's was last. It would be introduced by the mayor of their small town, emphasizing it as the most important of all the awards being offered.

He might be uncomfortable with it, but she could tell his family was swelling with pride, the closer the time came for the award to be presented.

Mayor Wilma Bergin took the stage. A distinguished looking figure in her fifties, she'd softened her brisk look tonight with an elegant green suit, a spray of white flowers pinned to the lapel. Daralyn wondered if the mayor's husband had given her a corsage as well. She liked that idea.

The mayor discussed the history of the store, how Elaine and Robert Wilder had started it, and how it had become an anchor in their community. She was respecting Rory's request that the award should honor his entire family, not just him. Only as she drew to a close did the mayor turn her attention to Rory's part of the legacy.

"Many of our young people leave here to do amazing things," she said. "They go with our blessing, our gift to the world at large. But when one of them chooses to stay, give his time and energy to the community, show his love of it, we rejoice in the chance to acknowledge his value and contribution. So Mr. Rory Wilder, would you please come accept your award, for you and the whole Wilder family?"

That was when Daralyn realized the problem. So did Elaine.

"Oh no," Elaine murmured. "Rory..."

In all the planning that had gone into the evening's elaborate event, someone had forgotten. The stage had no handicapped access, only four steps up to the platform on either side.

However, whatever initial tension Rory might have had about it seemed to have disappeared. He shrugged, gave the table a "not a big thing" smile and casually pushed himself from the table. Instead of heading for the stairs, he moved toward the front edge of the stage. Daralyn realized he was going to take the award from the mayor's hand, let her reach down and give it to him.

Any tightness she detected in his smile, the set of his shoulders, was likely him steeling himself for the embarrassed pause that would result when the presenters realized their oversight.

The chair across from her scraped the floor as Brick rose. With several ground-eating strides, he intercepted Rory at the front of the stage.

The way Brick positioned himself reminded Daralyn of those yearbook pictures from their pep rallies. Him and Rory and the rest of the team hamming it up for cheering students wearing school colors. Now Brick's voice boomed through the auditorium, as easily now as she was sure it had then.

"Hold on there a moment, Flash. You remember those few times you scored us a touchdown? When you weren't fumbling the ball, that is."

Laughter swept the tables with his former teammates and rippled through the crowd, covering Rory's good-humored retort. Brick grinned, but then he looked toward the audience, particularly those at the front tables. "When he took the ball across the line for the win against the Jaguars, we carried him off the field. Let's give him a lift again, right here and now."

Cheers broke out, chairs scraping in unison as a half dozen men rose. Daralyn saw Brick tilt forward, say a quiet word to Rory. Making sure it was okay.

Rory's expression had shifted from amusement to a wealth of deeper emotions. He managed a quick nod, which Brick answered with a hard shoulder squeeze. Then Brick and three of the men had lifted the chair, two on each side, the extra two as rear escort. They put him on the stage in a move as smooth as a chair lift.

During that few handful of seconds, Daralyn thought Elaine had Marcus take a dozen pictures with his phone. Rory's mother made a tremendous effort to stay composed, though her face was suffused with emotion as strong as her son's. Daralyn suspected when Brick came back to the table, he was going to get a rib-cracking hug from her. If she could get her arms around that much of his massive chest.

Right now, Brick and the others had arranged themselves to the right of the stage. Daralyn had lingered over Rory's pictures in the yearbook more than once. Now she recalled a much younger Rory, a high school junior, standing at the mic, his teammates in this same, almost military precise line nearby, hands clasped before them.

Rory had moved to the podium. The mayor had the plaque in one hand, her other extended. Daralyn could tell she was offering a sincere apology, distress and regret in her dark eyes. Rory gave her a reassuring smile, the one capable of making any woman's toes curl. Including Daralyn's.

Wilma handed him the mic, stepping back behind the podium while he turned to face the audience from his position next to it. As far as Daralyn knew, he hadn't prepared or agonized over a speech. She'd asked him, on one of their lazy evenings in the hammock, if he was preparing one. He'd shrugged. *"Nope. If anything needs to be said, it'll come to me at the time."*

He gave calm and appropriate thanks to the presenters, to the town that he called home, the neighbors and friends who supported him, naming several in particular. He said he was proud to support all of them.

Then he paused, gaze sweeping over the audience and coming to their table. He let his attention rest on Daralyn a lingering beat before moving it to his brother, to Marcus, and finally his mother.

"I'm thankful for my life," he said, shifting his gaze back to the listening audience. "It's a funny thing. After my accident, like anyone going through something like that, there were a couple moments I wished the tractor had finished me off." He sent his mother a regretful look. "It was tough. But now I know I didn't know what tough is. I had every gift in the world, all the love and family support I needed, to get through it. And I have those gifts still."

His gaze shifted to Daralyn. "Tough is going it alone in the world when everything seems against you, and surviving anyway, with your soul intact, and a heart bigger than anyone's I've ever met."

She could feel eyes turning her way. This was a world who knew her story. The local customers who came through the store, the people she saw at church, whose houses and farms she passed when she rode her bicycle to work. It was a quiet awareness, though, nothing they brought up or dwelled upon in her presence. Rory had put her in the spotlight, but only for the moment, just long enough to make her heart pound harder beneath their regard and his. Then he smoothly moved onward, drawing their attention elsewhere.

"When I was told I was getting this award," he said, "I didn't want it. Not because of false modesty or because I'm uncomfortable with that kind of thing, but because to me, it was obvious that there were two particular people who deserved it more. The two who taught me everything that's important. My parents."

His gaze touched Elaine, came back to the silent crowd. "As we move through our lives, our parents are not only trying to guide us, they're trying to figure themselves out, too. And whether they realize it or not, when they give us a front row seat to that journey, they're influencing us in ways that can literally save our lives, put us on the paths that make life something better than we ever could have imagined."

Now when he turned his eyes back to his mother, he held there, so the words went directly to her. "I've had that front row seat, watching my mother deal with losing her husband, the love of her life, my father, way too soon."

Daralyn could see Elaine hadn't expected this. She also wasn't surprised to see Marcus and Thomas's arms overlap on her chair behind her, giving her support. Rory's gaze moved to them.

"Then she faced a challenge to some of her deepest held beliefs. She had to change course on her thinking about what love is. What it looks like. It was really tough for her. But because she taught us from the time we were born what love is, deep in our souls, Thomas was able to gift that lesson back to her."

A faint smile touched his lips as he inclined his head to Thomas, then Marcus. He sobered, glancing at the audience. "When I realized I'd never walk again, my mother was with me, at every point on that road. Hardest thing I ever had to accept, and I didn't take it well. Through my pain and anger, she thought I didn't see hers. Which makes it even more shameful that I didn't acknowledge it far sooner than I did. But she forgave me, and never stopped loving me."

His face was as serious as Daralyn had ever seen it. The auditorium was silent, as if the message he was speaking was being drawn from all of their hearts and experiences.

"But for all those incredible things my parents have done for me, there's something else that tops all of it. A few years ago, my mom noticed something evil happening. She told my dad, and the two of them did the greatest, bravest thing anyone can do. They did something about it, and they didn't stop at the devil's door. They marched right in, and pulled an angel out of hell. Brought that angel into our lives, into our community. One who's changed us all for the better."

Thomas's hand was on Daralyn's back, a gentle stroke as she quivered. Her stomach flopped uncertainly, but that heart Rory was talking about was full, aching. The look in his brown eyes told her if he'd been beside her right now, he would have been holding her hand tight. Telling her he was there and there was nothing to fear.

"Learning what we had all missed for so long shamed us as a community," Rory continued, "including my mother. But just like with me ending up in this chair, or her learning a bigger definition of what love is, it shed light on the most important lessons my mother and father taught me."

He took a steadying breath. "We're going to screw up. We're going to stumble. We're going to hurt one another. We're going to take wrong turns. There is good and bad in all of us, strengths we can embrace and weaknesses we *can* overcome, especially when we have people in our corner who never give up on us, who love us too damn much to ever give up on us."

His fierce eyes came back to hers, sending a message as strong as any command he'd ever given her. *Don't you hide from me, or this. From the truth I'm telling you.*

Which brought her back to Marguerite's words, about how Tyler felt about her. *Nothing could change how he felt about me... Our bond was something that existed no matter what forces came against it.*

Daralyn held her position with effort, her back straight and chin lifted, her hands knotted tight in her lap. The approval in her Master's eyes went straight to her soul.

He lifted the plaque, sent his mother an equally potent look. "So Mom, this is going on your wall. I earned it because of the type of person you are, the one you taught me to be, not just from your raising, but through the example of your life."

With the kind of timing Julie would say would make him a great fit for her theater, his expression eased into a smile, changing the intensity in the room. He let his attention land on Brick and his teammates, standing by the stage. "Truth? Much as I loved being carried off the field then, knowing you guys feel I'm still worth putting on your shoulders means a lot. Hope I'll always live up to that."

"If you don't, we'll kick your ass and remind you," Brick called out.

Rory laughed. "Yeah. That's what community is for, too. To take care of one another, to help, and to kick each other in the butt when we need it. To be the type of people we should be, for others and for ourselves." He nodded to the audience, gestured with the plaque. "Thanks for that, and for this. Thanks for letting me have the chance to help support that kind of community. And now..."

He tilted his head at Brick. "If adrenaline could do it, I'd jump off this stage like Patrick Swayze, right here and now. But if you guys wouldn't mind getting me back to the side of the most beautiful girl in the room,"—he pinned Daralyn with his intent brown gaze—"that would be appreciated. Thank you, everyone."

As applause thundered through the auditorium, Rory was lifted back down to the floor. Elaine had soaked Marcus's handkerchief, Thomas arm tight around her. Marcus rose and moved out of the way so Rory could approach her on that side, which allowed both of her sons to hold her the full five minutes she needed to pull herself back together. Once Elaine started scolding him for turning her into a weeping mess, they knew she was okay again.

When Rory met Daralyn's gaze over his mother's shoulder, she couldn't look away. Despite what he'd said about not preparing a speech, he'd obviously been thinking a great deal about what he wanted to say. And it had included her. His words had made her as wobbly as the usually stoic Elaine.

When he returned to her side, he bent to kiss her bare shoulder. Daralyn cupped his jaw, pressed her face against the side of his head, inhaling his scent, the aftershave he'd worn. While the rest of the table saw, it felt like that moment was just them, full of things that needed no words.

Thankfully, now that the awards ceremony was done, a light dinner was going to be served. It gave her and Elaine both time to settle, return to an even keel. Before long, the men at the table were bantering as usual and Amanda was teasing them, drawing Daralyn and Elaine in at key moments to "balance the testosterone," as she put it.

"Hell, he made it." Brick interrupted the flow of casual conversation to nod toward the far end of the auditorium. It drew their attention to a man who'd appeared in the doorway. A server guided him to an empty seat at one of the tables. Daralyn's impression at this distance was of a dark suit, a stubbled jaw, and eyes that shifted around the auditorium as if their owner wasn't exactly sure how he'd gotten here, or where here was. He sat down at the table gingerly and ignored the plate of food put in front of him, instead obviously ordering a drink from the server.

"Hayworth McNally." Marty grunted. "Well, he missed your speech, but he did make it. Lesser miracles."

"Might be better if he'd made the speech but skipped the dancing," Rory advised. "Get a couple drinks in him and he becomes way too proud of his pelvic thrust move."

Chuckles circled the table, and Elaine shook her head at them. Rory squeezed Daralyn's hand. Fran was back on stage, drawing their attention his way. "In about twenty minutes, we'll get this party started," she said. "Dessert tables will stay set up, in case you want to work off dinner before indulging. It's almost time to dance, so break out those high school moves, boys." She executed a spin at the mic that sent the points of her dress swishing around her calves. "Get ready to dazzle us girls."

"Or scare the crap out of them," Johnny hollered.

"Just like you did in high school, Johnny," she rebounded, setting off laughter and applause.

More comments volleyed back and forth, but Daralyn missed most of them, because the announcement had woken her stomach butterflies. They did a full takeoff as Rory met her gaze, his lips curving in a sensual smile.

The expression and the wink he added to it had special meaning, because when he'd officially asked her to accompany him to the reunion as his date, he'd set one condition on it.

She had to promise to dance with him.

Since she didn't know how to dance, he'd made it less terrifying by asking her to practice with him at night, or at lunch breaks in the store, in the weeks leading up to the reunion.

Their first lesson had happened on the paved square of asphalt under the oak tree behind her house. It had been a basketball court for the Hill children, though the basketball goal was long gone, replaced by a light pole to illuminate the area when needed at night.

"You have no reason to be nervous," he chided gently. "You aren't going with John Travolta here. Close your eyes. Get out of your head."

When she complied, Rory spoke in that low way he did that captured her attention completely. "Dance for me. Close your eyes, let me see the way you dance in your head, or when you're alone. Do you ever do that? Think of a favorite song and dance to that."

Thinking of one of the country songs he played that she particularly liked, she began to sway. Turn. Step forward and back, sway some more. A little more tentative and far less boisterous, but similar to how Julie and Les sometimes danced on their "slumber party" nights.

On one of the turns her hand landed in his. Her eyes opened, and he moved his chair around her, speaking a word of encouragement, showing her how to turn with him. They were doing well, and then she tripped over her own feet and stumbled to one knee.

She saw the frustration on his face when he grabbed for her and missed, nearly overbalancing himself, and she was immediately contrite. "I'm sorry, I—"

He shook his head, took her hand to tug her closer, examine her scraped knee. "I hate not being able to catch you when you fall. That's all."

"There's more than one way of catching someone when they fall," she said.

His jaw flexed at what she hoped he saw in her eyes. "Okay," he said.

He didn't get frustrated again, even though they had plenty of missteps during their practices, which included tripping over him or having her toes run over, but since the former occurrence usually landed her in his lap instead of on the ground, she couldn't object.

At the end of that first dance lesson, he finished up with a "slow dance," her curled up in his lap while he moved the chair in easy circles, rocking back and forth to a ballad he hummed in a sexy, off-tune rumble she'd choose over the radio any day.

When they moved their practices to the open floor space of the store aisles, he showed her more ways to use counterbalance to move together, that momentum pulling his chair into the turns and step changes. Occasionally a customer would come in and glimpse their efforts. Rory didn't let her get nervous about it; he helped her look past her self-consciousness to register the customer's delight at the chance to watch them.

He was a good teacher, and she loved dancing with him. The way they could touch, slide away, come back again. The more they worked at it together, the more they seemed to anticipate one another's movements.

She'd watched mating birds dance like this in the air. When she was dancing with Rory, she felt like she was flying. Sometimes, seeing the deep pleasure in his eyes when they danced, she thought he felt like he was, too.

CHAPTER TWENTY

"*D*ance with me."

Now she tuned in to the present. Rory spoke in her ear, so he could be heard over the music that had just started up. Seeing the glint in his brown eyes, the smile on the lips that could do so many things to her, and the true happiness in his face, made her feel the same. Whether it was alone or in the middle of a crowd, it was still just him and her. This night was turning out to be as good as it could possibly be. Her fears, though always there, couldn't push through all of that to touch this, make it any less pleasurable for her.

Rory shot a teasing look at Thomas. "Ready for me to show you up on the dance floor?"

Thomas snorted. "You can give it your best shot." He tilted his head at Elaine. "Mom, you want to help your firstborn son prove his dance supremacy? Despite the shocking miracle of my little brother discovering a silver tongue on stage, I know I'm your favorite."

She chuckled, but shook her head. "I've already promised my first dances to Miles Warner and Jeremy Stone. The two of them are determined to see which one can overload their pacemaker first. Dance with Marcus."

"You're definitely toast," Marcus said to Rory. "Because I'm a better dancer than you *and* your brother."

"That may be," Rory said, unruffled. "But I've got the ace in the hole. I have her." He squeezed Daralyn's hand. "And though this might bruise your delicate feelings, she's way prettier than you."

Marcus spread out his hands. "I'm not going to argue that one, but we'll see about the dancing."

They moved to the floor. It wasn't hard to carve out a space for themselves as people adjusted to allow Rory room for him and his partner.

Ceelo Green's "Bright Lights and Big City" was the perfect tempo for the different combinations of steps she and Rory had worked on. Despite that and her more optimistic thoughts at the table, the reality of so many people around them, the inevitable attention they were drawing, had her shrinking a little inside. Though she tried not to show it on the outside, Rory put pressure on her hand and pulled her down to him. Cupping her face to draw her eyes to his, he brushed his lips over her mouth.

"You look so beautiful," he said softly, and the heat in his eyes, his voice, told her how much he meant it. "You remember what I told you we're going to do when we get home tonight? You think about that. Show me how you'll move for me when your hand is between your legs."

At her flush, a devilish glint came to his gaze. She thought about smacking him, a startling thought, and then he grinned, as if the reaction had shown on her face.

He shifted his grip to one familiar to her from their lessons, and waited a beat to make sure she knew what he was about to do. Her nod confirmed it. He yanked, and she executed the turn into his lap, pushing off with her leg so she gave the chair the momentum for the spin he put it in. The turn ended with her reaching out with the opposite leg, and pushing herself back out of his lap, onto her feet and spinning out once more. At the full reach of their arms, the strength in his grip was enough to let her lean outward at an angle, like grass blown from a strong breeze, her free arm outstretched. Then he did another yank, spinning her back into the wrap of his arm, her hip against his side.

Exclamations of surprise and a burst of applause made him grin, and she found herself smiling back. He settled them into simpler steps, the ball changes, spins, turns and wheelies that were less showy, merely about enjoying the dancing together. A glimpse toward

Thomas and Marcus showed they were doing the same. Despite the teasing at the table, they wouldn't be doing anything to take the shine away from Rory tonight. Not that she thought that would have mattered to him. His attention was entirely on her, and he looked... happy.

When his tension about the lack of stage access had disappeared, she thought she knew why. Such things could still give him a momentary hitch, but he was past it. He'd become comfortable in his skin, in who he was. What he wanted, and what mattered.

What would it be like to reach that point? She had never believed it would be on her horizon, let alone within reaching distance. But she wanted him, wanted to be part of what made him happy, now and forever. She wanted to learn how to dance even more complicated dances with him, learn to trust his lead. Most of all, she wanted to break out of the prison that kept her from telling him everything she wanted with her own lips, her own words.

Tonight, she believed that eventually she would. She thought of the words he'd said up on the stage. Most of them had been for his parents, but that one part had been a straight arrow, fired right to her soul.

He was never going to give up on her. Never. She thought she could believe it, and though that belief might only hold through tonight, it was an important start, a foothold toward a more enduring belief and trust.

As Marguerite had said, for this moment, it was enough.

"Cake by the Ocean" by DNCE was next. Amanda, Johnny, Brick and other friends had closed in on their position. Couples broke apart so they were dancing as a group. Amanda bounced up to her and they were bumping hips, turning and moving to the rhythm. She showed Daralyn some other steps. Daralyn didn't even mind when Rory took Amanda's offered hand and put her into a spin.

Daralyn did a couple steps with Johnny, though Johnny didn't put his hands on her, merely mirroring her dance steps and shooting her a big grin. Then there was Thomas and Marcus. Elaine joined them with a new partner, and there was so much energy around them. Good energy, like the heat of the sun when her bones were cold.

She was surrounded by a group of people, and it wasn't frightening.

All she felt was love. No anxiety, despite the noise and people. Because all of it was charged with good energy, fun and love.

She met Rory's eyes, saw he was making sure she was okay. Even now, on his night, with his friends, he was thinking of her.

I love you.

She wanted to say it to him so much it was an ache in her chest, trying to claw its way out. As the feeling rose inside her, she realized the words, that one key desire, might be the thing that could break down a wall her back had been against for so long. It had always seemed immovable, because what was on the other side of it was something to be feared. If the wall was gone, it would leave her unsupported, the bricks that had held up her reality for so long broken to rubble.

Rory extended a hand, and she came to him, took it, held fast. She danced with him with that connection, and he never let her go. Not once.

After the dancing, Johnny and Brick drew Rory away to spend some time reminiscing with his teammates. Daralyn had rejoined Elaine at their table, so she gave Rory a nod, a little wave, telling him she was fine. He sent her a searching look, but with her sitting by his mother, he seemed satisfied, moving away with the men.

Elaine was trying to figure out how to get her cell camera to pan the room, so she could then call Les and show her what was going on. Daralyn concentrated on helping her, but the music had moved to a hiphop piece. The people noise was getting louder, more raucous.

The wave of feeling from the dance floor was still with her, but she wanted to keep it that way. She knew the warning signs. She needed a few minutes where it was quiet.

She didn't want to interrupt Rory, so she told Elaine where she was going, and left her with Thomas to help with the phone. They all understood she had to have those retreats.

"Go by the cafeteria area, see if they have some extra sleeves of plastic cups in the cabinets," Elaine said. "I heard Patsy say they were running a little low, but she hasn't had a chance to get away."

A task to do, to be helpful. Even better. Daralyn hurried out of the auditorium, taking a deep breath once she reached the wide hallway outside. It had a bank of windows with a view of the front parking lot, full of cars. People had washed their vehicles before showing up tonight, so the lot lights reflected off shiny hoods and windows.

A handful of people were chatting out in the hallway. At the exits, others took a smoking break, standing in the open doorways. She avoided those places and headed for the cafeteria. Finding it was easy, since there were signs to it.

As she moved past the display cases of school awards and pictures, she stopped for a few looks. Not for the first time, she imagined what it might have been like, attending school like a normal child. Having a group of friends to meet in the hallways between classes.

Once she was in the cafeteria, she leaned against the counter that held the cabinets Elaine had mentioned and took a couple extra minutes to breathe. She filled her mind with good thoughts. Dancing with Rory. How he looked in his suit. Elaine's happiness, realizing how content he was.

Elaine's breakdown was a rarity. She was a farmer's wife, a practical sort. Not gushy or sentimental. But while watching her son with his former classmates, her emotions had been there for Daralyn to see.

"There were days I worried he'd never be this happy again," Elaine had said softly to her. "I prayed over it, cried over it."

Daralyn had gripped her hand and Elaine put hers over it, squeezing. "You look happy tonight, too," Elaine said. "And I thought the same about you. God brings us hope in the darkest of times."

Thinking of those dark times, Daralyn remembered that she'd had no concept of God, except from biblical quotes her father and uncle had used to direct her according to their will. She'd associated whatever God was with them, since He seemed to reflect their feelings on things. When they took her to church to keep up appearances, she'd been wholly focused on warning cues of their displeasure, rather than the message coming from the pulpit.

Elaine and even Rory saw God as a loving source of comfort, a symbol of faith in the good in the world. But Daralyn wondered if believing in that kind of God could have made her darker times harder.

She'd only known daily survival, following her father and uncle's orders to eat, sleep, breathe. If she'd believed some all-powerful entity could save her if He wanted, but hadn't...she might have given up. Having that held out of her reach would have just underscored her worthlessness.

But she hadn't given up. She was here, and tonight Rory had danced with her. Maybe God was more like love. Something that didn't fix things, but helped a person get through the bad things, reach for all that was possible in life.

"Hey, there. Is that smile for me?"

She turned to see a man leaning in the doorway, a beer dangling from his fingertips. Hayworth McNally. He'd disappeared after the dinner, apparently not wanting to join the dancing. The suit she now saw close up was like a banker's suit, but he'd loosened his red and black striped tie. He was handsome in a disheveled way, with longish hair on top and a dark shadowed jaw. But his blue eyes seemed extra bright.

"You're the girl that Rory's family took in." He seemed to be fishing for her name, and she helpfully supplied it.

"Daralyn."

"Yeah. That's right. Wow, you grew up pretty." He joined her at the counter, trailing the beer along the veneer with a solid sliding sound. He studied the supplies on the shelves behind the open pass through. "Weird, huh? When we were in school, no students were allowed back there. Probably because they thought we'd try to get into the desserts. They had some good cookies." He lifted a hand, spread out his fingers. "Size of pancakes."

He looked up at the cabinet she'd opened, her fingers resting on the lower shelf. "I heard Patsy bitching about the cups. I assume you're needing the ones on the top shelf?"

At her nod, he reached up and pulled them down, putting them on the counter. "Handy to have a tall guy around sometime, right?"

"Yes. Thank you."

He slid a hand in his pocket and touched the bottle to the inside of her forearm, leaving a trail of condensation over the scar there. She took a step back, and he chuckled.

"It's cold, I know. Sorry. Here, I'll fix it." He fished out a handkerchief from his pocket and gripped her wrist. It was the one without the bracelet. He held her steady as he mopped the dampness off, but then he didn't let go. He moved his hand so her fingers rested on his wrist as his palm cradled hers. "So pretty," he said thoughtfully.

Her heart had started to thump. She should pull away, tell him... what? That she didn't want... That she couldn't...

She belonged to Rory. Just like she'd told him, the night Rory had implied her teacher might be interested in her. She'd been so quick in that moment, but the teacher hadn't been standing next to her like this, holding onto her. Demanding something from her. And Rory had been there, right with her.

When she darted a look toward Hayworth's eyes, the strange intensity was both foreign and chillingly familiar. He wanted something from her.

No is not an option, girl. You never say no. What you want doesn't matter.

Cold and darkness. No food, no water. Her father's voice, then her uncle's. When the lack of water made it hard to think, their voices would overlap, and she couldn't tell one from the other.

You'll live in this cellar until you understand that, until the very thought of what you want never crosses your mind. Never.

"So quiet. You don't mind being touched, do you?" He'd moved his other hand to a loose lock of hair on her forehead, was stroking it. She swallowed, still as a mouse, even as something way down deep was screaming. Just like in the cellar. Something had been driven so far down inside her, it had been lost in the silence. It had disappeared there.

What everyone else had, she didn't. A will of her own. And suddenly, she realized the terrible truth; without a will, she wasn't a person. She was an object. The thought shredded her heart and soul with sharp blades, but she couldn't do one thing to tell Hayworth to stop. She was frozen.

He leaned in, brushed his lips with hers. She trembled, and oh God, that made her lips move, as if she was responding. He cupped her face. "So pretty and sweet," he murmured and slid an arm all the way around her, his hand settling over her hip, spreading out over her buttock. She was dying inside, and she could do nothing in her defense. She would die inside this motionless prison of her body that he thought was okay with this. He wasn't being rough or forceful. He thought she was...compliant.

Or complicit. A far worse word. She wanted to black it out of her notebook.

"Best thing about high school reunions," he said, offering a chuckle against her mouth. "It's like time freezes and you get a hall pass to do some impulsive things. Why don't we take this further? I wouldn't mind putting you up on the counter and tasting what's between your legs. I'm good at eating pussy, and see, I got this..." He kept one hand on her while he fished a vial out of his pocket. "I'll sprinkle it on you, and you won't believe how good it feels. Know there's not a lot of recreational drugs of this caliber in this county."

That was why his intensity seemed familiar. Her uncle liked to take things that made his eyes like that sometimes. He was less careful with her then, and her father had usually intervened to ensure she didn't need to go to a doctor afterward.

"After you're nice and slippery, maybe you'll be nice to me. Offer some reciprocity." He chuckled as he got the word out, with effort. "See—if you can say a word like that, you're not really impaired. I've told cops that when they stop me, but they don't get it. No sense of humor, I guess. You've got a lovely mouth. You're so quiet, darling. But your eyes do a lot of talking. So soft and willing..."

He was gathering up her skirt in the one hand, working his way beneath it while he went back to kissing her mouth. His body was against hers, and she could feel his erection against her stomach. A strangled moan came from her lips and he growled in answer.

"What in God's name?"

Daralyn jerked at the sound of Elaine's voice, and Hayworth turned. Then all hell broke loose.

Because Rory was right beside his mother.

She'd seen Rory's temper unleashed, though never directed at her, unless she counted the day she'd been on the tractor, and that had been different.

This was rage, so hot it swept toward them like hellfire.

His mother called out, but Rory was already headed for Hayworth. Then Daralyn realized Elaine hadn't called out to Rory. She'd known the futility of that. She'd entreated other help.

Thomas came in, Marcus on his heels, just as Rory reached Hayworth. However, in instinctive self-preservation, Hayworth had grabbed Daralyn by the shoulders, put her in front of him. She was a puppet, unable to move on her own, detached from anything. Like a news program Elaine had watched, where people had been rioting in a park. Daralyn didn't like the violence, and so had fixated on a statue of the city founder, part of the park's offerings. A monument seemingly indifferent to what was happening around it. Now she wondered if the statue simply couldn't move, could only watch the violence ensue, its feelings irrelevant because it couldn't do anything.

Rory was looking at her, and she couldn't survive the rage in his face. She dropped her gaze to the floor, to his shoes. Hayworth's hands flexed on her, making her sway. She'd locked her knees, and was starting to feel lightheaded.

"She was okay with it," Hayworth said hastily. "She didn't say no."

"Look at her," Rory snapped. "Or are you too fucked up in your head to *see* her?"

She flinched at every word.

"What's happening in here?"

The authoritative voice pulled everyone's attention away except Rory's. And hers. His gaze was burning her flesh.

The sheriff and two of his deputies had attended tonight as guests, not law enforcement. At least not until this moment. Loud voices were making accusations, talking over one another. Thomas and Marcus had circled around, latched onto Hayworth and moved him off to a corner, leaving her standing like a rootless tree, about to topple.

She remembered when her father died and the sheriff had come and escorted her out of her father's home. Not this sheriff; that one had retired since then, but the new sheriff had been one of the deputies she remembered at the county office. She'd sat rigid in a chair, politely responding the same way to offers of a soda, candy. *No thank you. No thank you. Please call my uncle to take me home. I'm fine.* She'd seen her uncle cuffed and taken away, but it was what she'd been taught to say if ever she was separated from them, if anything happened that she wasn't sure how it should be handled.

Rory had given her a different default, even if he hadn't realized it. She didn't know if it was right or wrong, but as it went through her mind, it was the only thing she could make her body do, so she seized onto the idea with both hands.

She dropped to her knees in front of Rory's chair, bowed her head. The cold tile hurt her knees, snagged her hose. Probably ripped it.

I'm sorry. So, so sorry.

A long second of silence reigned, during which she died inside, because that silence overflowed with how she'd disappointed him, his family. Failed all of them. She was Rory's, and she hadn't been able to tell Hayworth that. She was staring down at the bracelet he'd given her, to remind her, and it hadn't helped.

If she looked at Elaine, she would see shame. Maybe even anger. She couldn't bear it. She wanted to curl into a ball at Rory's feet, but since her body refused to do anything else but kneel, she didn't cause him that additional embarrassment.

Please. I'm so sorry.

Rory's fingers brushed her hair. The tension in them made her ache. She couldn't tell if the lack of warmth came from him, or if she'd just gone so cold, she couldn't feel it.

The sheriff was there, standing at her side.

"Miss. Are you okay?"

A long pause. Rory touched her shoulder. "Answer him, Daralyn." The calm in his voice had to be taking a tremendous effort. That penetrated enough to give her the ability to speak.

"Yes," she said. "I need to go home now." She sounded like a robot, but she couldn't inject anything into her voice that resembled real emotion.

"I need to talk to her alone," the sheriff said. "You understand that, Rory? I need to know what's going on here, from her."

"It doesn't work that way for her, Owen." Rory's anger surged back out. "You know that."

"It's going to work that way right now. I need you to back off."

"How about I put my fucking fist up your ass? I'm not leaving her—"

"You want me to have my deputies haul you out of this room by force? Push me, and that's what it will be. There's a procedure here. I need to talk to her alone. Now."

∽

As Rory stared at Owen, rage and helplessness took him within a breath of throwing a punch. Being a cop, Owen sensed it, his eyes narrowing.

"Don't do it, son," he said. "That's not going to help her, either."

Even wearing a suit, not his uniform and sidearm, Owen carried the mantle of his job, and so did his deputies. The flick of his glance toward them said he wouldn't hesitate to do what he'd threatened.

Rory looked down at Daralyn, kneeling at his feet. The move had been so unexpected. Rory thought Marcus might be the only one in the room who understood the crazy mix of feelings it had invoked in him. It also saved Hayworth, because it reminded Rory of his most important job. To protect his sub.

To care for her, give her what she needed. The problem was, he didn't know exactly what Daralyn needed right now, and he wasn't being given the space to figure it out. The protective side of him was about to go full berserker on anyone keeping him from it.

Which wouldn't help her, either. So he did what would, though he didn't want to say it like this. He'd owe Daralyn a huge apology later. "She's not capable of communicating when it comes to things like this, Sheriff." Her flinch drove a spike through him, but he pressed on. "My mom has her psychiatrist's number, and Dr. Taylor has a call service to reach her after hours."

"We'll check into that. I still need to talk to Daralyn. And I need you all out of the room."

"No," Rory said.

"You're still acting like I'm making a request," Owen said, his expression hardening. "I'm looking out for her best interests."

"She didn't say no," Hayworth said desperately from the corner. "All I did was kiss her, touch her a little bit. That's it. I've never forced myself on any woman."

"Since you're high as a fucking kite, you might want to shut up," Marcus advised. His green eyes were colder than Rory had ever seen them, telling him Marcus was just as pissed as he was. Only whereas Rory ran hot in a temper, Marcus went cold as ice. He looked ready to toss Hayworth in a car, find a river and a few heavy rocks.

A glance toward the door showed Rory that Brick had arrived, as well as other people from the party, including Fran Potts. They were drawing attention from the auditorium.

Rory still had his hand on her shoulder, his thumb resting on her collar bone. He could feel her vibrating under his hand. How could he explain how much she needed him with her, to help translate what had happened?

The bitch of it was, if she said, "I want Rory to stay," Owen wouldn't be able to override him. But she wouldn't. Rory knew she wouldn't.

She couldn't.

The frustration, the anger, the helplessness, were tearing him up inside. The worst part of it was some of that frustration was spilling out toward her, even as he knew she couldn't help it.

He couldn't stop being human, but he could help her by pushing past that, past everything that had to do with him, because this wasn't about him.

"I get you don't want me with her. But please, Owen. I'm begging you..." Daralyn twitched as his voice roughened. "Let my mother stay and help her. Please. You know Daralyn's history."

At least he hoped he did. Owen had been a deputy when the sheriff removed Daralyn from her uncle's home. Beyond that, everyone in this town knew everyone else's business.

Owen shifted his glance to Elaine, then back to Daralyn. His mother had stepped forward. No matter what she was feeling, she projected a practical calm and earnest desire to help that couldn't have come at a better time. Elaine was friends with Owen's parents. His jaw relaxed slightly.

"Okay. Long as she doesn't interfere."

Rory stroked Daralyn's cheek. She hadn't lifted her head since she'd knelt in front of him. He wanted to stay with her more than anything in the whole world, and he wanted her to know that. He hoped his touch told her, as well as what he did next.

Every time the girl hit a bad moment, it was like she became a vampire. He shrugged out of his coat and draped it over her, snugged it over her shoulders. A second later, one set of fingers crept around a lapel, pulled it close. The other hand rested on his foot, fingers against his ankle.

"I'll be close, baby," he murmured. "It's all right. Don't worry."

Elaine moved forward. Now that she was closer, he saw the worry and strain in her expression. For him, as well as Daralyn.

Owen gave him the stare that said he was done waiting. He could go fuck himself, but Rory made himself back up. The hand that had been resting on his ankle fell limply away from him. Despite him having no feeling there, it felt like a strip of skin had been torn off.

Owen glanced at his deputies, jerked his head at Hayworth. "Take him to one of the empty classrooms and hold onto him for questioning. Keep them apart."

He didn't have to specify who he meant, since if Rory got within arms' reach of Hayworth, he'd knock every one of his damn teeth out. Thomas and Marcus looked fully on board with that.

It kept replaying in his head, seeing Hayworth's hands on her, up her skirt. Her hand had been resting on Hayworth's forearm. To someone who didn't know her, it might have looked like she was welcoming the embrace. But that was only if they hadn't noticed everything else, like the vacant look in her eyes, and how, except for a quiver like a struck tuning fork, she wasn't moving. The arm had been rigid, like the branch of a tree with roots planted in the cafeteria tiles.

The deputies had flanked Hayworth and were gesturing Rory, Marcus and Thomas out of the room ahead of them. Hayworth was still talking a mile a minute, making it even clearer he was high. Probably drunk to boot.

A night that had started out so well had gone to shit. But his anguish about that wasn't on his own behalf. As he reached the door, he couldn't make himself go any further, but Thomas was there, a hand on his shoulder, keeping him from going back to her.

"Mom will watch over her," he said in a low voice. "You know she will."

But that wasn't his mother's job. It was his. The man who loved her. Her Master. His gaze went to Marcus, because he knew Marcus understood.

"It sucks ass," Marcus muttered. "But she's safe. Give them a few moments, and then we'll deal with the next thing."

As they moved into the hallway, one of the deputies closed the cafeteria door with a thud that speared Rory's heart. He spun his chair around, nearly taking out Thomas's toes, and planted himself, staring at the closed panel as if he could send his thoughts and feelings past it to Daralyn. He was here. He wouldn't abandon her.

He'd seen her have panic attacks that took her beyond speech, a near-catatonic state. It had been a long time since she'd had one that bad, but he hadn't forgotten how terrifying they were.

When they were younger and he'd first witnessed them, his parents had worried she might someday retreat so deep inside, past caring or want, she'd never find her way back.

Even if it wasn't that bad, at times like this, she could be like an injured wild animal, dedicated to making herself as small and unnoticed as possible. She'd come so far, but this one night might send her back months. All because he'd decided to let his ego be stroked by some damn award he didn't need.

The deputies herded the curious and concerned back toward the auditorium, though Brick was the most difficult to move. At least until Rory met his gaze and gave him a nod that said he knew where to find him if needed. Only then did Brick go, leaving just the three of them and one of the deputies in the hallway. The other one had Hayworth in the classroom a couple doors down.

Fuck it. He could feel her pain, knew she was in that dark place of her nightmares. He started forward again, but before the deputy could intercept him, Marcus was there.

"Get out of my way," Rory said. "I don't give a fuck what he said. She needs me."

"Yeah, she does. You getting arrested for assaulting a cop isn't going to help with that." Marcus nailed him with that stare. "Put your dick away and use the right head for this. Think about how to help her under these circumstances, the way things are, not how you wish they were."

He wished they'd never left home tonight. But then, thinking of her dancing with Amanda, her laughter, he knew that wasn't a good thought. Marcus was right. He needed to take these few moments, frustrating though they were, to figure out the correct one.

Elaine helped Daralyn up with a firm hand under her arm, and guided her to sit down at one of the lunch tables. Elaine sat beside her, Owen across from them both.

Elaine held her hand, was chafing it between both of hers. She wasn't acting angry, so that was something. Daralyn held Rory's coat around her with her other hand. It still had the warmth of his body, but there was a barrier between her flesh and the cloth. Nothing was warming her.

She'd failed. Disappointed.

Owen was saying something, but she couldn't focus, not until Elaine squeezed her fingers. "Daralyn, the sheriff is asking you a question."

There was a sadness to her face. Daralyn had caused that sadness. Tonight was supposed to be a happy night. Daralyn had ruined it.

All those things Rory had talked about on the stage, what Elaine had gone through when Rory had been hurt, when Thomas had been torn between two worlds, when she'd worried Les would drop out of medical school to marry Bart, the senior who'd insisted they get married. All of them were the ups and downs of being a mother. Elaine had suffered on Daralyn's behalf, too. Treating her as a daughter. This was how Daralyn repaid her.

What she'd allowed Hayworth to do had not been right. Not even close to right.

Maybe Elaine was regretting ever bringing her into her home. Her uncle and father had told her she had to do everything right, everything they said, because she had no value otherwise.

Daralyn knew she'd come farther than that. She should know it. These thoughts shouldn't be able to hold her the way they did, but this situation, the noise, the people, Rory's absence, the riot of emotions pushing in on her from all sides, and a great geyser of it coming up from her own core...

The darkness had never left, just as her soul had always known. The abyss was waiting.

Put you in the hole...never take you out.

Everything Elaine had told her earlier, the tentative confidence Daralyn had felt, vanished before things she'd been told over and over again, been left to remember in darkness, cold and hunger.

"Miss..." Owen was fishing for her last name.

"Moss," Elaine supplied. "Daralyn Moss."

Moss growing green and close on a tree, deep in a quiet forest. It was a good image. It was also the maiden name of Daralyn's mother. Elaine had insisted on using it when she and Robert had become Daralyn's legal guardian. Not Moorfield, her father's name.

"Miss Moss," Owen said. "Did you want Hayworth to touch you?"

Elaine cleared her throat. Owen raised a finger, stopping her. "No interference," he said sharply. "Or you'll be escorted from the room, Mrs. Wilder."

His tone made Daralyn cringe, and he saw it. His voice softened. "Did you?"

Daralyn stared through him. The storm was building in her ears, a roar. Sometimes in the cellar, she'd imagined it bursting through, filling up the space, taking all her air, her body floating in it, finally beyond the wanting her father and uncle had said was wrong.

"I...I...fine. Okay. Fine. I need to go home now. It's fine." She held onto that word desperately. Maybe it would be enough.

Owen's brows pulled down low. He had steady, watching eyes. They probed, wanted things from her she couldn't give. Elaine made a noise and Owen shot her a look, but this time Elaine wouldn't be silenced. Her voice was calm, though, offering explanation, not defiance.

"Daralyn has difficulty expressing things in terms of what she wants, Sheriff. A different phrasing might work better."

A puzzled look crossed his face, but Elaine waited him out, patiently staring him down. At length, Owen sighed. Frowned. "Miss Moss, did you tell Hayworth no?"

"No." She hadn't.

Owen's brow rose, reflecting his surprise at how easily the answer had come. He glanced at Elaine, then brought his thoughtful gaze back to Daralyn.

"Did you push him away?"

"No."

"Did he hurt you? Frighten you?"

"No."

"Do you want to press charges against Hayworth for assault?"

"No." The surge of panic at the idea must have shown in her face, because when she looked toward Elaine, the older woman's hand covered hers again. "Please. I need to go home."

She just needed her room. Her cottage. A place to hide.

Elaine put her purse on the table, and withdrew a card, handing it over to Owen. "Dr. Taylor's number, Sheriff. May I say one more thing? Please. If you know anything about me, you know the last thing I would be trying to do is override Daralyn's will."

Owen picked up the card. Daralyn felt his regard, though she was looking at anything in the room rather than him. But she clutched Elaine's hand, so afraid Elaine would pull away and it would be the last time she'd ever let Daralyn touch her.

Owen nodded at last, giving Elaine permission to continue.

"You know where Daralyn is if you need to question her further. And I truly believe Dr. Taylor can explain the situation better." Elaine sighed. "Hayworth grew up with Rory and Thomas. You may already know he has substance abuse problems. I'm certain they interfered with his judgment in a shameful way tonight, but he doesn't have the kind of meanness that would have him forcing himself on a woman he knows doesn't want his attentions. Angry as Rory is with him, he knows that, too."

"And how do you know that?" the sheriff asked.

"If he did have that kind of meanness, my sons would have beaten him half to death before you could get to him." Elaine didn't blink.

Owen rubbed a hand across his face, looking between the two of them. Daralyn could tell he was undecided as to whether he'd done his duty. The dull ache inside her was expanding, taking up her air. She was going to start hyperventilating, drawing more attention to herself.

Music started filtering in through the walls, a heavy bass thump that she felt through the soles of her wedge heels.

"Sounds like they got the party going again. All right." Owen rose. "I'll go talk to Hayworth, and call you if I need anything further." He flicked Dr. Taylor's card between his fingers, but then he pulled out his own card, slid it across the table until it was in front of Daralyn. "If there's anything else you need to tell us, Miss Moss, don't hesitate to call."

"Yes. Thank you. I'm fine."

His gaze rested on her. "Yes, ma'am," he said, in a tone that said he didn't think she was fine. At all.

~

She remained in the chair as Owen left and Elaine stepped out into the hallway to speak with Rory, Marcus and Thomas. They were talking in low voices.

Daralyn thought of Rory's expression when he'd first seen them. Haywood's hands on her. Hurt, anger...then the realization that she hadn't wanted Hayworth's hands on her, but she couldn't tell him no.

It had torn her apart inside, watching him understand that in a way she didn't think he had before. That changed things, didn't it? And not just for him.

She belonged to him, yet she hadn't told Haywood that. She'd been frozen, even Rory's hold not enough to thaw it.

She'd thought it would be. She'd convinced herself it would be, like a vase sitting on a shelf, believing it couldn't be broken because it had never fallen off the shelf before.

Now she'd never felt so broken in her entire life, sitting here like an inanimate doll in her dress and sparkling jewelry. A tangled ball of embarrassment, pain and shame rested within her. When the night had started, she'd come to the party on Rory's arm. His girl-friend, in pretty clothes, with the right hair and makeup. She'd danced with him, and people looked at her the way anyone was looked at, when people liked seeing two people together, in love, having fun.

Then this had happened, and now everyone remembered who she was. The thin, dirty, practically mute girl taken out of a rundown house. The kind to be pitied, whispered about.

She hadn't realized she knew what pride was, but she suspected the stinging in her gut was something like that.

Mostly she was tired. She wanted to go home, to her cottage, close the door, lie down on her bed, pull the covers over her head. Believing she'd come so far and then realizing she'd never really left the spot where she'd been standing was like a cruel joke she'd played on herself.

That part she could handle, eventually. The problem was she'd played it on the people who had offered her their home, their hearts. She'd let everyone down. Rory deserved better. Far better.

She rose, moved toward the door. Elaine had left it open while standing in the threshold, probably so she could keep Daralyn in sight. Now she turned as Daralyn reached it, saw past her to where Rory was, Marcus and Thomas. Rory's gaze immediately latched onto her. He looked so handsome tonight, particularly now, when he wore just the dress shirt and loosened tie, his hair tousled over his forehead, his eyes full of so much life and emotion.

One deputy was still in the hallway. Owen was in with the other one, talking to a nervous-looking Hayworth who she could see through the upper pane of glass in the classroom door. She wondered if the lone deputy stood near that door to give Owen and Hayworth privacy, or to ensure, if and when Hayworth emerged, that Rory would let Hayworth return to the party in one piece. Or go home.

Hayworth probably wanted to go home now, too.

She didn't know the deputy guarding the door, but his expression said he didn't know what to make of her. Was she a liar who liked getting men into trouble? Or was she simply...not capable, when it came to a situation like this. Rory had described her that way.

Either way, the deputy looked at her as if she couldn't be trusted. She put her hand on Elaine, a brief touch before she slipped past her and began to walk down the hall, away from all of them. Her skirt slipped against her legs, light as a breeze.

"Daralyn?" Rory caught up to her in a few heartbeats. "Where are you going?"

"Home," she said, not looking at him. "I need to go home."

"Okay. But the parking lot's out the other exit. This just leads to the bus lot."

"I'll walk home."

"Daralyn, it's eight miles and it's nearly ten o'clock."

"It's okay."

The roads were quiet here, safe. She'd walked them at night plenty of times since she'd moved into her cottage. She often walked the perimeter of the fields, the side roads, when she couldn't sleep.

No one knew that. Well, except Marcus. He didn't sleep much either. When he and Thomas were at the North Carolina house, he sometimes followed her, at a distance, giving her privacy, but watching out for her.

She saw deer when she walked, bobcats and coyotes hunting, foxes slinking through the brush. In the country, there was a whole world at night most people never saw. She moved through it, unnoticed and unbothered, because she wasn't their prey, and she was nothing for the prey to fear. She stood between both worlds, a presence like a tree or a pond. She liked that feeling. Nothing demanding.

"Daralyn." Rory maneuvered decisively in front of her, brought her to a stop. She stared at one wheel, and he put his hand out, gripped her wrist above her bracelet.

Her heart cried out in actual pain, though no one could hear it except her. She couldn't feel his touch the way she normally did. Her skin was aware something was against it, but she felt no reaction. It was a loss she couldn't bear.

She wondered if that was what it was like when someone touched his legs.

She wanted Rory. So much. She'd relied on him to understand what she wanted and needed, and he did. She hadn't really realized until this moment that it wouldn't be enough to let her love him the way he deserved. It didn't matter what she wanted when she was in darkness, her voice taken away. How could she find her way through that darkness? How did she find a light in herself that might have been extinguished long ago?

"You are not walking home by yourself," he said firmly. "I'll take you home."

"Okay."

"I'm going to stay with you."

She kept her eyes on his wheel. "I'm going to call Dr. Taylor and talk to her."

"That's good." He sounded slightly relieved. "Sounds great. I'll hang out at Marcus and Thomas's, if you need privacy while you do that."

She didn't say anything, but if her silence ended up convincing him that was the thing to do, that would work.

Because by morning, she knew she'd be gone.

CHAPTER TWENTY-ONE

*R*ory sat at Thomas and Marcus's living room window, watching Daralyn. From this vantage point, he could see through her picture window in front. She'd dialed Dr. Taylor while in her kitchen, sat straight in her chair as she held the phone to her ear. She was on it for a while. Sometimes talking, sometimes listening. She didn't give much away, her body and manner rigid, as if she held something in a tight grip, all her focus on not letting it go.

He was aware of Thomas and Marcus moving around, keeping an eye on him. But he had eyes only for her.

Eventually, she put down her phone, took a breath. She looked toward him. He was sitting in a darkened room, because he hadn't wanted her to feel like he was spying on her. But he hoped she was looking toward the house because she was looking for him. Before he could back up and head for the door, his phone rang.

He wanted it to be her, but she wasn't holding a phone. It was Dr. Taylor.

"You've had an eventful evening." The doc's voice had its usual professional tone, but there was a thicker softness to it, maybe because she was at home, not in her office. People used different voices depending on where they were. Home, work, in the grocery store. Daytime, nighttime.

Right now, the place and time he was at in his head, he was sure

347

his voice was all kinds of rough and on the edge of some not-stable things.

When he'd watched Hayworth talk to Owen, so many things had gone through his mind. If Rory could have reached him, he would have hit him, and kept hitting, until the man was nothing but bloody meat. Fortunately, his brother and Marcus had kept him from that course of action. Brick had taken Hayworth back to his hotel and would get him sobered up.

"He'll probably want to call you tomorrow and apologize," Brick had said in parting. "You know how he is after he comes down."

"Don't let him. Not this time. I don't want to talk to him. Not now, and possibly not for the rest of our lives."

He'd pushed past that. It was still true, but whatever happened with his tragically fucked up teammate wasn't even on his radar. It was in the past, except for how it was affecting Daralyn's present.

"Congratulations on your award," Dr. Taylor continued. "Daralyn told me."

"Thanks." He managed to keep the impatience from his tone. "How can I help her?"

Dr. Taylor paused, then spoke slowly. "By doing something extremely difficult, Rory. That's why I'm calling."

"Okay." He held the phone tighter. There must have been something in his tone, because he was aware of Thomas, coming to stand in the doorway of the living room, which meant Marcus wasn't far away. They were giving him space, but staying close.

"Daralyn has asked to be checked into my treatment facility in Raleigh. She'd like to stay there for a few weeks to undergo some concentrated therapy, particularly regarding the issues that came up tonight. After hearing the details, from her and from my call with Sheriff Wright, I have agreed."

"Is there something I should have done? Could have done differently? Can I fix this?"

"No," Dr. Taylor said, not unkindly. "I told you recently that, the better things were going, the more likely it was that Daralyn would run up against some of her deeper issues. Do you remember?"

"Yeah. I remember."

"She's still on your mother's health insurance as her dependent, so it will be covered," Dr. Taylor continued, as if that was a sufficient answer to what was burning a hole through Rory's gut. "While she's there, we recommend that she not communicate directly with any of her family or friends. It's part of the program, reducing any outside distractions. She's certainly allowed to reach out if she wishes to do so, but we ask relatives and friends not to initiate contact, to avoid influencing or putting any pressures on the patient while they're undergoing the therapy."

"Okay." It wasn't okay. Not at all. But he didn't know what else to say. Daralyn had gone into the bedroom while he and Dr. Taylor were talking. Now she'd come back into the kitchen. She'd changed out of her dress and into jeans and a T-shirt. Her hair was pulled up in a ponytail. While she was on the phone, she'd still had his coat around her shoulders. It was gone now, probably lying neatly on the bed. She looked tired, sad. Beaten.

She was carrying a suitcase.

Alarm stabbed his gut. "She's going tonight?"

"Yes. I've called her a cab. She'll stay in my guest room and I'll take her to the treatment center in the morning. Normally I'd tell her to wait until daylight and pick her up then, but in her current frame of mind, I feel better taking action now, having her under my direct supervision. She's in a very precarious place in her head, Rory."

He swallowed. "I can help."

"Yes." Dr. Taylor's voice firmed. "By stepping out of the way and letting this happen. I know it's very, very hard to hear that. You're going to have to trust me on this. Let her go."

"For a few weeks."

"For as long as she needs."

That sounded as ominous as it felt. And it felt like being rammed in the gut with a bowling ball.

"Rory, you and your family already knew Daralyn lacks some key skills for operating independently in the world. Tonight highlighted a very important one. We've all been able to work around it as she's undergone sessions with me for resolving that and her other issues. But being an equal partner in a long term, healthy relationship requires the ability to express her desires, doesn't it? Until she has that skill, won't some part of you wonder if she's with you primarily because she doesn't have to do that?"

His temper flared. "It's not like that with us, and you know it, Doc."

Just like his upper body being much more sensitive after his accident, falling in love with her had enhanced his awareness of her in every nerve ending, with every brain cell. All of them attuned to her, and the way she responded to him. He knew she wanted to be with him.

Dr. Taylor's voice softened. "You're right. I can't speak to what's true between the two of you. But Daralyn is my patient and my priority. She is very lost right now, and it's a hazardous labyrinth. Let me do my job, Rory."

Thomas had closed the distance between them, was standing within arm's reach. Maybe he could feel the volatility emanating from Rory as he stared through one pane of glass at the slim woman standing behind another. Her face was blank, but he could feel her pain.

"If you tell her not to go, she won't, Rory," Dr. Taylor said. The urgent note in her voice was something he wanted to ignore, but couldn't. "You know she won't. I am asking you not to do that to her. If you love her, let her go."

He cut the connection, held the phone in a tight fist. Then he hurled it across the darkened room, hard enough it hit a picture on the far wall. It knocked it off its hook and broke the glass, sending pieces scattering across the wood floor. "No," he said. "Fucking hell, no."

He went to the door, ripped it open and thumped out onto the porch. It took so damn long to get around to the ramp, and another two corners to get back on the drive between the house and the cottage.

The taxi was pulling in. It was Teller Williams, who ran an evening cab service when he wasn't working at the Walmart. He gave Rory an affable wave Rory didn't return as Daralyn stepped out onto her porch, holding the suitcase.

She stopped when she saw Rory. Froze, really. He lifted his casters up, wheeled over the gravel to her, let them come down with another solid thump a few inches from the patio edge.

She met his gaze, then shifted hers to his shoulder. Her hazel eyes were full of brilliant pain, fear, longing. And a numbness. She wet her lips. "I'm sorry," she said, and all those things were in her voice, too.

He wanted to tell her she hadn't let him down, that she'd done nothing wrong. He wanted to tell her if she got in that cab, he'd go dead all over. Like he would have if the tractor had rolled over a place far higher on his spine, severing feeling below the neck completely. Leaving only the agony of what was happening in his heart. He needed her. God, he needed her so much.

If you tell her not to go, she won't.

So many times since they'd started down this road, he'd told himself if the road to her happiness led away from him, he'd let her go. He loved her that much.

But saying something and actually doing it, well that was the bitch of it, wasn't it? It was the difference between some asshole telling his girl he'd die for her, and actually dying for her. Which was what this felt like.

Plus, in his thoughts of noble self-sacrifice about letting her go, he'd imagined her happiness looking like happiness. Not like her struggling just to keep her head above water, and him withdrawing to let her drown.

The taxi's lights were on him. She held his gaze, and he extended a hand. She put down the suitcase and came to him. Quietly, no emotion in her face. Nothing. Her hand was cold, as always. She was standing on the edge of a cliff, her heels off the back edge, just waiting to see if he was going to push. She still wore his bracelet. That was something.

He tugged her hand, bringing her down to him, and threaded his fingers through her ponytail as it fell forward over her shoulder. He curled it over his knuckles. "I love you," he said. "I'll be here for anything you need. Go do what you have to do."

Wariness entered her gaze. Her lips parted. "Rory..."

"Go," he said harshly.

She drew back, startled. "Doesn't mean I'm not pissed about it," he said. "But I support you a hundred percent. Get your ass in that cab, now. And go."

Tears spilled out of her eyes, but before he broke and lunged for her, which probably would have had him sprawled on the gravel, she retrieved her suitcase, dashed to the vehicle. Teller had emerged to help her. She ducked into the cab while he put the suitcase in the trunk. Then he was back behind the wheel and they were leaving, the car backing up.

Rory turned toward the cottage, looked through the window at her kitchen table. One chair. She kept the other pushed to a corner now, because of how often the two of them were together there.

He didn't turn away from the sight as the cab reached the road. She might have expected him to look toward her, but he was only so strong, honestly. He shifted his gaze to the chimes she'd hung over her patio as the wind moved them. He heard the car drive away, recede with that soft rush of noise, the hum of an engine.

Only then did he move. He went to the road, watched the tail-lights recede. From the shadow in the back, he thought she might have looked back, seen him there. Then the car disappeared over a hill, out of sight.

He started to move. He didn't have his push gloves to protect his hands, and this wasn't a chair designed for miles of road travel, but he didn't care. He started to push faster, and faster, up the hills, headed down, taking the curves without care for his speed, not even feeling the burn in his hands on the rims when he did have to slow enough to keep from toppling. His breath started to sob in his throat, squeeze out of his lungs. His shoulders and back were on fire. He didn't care.

He followed the roads by muscle memory. His mind's eye was full of her. The various versions of her shy smile, her resolve as she woke up and faced a world every day that terrified her. She'd let him help with that, had let him stand with her. Seemingly overnight, it became the role he wanted for his entire life.

He inhaled her scent with every gasping breath. He heard her voice, the little erratic breaths she made when he pushed her to climax. The way she'd fallen to her knees before him in the cafeteria, as if she was throwing herself on his mercy.

Her bowed head, the slump of her spine, had said she thought she'd done the unforgiveable. But what worried him more was thinking she'd lost hope that she could ever overcome the fear, the shape of the person she'd been forced to be. It might pose the greatest obstacle to their relationship, but he had no doubt it posed the greatest danger to her soul. To her survival.

Was the treatment center an effort to change that? Or her way of giving up? Disappearing into a structured world, which, while safer and better than her childhood by a long shot, might just be a different version of a world with no choices to make.

He usually did the steep grade on Lichen Road at the front end of his workout. He had no idea how far he'd gone when he reached it, and it didn't slow him down. Not until halfway up the incline, when dizziness swamped him.

He snarled, made himself reach the crest. But his hand slipped off one rim, jerking the chair to the right. The wheel hit a rough spot on the pavement and the chair veered off onto the shoulder. The impact pitched him out of the seat, and he hit the slope, the clumps of weeds. His legs landed in the drainage ditch with a splash, since the last rains had left a shallow amount of water. With how his luck was running, there'd be a nest of copperheads hanging out there, just waiting for something to bite.

He heard a screech of brakes. Staring up at the sky, his chest heaving, he noticed it was a dark night, no moon and overcast. None of the rural roads outside of town had streetlights.

And yet he'd had enough light to navigate. That was when he realized he'd had a vehicle following him for some time, lighting his way. Thomas was jogging toward him, silhouetted by the headlights of his Nova.

He crouched next to Rory, his concerned eyes all over his brother under the flashlight Marcus held. But Rory gave Thomas credit. He spoke as casually as if they were in their mom's kitchen. "Hey, little brother. Can I give you a lift home?"

"Yeah." But Daralyn wouldn't be there. Which made the word home mean a lot less.

As Marcus righted his chair, Thomas helped Rory sit up. Rory wouldn't say he buried his face in his older brother's shoulder for a long moment, or that Thomas wrapped his arms around him, held him tight. He wouldn't say that it might have been the only thing that gave him the strength to get up one more time. Keep going.

That was okay. Thomas wouldn't be saying it either. The truth really didn't need words. Words usually just fucked it up.

~

353

So life went on, as it did. Thomas came and helped out at the store. Rory knew that he and Marcus were delaying their return to New York. Thomas said the loft was a better place to work on his newest project, and coincidentally it gave him the opportunity to pitch in, since Rory was down an employee. Rory let it pass, though if his brother and Marcus didn't leave soon, he'd give them the necessary nudge to do so. They had a busy life and other demands on their time, and they couldn't put them off indefinitely, no matter what Thomas claimed.

Rory was fine. He couldn't seem to make anyone believe that, though.

His mother stopped by daily. Sometimes twice. She'd make dinner for him. Good stuff, his favorites. It all tasted like sawdust. He'd come home and pick at it, say the right things, make conversation, watch a little TV with her, then return to the store, work on fuck-all until past bedtime.

She was talking to Dr. Taylor daily, getting updates on Daralyn. Which was pretty much the same thing, every day.

Daralyn was working through an intensive program she and Dr. Taylor were developing and adjusting, day by day. Sometimes it was two steps forward and five steps back. She had good days and bad days. She missed them.

Since he could imagine what those backwards days looked like, Rory stopped asking for the updates, figuring his mother would tell him if the broken record changed.

When he exhausted himself, he went home to bed. Once or twice he went to Daralyn's place and slept on her bed. He didn't like being at her place without her, though. This was her space, that she'd filled with the things she'd allowed herself to enjoy, to express herself. When he was there alone, it felt too much like the house of a deceased relative, someone he wasn't expecting to come back.

She'd had one of Elaine's cookbooks sitting on the counter, and when he opened it up at a bookmarked page, he'd found a recipe for chicken-fried steak. The bookmark was a post-it note in Daralyn's handwriting.

Make this for Rory's birthday. Elaine says it's his favorite.

He didn't return to the cottage after that.

He reminded himself to shower, do his skin checks, do his workouts, his PT and training with Red. He did those things mainly to keep his family and friends from worrying about him.

They tried to get him to talk about it. He found himself realizing —and perversely admiring—how often Daralyn managed a conversation, avoiding unwelcome attention on things she didn't want to discuss. He wasn't as good at that, sometimes so abruptly forcing the subject toward more casual topics he earned a startled look from whichever friend or family member was trying to open him up.

They didn't have a can opener big enough. No one did, not even himself. The only person who might wasn't here.

He didn't want to think about what he was thinking about. He just wanted to keep moving so he didn't have to think at all. They didn't need to worry. He could take care of himself, be an adult. He'd had his wallowing period after his accident. He wouldn't become that person again. He wouldn't do that to his family.

But he had nothing to give to anyone right now, because it was taking everything he had to take care of himself. Be that adult, trying not to burn his world down because the woman he loved had put herself out of his reach, beyond where he could help her.

She was trying to figure things out. But she'd shut him out, and it was hard not to take that personally. Also impossible not to keep replaying that moment in the cafeteria, when he was sure he'd failed her somehow. Dr. Taylor had said he hadn't, but she couldn't replace his gut.

Daralyn had been an animal in a cage. That was how Dr. Taylor had described her. Born there, no memory of anything but confinement. She'd lived at the whim of two men who never considered her care a priority, except for how it served their purposes. She'd lived and survived without hope. When she'd finally been taken from them, a light had started to burn in her previously lifeless gaze, proof that miracles existed. Hope had found a way in, and life's possibilities had fueled it, made that light burn brighter.

In the cafeteria, that light had sputtered. In the driveway, before she left in the cab, he hadn't seen even a flicker of it in her. Something had taken hope away from her.

He was her Dom. Her person. The man who loved her. He should have been able to prevent that. Kept the light burning.

Dr. Taylor said the solution had to come from her. He knew that.

Told himself, over and over, this might be the best thing for her. He needed to be supportive. He passed on encouraging messages for Dr. Taylor to share with Daralyn, if she thought they'd be helpful. They felt like empty greeting card sayings that made him cringe just to recall them.

Getting up every day was getting harder, but he did it. When she needed him again, he was going to be there. But every day that passed without her return, without any kind of message from her, made the voice in his head get louder. It said what she needed might not end up being him. He might have just been a waystation, after all.

He wanted the very best for her. He wanted her to be happy. But if that meant a life that didn't involve him being with her, the pain of accepting that might just be the stroke that finished him off.

~

"Mom doesn't know what to do."

Thomas had spent the morning in the store, but he came home to eat lunch with Marcus. Marcus had made them a robust portabella salad, plenty of chopped ingredients. Thomas scattered a handful of pumpkin seeds over his dressing as he spoke. "He's running the store, taking care of himself, handling customers, but he's a robot. Completely shut down. Just gives me this cold stare if I try to get him to talk about it. Says, 'There's nothing to talk about.'"

Marcus lifted a shoulder, made a noncommittal noise. Thomas shot him a look. "That's pretty much been your response since she went to Raleigh."

"Just being supportive. Letting you talk it out."

Thomas leaned back in his chair, eyed his husband. Marcus was studiously slicing up the fresh tomato that Thomas had brought back from the store's produce stand. "You are many things, but laconic isn't usually one of them. Care to enlighten me on why you don't seem as worried about him as the rest of us?"

"I am worried about him. Very much." The flash of frustration in Marcus's eyes confirmed it. Unfortunately, that only made Thomas more concerned, since Marcus also wasn't the type to overreact.

"I just know there's nothing that's really going to get through to him but her...or a shitload of time." Marcus sighed, set down the knife. "I haven't said anything, because it's hard to explain. He's a Dom, Thomas. And it's not a middle ground or light side of the spectrum thing. We're used to seeing people grow into it, but I think Daralyn brought it to full life in him, because she's the same, on the sub side. Not learning to be one, not growing into it. Whether it was from nature or the lack of nurturing, or some clash between the two, it doesn't matter. It runs soul deep for her. And the kind of sub she is, needs the kind of Dom that Rory dug out of his soul to be for her. Remember the moment in the cafeteria that shocked the fuck out of Owen and your mother?"

Thomas wasn't likely to forget it. That flash of despair and desperation on Daralyn's face before she'd collapsed on her knees in front of Rory's chair. Thomas had recognized the gesture like a shot to the gut. When a sub couldn't figure out how or where to go, all avenues equally desolate, the only solution left was turning to your Dom, hoping to find in his strength and your submission a way to figure things out. In that moment, even if the sub didn't consciously realize it, they'd let everything go but faith in the bond between Master and sub. In the love that formed that bond.

"She made a choice to remove herself from his care and put herself beyond where he can help her." Marcus gave him a steady look. "Sound familiar?"

Thomas grimaced. "You figured out a way to bull yourself into that china shop."

"Yes, I did. But it took months to reach that point. I had to give you space to self-actualize and realize what parts of your method weren't working. Or find enough rope to hang yourself. Though it really wasn't that deliberate on my part. In hindsight, I think I just decided enough was enough. Maybe it's all the same thing, some tangled ball of fate, cause-and-effect bullshit. Why did she leave?"

"Because of what happened at the reunion."

"That's the catalyst. Why did she leave? The key is when Rory walked in and saw them."

Thomas thought it through. Marcus took a couple bites of salad, tore off a hunk of fresh French bread and put it on Thomas's bread plate. He had the back door open, so Thomas heard a crow's rasping call in the field behind the house. He could also hear the faint noise of Daralyn's chimes, adding music to the bird's cries. One of them had fallen down yesterday, pushed off its hook by the wind. When Marcus had walked over there to hang it back up, Thomas had been in the loft. He'd watched Marcus run his hand over the strands of sea glass that formed it, then stand there a couple moments.

They both missed her intensely. Yet when their eyes met across the property, Thomas remembered what it had been like, thinking he had to give up Marcus forever. Their reaction to Daralyn's absence had to be a mere shadow of how Rory felt. That glass was sitting in his brother's heart and being churned like a blender, slicing and cutting him every waking hour.

The light dawned, and he met Marcus's gaze. "She couldn't say *no* to Hayworth, tell him she belonged to someone else. To her Master. Not being able to be everything she wanted to be for Rory, discovering it was literally beyond her abilities, was something she couldn't accept. It tore her apart."

Marcus nodded. "With that kind of submissive, it doesn't matter how demanding the Master is. No one demands more than the submissive herself. The irony of this is that by leaving, a pretty drastic and decisive step, Daralyn *did* decide what she wanted."

A grim smile touched his mouth at Thomas's startled look. "She wants Rory, and she wants to be able to tell him that. I expect Dr. Taylor was smart enough to figure that out, and will use it to help her. I wish it could help your brother."

Shadows crossed Marcus's gaze. "I'm sure he's thought of it, but other things, his own issues, are likely making it hard for him to see it as a hopeful sign. And since it could go a lot of ways..." He lifted a shoulder.

"Wow." Thomas blew out a breath. "Hell. So...time."

"Time. It's a total bitch." Marcus gestured with his fork. "And patience is not your brother's best trait."

"What is?"

"Since he wears it on his shoulders a lot, I've gotten a close look. He has an excellent ass."

Marcus chuckled as Thomas shot a grape at him. Thomas shook his head. "Mom's pretty upset. She has that two-week trip to Flagstaff with her church group, and Rory wouldn't let her cancel it. He also told me this morning, before I even brought it up, that if I didn't keep the San Diego show date, he would fucking shoot me. Quote unquote."

"He needs time and space, Thomas. Let's give it to him."

Thomas knew he was right, but it didn't dissipate his worry. Marcus reached across the table, closed his hand on Thomas's. "We'll check in with him. Give Johnny and Amanda our cell numbers just in case."

Thomas made a face. "I know he's a grown man. I guess I can't stop being a big brother."

"Nor should you."

Thomas looked across the corner of the table at Marcus. No matter that time had healed it, he still felt the pain of their shared past. "Did you feel like Rory feels now?"

Marcus's eyes flickered. "Yes. I did. And though you had your family, I knew you had isolated yourself from them emotionally, because they couldn't understand. So you were dealing with everything seemingly alone, and you'd told me you didn't want my help. There might be nothing worse for a person to hear, whether they're a brother, spouse, or lover. But for a Dom in particular, it's tough as hell."

Thomas moved his foot under the table, covering Marcus's. "I'm a grown man," he said seriously, "But I didn't know how to handle the pain of being without you while caring for my family. Which is how my ulcers got worse. I knew something was wrong, but when you're between a rock and a hard place with nowhere to go, sometimes embracing that physical pain is the only distraction. That's what concerns me. In focusing on how much Daralyn needed him, how his strength helped her push her own boundaries, I'm worried that we're overlooking just how much he needs her."

Marcus studied him. Inclined his head. "If you want, we'll cancel the trip."

Thomas considered, struggled with it, then shook his head. "No. You're right. We need to give him space." A wry smile tugged at his mouth. "Plus, he really would shoot me. Rory loves any excuse to pull out his guns. But thanks. I know exactly what a pain in the ass that would have been, cancelling our show appearance."

"Well, every time you cause a pain in my ass, it gives me a reason to inflict pain on yours." Marcus's green eyes flickered, a light smile on his dangerously sensual lips. "So that's sufficient compensation."

～

Initially, it was a relief when his mother departed for her trip, Marcus and Thomas heading off to San Diego a couple days later. Though he had to handle more texts and calls from them than would have been the norm, Rory was relieved to have the house to himself. Now Amanda and Johnny were the only ones physically present who might try to push. Everyone else he could keep at arms' length with canned friendly interaction.

His mother had said she'd continue her daily calls to Dr. Taylor, and let him know if anything had changed. Nothing had. Nothing did.

So here he was, eight days later. He'd closed up the store for the night, gone home, eaten a sandwich for dinner. He didn't want to watch anything on TV, so he sat on the screened porch and stared out at the garden behind the house, the neighbor's harvested corn field stretching out behind that. Why was the ache in his chest expanding, getting worse? Even talking was an effort.

He didn't want to think it, acknowledge it, but he knew the signs.

He'd fallen out of the boat and was sinking.

Back when he'd found out he'd never walk again, he'd reached that point without knowing that was where he was. For way too long after that, he'd only done anything thanks to serious bullying from his mother. His reaction to it had been inexcusable. If his father had been alive, Rory wouldn't have had to worry about how to go on living. His dad had one rule not one of his kids ever broke—not if they wanted to keep breathing. No one talked disrespectfully to their mother.

During that time, Rory had been even less restrained with Thomas. Thomas didn't care; he'd practically dragged him out of bed to make him work in the store again.

Eventually the who-gives-a-shit lassitude had been replaced with anger, and anger, destructive as it could be, had started him up the mountain he needed to climb to get where he eventually needed to go.

Now he'd been blindsided by something he hadn't expected. He was tumbling back down the rocky slope, without the will to catch himself, stop the fall. Not even the anger was there to help him.

He hadn't asked, but he was pretty sure Dr. Taylor hadn't given Daralyn his messages. She'd said no contact right now, no distractions, and Rory had accepted that. However, maybe because she'd recognized where he was—or his mother had expressed her worries—the doc had suggested Rory could write to Daralyn. For himself. Later he could give Daralyn those missives, or not. It would be an outlet either way.

He wasn't much for writing things down. But he tried, and all he ended up doing was writing down the basic, inane wishes of the heart. *I'm sorry. I miss you. I need you. I'm fucking losing my mind.*

When he'd fallen in love with Daralyn, he'd overlooked the downside of cracking open his heart. It made him vulnerable to attack in ways he'd thought he'd overcome.

He stared up at the night sky. "Come back to me, baby," he murmured. "I love you. Whatever you're going through, know that you did nothing wrong. Not a damn thing to make me love you less. There's no possible way you could ever do that. I really...I'm lost without you."

It was like praying, wasn't it? If so, he was fucking it up. This was supposed to be about her. It should be about him praying for her happiness, whether that included him or not. He should ask God for strength to let her go, if that was what was best for her. For the strength to continue to be the best brother, son and friend he could be to the others in his life who counted on him.

He needed to go to bed. He didn't. He left the porch, pulled the axe out of the stump that served as a block and began to chop wood. The simple act of swinging and letting the cord of wood split, an ongoing chore for his mother's wood stove and the fireplace they used in the winter, kept his mind occupied and numb.

He worked himself into a sweat, long past when exhaustion told him to quit. The ache was still there, and he'd keep going until it became bearable.

It didn't.

He fell asleep in the chair, the axe balanced on his lap. He hadn't worn gloves, so the blisters had formed and broken. He embraced the pain.

He didn't rouse until he felt a hand on his shoulder, a shaking that became more insistent as he didn't immediately care to respond. "Rory."

Johnny's voice, sharp. Rory raised his head, blinked. It was past sunrise. Well past. Fuck. "Hey, Johnny." He coughed, straightened. "Hell, sorry. What time is it?"

"Nine-thirty." His friend's bearded face was grave. "I would have been here earlier, but Tim brought that grain delivery and we had those orders to fill. You left a note that you might be in late, but I thought I'd come by anyway."

Rory managed a smile. "I looked that bad yesterday, did I?" He coughed again, shifted. Shit. The autumn chill had gotten to him. Big surprise, with him sweating through his shirt, then sitting out here all damn night, hunched over.

"You've looked better." Johnny peered at him. "You been burning it at both ends, and pushing yourself on your workouts. The other night, you didn't even hear me honk when I passed you on Gordon Road." He sobered. "I know you don't want to talk about it, but we know it's tough on you, being without her."

Rory gazed at him distantly. Yeah, that was a word for it. Tough. He shouldn't be letting it knock him down like this, though.

"I'll go get a shower. Then I'll get to the store." He coughed again.

Johnny looked at him dubiously. "Okay. But if you change your mind and want to take a day, just text me, all right? We'll cover you."

"Got it. Thanks."

Rory pushed himself into the house. Handled the bathroom stuff, then pushed himself over to the shower. He sat there for a while, looking at it, imagining the effort to slide himself onto the shower chair, bathe, get back out.

Slowly he turned, went back to his room. He transferred himself into the bed, sent Johnny that text. Then he rolled over, not caring about putting a pillow between his knees like he usually did. He probably had pressure sores forming on his ass and backs of his legs, because he hadn't been keeping to his regimen of shifting and lifting his weight throughout the day like he was supposed to. He needed to pay attention to that.

He needed her.

Maybe if he went to sleep long enough, he'd figure out a way to bring her back to him. Or maybe he'd sleep long enough she'd come back to him on her own. He just wanted to talk to her. Hear her voice, know she was okay. Know that he hadn't done this. Making her feel like she'd let him down, when he was pretty sure the opposite was true.

Especially right now. Why was it so hard to think? Every day since she'd gone, as the feelings had expanded like an aggressive cancer, he'd tried to shame himself out of acting this way. Telling himself he was acting like a damn two-year-old who'd had a favorite toy taken away.

The truth was, he was a man in his twenties with half a body, who felt like his heart had been ripped out of his chest.

The truth was—just like for Daralyn—even his best day meant a bigger effort to do what everyone else did without a second thought. He had to talk himself through things, over things, around things. There was a millstone always waiting, eager to yoke itself back around his neck, tell him what he'd lost. And losing her meant that millstone had doubled in size and taken him back down, even deeper than before.

The truth was, suddenly those things he was so proud of himself for proving he could do, embrace a good life, take stock of his blessings, didn't seem to mean much.

The truth was, he couldn't handle losing something *again* that meant as much to him—more, even—than his legs.

Ever since she'd left, that was the feeling that had been growing inside him, taking up every spot until he had nowhere else to contain it.

Fuck, he needed her so much. But he couldn't reach out to her, couldn't do that to her.

If you tell her not to go, she won't.

He was afraid he'd have to live up to what he'd promised himself. He'd have to let her go permanently so she could be happy, healthy. Strong.

If he had to do that, he could survive, keep moving, keep doing. He just wouldn't want to.

He drifted through the day, lying in the bed, staring blankly out the window. Coughed. Thought about getting up and finding water for his dry throat, then decided against it. He sent some texts. Short stuff, to reassure his brother and mother.

Staying busy. Hope the trip is going well.

For Johnny and Amanda. *Feeling a little under the weather, so might need a couple days.*

Don't know.

That last one was for Brick's text, which came in later that afternoon from Richmond.

Any word on when your girl's coming back?

He'd answered two questions in one. Because he also didn't know if she was his anymore.

~

He woke at three a.m., having trouble breathing. He managed to push himself up to a sitting position, and his head swam. He was feverish.

Shit. Shit. *Shit.* He knew better than this. Apathy was an indulgence his body couldn't afford.

He dragged himself into position to transfer himself to his chair. Dizziness assaulted him, but he trusted muscle memory to get him from point A to point B. Which would have worked, if he'd braked the damn chair properly. It shot out from under him and he hit the floor. The weight of his legs twisted him around, and he couldn't stop the momentum. His forehead hit the corner of the foot board with a resounding *thwack*.

He saw stars, tried to steady himself. His phone had been left on the nightstand on the other side of the bed, out of reach unless he got himself back in the chair or could drag himself over there. Fear trickled through him, an unwelcome companion he knew too well from his earlier days in the chair, when he was weak and helpless.

"Damn it," he snarled. The rage didn't help. He felt nauseous, and his body wanted him to lie down, go to sleep. He was smart enough to fight it, but he was alone in the house, it was the middle of the night, and he might be too weak to get to his phone.

If he had a concussion, he could die down here.

No, he refused to think that. He wouldn't do that to his mother, to his family. To Daralyn. Damn it, she'd think it was her fault.

He was better than this. He could be better than this for her. Nothing like a near-death experience to help a guy do a one-eighty and pull his head out of his own ass, but the lesson would be lost if he became a corpse on his bedroom floor.

"I'm sorry," he mumbled, laying his head against the mattress. Weird images were swimming around on the floor, and God, he felt sick. "Please...don't let me do this to them. I'm sorry. I just miss her so much. I can't be without her. Daralyn..."

He whispered her name, felt the tears come, the anger slipping away. He'd figure this out in a minute, be strong. She should be able to expect him to be strong, except he was having trouble pulling air into his lungs in his slumped-over position. He needed to move.

A door opened somewhere in the house. The kitchen door, maybe? As he strained his ears, he realized he could be hallucinating, caught in a delirium of wishful thinking. It was the middle of the night, after all.

No, those were footsteps on the wood floor. Quiet ones. Whoever it was thought he was asleep, was trying not to wake him. They'd turned on the hallway light.

He tried to push a word out of his throat. "Help..."

Instead, he choked on a near laugh. Wouldn't it be a fucking joke if it was a burglar? He kept a handgun in the nightstand. His hunting rifles were in a locked case in his closet. They did him just as much good as the phone.

The person was at the doorway, a silhouette. A woman whose slight figure was so beloved and familiar, but not at all expected. Great. He really had moved into hallucinations. It was all right. He'd take her anyway he could get her.

"Daralyn..." He spoke her name hoarsely.

"Rory." She flipped the light switch, turning on the lamp beside his bed. She was wearing her jeans that were a faded light blue color, and the store T-shirt, the women's version in a salmon color with yellow lettering. She had an oversized cardigan over it that gathered at her forearms. Her long hair was braided in a tail that rested over her right shoulder, on her chest.

While he took that all in, he was vaguely aware she made a little cry at the sight of him. Then she was at his side, her hands on him.

She was real. As he realized it, he gripped her, so fast and hard it startled her, but he couldn't ease up. She was real, her softness, her scent. That scent he'd know anywhere. He wanted to bury his face against her throat, her hair, but he was suddenly way too aware of how disgusting he must smell right now.

"I'm here." She touched his face. He realized he couldn't open his right eye because water was dripping into it. She took the hem of her T-shirt, wiped it, and he saw the blood stain the fabric. "You banged your head," she said.

He must look pretty out of it if she was explaining the obvious.

"Yeah." He coughed, and then the cough took a firm hold, bucking him forward against her. It made his head hurt worse. She held him, moved around him, showing surprising strength as she shifted him into a full sitting position, back straight against the foot board, which helped him breathe better.

She kept her hand on his shoulder as she pulled her phone out of her back pocket. As she lifted it to her ear, she was standing on her knees next to him. He let his face drop against her bosom, kept inhaling her. She stilled, then her free hand lifted to caress his hair, his bearded jaw.

He heard her calm voice as she spoke into the phone. "We need an ambulance."

CHAPTER TWENTY-TWO

The EMTs put an oxygen mask on him because his sat rate was low. On the way to the hospital, they checked his head, cleaned it up. They let Daralyn ride with them, and she held his hand.

At the hospital, they gave him a good once-over in the ER. Found a bad pressure sore that had broken open on the back of his thigh, same place he'd had the stitches not so long ago. They said he had the beginnings of pneumonia. The doctor gave him a firm talking-to, bordering on an ass-kicking, which he knew he deserved. He could have told her everything she told him, and in far greater detail.

"Over the past year, your personal physician and PT have been glowing about your management of your disability and self-care." She had the tired but shrewd eyes of an ER doc, and was a stout, middle-aged woman with a straight shooter personality he appreciated. "What I'm seeing tonight doesn't reflect that. Have you had a recent setback, emotionally? Would you like to speak to one of our counselors while you're here?"

He sensed Daralyn's troubled gaze on him. Without looking, he found her hand, gave it a firm squeeze. He wouldn't allow her to think she was the cause of this in any way, because she wasn't. He'd done it to himself.

"No ma'am," he told the doctor. "But thanks. I'm good."

She gave him a dubious look and typed in another note. "This report will go to your personal physician. Depending on your condition tomorrow, I'll be recommending a follow up with him in a week, so he can check the healing on that sore and verify your pneumonia is clearing up."

Rory nodded, turned his attention to Daralyn. When they'd suggested she could stay in the waiting room, he'd said he wanted her here. He told himself it wasn't simple, cold fear she'd disappear again. That he wasn't worried that her showing up was merely because she'd come home to pack, after which she'd head back to Raleigh for a prolonged stay, or even move there.

All sorts of crazy ideas filled his head, with only one sure answer. He really didn't want her out of his sight.

She leaned against the wall, her mouth tight, gaze worried. He'd gone over a hundred scenarios for her return. All of them had featured him as a guy in charge, capable of handling things. Someone who could support whatever decisions she needed to make for herself, with no need to be concerned about how it would affect him.

So much for that.

She listened so carefully to everything the doctor told him, he expected she could recite it like a parrot. "I'm going to admit you for the night," Dr. Halford said. "I want to monitor your oxygen levels. If you improve enough in the next twenty-four hours, I'll discharge you, but only if you have someone at home with you for at least a few days. I see your mother lives with you."

"Yes, ma'am." He wasn't going to tell her that his mother was traveling. He also wasn't staying. He could sign himself out against medical advice, and would, if they tried to hold him. He'd rather go home tonight. Be with Daralyn alone. "Staying overnight isn't necessary. I'm pretty experienced in caring for myself."

"I see that here," the doctor responded, holding up the tablet, but then gestured to his general state, the cough that kept grabbing him, even now as she spoke. "But not here. Give it one night, Mr. Wilder. I think it's a very good idea."

"I think your mother would agree," Daralyn said.

He glanced her way. Her expression was hard to read, but the emphasis she put behind the words had his brow rising.

That had been a threat. If he didn't agree, she'd call and tell Elaine.

She met his gaze only a second before she demurely glanced down and away, folding her hands before her. It didn't change the set of her mouth at all. She meant it, and wasn't backing down.

He narrowed his eyes, but brought them back to the doc. She'd apparently picked up the veiled threat as well, because amusement was laced with the concern.

"Sounds like it's three against one. It's difficult to resist a woman's will, Mr. Wilder," she said.

"Tell me about it," he muttered.

~

By the time they settled him in a room, he was so tired, he was practically unconscious as the orderly helped him onto the bed. He slept, though a recurring prick of urgency roused him every once in a while, his need to ensure Daralyn was still there, that he hadn't imagined her.

The room had a sleep chair, and she set up operations there. She'd called Johnny and Amanda first. Then, once it was a reasonable hour in their time zones, she'd called his mother and brother. He tuned in for some of it, but kept drifting in and out.

"No, he's okay, Elaine. He really doesn't want you to cut your trip short. Johnny and Amanda will help with the store, and you know there are plenty of neighbors who will help if I need it. Please stay there, finish your trip. I'll take care of him." A pause. "I promise. When he wakes up, he'll want to call and talk to you, I'm sure."

The hope being that he wouldn't be hacking like a pack-a-day smoker by then. Which was how he'd sound if he talked to his mom now.

Daralyn was franker about his condition with Marcus and Thomas. While they'd be more likely than his mother to listen to her when she said they didn't need to come home, he suspected she wanted a second opinion on his condition, and how she was handling things.

She'd always been the type of person who, once she knew her help would be welcome, would quietly step in and handle something. But as he listened, he realized there was a different quality to this. In the past, she'd projected a certain jumpiness. Any indication her help wasn't welcome would make her back off immediately.

He couldn't pin down what the new ingredient was in her manner, so he gave up trying to figure it out for now. When she was done with the calls, she turned on her side so she could reach out from the chair, lay her hand on his forearm.

They had him turned on his side, keeping him off that pressure sore, pillows propped between his knees. The doc had said he'd been close to getting a couple there, too.

Amazing, how having her back here with him could bring total clarity. He really had been such a dumbass. He knew it. Shame would eventually set in, but that was the nice thing about exhaustion, drugs, relief, and the sight of his girl close by. Right now, things were okay.

"Wasn't the way I wanted you coming home to go," he mumbled. "Are you...home? Or just visiting?"

The question was out before he could stop himself. His heart about squeezed itself into pulp, because her expression didn't immediately change, holding that thoughtful but hard-to-read look.

"Dr. Taylor and I agreed I was ready to come home," she said at last. "I was planning on coming home today, taking a morning bus back, but then...I just couldn't wait. One of the staff at the treatment center was driving to the beach after his shift last night. He offered to take me home."

Her expression darkened, and she traced a line down his arm, then up to his face, fingers stroking through his beard. It was a little tangled and thick. He usually kept it clipped and groomed. He needed to tend to it. "It felt like I needed to be home tonight," she said. "The closer I got, the more urgent it felt. Then I saw you on the floor..."

She was sensitive to moods, and had a way of gravitating toward customers who might not be having the best day, lifting their spirits. He didn't typically believe in psychic intuition, but he knew one thing for sure. If Daralyn hadn't come home when she did, he would have been in far worse shape. The thought brought a harder twist of guilt.

"I'm sorry," he said.

She put her chin on the back edge of the sleep chair, her fingers sliding up and down his arm, up and down. Back to play in his beard. "What happened?"

He stared at her. "I'm not as strong as you are," he said simply. "I thought I was. I was wrong."

Her brow creased. "That's not true," she said quietly. "Everyone stumbles. You just stumbled."

"Daralyn, I can't walk. I can't stumble."

The lines around her hazel eyes creased in response to her small smile. "You know what I mean."

There seemed to be this bubble of softness around them, making everything okay to say, but he still hedged on it. "Thanks for making sure my mom didn't come home," he said. "She was really looking forward to that trip. Didn't mean to put taking care of me on you, though. Once I get out of here tomorrow, I can handle things. I'm not looking to turn you into a nurse."

That was the last thing he'd ever want to ask of the woman he loved. Yeah, when he hit middle age, things might happen where he'd need more help, but that was all down the road, a different version of the same challenges that everyone faced as they got older. Not right now. But something like this cast doubt on that, would drive most women off. Or attract the ones who had an unhealthy and excessive need to be needed.

Or make a natural submissive believe that caring for her Dom's physical needs was the main role he wanted her to serve.

Hell, he was stirring up a variety of unpleasant feelings. Now wasn't the time to deal with this.

Daralyn studied him, then she rose, circled around the bed. She slipped into it, scooted close so she could curl her body up behind his. She slid an arm over his chest, letting him find and hold her hand, tangle their fingers together. Fuck, she felt so good, pressed up behind him.

She laid her head between his shoulder blades, her lips on the bare skin revealed between the ties of his hospital gown.

"You are so stupid," she said distinctly. "I love you."

He slept fitfully, woken by those harrowing coughs, interfering with his need to breathe. Each time he roused, Daralyn stroked his hair, his back, until he settled, dropped into sleep again. He was reluctant to let go of her hand, held it against his chest. Her fingers moved slowly over the cotton of the gown, feeling the man beneath. It was the first time she'd ever known him to be cold, and he alternated between cold and hot, still battling fever.

Even with the worries all that caused, the second she'd laid down in the bed behind him, the tight fist around every vital organ she had eased. She was back where she needed to be.

It had been a long time since she'd felt the kind of fear she'd experienced when she saw him crumpled on his bedroom floor, the blood on his face, and heard that horrible struggle to breathe as he tried to speak to her.

Though he probably didn't realize it, she was now almost as familiar with his daily health requirements as he and Elaine were. She'd always paid close attention, and being more intimate with him had only expanded her knowledge.

She knew he wasn't aware he'd soiled his bed, his clothes. That had frightened her the most, how disoriented he'd seemed. But once the doctor looked him over, and they had cleaned him up, gotten him into a hospital gown, put an IV in to hydrate him, he'd started talking more lucidly. It had made her feel better. It was also good that it had happened before she made the calls. Otherwise she would have told Elaine and Thomas to come home.

Thomas had helped settle her nerves, in his usual calming way. During her conversation with him, Rory was out of it, sleeping deeply, allowing her to fill in some blanks she was missing.

"Did he have a cold? How did he get like this?"

Thomas's guilt had been palpable, but she heard Marcus speaking in the background, forcefully enough that it reached her ears, even as he aimed his admonition at Thomas.

"He's an adult, allowed to act like an idiot without you being responsible. You should relate to that."

Thomas took a breath. "Truth is, Daralyn, being without you threw him for a loop. I don't think he realized how hard that would be."

"Why didn't he call me?" But she knew why. Dr. Taylor had explained it. But if he'd really needed her, he could have called. Then she thought of everything she knew of Rory, of how he felt about her, how he put her well-being far above his own.

"You know the answer to that," Thomas said, confirming her

thoughts. "He didn't want how much he needs you to interfere with anything that helps you."

"But how much he wants and needs me.. that helps me so much." It was key to what had made her *able* to want and need things.

She'd told him she loved him. She'd said it. Finally, something she'd felt for so long, so deeply, it should have shown on her face like a billboard. She suspected it had, for him. But saying it still meant something.

"Sounds like you two have some communication issues to work out." Thomas paused. "Give him total hell, Daralyn. You deserve better than him falling apart because you had to take a little me-time." His voice softened. "But I think he convinced himself you weren't coming back. Not in the same way, at least."

"I'm not the same," she said. "Now I'm sure being with him is exactly where I should be."

The smile in Thomas's voice came through on the phone. "I expect he'll be glad to hear that. But don't tell him too quickly. The little prick deserves to suffer some for giving you that kind of scare."

She knew he was teasing. But she realized she was actually...mad. Rory knew so much better than this.

He was a proud man. If his mother had rushed home to care for him, it would have upset and humiliated him. Normally that would be enough of an incentive for him to care for himself properly.

He didn't realize how hard it would be without you...

"He loves you, and it tore him apart that he couldn't help you," Thomas said into the sudden silence. He paused, as if deliberating, then spoke plainly. "He's your Master, but that doesn't mean he doesn't need you sometimes, desperately."

His voice dropped to a lower tone. "Sometimes I think they actually need us even more than we need them, but you didn't hear that from me. And since I need Marcus so much I can't imagine breathing without him, that's saying something, right?"

She put her arm around Rory now, tunneling under the gown so she could put her palm against his bare chest, stroke through the layer of curling hair there.

Yes. It was saying something.

He was so strong. She wondered if he knew she felt that way. She'd watched him grow into handling and managing the store, becoming the head of the family with his mother and sister. He'd extended that mantle of care and protection over her as soon as that path had opened between them.

She'd told him she didn't see the chair, and she didn't. But the chair was still there. It was part of his life, part of who he was. Every day he managed life with a body that didn't work like most people's, in a world that was structured for people who could walk.

Seeing his strength, she'd thought her presence or absence would mean little in terms of its effect on that strength. If she'd been wrong, and that was the reason this had happened, Rory would never want her to know it. The why of that wasn't hard to figure out either. He'd never want her to feel like she had an obligation to care for and protect him.

The idea that he would think that stuck a thorn in her anger, goaded it. And that anger rested squarely in fear, from how quickly his lack of attention had put his health in a precarious place. That could never happen again.

The nurse had come in to check his vitals. "Those medications finally kicked in," she noted with satisfaction. "He's breathing better, and he's well and truly asleep."

Daralyn pushed herself up on one arm, gripped his shoulder. "Do you think he'll be okay for an hour or so? I need to go home and take care of a couple things."

"Sure. I'll keep an eye on him, honey."

When Rory finally pushed out of his drug-induced sleep, it was late afternoon. Good. Though it hadn't been twenty-four hours, maybe it had been long enough he could get himself out of here for an evening check-out time.

He was weak, fuck it all. And then he got another leveling blow. Daralyn wasn't here.

"They had your diet cherry Dr. Pepper," she said, coming in the door carrying one of those small squat cans that only hospitals ever seemed to have. She'd changed clothes, and was wearing her blue cotton dress she often wore with white canvas sneakers, no socks, as she did now. It was a breezy kind of outfit. Her hair was pulled back in a barrette, but loose so it framed her face in soft waves.

The constricting band around his chest loosened. He was glad to realize the breath he took was also much easier than it had been last night, though he was far from a hundred percent. He coughed a little, but fortunately it didn't set off a spasm of hacking.

She brought the drink to the bedside table and opened a straw, sticking it into the can. He took a sip, eyed her. She looked quietly content but tired.

"You didn't get much sleep," he said.

"I will at home. The doctor was pleased with your oxygen saturation. It's closer to normal. Not quite where she wants it, but I told her you had monitoring equipment at home and could keep an eye on it."

More important details about last night came back to him. Him waking, falling. Daralyn there. He'd stayed in that bed for hours, and then on the floor...

Holy crap. He had some clean up to do before he would let her come back into the house.

"Yeah. Don't worry," he said casually. "We can share a cab, but I'll drop you at your place, let you spend a little time there while I get myself straight. I'm sure you've missed being at your place."

"Hmm." She brought his chair from the corner to the side of the bed. "The shower is set up for you, and I brought you some fresh clothes."

She gave him a level look, and he felt the stirrings of irritation. "Okay. You know, actually there's no need for you to wait on me. Why don't you head on home and—"

"They're not going to discharge you without someone here with you," she pointed out.

"They will if I tell them I'm leaving," he said edgily, "with or without their permission."

Her lips pressed together. "I've already been back to your house," she said. "I cleaned up your room, washed the linens. It's okay."

No. That definitely was not okay. "I could have done that."

The expression on her face said no, he couldn't have. No more than he was going to be able to get himself into an unfamiliar shower without an orderly's help, in this condition. Her being right didn't help, but he managed to check himself a breath before snapping at her.

All he'd wanted was her to be back, and now he was pushing her away. Because he'd wanted her back on the same terms. Him in control of things.

As their gazes met, he saw she'd already figured it out. "Is it easier when I'm more broken than you are?" she asked quietly. "When you're the one taking care of me?"

He set his jaw, turned the Dr. Pepper around in its circle of condensation, trying to think of the right reply, but she wasn't done.

"Do you think it would change how I feel about you, if I sometimes have to help care for you, the way you care for me?" A little break entered her voice. "Or is it that you don't want me if you can't be the one always doing the caring and protecting?"

If she'd swung a bag of bricks at him, she couldn't have gotten his attention any better. His gaze snapped to her. "I want you no matter what," he said. "Always."

He held out a hand and, after a moment's hesitation, she took it. He squeezed it. Took a breath. "Say all of it. Everything going through your head, causing that tight set to your mouth. You want to fuss at me. I know the look of a woman who wants to fuss."

She looked surprised, but he was the surprised one when she took him at his word. "All I could think about these past few weeks is being back with you," she said. "Did you think I wouldn't? Why would you lose faith in me like that?"

He hadn't thought of it like that at all, but he could sure see why she would think it. Fortunately, she was pushing on, rather than requiring a response from him yet.

"I realized that night, with Hayworth...that it was like the first time you told me that asking questions would help you. A relationship doesn't work if it's one person taking total care of the other. I have to be able to take care of you, too. That means being able to stick up for myself. Being able to say, 'I want'... whatever it is I want."

She'd taken a breath before she said that last part. He saw how difficult it was for her to say it, even talking in theory. But she'd said it.

Hot damn, his girl had said it.

Even though she had to stop right afterwards, take another

steadying breath. Close her eyes. He waited her out, holding her hand, stroking her knuckles. When she finally lifted her lashes, she gave him her shy smile.

"Dr. Taylor gave me this idea. Every time I'm confronted with a situation where someone wants to know what...I want, I visualize that I'm somewhere I feel safe and completely unafraid. First, though, she had me practice saying it in my head. Not out loud. Then she gave me a tape recorder, told me to tape it and listen to it."

He couldn't say a word, because he'd never seen so many rare emotions openly showing themselves at once in her face. He just wanted to watch, afraid he'd miss a single one of them.

"It was really hard," she said, her voice trembling again. "It still is. I don't know why, I can't explain it. But when I try to...form those words, this overwhelming feeling of dread takes me over. Every time. But she and I kept at it. I failed, a lot. I threw up so often she made me back off of working at it so hard. Said I was pushing myself too much."

"Imagine that," he said in mild reproof, but his hand was tight on hers.

She squared her shoulders. "Then I did it. Maybe only once a day, and only something really easy...for everyone else. Like telling the staff what I...wanted for lunch."

"You're talking to a guy who had to learn how to put his shoes on without taking a header out of his chair. I get it."

She met his gaze, smiled. "Yes. You understand things like that. Which is part of why I think we fit so well sometimes. You understand how hard it is. You also know how it feels...to want it so badly. For it to be easy, the way it is for everyone else."

Yeah, he did. Her hand was holding his just as tight. "I wish I could have been there to help you," he said.

She gave him a surprised look. "You were. You did." She laid her other hand over his, holding it between both of hers. Her mouth was soft. "The safe place I imagined, where I feel completely unafraid, was your arms. That's the way I feel, every time you're holding me."

Well, hell. He pushed the bedside table out of the way so he could tug on her, pull her onto the bed and wrap her up in those arms she was just talking about. He wanted to kiss her, but thanks to the meds and everything else, it felt like a skunk had died in his mouth. There was only so much he'd inflict on the woman he loved. Plus the rest of him smelled like a sponge bath with hospital soap.

It didn't matter though. With those words, the way she looked at him, she told him she was back to stay. She wanted to be with him. Which meant he had every reason in the world to get his act together.

She let out a little sigh, relaxing. "I'm so mad at you," she said to his chest. "You can't ever do this again. Not ever."

He'd never been so thrilled to hear a woman say she was pissed at him. He managed to contain his ebullience with a grave smile, though. "You got it."

He realized then what was different about her. Confidence. Daralyn had discovered confidence in herself, over and above the darkness that clutched her. The tool she'd been missing in her arsenal. She'd figured out a way to get it, forged from her own will and determination.

As he'd always said, she was stronger than all of them.

She might occasionally swing and miss with it, or find it too heavy to lift on her own all the time, but she had it. And she had him.

He eased her back to meet her gaze squarely. "Okay, listen. I know I'm a stubborn ass. However, despite current evidence to the contrary, I have a good grasp of the condition I'm in, and what I can handle. I'd really like to take a shower at home, with my own set up. If you wouldn't mind being around for that, I could use..."

"A spotter?" She gave him a smile, her eyes warm.

He nodded, although he also gave her a harder look. "But you're not my nurse. Got it? That's not in your job description for this relationship."

She tilted her head to the side, her hazel eyes thoughtful. Her hand rested on his shoulder, her thumb tracing the line of it, up to his neck, and it felt damn good. "But we can take care of each other, right?"

"Yeah. We can do that." He cleared his throat. "Fair warning, though. I'm not great about someone taking care of me."

"Imagine that."

The light in her eyes said his girl was teasing him. God, he loved her. He loved her so much.

"Smartass," he said with a gut-easing grin, pinching her. Then he sobered. "Part of it is what you'd expect. Guy, lots of testosterone, doesn't like to be babied. But the other part of it is when I was wallowing in self-pity, I let my mom and others care for me like I couldn't do anything for myself. So I associate accepting someone's help as regressing toward needy, selfish asshole again. I'll try to recognize when that's happening, if you don't mind being patient with me while I'm learning."

"All right." She nodded. She'd put her other hand on the opposite shoulder, was sitting facing him, her hands spread out on him like she didn't want to stop touching him any time soon. Her scent was earth and water, lavender and clean, female things. It was all he could do not to crush her to him, hold her a couple hours.

"I can't imagine your mother letting you wallow," she said. "She was so good about not letting me get bogged down in things."

"She figured it out for you before she figured it out for me." He shot her a wry look. " Maybe because I'm a boy and mothers are weird about their sons. They tend to coddle us when they should kick us in the ass. But she got there eventually, thank God, though I deserved more kicks than she gave me for pushing her to it."

And on that note... He cleared his throat. "Thanks...for cleaning up my room. For all of it."

At her soft look, he wrapped her up in his arms, humbled by everything she'd said, done, and obviously meant so fervently. "Most of all, thanks for coming home to me."

"You *are* home to me," she whispered.

He couldn't have asked for a better home health assistant. Most people automatically tried to get ahead of him, make suggestions, be proactive because that was how they thought they'd be most helpful. They didn't stop to think that he'd been doing this a while and likely knew the best, most efficient way to handle the task. She followed his direction to the letter.

Once he was sitting in the shower, he noticed her lingering, leaning in the doorway. He thought of how her hands would feel on his shoulders and chest, his back. He wasn't up to sex, but having her naked and close enough to touch...he'd have to be dead not to be up for that.

"Take off the dress," he said.

A quiet, weighted moment, then she pulled her dress over her head, her pulled-back hair funneling through the neckline and then falling to her back. She was wearing a light blue bra, the straps etching her delicate shoulders. The matching bikini style panties outlined her mound and point of sex in the same sweet cotton fabric.

He swallowed, staring at her. He wanted to touch her, hold her, inhale her. Be with her. He remembered, forcefully, just how much he'd missed her.

After all that had happened in the past day, he might have doubted he'd have the brass tacks to let this side of himself come forward, but he guessed this proved it wasn't a switch he turned on and off. A Master's desires rose up hard and strong in him, craving to be voiced. Refusing not to be.

His gaze locked with hers. "Take it all off," he said. "I want you in the shower with me."

The words made her get still all over, except for her lips, which parted, and her hazel eyes, which flashed with joy and hunger. She wanted that from him, too. Maybe she, too, had worried that things had changed. The way she trembled, the light in her eyes becoming a deep shine, told him she'd needed to hear that demand from him.

And seeing that nothing she'd done to care for him had diluted the Master-sub feeling between the two of them? That was something he'd needed, too.

She unhooked the bra, folded it onto the dress she'd left on the counter. Slipped out of the sneakers and panties. She looked so good to him. He repositioned his feet so his knees were spread. He was already reaching out to her as she eagerly crossed the bathroom and joined him in the shower.

He banded his arm around her waist, spread his hand out on her buttock as he brought her close. He nuzzled her small breasts, teasing one nipple with his lips before simply pressing his face there, feeling her hands rove over his shoulders as he held her tight.

"I love your shoulders," she whispered in his hair. The spray of heated water mixed with her voice, matching the fluid rush of feeling through him.

"I love all of you," he said. He was caressing her with his mouth, his hands, just needing to touch her everywhere. And that scent...he was never doing without it again.

At length, he made himself ease back, found the soap and handed it to her. "You deserve a clean guy."

Smiling, she took the soap, turning it in her palms to create a lather. Then, with a flick of her lashes at him, she dropped to her knees. If she'd intended to incite a pure male groan of need, that gesture would have done it.

He'd installed a mirror on the back wall of the shower, a practical decision that helped him do skin checks while bathing. As a result, he now had another view he'd gladly exchange for the promise of heaven, because it was already here, kneeling before him.

She started with his feet. He watched her run her fingers over them, then up his calves, knees and thighs. When she soaped his genitals, his cock hardened in her hands, so she was thorough there. He tipped his head up to the spray, closed his eyes and let what she was doing spread out inside him in the places he could feel it.

Then she was moving again, standing between his legs, sliding her hands without hurry over his chest, upper arms. He took that time to put his mouth on her breasts again. A slow open-mouthed teasing with tongue and teeth, deep suckles that had her breath drawing in and her body leaning into the cradle of his. She circled her arms over his shoulders and back again, fingers digging into his hair.

She'd missed him, too. He could feel it in her hunger, every bit as strong as his.

He curled his arm around her, hand cupping her buttocks, kneading the soft flesh there as he suckled. When the soap dropped out of her hand, he smiled against her flesh. The soap swooped down toward the drain, stayed there.

He didn't have the strength to have sex, do the things to keep himself hard, and then hold her on him, help her rise and fall in the way that would bring her to the peak he wanted to see. But the desire to do so would give him the incentive to get his ass back on track, get better sooner than later.

In the meantime, there was a reason why God had given him ten very clever fingers. And an active imagination.

"Get the soap," he said.

The drain was behind his shower chair, so she had to lean around him and down, past his arm. When she did, he shifted his grip to keep her there, hold her over his thigh as he did a more thorough exploration of her backside. He wet his fingers in his mouth, providing lubrication the water lacked, but that was just to get him past the opening to her sex. A well of slippery honey was waiting for him, sucking his fingers in. He muttered a reverent oath as he slid three in, slow and easy.

She'd pulled in a breath, her fingers spasming on his biceps. The soap was forgotten as she braced herself against the shower wall with a flat palm. When he ran a thumb over her clit, began to tease it, he heard her hand slip a few inches over the tile wall. Another gasp broke from her lips.

Glancing toward the mirror, he saw her lovely bottom poised for the flat of his hand, the folds of her sex visible between her legs, his fingers buried between them. It gave him the spurt of adrenaline necessary to keep holding her.

From the way her body began to ride his fingers, her rhythmically clenching muscles, he knew he was on the track he desired. He kept going until he noticed the trembling in her back and thigh muscles, how she was trying to maintain her footing. He slid his fingers out of her reluctantly, but before he brought her back up, he tightened his arm around her to hold her in place one more moment.

He smacked her ass, hard enough she yelped. As he guided her back to her feet in front of him, he leveled a hard gaze on her.

"You had to take care of yourself, and I respect that," he said. "But I still get to take it out on your ass for leaving me. You're lucky I don't have a belt close to hand."

Though if he did, the image that came to mind wasn't striking her with it. Instead, he thought about roping it around her hands, strapping her to his headboard and feasting on her, caressing her, bringing her to climax several times, until she begged him for mercy. The potential for dishing out sensual punishments was limitless. When he was done, she'd have some enduring memories to remind her not to leave him again.

Her startled look had resulted in a biting of her bottom lip, and a mix of emotions on her face. She was wondering if she needed to apologize to him for leaving, but he fixed that.

"All you need to do right now is listen, and do what I tell you. Got it?"

He held her gaze, clasped her hand. Water droplets clinging to her lashes were freed to trail down her cheeks as she lowered her gaze. "Yes, sir."

He put his other hand on her hip to turn her away from him. Then he brought her down on his knee, her legs split over his thigh.

"Lean back against me," he said.

He slid an arm around her, pressed his lips to her throat and bit her. Her breasts, slick with the water beating on them, rose high as she drew in another breath. Her legs were spread for him, her feet pressed to the outside of his. "Before I go to bed and become comatose for the next few hours," he growled in her ear, pressing his nose to her wet sheet of thick hair, "I want to make you scream for me. Hard and long enough the echoes will become part of this room, reminding me of it every time I come in here. Put your arms around me."

The delicate lines of her neck shifted as she linked her arms around his neck and shoulders. It arched her forward into his hands. He teased her breasts, plucked at her nipples as she squirmed and moaned, as he laid kisses along her shoulders. When he gripped her throat in one hand, he felt her violent quiver, watched her body writhe below that hold.

He had to have the strength to see this through, and if he exerted himself too much, he'd set off an ill-timed coughing fit. But "make lemonade out of lemons" had been a favorite saying of his father's. A slow pace worked just fine for his purposes. Rory touched her everywhere, taking his time working his way down.

As a result, by the time he reached his goal, she was moaning with need, her beautiful body doing a sinuous dance against him. She was rubbing her sweet pussy against his thigh, telling him it wasn't just the water slicking up his skin. She noticed how he was staring at her in the mirror, watching her, and she almost stopped.

"Don't you even think about it. Keep rubbing yourself on me."

He made her do that for him for several minutes before getting involved, playing his fingers over her cunt, dipping into it, stroking, tugging on her clit. Spasms bucked her up into a deeper arch, her thighs trembling and fingers clutching him. Her hair was wet and sleek against his shoulder.

As he stroked and played, whispered to her, she was losing her mind, pleading without words.

It made him feel even less merciful.

"Did you touch yourself when you were away from me? Bring yourself to climax?"

She shook her head.

"Tell me. Say it out loud."

"No...no, sir." Her voice elevated as he flicked her clit, a more aggressive touch. Another ripple went through her.

"Did you want to?"

"Yes...a lot."

He concealed his fierce satisfaction as she didn't get hung up over the words, too aroused to be snagged by it. Like the night she'd said she wanted the ropes. "Why didn't you?" he demanded.

She sent him a desperate look, and he tightened his grip. "Yeah, I know you're having trouble talking because of what I'm doing to you. Which is exactly why I'm making you talk. Answer me."

"It felt...wrong. Without your permission."

"Right answer."

He pushed it as far and as long as he knew he could, and then he tipped her over that edge. He gave her every ounce of pleasure she could handle and then pushed her past that, demanding she go even further. Just as he'd promised, he made her screams echo off the bathroom walls, refusing to let her hold anything back. Her movements became so violent he had to cinch his arm harder around her waist to hold her still.

There was a God, because the shortness of breath and coughing didn't hit him until he'd finished her the way he intended. By then she was limp in his arms, draped back against him. It did a hell of a good job restoring his sense of himself, no matter how caveman that sounded.

She'd kept her arms wound loosely around his neck, and so stroked his nape and whatever else she could reach as he held her, coughed it out, caught his breath. Before she could marshal enough strength to say anything herself, try to turn and check on him, he brushed his fingers over the tender, sensitive lips of her pussy. He cherished the little quiver that went through her, the tiny sound that escaped her throat.

"I've missed that," he said. "Missed holding you and touching you."

"Me too," she whispered. "So much."

Reluctantly, he let her go, though he kept his hands on her, steadying her until she stepped out of the shower, found them both a towel.

His body let him know in no uncertain terms he'd exceeded his limits, and he'd aggravated that pressure sore under his thigh some, but he wasn't going to regret any of it, not while she had that dazed, soft look to her face. She kept touching him, random, impulsive caresses, and he did the same, neither of them wanting to go without touching for more than a blink of time.

Eventually, though, he needed to handle the bathroom stuff and tend the sores with ointment before he could lie down. "Go pick out one of my shirts to sleep in," he told her. She hadn't brought night-clothes, and he didn't want her to be cold. The farmhouse could be drafty.

When he emerged, she was perched on the edge of the turned down bed, waiting for him. She'd chosen his Tennessee bike marathon shirt. The faded design indicated it was one of his favorites, and seeing how the soft, worn fabric molded to her shape only increased its status.

He pushed himself to the side of the bed, hooked an arm around her waist, nuzzling the tip of her breast through the cotton as he smoothed a hand over her backside. She threaded her fingers through his hair. Lifting his head, he gave her a lingering kiss, and felt her touch on his beard, now clipped and groomed again.

"Wanting you is going to kill me," he said. "And I'm okay with that."

She gave him a half smile, but as he coughed on the end of that statement, he saw her worry. He wasn't going to put up with that. But he was aware his exhaustion was showing. He was having trouble sitting up straight, not slumping in the chair.

"Nothing wrong with me now that can't be fixed with rest," he said. "Come to bed."

She did, as soon as he transferred himself over to the mattress and adjusted the pillows where they needed to be. She fitted herself against his side, resting her head on his shoulder. They lay there for a while, and he knew she was giving him the opportunity to drift off again. Which he would, soon, but he detected tension in her. Adjusting his head and tipping up her pensive face, he gave her chin and jaw a little squeeze.

"Tell me how to help you to stop worrying. And I don't mean me not pulling this shit again. We've covered that. What's in your head that you're not letting go? I need you to tell me. I can handle anything but causing you pain."

Another silence, during which she drew a couple circles on his chest. He'd donned T-shirt and shorts to sleep, so she was creasing and smoothing the fabric. "I know I asked, but the answer, why this happened...it didn't feel like all of it. And this scared me, Rory. Really, really scared me."

He held her closer, pressed his lips to her forehead as she held him back, shuddered. "You'd never have known it. You took charge and handled things like a pint-sized general."

She put her mouth to his throat, her breath shallow and warm there. "But if I could understand better...it would help me feel like..."

"You could head it off next time?" He gave her a squeeze. "You're not in charge of this, Daralyn. It's like you going to Raleigh. There are decisions we each make, obstacles we face...having support makes all the difference in the world, but the solutions have to come from within us, you know?"

Dr. Taylor had told him, sure, but until it stared him in the face in his own behavior, he guessed he hadn't really internalized it. Or the significance of what Daralyn had done.

She'd left to become a stronger, better version of herself. And she did that because she *wanted* to be that person. For him. And for herself.

Which meant he owed her a nothing-held-back answer to her unspoken question. He took an additional beat, figuring out how to put it into words, but he didn't have to seek the answer itself. He'd known it all along.

"When your whole life changes in a blink, and you come face to face with how much can be lost in that blink, it does some things to your head that can't be undone. You can manage it, handle it better, but it still fundamentally changes something, deep inside. I expect you get that, better than anyone."

She was looking at him again and he tipped his head back down to meet her thoughtful hazel eyes. He stroked her shoulder, down her side, felt the nip of her waist and flare of her hip. "Pride's close to anger. So's fear. They were all wrapped up in it, this tug of war between me knowing I'd let you go if that's what you needed, and not being able to figure out the next step if I'd lost you. These past couple years..."

He shook his head. "I've been in love with you for quite a while. Long before that Christmas kiss under the mistletoe." He smiled at her. "But until you left, I didn't realize how deep inside me you were. All of a sudden, I saw how much of my life was built out of a picture with you in the center of it. And suddenly, no matter how crazy it sounds, I was waking up in the hospital again, discovering the life I'd planned to have was going to look way different. Only this time, the most important part of it, the thing that filled my heart and soul, wasn't going to be in it. Do you understand?"

Her face filled with emotion. "Yes," she said, her voice barely audible. "I understand how that feels. Realizing things could change in a blink. Only for me, it was the opposite. Suddenly, life went from being dark and difficult, where I was alone, to a place with love, and encouragement, light. So many things to learn and see and know... It was marvelous, and terrifying, because I didn't trust it."

She shook her head. "I didn't believe it wouldn't disappear, that it wasn't all a lie. That fear hasn't left me. But trying to figure out what was expected of me, so it wouldn't be taken away... It's exhausting. Some days managing that fear is all I can handle. But then there was you."

Her fingertips slid along his throat, down to his collar bone. "You...the way you felt about me, how I felt about you, it changed all of it. What happened with Hayworth showed me that I really could lose everything, but not in the way that I feared. I had to figure out how to hold onto what mattered. Give you everything."

She adjusted closer, and he banded both arms around her. Her voice was muffled against his chest. "Ever since the first time I looked at you and knew you noticed me...the way I noticed you, I knew what mattered the most to me."

She shuddered. The more words she pushed out, the more he could tell she was fighting that involuntary reaction, the nausea and fear. He understood the steps a person had to take, when coddling them wasn't helpful. He also understood when a person was asking too much of themselves all at once. Fortunately, that intuitive part of him that was getting stronger all the time knew a Master's job description included putting on the brakes when a sub was doing that.

He tipped her face up again, brushed his lips over her nose, her eyes, her cheeks. "I want you to embrace everything you want for yourself," he said, giving her a steady look. "But you can take all the time you need saying aloud something you tell me a hundred other ways. Be at ease on that. I love you.'"

Pain and relief were in her smile, but also joy and hope. They were okay. When she wrapped her arms around him, he held her, and that contained all the things they needed to say to one another for now.

They were both okay.

CHAPTER TWENTY-THREE

"*I* could get used to this," Rory said.

"You don't make enough money to get used to this. Neither do I. I'm just lucky to have a rich female friend."

Brick smoked a cigar, lazily reclining on a giant unicorn float in the heated pool. Rory, drifting with a pair of blue swim noodles under his arms, sent him an amused look.

"What did you do to earn the privilege of using her house while she's in Spain? Are you her boy toy?"

Brick snorted. "Gutter brain. She's seventy. Admittedly a very hot seventy, but she's told me to keep my hands to myself." He smiled fondly. "We're cut from the same cloth, anyway. Even without the age difference, we're too compatible to be together. But I helped get an arson case involving her son solved, after it had sat on a cold case pile for a couple decades. We became friends."

He gave Rory a critical look. "You're looking a lot better. Sound better, too, than when we talked on the phone." He tilted his head toward the other side of the pool. "You've got a good nurse."

"She's not my nurse. She's a ninety-eight-pound tyrant with more eyes than a spider."

"She looks great in that swimsuit, though."

"You can keep your hands to yourself there, too." Rory pointed a loaded finger at him and Brick held up both hands, grinning.

Not that he'd needed any encouragement to look in that direction, since he did it about every minute or so, but Brick's comment inspired Rory to follow his glance. While he and Brick had drifted to the deeper part of the pool, Daralyn had stuck to the four and half foot end. Today had been her first swim lesson, and while there were plenty of swim noodles to use as flotation devices, she'd been practicing stroking where her feet could still touch.

She did look good in a bikini. It wasn't overly skimpy, but nicely revealing, and a cherry red that looked good with her brunette coloring. Amanda had helped her pick it out when Brick had invited them to meet him here for the day. The house in Waxhaw was a millionaire's version of a log cabin, with lots of screened porch, natural wood, and a thick cluster of surrounding forest to buffer the eight-acre property. The enclosed and heated pool was well vented and surrounded by windows so clear it didn't have that usual stuffy indoor pool feeling Rory disliked.

Brick dropped off the float and moved over to the side, all the while puffing on the cigar. He removed it from his mouth, gestured. "I'm headed back in to handle some work stuff. Probably take me about an hour or so."

When Rory lifted a brow, Brick met his gaze with a twinkling one of his own. "In case you don't understand the language of Obviousland, you're not going to be interrupted for a while. Do what you want with that."

As he watched his friend lift himself out of the pool, those insanely thick muscles rippling over his back and arms, Rory shook his head. "You know, you're not as much of a dick as everyone says."

Brick put the cigar out and palmed the stub. "Just remember all that love when you become my brother-in-law."

"Thomas is already married. You'll have to kill Marcus to get him, and my money's on Marcus."

Brick flipped him the bird on his way back into the house.

As Rory smiled, he gazed thoughtfully after his friend. Brick's cigar smoke hadn't seemed to bother Daralyn the way cigarette smoke did, but Rory knew Brick would have doused it in a second if it had.

From the time they'd met in high school, they'd gotten along. But they'd become even deeper friends after his accident, not the usual thing. Disabled people often lost friendships they had before their injuries, or the bonds of those old friendships loosened. Priority and perspective changes forked them onto a path separate from the things that had kept them linked. But Brick had moved from the old circle into the new, becoming a key bridge between them. It was largely because of him that Rory's local high school buddies had remained current friendships. Brick had helped them regain a comfortable footing with one another, find a new look to their connection.

If he had no blood family left in the world, Brick would be the closest thing Rory had to a brother. A day like this just reinforced it. Brick had learned about Rory's close call when he called to check in with him about Daralyn's status, pleased to learn she'd returned home. As such, it hadn't surprised Rory that several days later the firefighter had called back, casually suggesting they come spend the day with him at his friend's pool.

Normally, a pool party wasn't the best option for a guy getting over a brush with pneumonia, but a heated indoor pool in this kind of setting? That was a different matter.

Rory lay back on the noodles, just floating. The sun coming through the windows was warm on his wet skin, and he was relaxed, breathing easy. He could get back to his normal workouts in a couple days, start rebuilding his strength where he wanted it. He had definite plans for that recuperation.

His lips curved as a fine-boned hand slid along his back, his side, up to his shoulder. Daralyn emerged on his right, brushing her lips against his biceps. He curled an arm around her, the noodle giving him the support so that he could bring her close to his side, let her twine her legs over his under the wavering, sun-sparkled water.

"I have my own personal mermaid," he said.

"If you can catch her," she said, sliding out of his hold to circle him, displaying her newfound swimming abilities. She enjoyed the water, was comfortable in it, turning and twisting like a mermaid in truth. As she backed away, she sent him a teasing look beneath her lashes.

She was flirting with him, his shy girl offering a delightful glimpse of her inner female minx. He gave her an unimpressed nod, laid his head back to feel the sun again and then struck, lunging over the right noodle to snag her around the waist. She let out a little yelp.

He'd timed his attack, the momentum carrying him and her in a turn that brought him to the ladder in one or two strokes. He hooked himself with one arm, pushing her full up against the ladder steps. With his free hand he took a nice handful of her ass, curving his fingers under the edge of the red bikini bottoms to stroke.

Her lips parted, her eyes darkening. He felt where every one of her fingers pressed into his wet shoulders, against his neck, and as she moved them to curl in his short hair. Relishing the give of her breasts against his chest, he touched his mouth to her neck and tasted Daralyn, chlorine, and the faint coconut scent of sunblock.

"Wrap your legs around me," he told her. When she did, she also wrapped her arms tighter around him, holding him close. He felt her love everywhere. It was all the proof he needed of the existence of the soul, a full-bodied thing that transcended the physical.

He didn't mind indulging the physical side of things, though. He eased back, so her hands slipped to his abdomen. She gazed at him as he sent a meaningful look to his firm grip, now on both sides of the ladder. "Caught my mermaid," he said softly. "Turn around. Stand on the bottom step."

He'd never get tired of that light flush in her cheeks when he took control, the way she swallowed, how it made the fragile lines of her throat move.

When she complied, the tension of standing on the ladder gave her pert backside an intriguing lift, square in his view. She looked over her shoulder at him, her sleek hair spread over her shoulder. The valley of her spine, the curve of her back and slim lines of her shoulders, also filled his vision, but that sweet ass stayed front and center. Her lips were temptingly wet.

"Lie down on the concrete," he said. "Hips hooked over the lip of the pool."

And there came that sexy little quiver as she understood what he was intending. She stretched out on the concrete. It would be warm from the sun coming through the windows, and he confirmed it when he saw how she flattened herself to it, pressing her hip bones just over the lip of the pool as he'd commanded.

Her heels brushed his sides as he used his grip on the ladder to push himself down further in the water, bringing himself level with her thighs.

"Spread them wider," he said, a low rumble.

She did, which meant her feet left the bottom step of the ladder, floated free on either side of him. He put his grip on the ladder over her legs, so both his arms and his body would keep them open as he desired. Then he moved in, putting his mouth on that red damp crotch, breathing heat on what was beneath. She shuddered, and he saw her fingers curl against the concrete.

"Rory..." she breathed.

"Let me tell you something," he said, brushing a kiss on her upper thigh, right at the crease with her buttock. He nipped her with teeth, watched her jump. "For the past week, you've made sure I took medicines, checked my vitals, helped me do all the things the doctor told me to do. I told you I didn't need a nurse, that I could take care of myself. And I have and I do. But you still helped, because you care. Because I needed the help, and you're a friend. You're family. You love me, and I love you."

She licked her lips, her gaze flicking down to him and then away. She knew the other shoe was about to drop. He let the pleasure of it build in his gut, move up into his chest. Gave her another nip.

"But I think you need a reminder of who's in charge here. Don't you?"

She nodded, her lips pressing together. He treasured the sensual anxiety in her hazel eyes, even as he sharpened his tone.

"Sorry, I didn't catch that."

"No, Rory. No, sir," she added hastily as he nipped her, harder this time.

"So who's in charge here?"

"You are."

He brought his mouth back to her cunt, tonguing her through the fabric, pushing. Her buttocks tensed, her heels digging in to his sides. He nudged the elastic aside, dipped beneath it with teeth and tongue, and leisurely enjoyed eating her out, tasting the slick arousal. She jerked, shuddered, made little cries. All of it filled him with a deep male satisfaction, a fierce possessiveness.

He took down the bottoms to reveal her pale pink buttocks. He cupped water in his palm, letting it trickle over them, then down between her legs, giving her the contrast of the wet heat of his mouth and the cool water. When she was gasping for air, eyes closed, he backed off enough to slap her ass with a wet palm, knowing it would change the nature of the sting, make it stronger.

She cried out. Then her buttocks lifted, asking for more.

He liked to give her more.

He did it until he saw her squirms become less on the pleasure side and more on the discomfort side, and then he did it another half dozen times. Proof that she'd bear more for her Master, and him testing that obedience. Then he put his mouth on her again.

He loved the taste of her. He wanted to let go of one side of the ladder, run his hand up her back, let her feel his palm there, but he needed to keep his balance to work his mouth on her just the way she needed. Afterward, he'd have her lie on a lounge chair and stroke the supple line of her back, the damp hair, and watch her turn into a drowsy kitten. Now he engaged the other side of her, the writhing, begging, panting aroused woman, straining toward the climax he held in his control.

"Rory..."

"I like to hear you beg," he said. He pulled himself up on the ladder, curved his body over her, putting some of his weight down on her frame. He watched her press her ass into his pelvis as he laid a kiss between her shoulder blades. Then he lowered himself back into the water. "Sit up and turn around," he said.

When she did, he nodded to the space in the water between him and the ladder. "Bring yourself down into the water and wrap your legs around me," he said. "Stare into my eyes and rub yourself against my cock. Make yourself come. Don't look away."

She obeyed, sinking back into the pool. The space was small enough she slid against his chest, his stomach and everything below. Lifting her legs, she wound them around him. Leaned back on her elbows on the top step and began to do as he'd commanded. He stared down in the water, watched her align herself with his groin and begin to lift and lower herself there. He should get rigid enough to provide interesting friction for her, and he could tell when he had, not just by seeing his erection push against his swimsuit against her, but by the way her breath rate increased, and her eyes got that glazed look. Her nipples were hard points against the swimsuit. Her arching back made it even more noticeable.

"Cup your breasts and press them together," he said. When she complied, he put his mouth in between them, let his tongue play in that crevice and then nuzzled the tender curves. Her cries strengthened as he suckled the points through the fabric. Her hips were sliding up and down on him, short strokes whose speed was increasing as her climax bore down on her. The water rippled around them.

Her gaze clung to his, as he'd commanded. She was struggling to do it, and he watched her, unsmiling. She was feeding on the commands, the sensations. The unspoken knowledge that he wouldn't let her look away, that it was up to him when she went over, and he relished watching her struggle between her body's desires and her Master's will.

When she reached for him, he allowed it. She slid her fingers over his abdomen, up his chest, over his nipples, and down again. It was erratic, no finesse to it, but because it was all driven by raw desire, it drew an equally strong response from him, particularly with her providing that stroke against his cock. He could feel his own response building and knew she might just make him climax as well.

"Now," he growled, and she went over, body shuddering, arching, skin flushing like a pale reflection of the bold color of her suit, the fabric creasing over her body, her hip bones, the slope of her ribs, the line of her neck.

She was crying out her pleasure, her lips stretched open, her lashes fanning against her cheeks, brow creased with the power of what swept over her.

He clutched the ladder as her movements against him, the touch of her hands, brought his orgasm forth, no surprise. Later tonight, he'd have her put him inside her, because he wanted that sense of joining, and knew she needed it, too.

But right now, he couldn't imagine feeling any closer to her, as they watched one another, rode that wave together, her desires under his command while he answered all her needs with more pleasure, more sensation.

"Rory..." She was whispering his name, her body still vibrating. Her fingers were stroking him, little needy clawings.

"That's my girl," he murmured. "You're so beautiful. The most beautiful mermaid I've ever seen."

He reclaimed the noodles he'd left on the concrete, fitting them under his arms before he scooped her up against him and floated them away from the ladder. As she rested against his chest, he gathered her hair in one hand, brushed her temple with his lips.

"Just for the record, you look positively smoking in that bikini. Brick said so."

Her gaze lifted to his, hazel eyes serious. "It doesn't matter. I belong to you."

"Yeah, you do. Did I mention how lucky I am? But you're still a tyrant when you're playing nursemaid." He tugged her hair. "Doesn't matter if you do it with shy smiles, big eyes, and sweet talking 'suggestions.' I'm not fooled."

That shy smile appeared, and she twined her arms around his neck. "I'm still yours."

"You bet your sweet ass you are."

Thanks to some additional discounts the trip organizers dug up, Elaine had the opportunity to stay an extra week out west, and Rory had encouraged it. As a result, by the time his mother returned, he was almost a hundred percent again, which was good. But he wondered if she was still upset about what had happened, because on the way back from the airport, he sensed some tension under her warm greeting for them, the chatty discussion of the details of her trip. They'd brought his van, so Elaine had the front while Daralyn sat in the second row seat that could be flipped up next to his anchored chair.

Rory noted his mother kept glancing at him, then looking toward Daralyn, with an oddly frustrated and worried glance.

"You okay, Mom?" he asked once, reaching out to touch her hand at a stoplight. His mother latched onto it, giving him a hard squeeze before the green light required her to let him go.

"Yes," she said. "Glad to be home."

He met Daralyn's gaze in the mirror. Neither of them was fooled, but whatever it was, his mother didn't want to talk about it right now, so he let it go for the moment.

Daralyn had fixed a lunch, so while she went to the kitchen to work on setting that out, Rory debated whether to help or follow his mother to her room. Daralyn helped him decide.

She put the potato salad on the counter and glanced in the direction Elaine had disappeared. "Maybe she'll talk to you alone," she said. "About whatever it is."

"Yeah. Let me go see." He briefly gripped her hand, their fingers tangling, then he pivoted the chair and made his way down the hallway.

Elaine had opened her suitcase on the bed, but had sunk down next to it. She hadn't taken anything out yet, which told Rory there was definitely something off. She was an obsessive nester, always insisting on getting everything unpacked first thing after a trip.

"Mom?"

Everything she'd texted or called about while traveling had suggested the trip had gone well, and she'd had a great time. So he braced himself for a lecture and marshaled a reassuring rebuttal, since the only thing he figured could be upsetting her was being away while he landed up in the hospital.

When she began to speak, he wished that had been it.

"I received a call from the ADA who handled the prosecution of Daralyn's uncle," Elaine said, meeting his gaze. "We should be getting a letter from the Department of Corrections in a few days. Daralyn's uncle is being released in a few weeks. Health reasons. He has terminal liver cancer."

Son of a bitch. As he digested that, her gaze went from him to the hallway behind him. He inhaled her scent, knew Daralyn was there. No surprise, since Daralyn had likely been listening, worried about Elaine and wanting to know how she could help.

Without looking her way, Rory lifted a hand. Elaine's gaze flickered as Daralyn stepped into the room and took it, leaning against him in his chair.

"You can talk to us both, Mom," he said. "She can handle it. She can handle anything."

Regret crossed Elaine's features. Her gaze shifted to Daralyn and she nodded, an apology. "Of course. I'm sorry, honey. I should have asked you to come in here before I said anything. I'm just...I know you're not a child anymore, but I'm just so very tired of you having to handle so much."

She wasn't the only one, but Rory's whole point in having Daralyn stand next to him, where he could put his arm around her waist, have her rest hers around his shoulders, was to confirm for her that it was okay. A reminder that Daralyn could trust that this life she'd built for herself wasn't going to disappear. They wouldn't let it.

Daralyn looked at him, then at Elaine, and there was resolve on her face. "But I don't have to handle so much," she said quietly. "Not alone. I haven't had to handle anything alone for a long time, thanks to all of you."

Rory shot his mother a tight smile and Elaine shook her head. "All my children are growing up," she said. She took a breath. "I can't anticipate what he'll do, but he believes he has a claim on your father's house. It's likely he'll come here."

It wasn't the first time Rory had thought of it. In the back of his mind, he'd kept a mental countdown of when Burton would be up for release. He was sure his mother had done the same. Unfortunately, that timetable had just been stepped up by a couple years. He expected the state didn't want to have to pay for cancer treatments. Easier to put him on a sex offender list and cut a dying man loose.

Despite Daralyn's calm words, hearing that her uncle might set up house here had made her face pale, and put a tremor in her suddenly stiff body. Having him in the same county, only a few miles down the road, knowing she might run into him while on her bike, at the store, at community events?

That sure as fuck wasn't going to happen.

He thought of her coming to him in his room, getting him to the hospital. When strength had been needed, she'd found it. She'd always found it.

But there were certain things she could expect from him, that he would handle, and nothing she said or did could keep him from it.

Still holding onto Daralyn, he used one hand to push the couple of feet to the bed and take his mother's hand. Then he looked up into his girl's face and met her gaze with a solid and steady one of his own.

"Let him come," he said. "We'll deal with it."

CHAPTER TWENTY-FOUR

*I*t was mid-morning when the text came in on his phone. Rory glanced at it, lifted a hand to catch Johnny's attention. It also drew Ralph Peterson's, who was here to pick up some fire ant powder. "About forty-five minutes," he told them.

The two men stopped what they were doing. Peterson headed out to his truck and Johnny turned the sign to *Closed*. About that time, Daralyn came out of the back. Her expression told him she'd heard him.

As she approached the front counter, Rory put his hand out on it, and she put hers in his grasp. Her eyes were thoughtful and dark, an abyss. He tightened his hold, telling her he had her.

"If it was my choice, you know I'd tell you to stay here," he said. "But it isn't."

He'd wanted to make it his. Only a talk with his mother had kept him from being an idiot about it. He'd brought it up with her one night when Daralyn was at school. He'd discussed it from several angles, but then it had boiled down to one major point.

"That first year, when I was hurt, you didn't want me out of your sight," he'd said, meeting his mother's gaze over the dinner table. "I'm ashamed how I let you wait on me hand and foot, not realizing how much more helpless it was making me feel. Not your fault. You did it out of love. But I'm afraid of doing the same to her, Mom."

"What snapped you out of it?" she'd asked sagely.

"Marcus, when he threw the bag of grain at me—"

"Yes," she interrupted. "That was the straw. But it had been happening before then. You were getting more irritable, more restless. Even caught up in your head, there was a part of you that knew your own heart, the man you wanted to be. That you wouldn't deny yourself. The man you are."

She met his gaze, smiled. "Marcus's challenge to you was the catalyst, but it was one you were ready to hear, in that moment. And we all learned something important. To trust the strength you had within you to set your own path the way it was meant to go."

Reaching across the table, she put her hand on his. "You need to trust her the same way, despite how protective you are." A fond smile crossed her face, one that spoke of the woman she was, as well as a mother. "Your father was the same. Didn't even want me to go up a ladder without him being right there with me.

"The men of this family have always been strong, traditional men, but with room in their hearts for change. Through love and the sense God gave you, and your mother and father encouraged you to have, to think for yourselves."

While he and Daralyn discussed it several times over the past couple weeks, him trying his best not to be that "traditional man," he hadn't pushed her to make a decision, and she hadn't indicated what it would be. Until now.

"I think...I have a couple things to finish in the back," Daralyn said after a long moment.

"Okay." Rory suppressed a strong sigh of relief and stroked her cheek, her mouth. Held her gaze. There weren't words for moments like these, but he showed her his feelings, his will. "There may be fire burning all around us," he said, "But around you and me, there's a circle, and nothing gets past it. Got it?"

She nodded. Then she slipped away, returning to the back with precise steps. She hadn't said much, but he could tell a lot was going on. He'd realized that deep place she'd carved inside her head was a place she went to deal with things. Which made sense, since it had been the only place she could live, be something other than what she'd been forced to be. She didn't hide there, not so much anymore. Now it was where she went to work things out.

When she was ready to be held, when she needed him to take control and bring her out of that place, he'd be there.

He pushed himself out into the parking lot, got into his van and followed Johnny in his pickup. When they reached the stretch of rural two-lane highway that was the main artery into their small town, he saw they weren't the first to arrive. Over thirty people were already here, including Thomas and Marcus, who'd returned from New York specifically for this. His mother was with them. More were arriving, a convoy of cars parking on either side of the road.

If he'd had their town's phone tree, Paul Revere and his cohorts could have saved themselves a hell of a hard night's ride.

Rory didn't say much to anyone as he left the van and moved to where Thomas and Marcus were. When Elaine embraced him, her eyes were serious, her mouth set. She didn't comment on Daralyn's absence, but all his family looked as glad as he was that she'd decided to sit this out.

Everyone was quiet, most gazing down the empty stretch of road. Anticipating, watchful. Other community gatherings were noisy with laughter and local gossip, but the purpose of those events was socializing. Celebrating.

This was an army, waiting for the enemy to show himself.

They didn't have long to wait. He saw the car coming, a nineties-era dusty black Chrysler sedan. His heart thudded like a hammer. He remembered that same car, occasionally parked in town as Burton or Oscar came to the grocery store, the bank. Even more infrequent had been the times Daralyn was with one or both of them, a shadow that stayed close.

They'd rarely come into his parents' store. Maybe once or twice, but the Moorfield brothers probably sensed his mother's eagle eyes, her growing suspicions about Daralyn.

Burton had three cars trailing behind him, far enough back that it looked like he'd simply picked up some traffic on his way into town. One of them had Brick in it, who'd sent the text to Rory. He'd volunteered to be the one to drive from Richmond to Tabor City and dog Burton once he'd left the prison, confirm his first stop was their town. The last text he'd sent Rory, the one he'd received at the store, had been brief.

Forty-five minutes. Doesn't seem to know he's being tailed.

Rory figured Burton wouldn't expect a tail, so he hadn't been looking for it. The other two cars following Brick were town residents who'd fallen in behind him a few miles back. One of them included the Baptist preacher, Reverend Mueller, and his mother. That was the church Burton and Oscar had gone to, only a stone's throw from the Catholic one that Rory's family attended.

Rory rolled to the center of the road. He didn't have to look to know the now nearly seventy people had followed his lead. They were gathering and spreading out behind him, a human roadblock. Thomas and Marcus were closest to him, just ahead of his mom. Thomas had probably exhorted her to stay back a little bit, and she'd graciously accepted the protectiveness, while staying close enough to go mama bear if needed. At another time, that thought would have made him smile. Not right now.

The Chrysler slowed but kept approaching. Burton probably thought it was some local festival. As he drew close enough to realize it might be something different, the car slowed further. That was when Brick and the other two cars behind him drew closer to his tail and fanned out, blocking his retreat and parking in a loose semi-circle behind him. There were drainage ditches on both sides of the road, and the two flanking cars covered the shoulders. He wasn't leaving.

The Chrysler had come to a full stop. Burton Moorfield was a shadowed silhouette inside, but Rory noted a scruffy beard, and the glitter of calculating eyes. Then the door opened, and he emerged.

He hadn't missed a meal during his prison stay, a gut hanging over the waistband of his pants. Though Rory had done all sorts of practice runs in his head to ensure he could keep it together during this, he couldn't keep the teenage memory from springing to mind. Daralyn changing her clothes, exposing the sharp jut of her vertebrae, the stark lines of her ribs. How she struggled to eat more than a half a cup of food at a time.

She wasn't allowed to want.

Rory gripped his wheelrims and reminded himself of their purpose here. It wasn't to kick the shit out of the man, much as he deserved it. And he took some admittedly mean-spirited satisfaction in acknowledging cancer would take care of that weight soon.

Burton's clothes were worn, a stretched golf shirt, rumpled khakis, and a faded bill cap. His hair hadn't been cut in some time. When

Daralyn's father had been alive, Burton usually looked clean and put-together. Oscar really had been the glue that kept this piece of shit from looking exactly like what he was. Good. It was better when bad guys looked the part, especially sexual predators.

Burton's expression had tightened, because his gaze had lighted on Elaine. His mouth twisted, but before he could say a word, Thomas stepped even with Rory. His eyes were flint, his expression formidable.

"Say one word against our mother, and this is going to get ugly a lot faster."

Burton's jaw flexed. "I don't want any trouble. I'm just headed home."

"You don't have a home here." Rory pushed his chair forward, making it clear Burton's fight was with him.

Surprise crossed the man's face as he assessed the chair, squinted at Rory. "Elaine's boy. Didn't know you'd ended up in a wheelchair. Sorry to see that."

Rory offered a mirthless smile. "Hasn't slowed me down any. And I'm not interested in your feelings about it. You're not welcome here. Not now, not ever. You're going to get back in your car, turn around and choose somewhere else to go that doesn't take you through any part of our town. You won't be coming back."

Burton's gaze shifted past him, took in the force rallying against him, the resolve in their faces. Whatever he saw rattled him; Rory detected the flash of uneasiness, but the man had a stubborn asshole streak. Or nowhere else to go, more likely. Also not Rory's problem.

Burton's mouth thinned. "I have a right to live in my own home. I've got a niece here. Family."

"You don't have shit here," Rory said. "You gave up the right to call her family a long time ago. We're her family now." He shoved the chair forward another few feet, coming right up on Burton's toes. "She's with me."

Burton blinked. "So that's how it is. You think you have a claim on her. You don't." He leaned down, his eyes a hard glitter, the ugliness showing itself. "This isn't your business, boy. You brought backup to keep me from coming back to what's mine. But backup isn't always there." His gaze swept the chair. "And I'm not seeing how you're going to stop me."

Rory hooked Moorfield's collar in one hand and jerked him forward. Which meant when his face plowed into Rory's fist, the momentum came from both sides. The nose broke like glass under the blow, but Rory still had him, and he landed several strong punches. He was ready to break all of it. Eye socket, jaw. Turn the bastard's face into a pile of broken pieces. He knew just how fragile bones could be under the right amount of force. But he made himself let him go after those three punches, shoved him away. Watched Burton fall on his ass to the pavement.

But he wasn't done. Rory closed the distance once more, gripped his leg to lift it and drive it down, ramming his work shoe into Burton's abdomen.

Air left the man in a wheeze. Reflexes had him curled up in a fetal ball, while self-preservation made him simultaneously try to crawl away, get clear of Rory.

Now Rory held his position, not following. Inside, he was shaking with rage, but outside he kept everything locked down. He had to be here for her. He would be here for her.

"You mistook why I have backup," he said coldly. "They're here to keep me from killing you. Call me 'boy' one more time, talk about any kind of claim you think you have here, and they won't be able to stop me."

He was aware Thomas and Marcus had joined him, standing at his back and underlining the declaration with the darkest of markers.

When Marcus moved forward and gave Rory a look, Rory nodded. Marcus stepped over to the crumpled man, hauled him up by the collar. Since Burton was like a fat, unsteady gnome, Thomas went with him to flank the other side.

"I wouldn't count overly much on our willingness to stop him." Marcus's eyes were shards of green glass. "We'd be more than happy to help him get rid of your body and be his alibi. The whole fucking community."

Thomas jerked his head at the assembly of men and women. "This town looks after its own. And Daralyn is ours. Don't come back. We'll be watching."

Then Rory saw his brother's eyes shift to something behind him. Thomas's gaze sharpened and moved to Rory, a warning. Rory heard a quiet stirring among his neighbors. They'd agreed that they would all remain quiet, here as witnesses and reinforcement while they allowed Rory and his family to handle this. So there was only one reason they'd be murmuring among themselves. Something unexpected had happened.

Shit. Rory turned to see Daralyn approaching the group on her bicycle. In her jeans and pink knit shirt, she was an unlikely pastoral picture. He bit back a curse, but as his gaze briefly met his mother's, he knew he had to stand by what he'd said to her, and to Daralyn. Much as he wished he could keep her from it, Daralyn had every right to be here.

She walked through the group, steady and quiet. Many spoke a quiet word to her, reached out to touch her arm. Elaine slipped an arm around her waist, squeezed. Daralyn never looked at any of them, but she paused for each acknowledgment, as if drawing strength from that before proceeding. Her gaze stayed locked on Burton, bleeding and slack in Marcus and Thomas's grip.

Only when she reached Rory's side did her attention shift from her uncle to him. He held out his hand and she took it. She was ice cold, and he felt the tremor. The protective side of him, still backed by rage, immediately demanded that he get her out of here. She wasn't up for this.

He told that side of himself to fuck off. She was stronger than anyone here, including him. He put it in his expression, his grip. *We're here. We've got you. Do what you have to do.*

Her gaze flickered, and she gave him a slight dip of her chin. Then she turned back to her uncle, studied him.

Rory couldn't read anything from her face. She was a blank page, except for the hand that stayed in his grip. Her thumb rubbed over his slightly reddened knuckles, her gaze moving briefly to them, then she looked at her uncle, taking in the damage to his face, the bleeding nose and swelling eye.

She released Rory and moved forward, toward Burton. Rory tensed, but Marcus and Thomas were on it, their grip tightening on their captive in emphatic warning.

She stopped a foot from her uncle, met his gaze squarely, her back straight, chin up.

"This is my home," she said. "My family. I don't want you here."

She said it clear and strong. Nothing outward indicated the effort the declaration might have cost her. Maybe in this one miraculous moment, it didn't cost her at all.

It freed her.

"I don't know why you did what you did to me," she said. "But I don't think you know, either. Because you don't have a soul. You have to have a soul to know why." She extended her hand, her voice as firm as Rory had ever heard it. "Give me the keys to the house."

Elaine had come to Rory's side. She put a hand on his shoulder, squeezing hard, her tear-filled eyes brilliant with pride and pain both.

Several weeks ago, Elaine had shown Daralyn the simple hand-written will her father had left. "'My worldly belongings go to my closest kin,'" Daralyn said now, quoting it. "That's from my father's will. That would be me. Not his half-brother."

Thomas shifted his grip, obviously intending to search Burton's pockets, but Daralyn stopped him. "No. He has to do it. Please."

When Burton stared into Daralyn's face and she didn't so much as flinch, that was when he knew he was beat. Rory saw his gaze sweep back over the assembled townsfolk and their united front. Which included Owen.

The sheriff wore his uniform and leaned on the bumper of his patrol car with an impassive expression, arms crossed over his chest.

Burton shot a nervous glance at Marcus and Thomas, then brought his gaze to Rory's face once more. Rory knew he saw that they weren't bluffing. If he came back again, he wouldn't leave here alive. And Rory wouldn't lose a moment's sleep over it.

He'd been raised to believe in God's judgment. Which meant he fully believed God sometimes used other people to mete out that judgment. He'd pay good money to be Burton Moorfield's.

Burton reached down, fished in his pants pocket. Pulled out his keys. The keychain was an orange car-shaped piece of rubber, probably from the mechanic's place where he'd last had his beater car serviced. He took two keys off the ring and held them out. "Guess it's yours now, then."

Daralyn took the keys from his hand without touching his fingers. "Goodbye."

She turned, walked back through the group. Everyone watched as she reclaimed her bike, straddled it and pedaled away, her ponytail fluttering.

Brick assisted Marcus in escorting Burton back to his car, while Thomas returned to Rory. As he stood on one side of Rory's chair, Rory's mother on the other, Thomas squeezed his shoulder. "Go be with her," he said.

Rory didn't hesitate. He'd done what needed to be done for Daralyn here. Now she needed him for something else. He could trust his family to have their backs.

~

He knew where she was headed, but since her childhood home wasn't far from where they'd set up the blockade, she beat him there. As he pulled into the driveway, a scattering of gravel taken over by weeds, he saw her bike leaning against the warped boards of the front porch.

He hadn't wanted her to go in by herself, particularly in her current hard-to-read mood. But maybe she'd wanted a few minutes on her own; otherwise she probably would have still been standing outside.

When she'd lived there, her father and uncle had only done the bare minimum to take care of the place. Never any decorations or homey touches. The only thing he remembered was a candle in the window at Christmas time, and Thomas mentioning a brief glimpse of a straggly tree, when he accompanied Elaine to drop off some cookies and a Christmas card. Thomas had thought those had been Daralyn's efforts, not the men's.

After Oscar's death and Burton's imprisonment, Rory's father bushhogged the area around the house a couple times a year to keep nature at bay. His mother kept a line item in their account books for termite service and HVAC maintenance on the place, as well as anything else needed to keep the structure sound.

He probably should have put those things together a long time ago to realize the house was Daralyn's. If it had belonged to Burton, his parents would have let nature and the wildlife have it.

There were only three steps up to the porch. He put his ass on the second step, hauled his chair up to the porch, then put himself back in it.

She'd left the door open, either to help her feel less closed-in, or because she expected him. As he pushed over the threshold, he was able to take in most of the fifteen hundred square foot floor plan at a glance.

It was a two-bedroom one-story, with a bathroom, living room and kitchen. The living room had a couple pieces of furniture, upholstered in faded-to-colorless fabric. The walls had the same gray tint, though in sunlight and with a proper cleaning they probably were some shade of white.

No pictures on the walls. It was the habitat of two men with no evidence of a female occupant. Unless one knew where to look.

He noted a narrow twin bed in a skinny room he realized had likely been the laundry room or pantry. Her bedroom. The bed told him that, as did the lack of a door.

Plus, Daralyn stood in front of it. She was as motionless as the furniture that rested in the haze of way-too-undead memories floating in the place.

As he moved closer, he saw a scarred side table and a lamp jammed in behind the bed. "Daralyn."

She started, but not in a way that suggested she hadn't known he was here with her. It was as if his voice amid the other ones happening in her head had been unexpected.

He reached out, touched her rigid hand. Nothing about her said she was ready to be coddled. She gazed at him, then pivoted and walked toward the kitchen. He followed.

There was a mudroom. It was in that room he recalled there was one other door in the house that had been left intact, other than the ones to her father and uncle's bedrooms.

They punished me for misbehaving by putting me in the cellar without food or light, usually for a few hours or overnight... Three days, I think. I lost track.

As she stared at the trap door, her hands half curled, horror spiked in his gut.

"Daralyn. Don't go down there."

"I need to get something." She lifted her head, gazed at him steadily. "It's just a cellar."

But he could see the paleness of her features, the pulse jumping in her throat. He took her hand. "I'm here," he said. "Nothing here is going to hurt you."

She blinked. Swallowed. She tightened her grip on his before it slipped away so she could pull up the cellar door, revealing a narrow wooden ladder that descended into darkness.

She'd seemed so calm, he wasn't ready for it. As the stale, trapped air wafted up from a room that hadn't been disturbed in years, she lost all color, as well as whatever resolve had driven her to open the door. Her knees gave out.

His heart leaped as she swayed precariously over that opening. Fortunately, she was reaching for him at the same moment he grabbed for her, so she mostly collapsed into his arms, one of her bent knees against his wheel as the other rested on the floor. Her forehead and face were pressed to his biceps.

"Can't..."

She was clinging to him as if she thought she was on the edge of a cliff, prepared to fight off the pull of gravity with teeth and nails.

He tipped up her chin and forced down fear at the naked wildness in her face. In a blink, all that detached calm had given way to the look of someone lost in a tornado, no sense of how to find her way out. It made him speak sharply.

"Daralyn, pay attention to me. Right now."

That helped, after he repeated it several times. He watched her come back to him, her hazel eyes showing her struggle. "This is too much," he told her. "You've already handled enough today. We can come back."

Her gaze was glassy. "But I really need what's down there. I can't explain why..."

"You're not going down there. We'll call someone to go down there for you. Tell me what we're looking for."

She shook her head. She was pulling herself together by millimeters, but since he could track the subtlest changes in her expression, he saw it. "I have to do it," she said. "Please. Please help me do it."

He wanted to tell her hell no, but the request was so plaintive, so desperate, he couldn't deny her. "Okay." He gave it some thought. While he did, he shifted her so she was fully in his arms, on his lap. "Hold onto me a minute first."

She did, clinging to him like she was about to be torn away from him by that tornado. Fuck this. When it mattered, he tried never to overrule her, but she was asking too much of herself. Shit.

Shit, shit, shit.

He shoved the Master to the side, every protective instinct that came from the man he was, who loved her so much he couldn't tolerate anything that caused her distress. He re-channeled it in what he hoped was the right direction.

"You can do anything," he said roughly into her hair, stroking it. "You're right. It's just a goddamn cellar. I am right here. Say it."

"I can do anything. You're right here. It's just a goddamn cellar."

She rarely cursed, so the parroting gave him an unexpected smile. She saw it, and amusement flitted through her gaze. It was like a moth buffeted by a storm, but it was there.

He tugged her hair. "You belong to me," he reminded her. "Right?"

That steadied her even more, which steadied them both. She lifted her chin. "I belong to you."

"Okay." Since he didn't see anything resembling a light below, he twisted around, fished in the pack hanging from his chair and pulled out his store keys. The ring had one of those keychain flashlights on it, which he detached and put in her hands. "Go get whatever it is and bring your ass back up here. Don't overthink it. Just go. Now."

He propelled her off his lap and toward the ladder, a little push. Since that near-topple over the opening was way too fresh in his mind, he kept his hands on her until she descended. She seemed pretty steady now, though, moving quickly. He thought she was hurrying, trying to do what she needed to do before the visuals they'd planted in her head to handle this were overwhelmed by other things.

As he moved closer, he could see the space where she was descending. At least for this moment, these purposes, he was relieved to see it wasn't large, more like an underground walk-in closet. There was nowhere down there she'd be outside his view, which might partly explain why they'd never bothered to put in a light.

She stopped in front of a set of empty shelves, and her gaze went down to her feet. He adjusted to see what she was looking at, and saw a space just big enough to shove a sack of flour, to keep it fresh and cool. As she dropped to her heels, she gripped the shelf above that alcove, and laid her palm on the ground beneath. Her shoulders rounded, her head bowed, and he saw her body jerk, as if caught by a sob.

Damn it. He bit back an order for her to return now, and instead waited her out. He was here. Whatever she needed to do, she needed to do it.

She went to her knees, putting both hands on the cold concrete floor. Anguish and fury struck him in the gut as he realized the spot was big enough for a child to hole herself up, try to shield herself against the dark and what she might imagine inhabited it.

"Daralyn," he said.

She didn't respond. She hadn't heard him. He was trying to figure out the impossible, how to get himself down the ladder, when she shook herself out of it, lifted a hand toward him, an acknowledgement. Then she rose and came back up to him. She sank down on the floor, her feet on the top step of the ladder, her hand on his foot. Her face was ashen, her eyes bright with pain, a brittle coldness to her face. Her hands were empty.

"Did you not find it?"

Her gaze cleared, though she looked puzzled by his question. Then she understood. "It wasn't an object. It was me. I needed to tell that version of myself that it was done. That she isn't trapped down there anymore."

Her hazel gaze rose to his, and suddenly that lost look vanished, swallowed by something feral as a wolf, as focused as a dog on a scent.

She bounded to her feet, squeezed past him and charged into the kitchen. When he backed out of the mud room, he saw she was yanking open the drawers, one after the other. She found what she was seeking under the kitchen sink.

A hammer.

She moved back into the mudroom, fell to her knees and attacked the hinges of the cellar trapdoor. She knocked the pins loose with impressively precise swings. But when the door came loose, that was where any control to her movements gave way to that wildness again. She yanked the door free with a strength fueled by something far beyond the physical, and hurled it down that narrow opening. It bounced off the ladder, landed against the empty shelves with a loud clatter and landed on the subterranean floor.

"No door for the cellar. Never again," she said.

Then she collapsed to her knees, buried her face in her hands and started to rock, making a keening noise.

"Ah, baby." He locked the chair, lowered himself to the floor so he could collect her against him. She toppled over, a tight human coil in his lap. Curling over her, he wrapped his arms around her, holding her. She wasn't crying. She was literally like a wounded animal, expressing pain with a quiet, heartrending noise.

As he murmured to her, held her, he lifted his head and noted the rear door led to a back porch. Outside, the sun was hitting early afternoon. It was a memorable fall day. The trees in the backyard were an assortment of maples, red and yellow, their color shining in through the window.

He was glad she at least had had something like that to look at during her bleak childhood. The woman he was holding loved the outdoors, all the different things nature could offer the senses. It would be the best thing to help balance what was in her head.

"Come on," he said, when she seemed to be easing up, seemingly more aware of her surroundings. She was also holding him as much as he was holding her, her arms clutching his back. "That's enough for today. Let's go to the back porch."

She straightened with an uncertain nod, her face flushed and strained, hazel eyes weary. He put himself back in the chair, clasped her hand to help her to her feet. She put her hand on the scratched knob and opened the back door.

As he followed her out onto the porch, he saw, just like the front, the screens had been ripped out long ago. However, the view through the trees was good, showing an open meadow with autumn gold grass, and a small pond.

Off to the right was a storage building, the door padlocked. He noted it was the only thing on the property that looked well-maintained.

Daralyn followed his gaze. "When my uncle went to jail, your parents and some of the neighbors stored everything but a few pieces of furniture and tools in the storage building," she said. "Your mother said it would be there if I wanted to go through it. At the time, I was afraid they'd keep asking me about it. It made me sick to my stomach, until I realized they were never going to bring it up again, unless I did. They were fine waiting forever for me to choose."

He pressed her hand in understanding. Without the screens, the air was fresh, the afternoon breeze touching their faces. It was a welcome change from the stale interior of the house. Daralyn sat down, her backside on the porch boards, her feet propped on the steps to the yard. Since he stayed at her side, she leaned against his leg. He put a hand on her hair, her shoulder, stroked.

He waited her out, wanting her to decide if there was anything she needed or wanted to say. And he gave her the quiet if that was what she needed more.

She gazed at the view for a long while, laid her head against his knee. Her breathing settled.

"I don't remember much about my mother," she said at last. "She was a shadow. A touch. Not always gentle. Not unkind. More...shaky. She wasn't well."

He nodded, and she continued. "She left a stack of old magazines when she died. I couldn't read them, but I liked looking at them. I wasn't allowed to change the TV channel, but my father fell asleep with the TV on...always so loud, and never off, never quiet. But early in the mornings, Sesame Street was on the channel he fell asleep to. They'd do that part about the letters, how to sound them out, what they looked like. I didn't learn to read well, but enough to recognize some words."

Her ability to acquire skills simply by listening and watching had always been exceptional. But hearing proof she'd strived for it, with no adult providing any type of encouragement, made it even more impressive to him. Dr. Taylor had mentioned it herself.

A lack of early childhood development from a nurturing source creates myriad learning and interpersonal relationship problems. But Daralyn's innate intelligence compensated in extraordinary ways.

Extraordinary was the right word for her. He didn't need anyone to tell him that.

"They were always watching me," she said, staring at the pond. "Even when I didn't think they were. They figured out I was watching Sesame Street, was spending...too much time with the magazines. Daddy started turning it to a different channel before he fell asleep, one that had a hunting show first thing in the morning. My uncle collected all the magazines in a trash bin and burned them."

Her fingers brushed the scar on the inside of her forearm. "It was one of the few times I fought. I screamed, put my hand in the bin, grabbed one out, held it to me, even though it was on fire. He took it away, tossed it back into the trash bin. Dragged me to the cellar. That was the first time he left me there a full twenty-four hours."

"Fucking hell." He lifted her forearm, pressed his mouth to that burn scar. Her hand trembled. "You've never acted like you're afraid of going into the cellar at my mom's house. Or Thomas and Marcus's."

"They're different spaces. A whole different feeling. And they have lights."

Another silence ensued before she spoke again.

"I didn't know giving up was an option."

He saw her gaze was fully caught in memories, not her surroundings, though her fingers curled over his hold, a lifeline to the present.

"I wasn't that...self-aware, and maybe that was good. But I do remember something broke inside me that day. Something that really, truly hurt. I couldn't...I didn't get out of bed for days, it seemed. Except to do the chores and whatever they told me to. I didn't take the shower I was allowed every two days."

A faint, grim smile touched her lips. "I guess it worried them. Uncle Burton brought me home one new magazine and a Hershey bar. For a whole week, they didn't make me take care of their...physical needs. He said if I'd start behaving again, he'd take me to a movie. The first I'd ever been to. It was too big and loud, the kind they liked, with explosions. My uncle got angry because the sound frightened me."

She shifted. "I tried to focus on other things, like the people in the theater. There had been this lady at the popcorn stand who was kind, who had a quiet voice. It was a world different from mine, and I think some way down deep part of my soul took it as a sign of hope. Hope that my life could be something different. It was enough to snap me out of it."

Her gaze turned to him. "At least, that's what I think now. At the time, I didn't really know why going to that movie helped bring me back to myself. Your mother told me that God shines a light in the darkest corners. Even if we've never seen that light before, the soul inside us, that was made by His hands, recognizes it."

He smiled a smile that hurt him all the way to the core of that soul, and gripped her hand. "It's funny," he said thickly. "I don't believe as she believes, but her belief is so strong, I think it gives me my faith, by proxy."

"You experience it vicariously," she said, pronouncing the word carefully.

He loved her so much. "Good word."

She rose, her hand slipping from his as she went down the back steps. She stood there another couple minutes, staring out at the meadow. Her shoulders twitched and then she turned toward him. The pain was so stark in her face, so raw, it startled him.

"I want," she said in a strangled voice.

"What, baby? What do you want?" He wanted her back on the porch, within touching distance.

A smile, brilliantly painful, lit her face, made her eyes flash like lightning. "You."

Then her gaze shifted so she stared past him, at the house. "I want my life to be full of the choices I make. *Me.*"

She jerked into motion, coming up the stairs to sink down at his feet, her hands gripping his knees. She stared up at him with such a hunger he thought it could consume every bit of his heart and soul.

"I want you," she said again. Now her voice was trembling, and her eyes filled with tears. "Please. Right now. And forever after that."

"Okay," he said. "Come up here."

She did, and he pulled her forward, helping her straddle him. The way she kissed him was savage, so uncontrolled, it ignited the Master in him. He wrapped his hand in her hair, held her tight. She could be as out of control as she wished; he held the control for them both.

She drew back. His beautiful girl, his submissive, his heart, the center of his soul, wasn't done detailing her wants. He was happy to let her roll them out, and hoped she had a list longer than anything ever sent to St. Nick.

"I want this house," she said. "I want to make it ours. I don't know how, but I want to do that. I want to change it, so all the bad memories are driven out and every memory we make here crowds out all the bad ones. I'll pull up the carpet, paint it, inside and out. I'm going to put chimes in the cellar, a bunch of them, and a fan that will run, make them sing all the time, until every bad thing is gone from that space. Then it will be a food pantry, a proper one. With finished walls and it will be a bright color. I'll start an account at the store, and pay it back. Oh..."

She bounced off his lap, bolted down the stairs and disappeared around the corner of the house.

"What the hell—"

"I'll be right back," she called over her shoulder. She sounded excited.

He blinked, his lips curled ruefully. Then he pivoted, regarded the house. It was the last place he figured she'd ever want to live again, but she'd sounded determined, so he gave it a more critical look. Yeah, a lot of work, but the bones were good. And through her eyes, he imagined it transformed.

She was back. He vaguely remembered she'd had a folded blanket in her bike basket. It was the lap quilt that his mother had made for Daralyn, a housewarming gift when she moved into Marcus and Thomas's guest house. She kept it folded at the foot of her bed.

She clutched it as she came back up the stairs. "When I said I want you..."

The words stopped, and she stared at him. When her eyes lowered, he realized what had happened. Her wants were starting to move into a realm she felt crossed the line into telling him what to do. She wouldn't make decisions her natural submission wanted to give to him.

He'd learned how to respond to that. No, not learned. He'd always known, and she opened it up wide in him, an ocean of possibilities and need.

"Tell me what you want, Daralyn. I'll tell you if you can have it." Like he'd ever deny her any fucking thing she wanted.

"I want...you to be with me on my bed. Here."

The idea of doing anything so intimate and sacred in a place where she'd been treated so abominably initially repelled him. But he had to look at things like this through her eyes, not his own.

Which made him understand. This was the beginning, the way they would make the house theirs.

He brought her to him, put his hands on her hips, caressing. "Go spread the quilt out on the bed. Make it ready for us. I'll join you shortly. You wait for me."

She met his gaze, nodded. Biting her lip, she reached out, touched the front of his shirt. "Can I have this?"

He pulled it over his head, handed it to her. She held the balled-up fabric against her chest, eyes closed, nose buried in the shirt. Reaching out blind, she trailed her fingers against his flesh, and he covered her hand with his, let her palm rest against his heart, where she seemed to want it. Then she lifted her head, met his gaze and nodded, before hurrying inside to do as he'd ordered.

He found the bathroom functioning and clean, if dusty, and thanked whoever his mother was paying to maintain the house for keeping the basics running. He imagined what Daralyn would do with it, how she'd transform it. He'd help her. Two bedrooms and a bath were plenty of room for one couple, bigger than her guest house, and they could build an addition when and if it was needed. Or strip it down, keep the bones, and build a whole new floor plan.

He'd made the transition from being a man defined by his wheel-chair to a man who used a wheelchair. Today he thought she'd hit that fork in the road for herself and made a definite decision of which way to go. She'd discarded the label of victim, tossed it into the wind by confronting her uncle, and by the fierce declaration she'd just made in the backyard.

I want.

She was a woman whose childhood had included horrific abuse, but her life, who she was, was so much more than that, too.

He went to her room. The quilt was on the bed and she was on it. Kneeling, her bare legs folded up beneath her, because all she wore was his shirt, the neckline exposing the delicate line of her collarbone. Her hair was loose.

Would she ever understand what it did to him, looking at her like that, waiting for him, wanting his care, attention and love?

He could show her. It was time to do what he'd wanted to do with her for so long. In the weeks since his hospital stay, he'd built up his strength again, and he was glad he hadn't shirked on that, so he could act on it now, at this very important moment.

If he let himself get caught in what this place had meant to her for so long, the darker side, he'd approach this as something to get done quick, so he could get her out of here. Until they could change it, make it reflect what she wanted it to look like.

But while he was in the bathroom, he'd heard her thumping pillows, telling him she was shaking the dust out of them out on the back porch. Despite the dismal look of their surroundings, with the quilt on the bed and the front and back porch doors open, letting in the fresh air, the sound of birds, he could focus on what mattered.

She wanted to make this into their home. He'd prove to her that it could be done. He could help give her that, starting right now.

As he transferred himself onto the bed, she adjusted to make room for him. He stretched out and took her hand, guiding her so she was leaning over him. He put his hand on her hip beneath the shirt, stroking soft flesh. Her hair framed her face as she gazed at him, the soft ends tickling his stomach. He tugged the strands. "This is getting long. I might eventually be able to tie you up with it."

The flicker of heat in her gaze brought back several recent, very good memories of things they'd done with rope. "You like it long," she said.

"Yes, I do. But I'd love it short, or anywhere in between. As long as it's on your head."

He moved his touch up her side, having plenty of room under his shirt to find her small curves, the lines of her ribs, following them around to her back so he brought her down to him. He cupped her face with the other hand, brushed his mouth over hers. Kissed her deep and long before easing back.

"Why did you want my shirt?"

"To remind me of who I am now. Not who I was then." A slight smile, tremulous. "To give me more courage."

"You look damn good in it. And I've never met a braver person in my life." He slid his touch down the front, found a puckered nipple beneath the fabric. Her breath drew in, those subtle signs of arousal that drew him in, made him want to give her less subtle ones. "Lie down on your back," he said, low. "And open your legs for me."

Her pupils darkened. She eased to her back, stretching out, keeping her hand on him, though she plucked at the shirt with the other hand. "Do you want me to take this off?"

"Yes. I'm going to cover you with me."

Her eyes widened, but the brightness in her eyes, the eagerness, captivated him as she arched in a wonderful way to take the shirt off. He was already turning on his side, their bodies choreographed to one another's movements. When she had it above her head, he gripped the shirt between her wrists, arresting her movement. He slid his other arm underneath her, keeping her in that arch as he descended upon her breast and took the nipple in his mouth, suckling deep.

A part moan, part cry was wrested from her throat, and she pressed herself more urgently to him. He kept her arms where they were with the pressure of his hand on the shirt, reveling in having her helpless like that, taking every bit of pleasure he could give her. His mouth moved over her nipples, her breasts, her sternum. Another time he'd enjoy what was between her legs, but she was aroused enough for where he wanted to go.

As he drew back to look at her, he opened his jeans, worked them off his hips. He pushed them down to his thighs one-handed, using his arm strength to lift his hips enough to manage it. When he took himself in hand, stroking, his cock responded quickly, telling him the prep he'd done in the bathroom was taking effect. He pulled the cock ring from the small pouch in his pocket, showing it to her before he dropped his hand down between her legs.

"Need you to slick this up some more for me."

She let out a breath as he pushed the ring inside her opening, worked it in her wet heat while playing with her swollen flesh with his fingers. Then he withdrew his touch reluctantly, but only to slide the ring onto his cock, fitting it to the base.

He gave himself another several moments of stroking himself while looking at the beauty of her trembling body. Then he lifted himself on one arm and maneuvered over her so he could brace and lower himself between her spread thighs.

He'd practiced it, and in this moment where it seemed everything was going their way, the shift on top of her was as smooth as he could wish. He did manage to plant his palm on that thick mane of hair. It held her head in place, pulled on her scalp. From the way her breath shortened at the hint of restraint, he thought she didn't mind it. But he didn't want to rip her hair out of her scalp as things became more insistent. So when he murmured the quiet command to her, she freed her hand from his shirt and swept her hair away and above her, him adjusting his palm briefly to make that easier.

"Put your hands on my forearms," he told her, and watched them settle on his braced arms. "Bring your knees up so they're brushing my ribs."

It would open her further. Even more importantly, he could *feel* her legs against his body. She did it, her hazel eyes luminous. "You're on top of me," she whispered.

"I am." A faint smile curved his lips but he knew the gaze he had on her was serious, intent. "I've wanted you under me like this for a long time."

She touched his face, a tentative, needy gesture. "It feels... wonderful."

"I hope it's about to feel even better to you. Guide me in, Daralyn."

He watched her move her hand between them, close her fingers around his erection. As she put him into her body, her lips parted. When he saw the flex of her stomach muscles, he knew she'd clenched those inner muscles on him, to keep stroking him. Fuck, he would love to feel it the way he once had, but there was nothing about this moment he would trade. Every live nerve ending he had was feeling this, ten times more acutely than before he'd been paralyzed.

His knees had stayed at the angle he'd planted them, also something he'd experimented with. He didn't want them slipping and taking him out of her at the wrong moment. As he started moving, using his upper body strength to thrust into her, he kept it slow and easy, also to make sure he held his position where it needed to be.

Slow and easy worked for her, because her eyes had already started to burn with need, her breath coming more rapidly as he moved. She was stroking his arms, sometimes curling in so he felt the bite of her nails.

When he whispered his permission, she moved her hands to his sides and down to clasp his hips, her thumbs pressing high enough he felt their pressure. Her grip on his ass would help him drive deeper into her. She was helping him stay with her, give her this. Give them both this.

She knew to be careful with her nails below his waist, but right now he didn't care if she forgot. He could check later. He didn't want anything to inhibit or distract her from where this was going.

"Mine," he whispered, gazing down at her. He'd feared saying that to her too often, or in the wrong moment. He hadn't wanted her to think she had no choice except him. But now he knew she understood choice. It still wouldn't come easy for her, maybe not for a long time, but she'd proven she could decide what she wanted, and make it known to him in the ways she trusted him to understand. So he had no more fear of telling her what *he* wanted.

"Yours," she said, matching his fierceness with her own. Her body was lifting to his, the two of them moving the way water moved, with no conscious thought. Nature simply existed, flowed, went the direction intended.

He was going to give Red a lifetime supply of mulch for his yard, because though he felt the burn in his arms, back and shoulders, it wasn't a strain. Every part of him he needed to make this work was a hundred percent on board.

Watching the climax build in her face, in the eagerness of her body, that burn faded, replaced by something else.

He would always remember how it felt to run across the football field, to soar, and have his body give him everything he needed, willing to give him even more. He'd never thought he'd feel that again. But that was just another gift love had given him. That Daralyn had given him.

"Come for me, baby."

Daralyn shattered, calling out her pleasure to the fields behind the house, taking flight with the birds. He watched it sweep over her body, that sensual helplessness that was nothing but God's gift, a way to lose oneself, let go of everything that didn't matter. Even if it was just for that moment.

But sometimes, when it was this good, that moment spun out, paved the path to a life of the same. The climax grabbed him then, too, and the way it made his body jerk, his arms tensing to hold himself, apparently spurred on her aftershocks. Her hands were on his arms again, digging in, and he relished watching her nails leave crescents there. Her legs locked high over his back to hold him tight. He didn't even care that it called for one more additional burst of strength from him, to hold them both.

Right now, he could carry the world.

⁓

After they rested some, they got dressed and headed back to her cottage. She was going to make dinner and Rory assumed they'd relax, do some of the usual things they did on a weeknight. They had work tomorrow and she'd have school in the afternoon.

Marcus and Thomas hailed them as they pulled in, though, and invited them to share the dinner they were making. Since he could tell she was amenable to that, they did. Afterward, instead of heading back to the cottage or his place, they found themselves on his brother's back porch. Though Daralyn was diligent about her studies, the day had taken its toll. When Rory moved himself onto the porch swing to share it with her, Daralyn eventually slipped from leaning against his shoulder to lying with her head in his lap, dozing while Rory shared a beer with Thomas and Marcus.

He'd lifted his legs into his nearby chair to provide a more even pillow for her. As he stroked her hair, he felt a deep contentment.

To confirm it was justified, he gave Thomas and Marcus an expectant look. They were sitting in the pair of rocking chairs facing him, Marcus's long legs stretched out so the toe of one bare foot brushed Thomas's, stretched out in his direction.

"Is she asleep?" Thomas asked, low.

Rory nodded. "She's exhausted. But in a good way, I think. Burton gone?"

"Absolutely." Thomas's eyes glittered. "Brick followed him sixty miles, then had his cousin in Monroe pick up the trail and follow him another hundred. Looks like he's headed to Asheville and the mountains. The mountain communities are a lot more close-knit than people realize, and Brick's cousin knows people. He'll spread the word. As a sex offender, Burton'll have to register wherever he settles. We'll make sure he does, so he'll be on law enforcement's radar. His cancer prognosis is about nine months, so hopefully we won't have to worry about it much longer."

"If we couldn't send him to hell, we at least sent him on his way," Marcus added. "Owen has his face pasted up on the wall at the office, and every one of his deputies has memorized it. The neighbors go without saying. Anyone sees him come back, we'll know."

"Good." Rory glanced down at the woman asleep in the curve of his arm. "But you know what? I think she did as much as any of us to convince him there's nothing for him here."

"Yeah. She's not going to be anyone's victim. Not ever again." Marcus tapped his beer to Thomas's and sent Rory a teeth-baring grin. "Don't discount your own contribution," he added. "You've got a hell of an arm. Next time I'm in a fight, I want you at my back."

"I think you should put him in front," Thomas said. "He hits harder than you do."

"Let's not get carried away stroking Cripdick's ego."

"No stroking involved. Just stating facts."

"I'm very uncomfortable with the topic of stroking around you two," Rory said, deepening Marcus's grin and earning a chuckle from Thomas. They were quiet for a while, drinking their beers while Rory played with Daralyn's hair, caressed the round shape of her shoulder, the slope of her arm, crooked over his thighs. The sun had set a while back, turning the sky all the usual brilliant colors, and now the stars were coming out over the open fields and the forest beyond. Lights from distant farmhouses, their neighbors, dotted the landscape.

He couldn't ask for anything more from life. He'd defended the woman he loved, stood by her, with the family and community who stood by them both. Tomorrow he'd work in the store his parents had started, and he'd continue to make successful. It was a hell of a good life.

"I want to ask her to marry me," he said abruptly. "But I think I should wait, give her time."

Thomas lifted a shoulder. "You have plenty of it. All the time you both need."

"When you do, it will only confirm what everyone else can see. Especially Daralyn." Marcus met his gaze. "She's yours, but it's pretty clear she sees you as hers, too. You're already bound to her in every way that matters."

Bound. Connected. Those were the right words. Several years ago, he never could have predicted this moment. A moment where he was happier, more content, than he'd ever been in his life, even when he had the use of his legs.

He wondered if Daralyn felt anywhere close to that, and then thought about what she'd said earlier, about hope. *I think some way down deep part of my soul took it as a sign of hope. Hope that my life could be something different.*

What was it Tyler Winterman had said? "Love can surprise you in so many ways."

When he shared that out loud, Marcus grimaced. "Probably

copped it off the cheesy inspirational wall poster of one of his corporate weasel friends."

Thomas grinned at Rory. "You won't get anything good from him about Tyler. Not until he has that sculpture."

"I'll buy it for pennies at his estate sale when he dies," Marcus said, unruffled. "Which should be soon. He's ancient. In his fifties or something."

"Says the guy who's hit his forties. Cradle robbed my brother." Rory chuckled as Marcus tossed a balled-up napkin at him. "Since Tyler seems to feel the same about you, I'm betting he has some clause in his will that it can't end up in your hands."

"I'll sweet talk it from Marguerite."

"Yeah." Thomas snorted. "Nobody sweet talks anything from that Mistress."

Daralyn shifted, turning so she was facing Rory's abdomen. She wrapped her arms around his waist and drew her legs up, snuggling in like a cat. Then she murmured something. Rory leaned in. "What, baby?"

She glanced up at him, her eyes heavy lidded and sleepy. "I would love to marry you," she said. "A spring wedding. Outdoors."

Then she subsided back into slumber. Rory stared down at her, distantly hearing Thomas and Marcus's chuckles.

"When a woman finally decides what she wants," Marcus said, "not even a Master can stand in her way."

CHAPTER TWENTY-FIVE

*T*hat was true, but Rory also knew stating things so directly was still new to her. A decision as big as marriage? He wasn't going to hold her to something she'd likely said while halfway asleep, after a really tumultuous day.

So over the next week, as they returned to a normal schedule, it was definitely in the upper part of his mind, but he didn't bring it back up. They did their work at the store, she attended her classes. She was already planning what she'd take next semester. Then there were plans for Thanksgiving and Christmas. Les would be home for a prolonged break, and Julie and Des would join them for both holidays. Rory's mother was making plans for it. Rory placed the Christmas tree order and started lining up the help he'd need to get them unloaded and delivered to the ordering customers.

In the middle of all those usual things, he and Daralyn had started working out designs for her reclaimed house. They obtained a copy of the existing floor plan from the courthouse and pinned it to a drafting table they set up in the back of the store. The tracing paper taped over it would reflect the renovation ideas they were bouncing back and forth.

On the day they'd added that tracing paper, Daralyn had set the tone for where they were going with the project. In the top corner, she abolished any past reference to the Moorfield brothers by printing four words in bold block print.

The Wilder Moss House.

When Rory saw it, he took the pencil from her. As she watched, a puzzled half smile on her face, he marked through what she'd written and wrote the correction below it.

The Moss Wilder house.

He handed the pencil back, closed her fingers around it. "I know why you put my name first," he said. "And I appreciate the respect. But this is you, reclaiming what's yours. Your name should be first."

The rest of that day she'd seemed thoughtful, but when he saw her stop at the drafting table, trace her fingers over the name, look toward him with a shine in her hazel eyes, he knew he'd made the right call.

As they worked together to sketch out the changes they wanted to the house—a more open layout that would require mostly gutting the interior, and customized options on the kitchen, bath and outside porches for full wheelchair compatibility—he pulled in contractors for bids on the changes that he and his buddies couldn't do themselves. He'd also revamp the storage shed, so it would be a workshop and workout area for him.

Des had already agreed to re-roof both the house and storage shed with architectural shingles. Their only cost would be whatever the shingles cost him. He wouldn't hear anything different from them on it.

Even so, their ideas required a budget that would take about six months of saving before they'd feel comfortable beginning the first major renovation step. While Marcus and Thomas were willing to front them the money, or even gift it, that wasn't the way Rory operated, and Daralyn was on the same page on that.

However, his girl did mention that, if the minor repairs needed to make the place inhabitable "could be done," it "might be nice" to go ahead and move in. She dropped the hint a couple times, in various ways.

Each time she did, he hedged on agreeing to it or setting a date. He didn't tell her why, which he knew was starting to cause a problem. It showed in the pucker between her brows that grew deeper each time. Though he was usually forthcoming with her on things, he wasn't on this. Instead, he would move on to another topic, or simply tell her, "We'll see how the repairs go."

He and Johnny did work on those minor repairs in the evenings and on weekends. And not just to give her a sense they were moving in the direction she wanted to go. When she decided to tackle the storage building contents, it gave him a reason to be on the property.

He was glad she asked his mother to help her, for additional moral support. Most of what was in that building were things that belonged to her father, so he wasn't surprised when she had a local thrift store charity cart off most of it. She found a couple small things that had belonged to her mother—a vase and a small music box—and kept those, but that was about it.

He knew she felt guilty about it, wanting them to carry away pots and pans and other things that were functional, but the first time she expressed guilt over it, he'd put an end to that, pulling her down on his lap and cupping her chin so she could see exactly how he felt about it.

"Anything in that shed that has a bad memory for you goes. I don't care if it's a teaspoon or a mahogany dining room set. Nothing comes into the Moss Wilder house that isn't something you want in there."

"Not even that vintage Winchester rifle I found?"

He did a double take, then saw the smile quivering around her lips. She was up and away with a shriek and a laugh as he grabbed at her, but that was okay. He paid her back for her teasing when he cornered her in their bedroom, after dinner that same night.

But later, when she was lying in his arms, he revisited the subject, because he knew the potential waste was bothering her. "The money from selling the stuff will help the charity," he pointed out. "And people buying it get something useful at an affordable price. They can create good, new memories with it."

Once the storage shed was empty, she and Amanda began making regular shopping trips to find secondhand furniture pieces that could be stored in the building until it was time to move them into the house. Sometimes he went with her, but since he wasn't as much into the shopping end of things, she often sent him pictures on her phone, to see if he liked her choices.

No surprise, she considered both their tastes when she was looking, so he had no problems with anything she picked out. But mostly he liked seeing how happy it was making her. If she wanted it, he'd have said yes to a faux fur hot pink sofa that made his eyeballs bleed.

However, as he and Johnny completed each repair, and space in the storage shed diminished, he was running out of reasons to avoid explaining why he wasn't ready to move into the house. From his mother, he knew Daralyn had put out feelers to make sure Elaine wasn't upset about Rory moving out. Just the opposite. His mom was near ecstatic about their plans. She was already helping Daralyn divide some of the plants at her cottage, as well as offering some of her own, to get the landscaping and future vegetable and flower garden started on the property. So Daralyn knew Elaine wasn't the hold up for him.

A couple days later Rory ran out of maneuvering room. He had just poured himself a late morning coffee and was talking to Johnny up front while Daralyn was in the back of the store. She was checking on a shipment for Betsy Dorsey, who'd called about it just after lunch.

"So after we get those cracks spackled today, the house should be occupant-ready," Johnny said cheerfully. "If you can get—"

He stopped at the look on Rory's face. He didn't realize what Rory did—that Daralyn had the hearing of a bat, and stayed pretty attuned to everything going on within a hundred yards of her.

As Daralyn emerged from the back, an expectant smile on her face, Johnny realized his mistake. He shot Rory an apologetic look—before escaping toward the back of the store.

"That's wonderful," she said, sliding a manufacturer's pricing note-book back on the shelf behind the counter. "So we can start to move in the furniture we've bought for the house this weekend, right?"

He shrugged. "Yeah, possibly. Can we talk about it after lunch? I need to run an errand."

And there came the little wrinkle in her brow. He really was going to have to come clean on this, because he was concerned he was starting to send the wrong message. He reached out, touched her hand, gave her a half smile that he knew didn't reach his eyes, but there was a coil in his lower stomach he couldn't explain to her. Not right now, like this.

"Okay," she said. He thought she might have said more, but fortunately several customers arrived, letting him off the hook. He was able to slip out a few minutes later while she and Johnny were involved with them, putting off further conversation about it.

Until he returned.

She was standing behind the counter, a conflicted look on her face that had him immediately concerned.

He lifted a brow. "Something up?"

"I don't know. Yes. Maybe." She folded her hands in front of her and looked directly at him. "I want to drive out to our house, please."

She still had an odd formality to her when she stated a desire so directly, as if she had to frame a support for it in her mind before she spoke the words.

"Right now?" He glanced toward Johnny and saw the *no clue, dude* look. Though his friend threw in an expression of male solidarity he probably considered helpful, a general commiseration on the mystifying nature of women.

"Yes, now," Daralyn said. There was unusual emphasis to the one syllable. Almost...impatience?

When Rory raised a brow and turned his gaze upon her, she lowered hers and added, "Please."

Which she charmingly never seemed to realize made it almost impossible for him to tell her no. "Okay," he said.

She headed out to the parking lot. When he glanced at Johnny, Johnny shrugged. "Call me after she cuts your legs out from under you. Metaphorically. That's one of her new words this week."

"I am so hitting you with a shovel later," Rory promised.

He backed the chair, turned and followed Daralyn out to the parking lot. She was already waiting by the van, but when he opened the door for her, she merely thanked him and got in, waiting in silence until he took the driver's side.

He thought about several topics of conversation, but whatever this was about, she was inside her head on it and he wouldn't disrupt that process. Not until he had more cues about what she needed from him.

Though he could guess what that was. His gut tightened around a wad of nerves, but he'd reached the fork in the road, hadn't he? Time to fish or cut bait.

When they reached the house, he circled around, opened her door. Since it was drizzling, he told her she didn't need to wait on him to go up to the porch. One of the planned changes was a paved driveway and walkway, but right now, it was a mix of grass and old gravel. It took him time to maneuver over the places they hadn't laid down plywood for a temporary fix.

She sat down on the top step. As he moved toward her, he saw she had her arms crossed over her body and her expression was pensive.

On closer inspection he realized it was deeper than that. The strain he saw in her features told him she'd been far tenser at the store than she'd revealed in front of Johnny.

His intention to take the ramp they'd added on the side of the porch vanished. He went straight to her, bumping his caster against the bottom step. He gripped the rickety stair rail, leaned forward to touch her knee. "What's going on?" he asked.

She took a breath and stared at his feet. "You remember the day you went to class with me?"

"Yeah, I remember it."

"It gave me courage." Her gaze lifted to his. "You've asked me to trust you a lot. How do I ask you to trust me?"

"Just like that. But I already do." Something was hurting her heart, and if it was the belief that he didn't trust her, he could fix that. He hoped. "Tell me what you're trying to say to me. Don't dress it up."

"I know my own heart," she said. "You helped me with that, but not just you. Thomas, Les, your mother, Marcus, everyone, but most especially myself."

She stared at him, and the words came out in a rush. "I love this life. I love standing out in a field, hearing the silence, the wind, the crows. People think you have to get in a spaceship to see the universe, but it's here, inside us, and orbiting around us, every day. Though I might like to go to Scotland sometime."

Rory blinked at the abrupt segue. "All those Scottish romances and men in kilts."

His comment gave her a faint smile. "Well, that, and this." The smile disappeared as she closed her eyes, obviously to recall the words she spoke next. "*But in high hills, and moorlands waste and lonely, The vast enchantment of her presence dwells. Wide sky, and sky-wide waste of thyme and heather, Perpetual sleepy hum of golden bees-- If you and I were only there together.*'"

"Wow. That's beautiful."

Her eyes opened. "'The Moors,' by Edith Nesbit. I like that word, moor."

"Unmoored," he remembered.

"With you, I feel moored, in the best of ways." She took a breath. "But that's the way my soul is. It's quiet there, but there's also a wildness...like a hawk."

Her gaze searched his. There was a nervousness there he didn't understand, but he linked his hand with hers and she looked at it, placing her smaller hand on top of it. Then she closed her eyes once more. The drizzle had stopped, the sun starting to re-emerge from the cloud cover.

This time she spoke in a quieter voice. "I swoop and glide, in perfect stillness. Always under the quiet eyes of my Master. When he lifts the gauntlet, I will fly to him in joy. He will give me a place of rest, happiness, until the wildness rises again. Then he will let me be free, and I will embrace life fully, while being loved fully. My peace and wildness will come together in my breast, my beating heart, where freedom and love live as one."

He blinked. "Who wrote that?"

"I did," she said shyly, opening her eyes. "In my creative writing class. We were supposed to write something inspired by Edith's poem. It's not as beautiful as hers, but I wrote it for you. And for me."

The way she tilted her head reminded him of a small, smooth-feathered goshawk in truth. "There are times...I can tell you're still worrying that you're holding me back. There are plenty of men in my classes. Nice men. Handsome men."

Another segue, and a more directed one, accompanied by an intriguing set to her jaw. "You try to get a rise out of me that way, you may not like where you end up," he said mildly.

The Master side of him could make her shiver, and it reassured him, seeing that jolt through her, but she still firmed her chin, nodded. "Me saying something like that gets you worked up, because in your heart and soul, you feel like I'm yours."

"Yeah. But I don't think I own you. Not like..."

"No, not like them," she said fiercely. "Never. And I never want you to worry about that. You're nothing like them. You're a strong man, a loving one."

Now her hands gripped his tightly. "One who loves me enough to shatter his heart worse than his legs, if the best thing for me is to let me go. That's what I didn't realize, until I came back that night and saw you by your bed."

He still felt bad about that, but before the inadvertent knife twist could make him say anything about it, she'd taken a breath and pushed onward. "You know things about me I have a hard time saying about myself. You've told me you can read my heart, that I don't have to work as hard to express my desires, and that...your caring for me, it never ends. It means everything. So for both of us, I need to say something."

The raw emotion in her voice told him what it was costing her to pull the words from her heart and soul, put them out into the air between them. It made his own heart ache for her, but he answered her in a steady tone. "Then I'm listening."

"I'm getting better at saying what I want. But there's a difference between want and choice. That was the real problem, wasn't it? They made me think I didn't have any choices. You, your family, you all taught me otherwise. There's a line...and past that line no one, not even you, gets to make those choices for me."

She'd kept her eyes on his chest as she said it, and he could see the quiver in her rigid shoulders. He leaned forward enough to put a thumb on her jaw, tip her face up. "Say it again," he said. "While looking right at me."

When she did, her eyes were bright, almost feral. "No one gets to make those choices for me."

She swallowed, and her fingers had that coldness to them, but he held them, warmed them, as he deliberately let his lips curve. "You bet your ass."

She stared at him. "You say that, but do you trust my choice? Will you let yourself believe I want you as much as you want me?"

The light dawned. Well, hellfire. That was why she thought he'd been hedging about moving in. He noted she'd added a little tilt to her chin at the end that made him smile, a painful thing. He withdrew his hand, but only to back up his chair. "Come stand in front of me, rebellious woman."

She gave him a curious look, but when she rose and complied, he looked up at her. It was as close as he could get to kneeling.

"I'm marrying you," he said. "So you'll know I believe you."

She jerked, her eyes widening. "I thought...I wasn't sure if you meant it that night, when I overheard you."

"So you didn't bring it up again. Waiting on me." He smiled again, easier this time. "And I didn't mention it again, because I didn't want to hold you to it. But I changed my mind. With one very important condition."

"What?" She looked off balance now, but in a very lovely way.

"You're going to promise me that whatever you want to do with your life, no matter how it changes, you'll always tell me. Travel, design a rocket, learn to be a surgeon. Whatever you want to be or do, I'm going to back you."

Her eyes sparkled, then softened as she sank to her knees and put her hand on his leg. "As long as you'll trust me when I tell you my favorite thing is just lying in a hammock with you, watching the sun set over the fields, hearing the breeze and the beating of our hearts. Oh..." Her eyes brightened even further. "We need to put a hammock out between those two maple trees in back. I forgot to add that to the plans."

He chuckled. "I have a million reasons for wanting to marry you. But here's the really important one. This can't be returned."

He fished out the ring. He'd grabbed it out of its box, wrapped it in tissue paper and shoved it in his pocket before he'd followed her out to the van. Hence Johnny's amused look, who'd known all along why Rory had been putting off the move.

Now he unwrapped the sparkling band and offered it to her. Since she was at his feet, he leaned forward enough to tunnel a hand under her hair to clasp her nape in a warm hand, rub his thumb there, that gesture that reassured her and pleased them both. He watched her eyes widen to saucers as she gazed at the ring.

The platinum band was what the jeweler had called a "bypass shank," a decidedly unromantic name for something that reminded him of the heart bracelet he'd bought her, the way the band swirled in a delicate curl around the solitaire diamond, holding it into place.

"They finished sizing it and called me to pick it up. That's where I went on my errand. It's what I've been waiting on, why I've held out on a date to move in together. I was trying to let it be a surprise, but if they'd needed one more day, I would have had to tell you. I never meant to get you upset like this."

As she raised dazed eyes to him, he saw the question in them. He lifted a shoulder. "If we're waiting for spring for the wedding, but moving in together now, I wanted something that said we're committed to one another. That we're not just shacking up. It might sound kind of old fashioned, but..."

He stopped as her tears spilled out. In the next heartbeat he had her up in his lap, holding her close. She'd clasped both hands over his, holding the ring, and had the knot of their interlaced fingers under her breast, her body curled over it as he held her in his arms.

"I feel silly," she said. "I thought...you were holding back on moving in together because of...what I just said."

He freed his hands from hers to take possession of her left one. As she watched, he slid the ring onto her finger, over her knuckle, held tight when her fingers curled over his.

"I want you," he said. "Today, tomorrow, forever."

More tears, but there was a smile in there, too. She would forever be a mix of strengths and fragility. A bewildered angel, but an angel nonetheless, with all the strength of Heaven behind her.

He slid both arms around her again, pressed his mouth to her cheek. Then her lips, when she tilted her head back and he could take that deep, lingering draught of her that made the world steady and wild at once. Like her poem.

As they eased back from one another, he met her gaze. "You weren't wrong. Your happiness is the most important thing to me. And so much is new to you. I can't help but consider that when I make decisions. If I hold back, it's because I don't want to stand in the way of your dreams, Daralyn."

"You're a part of those dreams," she said, sniffling. "Unless you mean you don't want to take that journey with me. When I imagine my dreams coming true, big and small, I imagine you sharing them with me. And what makes me feel even more wonderful is imagining being at your side when yours come true, too."

She looked at him with her big soft eyes, and he couldn't imagine his life without her. She wasn't settling for someone as broken as him, or him for her. It was believing he deserved someone as amazing as her, someone who had taken his broken pieces, same as he'd taken hers, and they'd formed a stained-glass window out of it.

His favorite part of church had been looking at those colored pieces of glass, the way the light was always different through them, at morning, high noon, or the full moon at midnight mass. Hell, the streetlight in the parking lot shining through it on a cloudy night.

"I have all my big dreams. I have the store, my family." His throat and chest felt weighted down with the happiness, and it was a good feeling. "You."

She glowed, but her expression became thoughtful again. "I think you have one more big dream. One you don't talk about. Will you trust me with it? I like the idea of sharing our dreams and knowing, even if we don't get all of them, we know one another, our whole hearts, every corner."

He nodded, looked away, then looked back at her. Said it out loud. "I want kids. Three of them. I don't care about them being our blood. That doesn't matter to me. Mom loves you as much as she loves Les and Julie, sees all of you as her daughters. It tells me blood doesn't matter when it comes to being parents." He set his jaw. "I know with me being in a wheelchair, and your psychiatric history, maybe we don't have a great shot, but maybe we foster. Like rent to own, something like that."

She chuckled. "I'm not sure if that's how it works, but yes. I would..." She faltered a little. "I would love to be a mother. Not right away, of course, but when we do... Do you think I would be a good one?"

"No doubt in my mind at all." He caressed her face. "And we've got a hell of a support network to back us up. Can you see Mom doling out her matriarchal wisdom? Les showing them how to appreciate the science stuff, while Thomas and Julie handle the arts. And Marcus..."

He paused, made a deliberate show of contemplating that. "Okay, maybe we don't expose them to Marcus's influence."

She laughed, and pinched his arm. "Marcus, the savvy businessman who brought himself up from the streets to become a very successful gallery owner. He'll teach our children how to be financially successful."

Rory held her close again, relishing how she curled herself tight against him, her feet braced on his push rim, her knees drawn up. They fit as perfectly together as the diamond did in its setting.

"We'll teach them that none of it matters without love," she said softly. "And faith. In yourself, your family and whatever it is out there that brought us together, that brought me out of that dark house and into your arms."

"You won't ever find darkness in them," he promised, and he knew that was his biggest dream of all. That she would always find what she needed in his arms.

WANT MORE OF THE NATURE OF DESIRE SERIES?
"I didn't come here for you to be nice to me."
Third year medical student Les Wilder has done the unforgivable. When she flees to the door of childhood crush and arson investigator Jefferson "Brick" McGuire, she doesn't come for comfort. With what she's done, she doesn't deserve to let love save her.

Brick feels differently. He's enough of a Master to know his shattered submissive needs more than pleasure or punishment. Though he will give her both, love is the only thing that will heal the wound that threatens her soul.

CLICK HERE TO READ NOW
IGNITION SEQUENCE

Reading this in print format?
Look for it at your favorite book vendor!

ABOUT THE AUTHOR

Having penned over fifty acclaimed BDSM contemporary and paranormal titles, which includes six award-winning series, *Joey W. Hill* has been awarded the RT Book Reviews Career Achievement Award for Erotic Romance. A submissive herself, Hill brings authenticity to her intensely emotional love stories.

She is grateful for the support of a wonderful and enthusiastic readership, which allows her to live on her beloved Carolina coast with her even more beloved husband and menagerie of animals.

- On the Web: https://storywitch.com
- Twitter: https://twitter.com/JoeyWHill
- Facebook: https://facebook.com/JoeyWHillAuthor
- Facebook Fan Forum: https://facebook.com/groups/JWHMembersOnly
- MeWe: https://mewe.com/i/joeywhill
- GoodReads: https://www.goodreads.com/author/show/103359.Joey_W_Hill
- BookBub: https://bookbub.com/authors/joey-w-hill
- Amazon: https://amazon.com/Joey-W-Hill/e/B001JSCIW0

ALSO BY JOEY W. HILL

Mirror of My Soul

Mistress of Redemption

Rough Canvas

Branded Sanctuary

Divine Solace

Worth The Wait

Truly Helpless

In His Arms

Ignition Sequence

Naughty Bits Series

Naughty Bits

Naughty Wishes

Vampire Queen Series

Vampire Queen's Servant

Mark of the Vampire Queen

Vampire's Claim

Beloved Vampire

Vampire Mistress *(VQS: Club Atlantis)*

Vampire Trinity *(VQS: Club Atlantis)*

Vampire Instinct

Bound by the Vampire Queen

Taken by a Vampire

The Scientific Method

Nightfall

Elusive Hero

Night's Templar

Vampire's Soul

Vampire's Embrace

Vampire Master *(VQS: Club Atlantis)*

Vampire Guardian *(VQS: Club Atlantis)*

Vampire's Choice